TOUGHER *in* TEXAS

KARI LYNN DELL

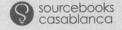

sourcebooks
casablanca

Published by Sourcebooks Casablanca, an imprint of Sourcebooks, Inc.
P.O. Box 4410, Naperville, Illinois 60567-4410
(630) 961-3900
Fax: (630) 961-2168
sourcebooks.com

Printed and bound in Canada.
MBP 10 9 8 7 6 5 4 3 2 1

In memory of Tal Michael, who loved bucking horses and being a pickup man.

Chapter 1

ALL OF COLE'S PROBLEMS WOULD BE SOLVED IF HE just found a wife.

The thought popped into his head at the exact instant that a ton of bovine suddenly bellowed and kicked, slamming into the steel gate Cole was holding and knocking him flat on his ass. If Cole hadn't stood six foot six, he probably would've lost some teeth. The gate caught him in the chest instead, and sent him sprawling in the dirt. His red heeler, Katie, barked once and launched herself at the bull to protect him, but Carrot Top just trotted off down the alley, more interested in checking the empty pens for leftover hay.

Cole scrambled to his feet and snarled as his gaze zeroed in on the bright-yellow cattle prod in the hand of one of the men who rushed to his aid. "What the *fuck* are you doing with that thing?"

The cowboy took a hasty step back, then another when Cole stalked toward him. "Just hurryin' things along."

"My stock moves just fine without a hotshot." Cole made sure of it, training them from birth to handle easily. The rodeo season was a cross-country marathon of long miles and strange places. Less stress equaled better performance, and even though the low-current buzz of the cattle prod was more startling than painful, Cole wanted his stock as relaxed as possible until the moment they exploded from the bucking chute. Carrot Top was an old pro. He'd earned the right to inspect the loading chute before setting hoof on the steep ramp.

And to come unglued when some asshole zapped him.

The cowboy ran out of room and backed up against the fence. Cole snatched the hotshot, busted it over his knee, and then tossed it back, the ends dangling by the wires that ran down the long shaft. "Pack that and the rest of your shit and get out of here."

The cowboy clutched the broken prod to his chest, jaw dropping. "But I'm your pickup man."

"Not anymore."

Cole turned his back and strode down the alley to retrieve Carrot Top. As far as he was concerned, the conversation was over.

Half an hour later, his cell phone buzzed. He was tempted to ignore it, but she would only keep calling until he answered. There was a strong undercurrent of stubborn in the Jacobs gene pool. He heaved a deep sigh and put some distance between himself and the rest of the crew before he accepted the call, holding the phone three inches from his ear in anticipation of his cousin's displeasure.

"What the hell is wrong with you?" Violet yelled.

"He used a hotshot on Carrot Top."

"So ban him from the stock pens. Hell, ban him from the whole rodeo grounds except when he's working the performances, but did you have to fire him?"

"He used a hotshot on Carrot Top," Cole repeated, slower this time.

"I understand. It was stupid. But what do you suggest we do next weekend when you're the only pickup man in the arena?"

Cole hadn't thought about that at the time. He'd been thinking about it since, but hiring contract personnel was Violet's job. If she was here like normal, he wouldn't have had to put up with a stranger. He wouldn't have to put up with any of this crap. He could go back to just taking care of his stock and leaving all the *people* bullshit to Violet. He couldn't say that, though, and as usual, his brain collapsed under pressure and offered up only the one sentence in his defense. "He used a hotshot on *Carrot Top*."

Violet huffed out a breath so exasperated he swore he felt the breeze on his end of the line. "You do realize the doctor sentenced me to bed rest because my blood pressure is through the roof, right?"

Cole ducked his head, crushing a dirt clod with the toe of his boot. He wasn't trying to aggravate anyone, especially Violet. She was command central for Jacobs Livestock. The hell she'd been going through had thrown all of them for a loop, Violet most of all. She hadn't been sick a day in her first pregnancy, though Beni had decided to make an appearance six weeks early. She'd been prepared to be cautious and watchful. She had *not* expected to be sick as a dog practically from the moment she and Joe had seen the telltale line on the home pregnancy test.

Besides, Cole was almost as excited about the baby as its parents. He loved being Uncle Cole, and now a little girl? He grinned at the thought of a future full of ponies and pink cowboy boots—assuming his family didn't string him up for driving Violet into another premature labor.

Cole huffed out a breath, leaning a shoulder against the back of the infield bleachers. Around him, the empty rodeo grounds looked like a hangover—garbage cans overflowed with empty bottles, corners of banners drooped along the fences, spilled popcorn and a smashed glob of cotton candy littered the ground. Katie nosed around under the bleachers and came out packing a half-eaten hot dog. It all looked ill-used and abandoned—sort of like Cole felt.

Yes, he had put them in a tight spot, but there were some things he wouldn't tolerate when it came to his stock. Okay, many things. *Obsessive-compulsive prick* was another way of putting it, though only Joe dared say that to his face. He was family. Plus, he was a lot faster than Cole.

"Don't try to say I didn't warn you," Violet said, her voice laced with grim amusement.

Cole froze. She couldn't mean... "I thought you were kidding."

"No, I was not, any more than I was kidding when I told you to make this one work, or *else*."

Panic churned Cole's gut. "Violet, you can't. There must be somebody else—"

"I refuse to even ask. This makes three perfectly good pickup men you've chased off. If you can't force yourself to get along, I'll send someone you can't fire."

"Don't. Please." He didn't hesitate to beg. If she followed through on her threat, he'd either be insane or under arrest by season's end in September. "Just one more. I promise—"

"Nope. I'm done. If you can find a replacement before tomorrow morning, I'll hire him. Otherwise..." He could hear her smirking, dammit. "Your new partner will meet you at Cuero."

"Violet, come on—"

The phone had gone dead. If he called back, it would go straight to voice mail. When Violet said she was done, she meant it.

He jammed the phone in his pocket and stomped over to his rig, his stomach rumbling right along with the big diesel engines of the stock trucks that sat idling, waiting for him to lead the procession to the next rodeo. Yet another reason he needed to get on that wife thing. He'd never realized how much food it took to keep this big ol' body of his fueled until he'd had to start rustling it up for himself. Living with his aunt Iris, there'd never been any need to learn how to cook. But she was with his uncle Steve in Salinas, California, at one of the most venerable rodeos in the country, always held the third week of July. They did the subcontracting, hauling the very best of the Jacobs string to elite shows too big for any single producer to handle.

Leaving Cole to handle all of the rodeos where Jacobs Livestock was the lead contractor. And starve.

He scowled into the fridge in his trailer—cold cuts, store-bought rolls, and plastic deli tubs of gooey macaroni and potato salad. He slapped together three sandwiches, grabbed a Coke, and kicked aside a pair of jeans that had spilled out of the overstuffed laundry hamper. His socks were turning gray and there wasn't a crumb left from the last batch of cookies Miz Iris had mailed to him. He hadn't had a homemade dinner roll since the Fourth of July.

"This is no way to live, Katie girl."

The dog gave a little whine of agreement.

He slammed into the cab of his pickup and tossed

one of the sandwiches to Katie in the passenger's seat. She ignored it. Even the dog was sick of cold cuts. At his growl of frustration, she cocked her head, the brown patches above her eyes creasing in concern.

He rubbed a hand over her head. "First, we call everybody we know and try to find a new pickup man. Then we're gonna figure out how to get us a wife."

Katie shot him a dubious look, then sighed and began to pick at her sandwich.

Chapter 2

As far as Shawnee Pickett was concerned, when most women went out to get a Brazilian, they were doing it all wrong.

Yawning, she stretched, then rolled over to admire the long, lean body sprawled beside hers. She trailed her finger down the dark bronze arm slung over the pillow, and paused to wrap her hand around his biceps on the off chance she might be able to absorb some of the brilliance humming under his skin. That arm was property of the hottest young team roper to explode onto the pro rodeo scene in years. Maybe decades.

Some people might not be thrilled about the Brazilian invasion of a sport they liked to think belonged to North America, but Shawnee sure wasn't complaining.

Her phone buzzed on the nightstand, then began to dance to the tune of Garth's "Friends in Low Places." Tori. Shawnee let it play a few bars, then peeled herself away from all that tempting bare skin and picked up. "Yes, Mother?"

"I slept in, had breakfast, and drank two cups of coffee. Then I read the Sunday *Dallas Morning News* front to back, so thanks to you I've lost what little faith I had left in humanity." Damn. Tori always made sarcasm sound so classy. "You've been holed up in that room for almost twelve hours. Don't you think you've had enough?"

"Says the woman who was just whinin' about not gettin' to wrap her hands around Delon's hot little ass for another week."

At the sound of Shawnee's voice, Joao Pedro Azeveda—alias J.P. because most people were too lazy to learn to pronounce his name—stirred. Without opening his eyes, he reached out and hauled Shawnee over to where he could nestle his face in her bare cleavage. She sighed.

"I heard that," Tori said. "I'm loading the horses right now. If you're not standing out in the parking lot when I swing by the motel, I will keep going and let you hitch-hike home."

Now J.P.'s hands were getting in on the action, despite the fact that he'd only slept for four hours. Lord. Twenty-two was a beautiful thing. Shawnee stifled a moan. Maybe a quickie…

"Don't even," Tori warned. In the background, Shawnee heard the sound of hooves thudding on the floor of the trailer as the horses hopped in. "If that boy is too weak to swing a rope at Bandera tonight, his partner will wring your neck."

Aw, hell. Shawnee caught J.P.'s wrist before either of them could get too heated up. He lifted his head and cocked it, questioning. Shawnee shook her head, pointing to the phone, then the door. He flashed her a coaxing grin as he slid his palm down her side and along her hip, pulling her against him so she could feel what she was missing. Her body responded in kind. She breathed a silent curse and shook her head again. He did one of those shrugs that was worth a thousand words, rolled over, and buried his face in the pillow.

"Ten minutes," Tori said.

"You know you suck, right?"

Tori gave an evil laugh and hung up. She didn't judge, bless her heart, but she also didn't make idle threats.

Nine minutes later, Shawnee hopped around muttering curses while she tried to tug jeans on over shower-damp skin. Might help if she had slightly less butt to stuff into them. As she dragged a comb through her wet mop of brown curls, she gave J.P.'s gangly body one last, lingering glance. Asleep, he looked even younger. Suddenly she felt every one of the eleven years between them, and for an instant she wished...

She shook off the weird little ache, grabbed her wallet, and headed for the door. This was how she rolled—keeping it loose and easy with guys who didn't expect her to be there when they woke up.

And yeah, she was aware that *loose* and *easy* were the most polite of the words tossed around behind her back. Well, fuck those sanctimonious assholes and the donkeys they rode in on. This was the life that had chosen her, and she was bound and determined to live it to the hilt. She didn't hear J.P. or any of his predecessors complaining.

She spared a glance in the mirror and winced. Without makeup, her face was a doughy blob with a couple of finger holes poked in it for eyes. Oh well. She could slap on a little something in the pickup.

J.P. didn't twitch when she opened the door. She didn't wake him to say goodbye. Spanish she could handle. So far, Portuguese had eluded her and J.P. had only mastered the bare bones of English, which wasn't all bad. When their paths did cross, they never wasted

time on chitchat, though she wouldn't have minded
hearing him explain how he'd learned to snatch up both
hind feet on wild, ass-slinging steers.

As she stepped outside, a pickup and horse trailer
rolled around the corner, right on schedule. After the
cool dimness of the motel room, the midmorning sunlight slapped Shawnee in the face like a hot, damp
towel. Still, her heart did a little happy dance at the sight
of the rig. All hers. *Turn 'Em and Burn 'Em Champion
Heeler*, the bold letters scrawled across the double-cab
declared. Three years, and she still got a thrill every
time she looked at it. Or its twin, which was parked in
Tori's driveway.

The icing on the cake had been the monster prize
money that came along with the pickups. Enough for
Shawnee to finally get rid of her granddad's rickety old
stock trailer and buy herself a decent used gooseneck
with a small but adequate living quarters in the front
section. Sure as hell beat camping in the back of her old
rust-bucket pickup.

The rig barely rolled to a stop to let Shawnee hop
in before Tori swung back out on the street and hit the
gas. Shawnee dug her sunglasses out of the center con-
sole, jammed them on her face, then squinted through
the blessedly dark lenses. Tori Patterson Hancock
Sanchez didn't look like the daughter of Texas's version of royalty. Her caramel-brown hair was yanked
through the loop of her baseball cap and she wasn't
wearing a scrap of makeup. Her jeans were smudged
with dirt from the previous evening's roping, though
her sky-blue tank top was clean. She filled it out better
than when they'd first met. Either Delon's chocolate

habit was contagious or being disgustingly well loved gave her an appetite.

Speaking of which…

"Can we swing past a hamburger stand? I'm starving." At Tori's impatient grunt, Shawnee scowled. "What, you're in such a rush to get out of town you can't spare three minutes to feed me? You got something against this place?"

Tori threw her a dark look. "My memories aren't quite as pleasant as yours."

In other words, she'd spent the last eight hours brooding because she'd missed their last steer and a shot at winning third place and a couple thousand dollars. Tori was good at many, many things, but failure was not one of them, which made her an excellent partner and an occasional pain in the ass. She took pity, though, and pulled over at the Dairy Queen on the edge of town. Shawnee had just dug into her one fast food fix of the week when her phone rang again, this time to the tune of Joe Diffie's "Pickup Man."

Shawnee's pulse kicked up its heels. "Hey, Violet. Fancy hearing from you on a Sunday morning. Does this mean what I think it does?"

Violet made a growling noise. "Can you be in Cuero by Wednesday at noon?"

Shawnee's pulse did another jig. She'd been both anticipating and dreading this call since Violet had asked her to be on standby. On the downside, keeping her promise meant no serious team roping for two months. Shawnee hadn't gone more than a few days without roping since back when…

She flicked that thought aside and concentrated on

the here and now, something she'd been doing so long
it was second nature.

She'd agreed to Violet's proposal because she was
ready for a change. Her life had settled into a groove
the last couple of years—rope with Tori, work at the
cattle auction, train some horses, hang out at the Jacobs
ranch when they weren't on the road—but a comfortable
rut was still a rut. Time to shake things up. Or in this
case, some*one*.

"I'll be there," she said, grinning as she hung up.

"Sounds like I'm losing a partner for the rest of the
summer."

"Yep." Shawnee tipped back her seat and got comfortable, munching fries and mentally making lists of
everything that needed doing before she could pack up
and leave. "You'll have your weekends free to chase
your pretty husband around the country."

After ten years on the rodeo trail, Delon finally had
his gold buckle—*World Champion Bareback Rider*—
and was well on his way to defending the title. Tori
certainly wouldn't mind missing a few ropings to spend
more time with him. Delon was a sight to see even when
he wasn't spurring a bronc, and given how long it'd
taken the two of them to get their shit together, they were
bound and determined not to let it get scattered again.

Shawnee jabbed a french fry into the ketchup so
hard it broke in half. All of her cronies were pairing
off, turning into husbands and wives, daddies and mom-
mies. She had accepted that it would happen eventually. She wouldn't pretend it didn't bother her at all,
but she'd learned to accept it—most of the time. It was
like being born knowing you were allergic to ice cream.

Just looking at it might be enough to make your mouth water, but as long as you'd never tasted it you didn't really know what you were missing.

"You should take my trailer," Tori said. "I won't be using it while you're gone, and yours is too small to live in for that long."

Shawnee debated for all of ten seconds. The living quarters in Tori's trailer were like a top of the line RV— four times the size of Shawnee's, with actual appliances and satellite TV. "That'd be great. Thanks."

Tori shot her a curious look. "Are you nervous?"

"Nah. Violet and her dad put me through the wringer at all those practices, and dragged me along to a couple of high school rodeos." Her grin widened. "Besides, it's a dream job. After all these years of just doing it for fun, I'm gonna get paid to irritate Cole Jacobs."

Chapter 3

THE PARKING NAZIS ATTACKED BEFORE SHAWNEE turned off her pickup. Red-faced and dripping sweat under their neon-yellow plastic vests, they waved their orange-painted sticks so frantically you'd think she'd landed a 747 in the contestant lot instead of her pickup and Tori's trailer.

She rolled down her window. "Is there a problem?"

"You can't park here," the taller one declared, jamming his thumbs in his pockets and thrusting his beer gut at her.

Shawnee ran a deliberate glance around the clipped grass field, dotted with live oaks like the one she'd parked beneath. Four hours before the first rodeo performance, only seven other rigs had arrived, all lined up with military precision along the back fence. "Looks like there's plenty of room."

"There is now." Beer Gut attempted to radiate pompous authority in a dime-store cowboy hat. "But it'll get crowded once the rest of the contestants arrive. We have to keep it organized so no one gets blocked in."

Shawnee gave him the closest thing she had to a polite smile. "Well, then, there's no problem. I'm with the stock contractor. I'll be here for the duration."

"Oh. Then you belong over there." The skinnier of the pair gave a dramatic wave of his stick, toward where the two Jacobs Livestock semis, an elderly travel trailer, and Cole's rig were lined up near the stock pens. They'd stretched a tarp between Cole's horse trailer and the nearest semi to shade the cluster of lawn chairs set up on a big chunk of outdoor carpet, exactly the same as they did at every rodeo. Cole probably had a diagram. There wasn't a tree within fifty yards.

"I don't think so." Shawnee turned off the pickup and opened her door, nearly clipping the big guy's chin with the side-view mirror.

They both jumped back, then blustered along behind her as she strolled to the rear of the trailer to unload her horses. "You can't just pull in and take the best parking spot!"

"Why not? My horses and I will be here all week. The contestants will come and go in half a day, at most." She flipped the latch on the back door and swung it open. The flea-bitten gray in the rear stall cranked his head around to show her the whites of his eyes. Shawnee stepped aside and waited, holding the door wide.

"But…" Skinny began, then faltered, as if he wasn't sure where to go with it.

"We got rules," Beer Gut announced. "Contestants park where we tell them to park."

"I repeat, I'm not a contestant." A few tentative thuds sounded inside the trailer as the gray attempted to find reverse gear in the confined space. "And if I were you, I'd take a step back."

The big guy stepped closer. "Listen, missy—"

Whatever wisdom he intended to impart was cut short by a clatter and a bang that rocked the entire trailer, then a huge thud as the gray took one big leap and missed the back edge of the trailer floor with both hind feet. His rear legs buckled from the twelve-inch drop that took him by surprise every single time. He plopped onto his ass, nearly squashing Beer Gut. The gray teetered on his haunches, looking shocked and perplexed, then flopped over onto his side. Shawnee caught the halter rope as the horse scrambled up and stood, legs splayed, quivering as if he wasn't sure the ground would hold him.

"He has issues," she told the goggle-eyed parking attendants. Among them, she suspected, a total lack of long-term memory. Or short-term common sense. The horse snorted and Beer Gut stuck out a hand to ward him off.

Shawnee slapped the halter rope into his palm. "Hold that, would you?"

He blanched like she'd tossed him a live cottonmouth.

She didn't wait for an answer, just stepped up into the trailer to trip the latch on the stall divider and release the second horse, a sorrel who eyed her doubtfully, then began feeling his way backward. At the edge, he extended one foot and waved it around, searching for solid ground. When he found it, he eased on down.

"Here." She tossed that halter rope to the skinny guy.

He fumbled to grab it, dropping his pretty orange stick. "Now, wait just a minute—"

Shawnee went to the front of the trailer and tripped the last latch. Her good buckskin, Roy, paused long enough to let her scratch his forelock, then ambled out of the trailer and calmly surveyed the latest of the innumerable stops they'd made together. Shawnee tied him on the shady side of the trailer and went to retrieve the other two.

Beer Gut practically threw the halter rope at her. "Look, lady. We already said you can't park here."

"And I asked why." Shawnee persuaded the gray that the grass wasn't actually quicksand laced with alligators and dragged him around to tie him next to Roy. "You haven't given me a reason, other than that *rules are rules* bullshit."

Beer Gut puffed up like an angry toad. "We were given our orders by the committee president. We have full authority to tow any vehicle in violation."

"Is that right?" Shawnee did a quick scan and located the rodeo office, a small white building to the left of the bucking chutes. "Let's just go have a chat with him, shall we?"

She strode away without looking back, ignoring both the outraged squawking and, "Wait! What am I supposed to do with this horse?"

—◦◦◦—

Cole hunched over the long table that functioned as the rodeo secretary's desk and jabbed his fat fingers at the laptop keys, entering the draw numbers for the team roping steers. Not his job, but easier than forcing his secretary to do it. He growled when he realized he'd transposed the digits, typing 198 instead of 918.

"Hey, I'm sorry," Analise said, looking anything but as she lounged in a lawn chair and fanned herself with one of the souvenir rodeo programs. "That guy who brings the steers needs to change the numbers. Make them start with eight, like the calves. Eight is rain on a tin roof. Nine sounds like a dying kitten."

She shuddered as if she could hear it now. According

to Analise, the color blue also tasted like antifreeze.
Cole had refrained from asking if she'd ever sipped
antifreeze. Her answer might be more than he wanted
permanently imprinted on his gray matter. He tried
to keep an open mind, but today she'd edged into
Creepyland, with a lip ring that looked like a skeletal
hand clamped around her bottom lip and matching skeletal feet dangling from her earlobes. Her hair was the
standard goth black pulled up into a schoolgirl ponytail,
which made her look at least five years younger than
her already infantile nineteen.

Violet had found her at a medical clinic, of all places.
Analise was deeply unhappy with her employer's dress
code, which oppressed her individuality. She was also
the only person who'd been able to force Violet's insurance to pay a disputed claim. Violet had offered her a
job on the spot and worked out the wardrobe guidelines
later: nothing profane, excessively revealing, or por-
traying graphic violence. Anything else was fair game.
Analise's single concession to rodeo life was a pair of
tall black cowboy boots stitched with delicate pink flowers and a grinning skull.

But she was almost as much of a nitpicking, compulsive perfectionist as Cole, and despite her age, the
cowboys never tried to mess with her. Cole figured it
was the piercings. Took some guts, getting a hole poked
in some of those places. And Analise's screaming
nines—formally known as synesthesia—were as real as
whatever screwed-up wiring made Cole unable to grasp
irony unless it was laid on with a cement trowel.

"The numbers can't be changed," Hank chimed in,
slumped bonelessly with one leg hitched over the arm of

the other lawn chair. "It's a rule. They have to have a permanent hip brand. You'll just have to deal, freak show."

Analise tossed him a scathing look. "From the idiot who throws himself in front of bulls."

He just shrugged. "It's my job to keep the cowboys from getting stomped. And I'm good at it."

Arrogant, but not wrong. In terms of pure physical ability and instincts, Hank was as good a bullfighter as they'd ever had. The problem, Aunt Iris liked to say, was that he'd been tended by everyone and raised by no one, the rodeo version of a latchkey kid. Which might account for why he'd never grown up.

Over in the corner, one of the truck drivers threw his cards down in disgust.

"You are such a sucker. You fall for that bluff every time." His mirror image scooped up chips from the oversized cooler they were using as a table.

Lester and Leslie weren't allowed to play for money due to the inevitable fistfights. Lester nearly always won, his poker face being the twins' only distinguishing feature. Their similarity and their fondness for playing switcheroo had led to most people just referring to them both as Les. Perversely, they seemed to like it.

At the other end of the table, their rodeo announcer, Tyrell Swift, made notes of the contestants' name pronunciations, past championships, and current rankings to add to his running commentary. "Have we heard anything from the new pickup...person?"

Before Cole could answer, he heard the sound of agitated voices, closing in fast. Katie scrambled to attention as the office door burst open, framing the female version of a Tasmanian devil—glittering eyes, wild hair, and a wide, malicious grin. One of the parking attendants huffed up behind her. Over their shoulders Cole spotted a second, skinnier guy holding a lead rope and standing well back from a sorrel horse that regarded him with equal distrust.

The parking attendant shoved into the office, his face frighteningly flushed, and zeroed in on Cole. "You're the contractor, right? Jacobs?"

"Yes," Cole admitted reluctantly.

"Well, this one—" The attendant jabbed a thumb at Shawnee, who gave a cheesy finger wave. "She claims she works for you, but she won't park in your area."

"I'm happier with the contestants. And shade. But if you insist—" She flashed Cole a smile so loaded with sugar it made his teeth ache. "I noticed there's an open spot right next to you. I suppose I can move if I have to."

He'd rather do CPR on the entire parking staff. Cole drew in a deep, supposedly calming breath. "Leave her be."

Shawnee made a triumphant *so there* noise.

The parking attendant *humphed*. "But the president said—"

"I'll explain it to him," Tyrell cut in. "I'm sure he'll understand."

People always understood when Tyrell explained, with his deep, mesmerizing voice and Denzel Washington smile. Life was easier for all of them if he ran interference for Cole whenever possible.

The parking attendant muttered and growled, but turned on his heel and marched off, leaving his bug-eyed partner to deal with the horse, which Cole assumed must belong to the natural disaster now surveying the office like she couldn't decide what to destroy next.

Cole heaved a beleaguered sigh and—ignoring Hank and the Leses, who already had the dubious pleasure— gestured toward the other two. "Tyrell and Analise, meet Shawnee Pickett."

Chapter 4

IF A MAD SCIENTIST HAD SET OUT TO DESIGN THE MOST intolerable woman on the face of the earth, he would've created Shawnee Pickett. Everything about her grated on Cole's nerves. Her voice, her language, her way of barreling in and assuming the world would get out of her way. Even her hair was outrageous, a mess of curls halfway down her back, waging war on whatever barrette or rubber thing she'd wadded them into. Cole never could fathom how she and Violet had become such good friends. Maybe all that attitude had seemed cool in college.

Not that Cole knew much about college. He'd barely scraped through high school. Even his ever-supportive aunt and uncle hadn't argued when he'd opted out of a higher level of torture.

He glared at Shawnee across the space between them in the arena—him stationed by one end of the bucking chutes, her at the other, waiting for the first bareback rider of the rodeo to nod his head. Shawnee was on Salty, a stocky white gelding and the most solid of Cole's string. The horse's strengths would help offset a rookie's weaknesses. Shawnee caught his eye and gave him a mocking salute. Cole ground his teeth and glued his attention on chute number one.

She was just too…everything. Everything except careful. And he was supposed to trust her with the safety of the cowboys and his stock?

At the ranch, he'd avoided her at the practice sessions by staying back in the stock pens, assuming she was just there for kicks. Shawnee lived for kicks. He should've known there was a plot afoot when he saw how much effort Violet and his uncle Steve were putting into coaching her, but as usual he'd been focused on his stock to the exclusion of all else. He should have been paying attention. Instead, he was paying the price.

And yeah, it stung, knowing his family had been so sure he'd fail without Violet that they'd spent months creating a backup plan.

He'd called around trying to find an alternative. That had been a waste of a full half hour of his life. His list of contacts was almost nonexistent. He'd never bothered to build one, because that was Violet's domain. Now, like most everything else, it was biting him in the ass. All he could do was put his faith in his uncle. Surely they wouldn't have sent Shawnee if she wasn't up to the job. Not knowing had anxiety nibbling at the ends of his nerves.

Cole wasn't good at assuming. And most of all, he hated having to fly by the seat of his jeans with only Shawnee Pickett as a safety net.

———

Shawnee caught Cole's glare and fired back a grin. From clear over there, he wouldn't be able to tell she was gritting her teeth to keep them from chattering—on a South Texas night that felt like being suspended over a boiling kettle. The nerves had slammed into her as the final strains of the national anthem faded away and she followed Cole into the arena. Saw the crowd. Heard the music. Her name. Suddenly, it all hit her.

Holy. *Shit*. This was the real deal. And it was *nothing* like the dusty practice arena in Violet's backyard.

Sponsor banners lined every square inch of the fences, representing the thousands of dollars that were up for grabs. The grandstand was packed, and so were the smaller bleachers that ringed the rest of the arena. Hank and the second bullfighter, Cruz, moved along the chutes, helping set flank straps on the horses as cowboys made final adjustments to their riggings. And not just any cowboys. Two of these guys were in the top ten in the pro standings. Another was a former world champion. And everyone expected her to know what she was doing.

What the *hell* was she doing?

She forced herself to breathe, slow and steady, but her heart screamed along with AC/DC, drowning out half of Tyrell's introduction. Lord, that voice, so rich and delicious that Miz Iris said it must have calories, because it made a woman's jeans feel a little snug. ". . . riding a National Finals bucking horse, Thunderstruck!"

Shawnee's hand clenched on the reins as the cowboy pounded his gloved fingers shut around the handle and eased up on the rigging. At least she didn't have to worry that they'd see her sweat. Everyone was sweating. She could feel it trickling down the inside of her calf, under the shin guards and stiff padded chaps that protected her from flying hooves. Another small river of perspiration meandered between her shoulder blades, plastering the royal-blue Jacobs Livestock shirt to her back.

A surprisingly silky shirt. She'd expected heavy, starched cotton, to match Cole's personality.

Focus. Breathe. She blinked away a drop of sweat that had dripped from her eyebrow, playing back Violet's last instructions. *I know it goes against your nature, but follow Cole's lead. Don't question him. Don't second-guess him. Inside the arena, he's always right.*

Follow Cole. Don't think. She could do that.

The cowboy cocked his free arm and nodded his head. With the swing of the chute gate, his feet lashed out, heels planted in the horse's neck as Thunderstruck took the first, explosive jump. Shawnee's thoughts dissolved and she just reacted, shadowing Cole as the bucking horse swooped first left, then right, rear hooves reaching for the lights and head disappearing between his knees each time his front feet slammed into the dirt. The cowboy fought hard, but with each jump he fell a little farther behind. Right at the eight-second whistle he got jacked back off his rigging. His hips twisted and his butt dropped off the side opposite his riding hand, leaving him head down, spurs up, the weight of his body trapping his glove in the rigging.

Hung up.

Hustle, hustle, hustle. She and Salty closed in fast on the lunging horse, taking the left side as Cole took the right. Coming astride, he reached down and grabbed for the back of the cowboy's protective vest. *Get the flank strap.* The bronc's hip slammed into Shawnee's leg as she leaned out and caught the trip mechanism with her fingers. The padded sheepskin strap fell away and Thunderstruck flattened out into a lope. Shawnee held her position, the three horses galloping abreast as Cole gave a heave, tossing the cowboy up and over the bronc and into her lap.

The impact knocked her sideways. She hooked her knee under the swells of her saddle and one hand under the cowboy's armpit—half rescue, half self-preservation—as he jerked his hand free of the rigging. Salty peeled away from the bucking horse. The instant they were clear, Shawnee lost her grip and dropped the cowboy square on his ass.

Oh shit. She glanced over her shoulder and saw him skid on one hip like he was sliding hard into second base, then pop up and throw both arms out in a *Safe!* motion.

The crowd roared. Shawnee exhaled for the first time since the chute gate had opened. Okay. *Okay.* Nothing like testing her right off the bat. And she had passed! Well enough, anyway. Like Violet's dad had told her, "As long as the cowboy walks away, you did your job."

She loped along with Cole, herding Thunderstruck into the stripping chute, where the crew would pull off the rigging. As they turned back at the gate, she glanced over to see Cole's reaction. Instead of a smile or an *Atta girl!*, his eyes narrowed and his jaw tightened. His chin jerked up a notch in acknowledgment. Then he reined Hammer off and trotted back to his position, ready for the next ride.

Shawnee bared her teeth at him. *Follow Cole's lead…*

All right, then. If he was gonna be a jerk, she could do that, too.

By the end of the bull riding, Cole was ready to bust a vein. Shawnee hadn't made a real mistake all night.

Hadn't given him a glimmer of an excuse to complain because—damn their eyes—they'd trained her to do everything exactly like Violet. Position, timing, even the cues she called out were the same. After the first dozen horses, he'd almost forgotten she *wasn't* Violet.

Until they rode out the gate and he had to look directly at her. She gave him another of those cheeky grins, a few stray curls sticking to the sweat on her round, flushed cheeks.

Her eyebrows cocked up into sharp, inverted Vs. "Well, boss? Do I pass?"

"You did okay." The words were sour and scratchy as hairballs, and nearly as hard to cough up. "You had good teachers."

"They showed me just how you like it." Shawnee steered her horse so close her padded chaps mashed up against his when she leaned in, lowering her voice to a suggestive purr. "Come by my trailer later, big boy, and I'll show you how *I* like it."

Cole felt his jaw drop. He tried to say…to say…Jesus Christ, what was he supposed to say to something like that?

Her laugh busted out, bawdy as a saloon girl, and she slapped a palm on her leather-clad thigh. "Oh my God! The look on your face—" She fired a triumphant finger pistol at him. "And me without a camera. Violet would've *loved* that face."

She flicked her reins and rode away, still laughing. Cole glared daggers at her back but they bounced right off, like everything else. He ground another millimeter off his incisors. *This*. This was why the woman should not be allowed in polite company. Or even impolite company. She was…hell, he couldn't even think of a word to describe her.

But if today was any indication, she was a passable pickup man. Okay, more than passable. She was good. Which meant—damn it to hell—he was stuck with her.

Chapter 5

DESPITE NOT CRAWLING INTO BED UNTIL ALMOST MID-night, Shawnee was up forty-five minutes before sunrise the next morning, saddling horses. She stopped to give Roy a thorough rub between the ears as she passed by to fetch the other two. He was a good stick. The best she'd ever had. Hard to imagine now, as he nosed her shoulder in hopes of extra grain, that there'd been a time when he'd as soon come at her, biting and striking. Just went to show, an unbroke colt in the hands of a soft-hearted, clueless novice was as dangerous as a gun. Horses were like people. They didn't have to like you, but they'd damn well better respect you.

In Shawnee's opinion, a whole lot of so-called problems would be solved if people did what had to be done, instead of what made them popular.

She led the sorrel and the gray to the arena, wading through predawn air as thick as lukewarm soup. Her thin, sleeveless T-shirt was already sticking to her shoulders. Eighty degrees and eighty percent humidity—this was why she'd never live in southeast Texas. They could have their greenery. She preferred air that didn't try to drown her one breath at a time.

She tied the gray outside the arena gate and took the sorrel inside. He snorted at the wide expanse of the arena, the brightly colored banners that rustled in the slight breeze, and the looming hulk of the grandstand. Shawnee gave him a couple of minutes to inspect his surroundings. Then she clipped the lunge line to his halter and clucked her tongue. Within a few minutes the gelding was loping smooth circles, stopping and turning on cue. When she was satisfied that they'd worked out the jitters, she bridled him and climbed aboard to put him through his paces.

Half an hour later, he dropped his head and walked sedately around the arena. Not bad. Tomorrow they'd rope the dummy steer she'd brought along. Too bad there was no one out at this hour who could be bribed into pulling it for her, but maybe next week would be cooler and she could work at a civilized hour.

Outside the arena, the flea-bitten gray paced and pawed at the end of his lead rope. She'd hoped he'd wear himself down, but it looked like he'd only worked himself into a full-on snit. She got him calmed down enough to clip the long lead onto his halter, but the instant they set foot in the arena, he tried to bolt. She dug in her heels and yanked him around to face her. He reared, stamped his feet, and shook his head. She snapped the lunge line, reminding him who was boss. He backed off, but when she stepped to the side and clucked her tongue, he bolted again. Shawnee yanked him around, hitching the line behind her hip and leaning her weight into it for leverage.

Sometimes an oversized ass came in handy.

From there, what was supposed to be a training session disintegrated into an all-out brawl. The dumb bastard would not weaken. At home they would have gone back to the smaller round pen where the fences would contain him until he located his brain, assuming he had one. Here in the big arena, it was all on her.

She hauled him around to face her yet again and they both paused to take a few heaving breaths. Sweat dripped from her eyebrows, soaked the strands of hair that escaped the wad on top of her head, and ran down to make muddy tracks in the dust coating her neck and arms. She was puffing like a freight train from alternately chasing and dragging the colt.

Finally, when she was so overheated her vision was starting to blur, he managed one decent circle. Then something caught his eye and he tried to stampede. Shawnee swore, dragged him to a stop, and shot a glare over her shoulder. Cole Jacobs stood, arms folded on the top rail of the gate. She could hardly blame ol' gray for spooking at the sight of the not-so-friendly giant, his canine minion peering under the fence beside him. Shawnee snorted, reminded of an old picture book illustration of a gnarly ogre with rotten teeth dangling a terrified horse by one leg over his open mouth.

Cole was big enough to eat a horse, but he was definitely not gnarly. Some women might even swoon over that extra-large hunk of prime American beef. At least until he opened his mouth. Or didn't, more likely. This morning he wore his usual nonexpression and an immaculate white straw cowboy hat. There wasn't a hint of sweat on his clean-shaven, square-as-an-anvil jaw.

"What?" she snapped.

"It's almost eight o'clock."

"So?"

"We run tonight's stock through the arena at eight."

The gray whinnied and sidled toward where his buddy was dozing on the other side of the fence. Shawnee yanked him around to face her. "I'll get out of your way as soon as Butthead here settles down and pays attention."

"It's almost eight o'clock," Cole repeated, his voice sharpening with impatience.

"You can't wait half an hour?" She scrubbed at her sweaty forehead with the back of one grungy hand. "It's not like it'll get that much hotter."

His face took on the obstinate, ain't-gonna-budge look that invariably goaded her into saying something rude so he'd get all stiff-necked and walk away. Yeah, she knew Cole had legitimate issues. Join the worldwide club.

"We always work the stock at eight," he said.

"And what, they turn into four-legged pumpkins at the stroke of nine?"

He scowled so ferociously his brows pulled into a single dark line. "I have a schedule. I like to stick to it."

"I'll be sure I'm out of your way in the future."

He just stood there, glaring at her. The dog glared, too.

Shawnee matched their heat and turned it up a few kilowatts. "I'm not leaving this arena until I'm done."

The furrows around his mouth deepened. "We can't work around you."

"Then *wait*." The gray tried to take advantage of her distraction. She jerked on the line to set him straight, then turned her glare back to Cole. "You of all people should know that when a horse picks a fight, you can't quit until you win. Otherwise, you're just teaching him to be an asshole. If you want to speed things up, take Butthead over there to the trailer where this mothered-up son of a bitch can't see him."

"I thought that one was Butthead."

She blew out a loud, exasperated breath. "They're all buttheads when I get them. As soon as they stop being buttheads I sell them, so there's no sense wasting time with names."

Cole frowned, probably debating whether to bodily remove her from the arena. No doubt he could, but she'd get in a few shots in the process. Finally he gave a single, curt nod and turned to untie the other horse and lead it away, Katie marching along beside him. Christ. Even his dog had a stick up her ass.

Shawnee glared after them for a couple of beats, then gave the gray her undivided attention. "It's just you and me, fleabag, and you don't even want to know how long I can keep this up."

By the time Cole came back, she had sweated out another gallon of fluids, but she had the horse trotting passable circles. She stepped out and flicked the line. The gray paused, then swung around to circle the other way. Intensely aware that Cole was watching every move, she worked the horse back and forth, made him stop, face, back a few steps, then start again.

Showing off, just a little.

Satisfied, she stopped the gray, brought him around to face, then walked up to rub his dripping forelock. She could feel sweat running down the crack of her ass, soaking the seat of her jeans. "Next time, you'll know better."

The gray dropped his head and whuffled as if in agreement.

She turned toward the gate and found Cole staring at her as if he'd never seen the likes of it. His eyes remained glued to her as he stepped back and swung open the gate.

"Thank you for your patience," she said sweetly, tossing him a mocking smile as she passed.

"Shawnee?"

"Yeah?"

"You should change shirts before you run into anybody else," he said, then strolled into the arena, closing the gate behind him.

She glanced down. Her white T-shirt was soaked through with sweat, her nipples clearly visible through her equally soggy white spandex. Damn bargain rack sports bra. She considered being embarrassed, then shrugged. Wasn't like it was the first time someone had seen her in a wet T-shirt, and she wasn't even dancing on a bar.

Then another thought struck and she huffed out a self-deprecating laugh. She'd been so sure Cole was in awe of her mad horse-training skills, and the whole time he was just staring at her tits.

She laughed again and started for her trailer. In the interests of public decency she kept the horse between her and a trio of committeemen chatting in the shade of the grandstand. Then again, they were good tits. They'd put a smile on more than one face. She should probably share the joy whenever possible, while she still had them. That shoe could drop at any time, especially now that she'd made it past thirty.

Cole, though—she shook her head. She'd figured him for the kind to toss her a towel and order her to cover up instead of hanging around to enjoy the view.

Huh. He might be human after all.

Chapter 6

COLE WAS NEVER GOING TO UNSEE WHAT HE'D JUST seen.

Prior to that morning, if he had been asked to describe Shawnee, he would have said something like stocky, or strong. He might have been thinking *round*. But not the kind of round that made a man raise his eyebrows and sketch her shape in the air with his hands.

Yeah, she was *that* kind of round.

Now he wouldn't be able to stop noticing. Ever. And it wasn't just her cleavage. It was the way she moved, the unexpected agility born of hours of the physically exhausting ground work he'd witnessed today. Cole had trained enough horses to know the strength and endurance it took. Shawnee had the muscle to show for it.

He should have walked away the instant he'd realized he could see through her shirt. He'd damn sure been raised better. His ears stung from the thought of how his aunt would react if she'd caught him. Honestly, though, he'd been mesmerized even before the peep show. The way Shawnee handled that horse—fierce, powerful, and...well, it sounded stupid, but exultant. As if she reveled in the challenge. Worshiped at the altar of *Equinus*, as some horse magazine liked to say.

Damn. Why did those useless snippets get stuck in his head? Now he was picturing her as a Greek goddess wearing nothing but a droopy sheet. But the way that

flea-bitten gray had all but bowed to her in the end—
words couldn't describe that moment, when a horse
gave you their complete trust.

And the woman was so focused she had no idea she
was as good as naked from the waist up.

Cole hissed a curse that made Katie's head jerk up
from where she was hunkered in the shadow of his
horse. He was never, *ever* gonna get that out of his mind.
And Shawnee would know. Probably use it against him
every chance she got. He yanked up on his cinch hard
enough to make Hammer pin his ears in protest.

"Sorry," he muttered, and backed it off a notch.

As he swung aboard the blue roan, Hank strolled in
from the stock pens. He flashed Cole one of the grins
that, along with his slender build and baby face, made
him seem like a perpetual teenager. "We took bets on
how long before you and Shawnee butted heads. Cruz
won—he's the only one who thought you'd make it
through the whole rodeo last night. 'Course, he hadn't
met Shawnee yet. She don't step aside for anyone."

Cole refused to growl, tempting as it was. "She didn't
know the schedule."

"So we'll be back to running the stock at eight from
now on?"

Cole shifted in the saddle, irritated. Shawnee had a
legitimate reason to use the arena and was willing to
get up before dawn to take advantage of the coolest part
of the day. Cole had to respect her dedication. He supposed there wasn't that much difference between eight
and nine as far as running the stock went. If he said so
now, though, it would look like she'd won.

"We're working out a compromise," he hedged.

"I wouldn't mind lettin' her compromise me." Hank's grin turned into a leer. "That's a woman who knows stuff, ya know what I mean?"

Cole snorted. "As if she'd look twice at a punk like you."

"I'm only a year younger than J.P. and she's got plenty of use for him."

J.P. Azeveda? Cole had to fight off a scowl. Figured, Shawnee would go for a guy who was a genius with a rope. Age aside, though, J.P. was Hank's polar opposite—polite, respectful, and thankful for every time he set foot in a rodeo arena. He'd come from Brazil with nothing but a suitcase and a rope. Six months later he was on track to qualify for the National Finals.

Yeah, he could see Shawnee with J.P. But Hank…

"I wouldn't put you and J.P. in the same class," Cole said.

"Yeah, he's just a team roper," Hank said with a sneer. "But it ain't like she's picky."

Irritation congealed into cold fury at the implied insult. "And you are?"

"That's different. I'm a guy."

"So you can stick your dick wherever you want, then call a girl a slut for letting you?"

A smart man would've backpedaled. Hank just shrugged. "I don't make the rules."

"I do." Cole leaned down, grabbed Hank, and hoisted him up until his feet were thrashing in the air as he choked and clawed at the fist bunched in his T-shirt. Cole hauled him close, so they were eye to eye. "If I hear you talk about a woman that way again, I'll take you out back in the bull pens and teach you some respect."

Hank tried to gasp out an answer. Cole let him work at it for a while, then tossed him on his butt in the dirt. "Get on my other horse. I need some help out here."

"I've got it," a voice said behind them.

Cole cranked around in his saddle as Shawnee led her buckskin through a side gate covered by a banner advertising the local Dodge dealership. Damn. How long had she been back there listening? And why was his face going hot, as if he'd been the one spouting off? "I didn't expect you."

"Why not? This is part of the job, right?"

"Yes, but—"

Her face was still flushed from heat and exertion. She'd barely had time to pull on a baseball cap and… *shit, don't look…*a dry shirt. She had to be down at least three quarts of fluid, some of which she'd replaced from the clear plastic water bottle in her hand. She stepped on her horse, polished off the rest of the water, and set the bottle on top of the nearest fencepost, all without a glance at Hank as he scrambled to his feet, knocking dirt off his jeans.

"Whenever you're ready, boss," she said.

If she'd heard even part of what had been said, she should be ripping Hank in two, with her tongue if nothing else. She just kept pretending he didn't exist as he hightailed it out the gate to the stock pens. Her silence should have been a nice change.

So why did Cole feel let down?

He reined Hammer around and signaled to the boys in the back pens. Ten head would buck in each event that night—bareback, saddle bronc, and bull riding—plus three extras drawn for possible re-rides if the first animal didn't perform up to par. They worked the stock through in groups of four, letting them trot around snorting and blowing as they checked out the fences, got a feel for the ground, and found the exit gate. Nothing killed the momentum of a rodeo performance faster than a horse or bull that refused to leave the arena. Plus, they'd be more likely to have their best trip if they were familiar with their surroundings.

After every animal had made the tour, the crew ran them through the bucking chutes and turned them out one at a time, testing every gate hinge and latch in the process. Overkill probably, but that was Cole's middle name. His job was to be sure the rodeo went off without a hitch, that every horse and every bull was prepared to give a hundred percent. If that made him an anal-retentive bastard, so be it, as long as the people in the stands got their money's worth.

Shawnee followed his instructions without a word, either plotting ways to murder Hank or on the verge of keeling over from heat exhaustion. The quiet was nerve-wracking. Cole kept trying to check her out without making her think he was, you know, *checking her out*. Which he wasn't. Intentionally. Could he help it if his mind jumped in all the wrong directions?

When the last bull had been herded out of the arena, Cole climbed off Hammer and loosened his cinches. Shawnee did the same. They both stepped toward the gate, then stopped, each waiting for the other to go first. Cole felt like he should say something about their encounter that morning. Apologize. Explain. Express his appreciation.

No. Wait. That was *not* what he meant.

She paused, then waved toward where Hank had hit the ground. "You can't fight that bullshit."

"Habit." When her head tilted in question, he hitched a shoulder and inspected the dirt between his boots. "You know, um, Violet…"

"Ah. Small town, single mom, big mouths."

He was blushing again, for God's sake. "I had to set 'em straight now and then."

"By setting them on their asses?"

"Sometimes."

She slugged him in the arm. When his head jerked up, she smiled, and for once he didn't feel like he was the butt of the joke. "Never thought I'd say this, but I like your style."

"Uh, thanks." As she started for the gate he blurted, "We can run the stock at eight thirty from now on."

"Damn. I should have flashed you sooner. As long as you're feelin' cooperative, what I'd really like is the key to the arena lights so I can be done before the sun comes up." She tipped her sunglasses down and cocked those eyebrows at him, her grin sharpening to its usual razor edge. "Get it for me and I'll show you my ass, too."

Cole stared after her, dumbfounded, as she sauntered away. And damn it to hell, he could not stop himself from looking at the ass in question. He turned, folded his arms on his saddle, and buried his face in them. What had already been the longest summer of his life had officially become eternity.

In hell. With his own personal demon.

Chapter 7

WHEN SHE'D FINISHED HOSING DOWN HER HORSES AND putting them away, Shawnee walked into her trailer and collapsed on the nearest horizontal surface—the massive couch that filled the entire slide-out of the living quarters. Tori's first husband had been a big man, and the trailer was designed to accommodate him. Shawnee pressed her burning cheek into the cool leather. The morning had wrung her out like a wet sponge—then smacked her upside the head.

Cole Jacobs had defended her virtue. Well, not exactly her virtue, but her right to be as unvirtuous as she damn well pleased. *Cole freaking Jacobs.* When Hank had mentioned J.P., there'd been something in Cole's eyes— just a flicker—that she'd read as disapproval. Then he'd slapped Hank down like a fence-jumping hound.

She'd have to think about that when her brain wasn't cooked to the consistency of a soft-boiled egg. God, she was thirsty. She tried to lift her head and measure the distance to the refrigerator, but even that took more effort than she could muster.

A knock sounded at the door, deep and heavy. *Oh hell. What now?*

"Come in!" she hollered without moving.

The door swung open and was immediately blocked by Cole's broad body. His dark eyebrows drew into the usual disapproving line as he inspected her. "Are you sick?"

"I'm resting. What do you want?"

"You left this at the arena." He held up her water bottle, his gaze narrowing on her face, which had to be the color of a ripe red tomato. "I shouldn't have let you help run the stock."

"Since when do you tell me what I can't do?" She meant to sound irritated, but her hackles weren't up to rising, either.

"Since you work for me." He jiggled the empty water bottle. "You need to drink something."

"No shit." She lifted a hand and let it flop back to her side. "Soon as I cool down a little. Might help if you weren't standing there letting the heat in."

He grunted, but instead of setting the bottle down and leaving, he ducked his head to step inside and waited for that damn dog to follow before he shut the door behind him. "You got anything in the fridge?"

"Yeah. Give me a minute—"

One long step and he yanked open the refrigerator door, pulled out the big jug of sweet tea, unscrewed the cap of her water bottle, and filled it to the top. The dog plunked down to watch, tongue lolling.

"Need help sitting up?" Cole asked, as he handed it to her.

"No. I got it." She wallowed around until her feet were on the floor and her shoulders propped against the couch cushions. Her vision went white around the edges from the effort. "I'm good."

"Drink," Cole said.

Words faded into the mental fog, making it impossible to argue. While she drank, he strode into the bathroom. She heard water running. A moment later he emerged with a wet washcloth in one hand. He tossed it in her direction, but her reflexes were shot and it landed on her chest with a chilly splat.

Oh Lord, did that feel good.

Cole found the air conditioner vent in the ceiling—*he* could reach it without even stretching—and adjusted it so the air flowed through her sweat-soaked hair. She took another gulp of tea, then pressed the cold bottle against the side of her neck as she picked up the washcloth and scrubbed the sweat and dirt from her face.

When she lowered the cloth, Cole's face came into focus, the sugar in the sweet tea already working its magic. He stuck a banana in her hand, swiped from a bunch on the counter.

"Eat that," he ordered. "Unless you feel like you're gonna puke."

"Yes, Master," she muttered.

He scowled at her. "You won't be worth a crap tonight if you don't replenish your electrolytes. Bananas have potassium."

She knew that. Nobody knew more about vitamins and minerals and antioxidants. She would make a smoothie chock-full of essential nutrients as soon as she got her legs back under her. "Well, thanks for your concern and all, but I can manage from here."

Cole folded his arms across his very broad chest and continued to loom over her. Geezus. The man could loom like no other, except his uncle Steve.

She gave him her best stink-eye. "Are you just gonna stand there and stare at me?"

"Until you stop looking like death? Yes."

The dog groaned and flopped onto her side, as if she

could tell he was planted deeper than a big ol' live oak. Shawnee gave an exasperated growl and ripped the end off of the banana. If she'd been in true fighting form, she would've done something profane with it to make him blush again—seriously, a man that size blushing was dangerously close to cute—but she was pretty sure even that wouldn't make him go away this time. She broke off a third of it, stuffed it in her mouth, and chomped like a belligerent eight-year-old.

There'd been no one to loom—or even notice—when she'd been knocked flat for three days by a case of food poisoning. She'd gotten so sick she couldn't crawl off the bathroom floor to find her phone and call 911 when she decided it actually might kill her instead of just feel-ing that way.

But that could never happen to her now.

She stuffed the next chunk of banana in her mouth, chewing more slowly as she considered her change of circumstances. Nowadays, she exchanged texts or calls with Tori, Violet, or both most days. If she didn't respond within a reasonable time or show up at Tori's to rope, someone would come knocking at her door. As if she'd asked them to look out for her.

As if she'd ever ask *anyone* to look out for her.

She wolfed down the last of the banana and chased it with a gulp of sweet tea. "There. Satisfied?"

"Yes—if it stays down." In case it didn't he slid the trash can over beside her, then finally stopped staring at her and inspected the trailer instead. "Not as fancy as I figured."

Shawnee followed his gaze around the interior of the living quarters. With the slide-out extended there was a good-sized chunk of floor space, with the couch on one side and the banquette-style table on the other. At the front, the nose that extended over the pickup box held a king-sized bed. At the back a short bar sectioned off the kitchen. In addition to a gas oven and cooktop with a microwave mounted above, it had double sinks and a good-sized refrigerator. The bathroom even had a full-sized shower stall. But none of it was fancy. Just functional.

Nausea rippled through Shawnee's stomach as it attempted to reject the banana. New beads of sweat popped on her forehead, but she refused to be sick. Not with Cole watching. She took a tiny swig of her tea and breathed carefully until the queasiness passed.

"If you're gonna hang around, find something worth watching on TV." She picked up a remote from the couch and tossed it to him.

He snatched it out of the air with one platter-sized hand and pointed it at the flat screen mounted on a wall swivel at the end of the bed. "Satellite?"

"Seventy-eight channels. Get a glass of tea and sit down, for Christ's sake. You're cricking my neck."

He hesitated, then poured himself a large tumbler. "Can I borrow a bowl for Katie?"

"Above the sink."

He found one, filled it with water for the dog, then settled in at the table to watch a show about rotational grazing on the ag channel. Shawnee closed her eyes and drifted, sipping her tea. Damn, he took up a lot of space. The whole trailer smelled like sun-roasted cowboy. Which wasn't necessarily bad, but…

When she woke up, someone on the television was

droning on about soil impaction in cornfields. Cole was gone so she keeled over, stretched out, and went back to sleep for another two hours.

After a shower, a couple more gallons of fluids, and a good meal, she was almost back to a hundred percent. When she arrived at Cole's trailer that evening to saddle Salty, he gave her one long, critical stare, then got on Hammer and rode away. Didn't even ask how she felt, the antisocial bastard.

But he had made sure she was okay.

———

At exactly two fifteen, Cole's eyes popped open, just like every other night on the road. Midnight might be the witching hour, but two a.m. was closing time, when idiots came out in force. Drunks wandering back from the bar or out of the beer garden, brains sufficiently pickled to drown their good judgment. Cowboys stoked up on beer bravado looking to settle a score, usually with their fists. And occasionally someone with truly malicious intent.

Cole pulled on jeans, boots, and a T-shirt and grabbed his flashlight and cell phone. Unlike Shawnee's plush accommodations, he could reach nearly anything in his living quarters while standing in the middle of the floor. He grabbed a silver key off the tiny banquette table and stuffed it into the pocket of his jeans before letting himself out into night air so humid it condensed on his skin.

On a Thursday postmidnight, all was reasonably quiet. A security light mounted on the power pole behind the announcer's stand lit the stock pens sufficiently that he didn't need his flashlight. Katie padded along at his heels as he worked his way around, bull by bull, horse by horse, senses tuned to any sounds or signs of distress. Sleepy eyes blinked at him, too accustomed to his nocturnal ramblings to do more than snuffle at being disturbed.

Somewhere on the rodeo grounds doors slammed, an engine roared to life, and hip-hop blared from a stereo. Cole waved at a car crammed full of young bull riders, headed to either an all-night diner or a motel. Or so he hoped. This was no time to be hitting the highway.

He moved on, checking the outer gates of the pens. Each was secured with a bicycle-style lock equipped with an alarm, triggered if anyone attempted to cut the cable or tamper with the lock, like when animal rights activists had invaded a rodeo grounds in Colorado, turned loose a herd of bucking horses, and shot off fireworks to send them stampeding. Four had been severely injured when they ran, panicked and blind, through a barbed wire fence, and three more died on the adjacent interstate highway, along with one motorist.

In the unlikely event of fire, flood, or other natural disaster and the even more unlikely event that Cole wouldn't be first on the scene, the Leses each had a set of backup keys. Plan B was an absolute necessity. Cole preferred to also have plan C, D, and even E, when possible.

He didn't expect human trouble tonight. At this rodeo, the parking attendants were on patrol twenty-four hours a day to be sure none of the rigs got a foot out of line—other than Shawnee's. Pompous bastards, but an excellent deterrent to anyone up to mischief, or worse.

Cole climbed the steps to the announcer's stand to check that the door was closed and locked, then walked

the entire outside perimeter of the arena, pausing to
look over the roping cattle, even though they belonged
to a subcontractor. He took his time strolling around the
back side of the grandstand and watched the final two
cars pull away from the now-darkened beer garden.

Completing his circle, he worked his way through
the contestant parking area, shining his flashlight down
the shadowy corridors formed by the fifty- to sixty-foot
length of the ropers' rigs. Halfway down the first row
of vehicles, he stopped short. A horse's head jerked up
when Cole's flashlight beam landed on him, mouth full
of the hay he'd pulled from a bale in the back of a pickup.

Recognizing the legendary escape artist, Cole laughed
softly. "Hey, Joker. Got yourself untied again, I see."

The horse gave what sounded like a guilty sigh. Cole
caught up his dangling halter rope, took him back to his
own trailer, and tied him with a nibble-proof knot. No
need to wake anyone. The only thing in danger when
Joker got loose was unsecured feed in the near vicinity.

Cole finished his patrol without further incident,
then turned toward the rig beside the big live oak in the
middle of the parking area—and grinned in anticipation.

Bam! Bam! Bam!

Shawnee felt as if she'd barely shut her eyes when
the series of loud thuds jolted her out of dreamland. She
was up and on her feet before she came fully awake,
heart pounding in time with the fist beating on her door.
She yanked it open and found Cole standing in the pitch
dark, his devil dog guarding his flank.

"Wha's wrong?" she mumbled, heart tripping as she

shoved the wild tangle of hair out of her face and hit
the switch for the outside floodlight. "Somethin' with
my horses?"

"No."

His gaze made a quick trip up and down her body,
but there wasn't much to see. She slept in an oversized
T-shirt and gym shorts, used to being roused by drunk
friends and, less frequently, equine emergencies.

Cole, though, looked odd. Not like himself.

Shawnee breathed through the adrenaline rush of
being dragged out of a dead sleep, blinking hard to
clear her head. It was his clothes, she realized, as a few
brain cells came online. Cole was always buttoned up
and clean-shaven. Now he had a definite shadow on his
jaw, and instead of his usual collar and long sleeves,
he wore a snug T-shirt that showed off powerful arms
and a matching set of shoulders. Under the floodlight,
his dark hair gleamed, mussed up as if he'd just rolled
out of bed.

The thought filled her head with visions of hard
muscle and soft cotton, hot kisses and whisker burns.
Eye to eye with an acre of well-developed chest, suddenly Cole's bed didn't seem like a horrible place to be.

What the hell?

Shawnee shook that craziness out of her head so hard
her neck popped. "If there's no dire emergency, why
are you beating on my door in the middle of the night?"
she snapped.

Cole held out his hand. She gingerly plucked the
weird-looking key from his palm.

"For the arena lights," he said. "Switch box is below
the announcer's stand."

She worked her eyes open and shut a few more times. "What time is it?"

"Almost three."

Her fingers curled around the key and she considered punching him right in those smug chops. She refused to thank him when he could just as soon have handed over the key after the rodeo. He must have had it. He sure hadn't dragged a committee member out of bed at this godforsaken hour to get the thing.

"Just so's you know, we do have to work the stock right at eight," he said. "The Exceptional Rodeo starts at ten and the committee wants us out of the way so they can set up. And if you're interested, we can always use more cowboys and cowgirls to help out."

"*We?*" She almost added something snarky about scaring the kiddies, but it might sound like she was poking fun at the special needs children who were the focus of the event.

He gave her a dead-eyed stare. "I like kids."

"Yeah? Why don't you have a passel of 'em?"

"I'm working on it."

Whoa. He was *not* joking. Naturally. Cole never joked. He waited a couple of beats, then gave her the usual clipped nod and turned away. She let him take a dozen long strides before she called out.

"Hey, Cole?"

He stopped and turned.

"A deal's a deal." She spun around, whipped down her shorts, and mooned him.

Chapter 8

WELL, THAT CERTAINLY HADN'T TURNED OUT LIKE Cole had planned. But what ever did when Shawnee was involved? Yet more proof that in a battle of wits, Cole was the guy in the red shirt who always died first.

Why hadn't it occurred to him that he was basically knocking on her bedroom door? Then he might've been prepared to come face-to-face with all that rumpled, sleepy woman, close enough to breathe in the scent of hand lotion and shampoo.

And a mouthwatering whiff of grilled chicken.

Twelve hours later, Cole was still obsessing about those breasts. As in, the package of chicken breasts he'd seen in her refrigerator when he was fetching her sweet tea. Plus fresh collard greens, red peppers, green beans, and two kinds of melons. God, what he'd give for a piece of meat that wasn't slapped between slices of bread and a big ol' heap of home-cooked greens. A fresh-baked roll on the side, dripping with butter.

He didn't even know if Shawnee was a decent cook. He did know she'd laugh in his face if he invited himself to dinner, and it wasn't like he could turn on the charm. He didn't even have a tap. Cole Jacobs, putting the *ass* in Asperger's for thirty-three years.

But at least kids liked him.

The one who currently had a death grip on his neck whimpered, and Cole gave his shoulders a reassuring rub.

"We're okay," he said softly. "We're just gonna go over here in the corner, and you can meet my friend Salty."

The horse was tied well away from where contestants guided the other kids around the miniature barrel racing barrels and taught them to rope and tie dummy calves. Hank and Cruz had a plush stuffed bull mounted on a wheelbarrow frame and were using it to chase each other and some squealing children as they demonstrated bull-fighting moves. And, to Cole's amazement, Shawnee was crouched next to a wheelchair, showing a little girl how to swing a loop.

The boy's mother gave him a tense smile. "Thank you. We came because Jamey loves animals, but all the noise…"

Cole glanced around the arena, filled with cowboys, cowgirls, and ear-splitting giggles and shrieks. He never missed the Exceptional Rodeos. This was the one crowd that didn't make him want to crawl in a hole and pull the dirt in after him.

"I understand." He hesitated, then added, "I'm autistic."

"Oh." Jamey's mother relaxed slightly. "Maybe that's why he took to you."

"Could be," Cole agreed.

Even after three years, it was hard to say out loud. He hadn't been diagnosed until he was thirty, and while it was handy to have a label for his particular brand of weirdness, it hadn't made much difference. He'd read all the books, visited all the websites, even done some therapy. None of it had transformed him from a tongue-tied frog into gallant prince.

Maybe it would've worked if they'd caught it when

he was younger, when his brain still had some flexibility. Before the head-on collision that had wiped out the other three-fourths of his immediate family, and the avalanche of loss that had buried him, depositing layer after layer of grief in the spaces between his neurons, where it hardened like the mortar in a brick wall.

In moments like this, though, with Jamey's slender body rigid against him, Cole was nothing but grateful. On the grand scale of things, he had it pretty easy. But he could still see the world through the eyes of those who had it worse. That's why he always zeroed in on the scared one. The rest would do fine with the regular people. This child needed more than an hour of fun and games.

Cole kept rubbing the boy's back as they moved away from the chaos, murmuring to him the way he would a frightened colt. He stopped beside Salty and the horse craned his neck around to snuffle gently at Jamey's arm. The boy squeaked in alarm.

"He just wants to get to know you." But Cole pushed Salty's head away, having allowed the obligatory sniff, and moved in so Jamey was sandwiched between his own bulk and Salty's warm, silky body. The horse stood stock-still as Cole matched the rhythm of his breath to the easy rise and fall of Salty's rib cage. After a few minutes, Jamey's grip on Cole began to relax. His head slowly turned. Salty gazed back at him from one dark, soft eye. They considered each other for a while. Then Jamey slowly, *slowly,* reached one hand out to press the palm against Salty's neck.

And he smiled.

Cole heard a breath *whoosh* quietly out of Jamey's

mother. When he glanced over, her eyes were shining with tears. She swiped at them with her fingers. "I'm sorry. It's just…it's been a really tough week, you know? I almost didn't bring him, but now…" She sniffed and flashed a watery smile. "Well, obviously you *do* understand."

Cole just nodded.

The loop flopped onto the head of the roping dummy, then settled around its neck. Shawnee gave a loud whoop and high-fived Amber. "You see? I knew you could do it!"

"I did!" The little girl's grin split her face. "Can I try again?"

"Honey, you can work at it 'til your arm falls off." She leaned in and lowered her voice, like she was telling a secret. "That's how you learn to rope like a girl. Then watch the boys try to keep up."

They exchanged a fist bump before Shawnee helped the girl build a new loop and stepped back. This throw was a little stronger and the rope hit the target with more authority. They whooped again and exchanged another fist bump. Then Amber's parents stepped forward.

"I'm sorry, baby," her father said, waving his phone to show the time. "Your brother has a baseball game."

Amber's smile faded. "But I'm just getting good at it."

"I'll tell you what." Shawnee retrieved the kid-sized rope from the dummy, coiled it up, and handed it to the girl. "You take that with you. Rope a bucket or a big teddy bear or whatever you've got at home, and next year you can come back and show…" She started to say *me*, but of course she wouldn't be here. She was temporary. Always. "Show everybody what you've got."

Amber still looked like she might burst into tears. "I won't remember all the stuff you told me."

Impulsively, Shawnee snatched the phone out of the startled father's hand and entered her number before handing it back. "There. You can send me a video once in a while. I'll give you a few pointers."

"Would you?" Amber's eyes widened and her smile crept back. "And maybe you could send me a video of the next time you go roping."

An annoying lump swelled in Shawnee's throat. "Sure. But it'll be a while, 'cuz I'll be busy being a pickup man until the end of September."

"That's okay." Amber reached up, leaving Shawnee no choice but to bend and give her a hug. "I'll wave to you at the rodeo tonight."

"I'll keep an eye out."

Shawnee crossed her arms tight over the ache in her chest as she watched the dad maneuver the wheelchair through the soft dirt of the arena, both parents nodding and smiling as Amber talked a mile a minute and swung an imaginary rope. What the hell had gotten into her, promising to keep in touch? But how could she resist those eyes? That smile. And the way it made Shawnee's heart feel like it grew two sizes.

That'd teach her to get sucked into this touchy-feely crap.

"They get to you," Cole said quietly, coming up beside her.

She glanced over and was caught by the softness in his face. A glow in his eyes—the same warmth that was toasting her innards. And an openness to him, as if he'd peeled off a Cole-shaped mask and she was really seeing him for the first time. She couldn't look away.

The moment stretched too long. Started to feel like a *moment*, and oh, hell no, not with Cole Jacobs, but—

A woman flung herself at Cole and sang out, "I'm ba-ack!"

He froze for an instant, then relaxed when he looked down into the face grinning up at him. Geezus. Who wouldn't smile at that face? She looked like she'd strolled off the cover of one of those cowgirl fashion magazines, all cheekbones and funky jewelry and end-less legs. Except you didn't see many women in western wear ads with skin the color of Miz Iris's chocolate silk pie, and unlike Shawnee's tangled mess, her waist-length hair was a glorious mass of jet-black ringlets.

"Aren't you supposed to be up north, kicking ass and taking names?" Cole asked.

The woman scowled. "My horse turned up lame. The vet found an abscess in his right front foot." She gave Cole another squeeze. "So I thought I'd come down and hang out with you for a while."

Tyrell strolled over and tugged on her arm. "Turn him loose. He's not a hugger."

"I know. That's why I do it." But she let herself be pulled free.

"I swear you're part cat." Tyrell tucked her under his arm. "Shawnee Pickett, meet my daughter, Mariah. She's gonna be my sound and music tech for a few rodeos."

What? Shawnee did a double take. This was the famous Mariah? Tyrell's pride and joy, who had just become the Washington State All-Around Champion

Cowgirl and finished in the top five in the barrel racing at nationals—as a high school junior? But that would make her…sixteen? Seventeen at the most? Shawnee blinked and stared some more.

Mariah Swift looked at least twenty years old. Possibly closer to twenty-five, when you threw in her deep, throaty voice, her clothes, and the way she carried herself.

Shawnee gave her head a slow, commiserating shake. "Geezus, Tyrell. Do you beat the boys off with a stick, or have you had to go with rubber bullets and tear gas?"

Tyrell made a pained face.

Mariah rolled her eyes. "I manage fine on my own, thanks. Boys my age are ridiculous."

"I'm sure that makes your father feel *so* much better," Shawnee said dryly.

"You have no idea." Tyrell scowled down at his daughter, then gave her a squeeze. "I have to keep telling myself she's not actually *trying* to drive me to drink."

Mariah grinned and hugged him in return. Shawnee had to wonder what the son looked like. He'd graduated last year and was attending Eastern Washington University on a basketball scholarship just like his parents—Tyrell imported from Southern California and his future wife recruited off the Shoshone reservation at Fort Hall, Idaho. If Mariah was any indication, their combined DNA must look like strands of gold under a microscope.

Mariah sniffed the air. "That barbecue smells so good. I am starving, and somebody refused to stop at an In-and-Out Burger on the way from the airport."

"I didn't want you to spoil your dinner." Tyrell

steered her toward the open gate, where Analise leaned against a post, waiting.

As they followed, Shawnee glanced at Cole and found him watching Tyrell and Mariah, his expression…odd.

"What?" Shawnee demanded.

Cole shook his head and looked away.

"You really do want kids," Shawnee said. Then, as an afterthought: "And a wife."

Heads turned as the others looked around in surprise. There was a beat of silence, everyone probably trying to decide how to reassure Cole that there must be a woman out there who could live with him.

"There's nothing wrong with wanting a family," Cole said stiffly. "Most people do."

Most people had a choice. Shawnee gave an elaborately casual shrug. "Yeah, well, count me out. I intend to wallow in sin for the rest of my days."

Tyrell covered Mariah's ears. "You are not allowed to listen to her for at least another ten years, or until I'm too old to see or hear. Whichever comes first."

Mariah swatted him away, focusing on Cole as they were all drawn toward the scent of grilled meat. "I'm really good with people. I can help you find your true love."

"Lord knows someone will have to," Shawnee drawled. "Otherwise some poor woman's gonna end up on a romantic stroll through the stock pens with Katie biting her ankles."

Tyrell snorted. Mariah laughed outright.

"No sense dating anyone who doesn't like my bulls," Cole said, sounding a wee bit miffed.

"What else is on the list?" Shawnee asked.

"What list?"

"Your requirements for a perfect mate. You must have a list." She raised a hand, extending her fingers to tick off the line items. "Number one—loves the smell of manure in the morning. Number two—tolerates that hell hound. Number three…"

"Bakes like Miz Iris," Analise chimed in. She was minus the lip ring today, but her black tank top featured a half-decomposed zombie with a red rose clenched in his teeth. "And hates the Dallas Cowboys. Cole won't even let Hank listen to the games on the radio when we're driving."

"Isn't that, like, blasphemy?" Mariah asked, wide-eyed.

Cole's shoulders crept up toward his ears. "I don't hate the Cowboys. I'm just not into football."

"You played all the way through school," Shawnee pointed out.

"I live in Earnest, Texas. There were ten boys in my class." He waved a hand, indicating his oversized body. "The coach started hounding me when I was in kindergarten."

Shawnee squinted, mental gears spinning. "But you never liked it? Not even as a kid?"

"No. It's too noisy and…" The corners of his mouth pinched as he caught her drift. He nodded, quick and sharp. "That's why I didn't go."

Or he'd be dead, too. The crash that had killed his parents and brother on a Sunday evening, coming home from a Cowboys game, had been so horrific no one could have survived. Violet had confided once that they'd been scared it might kill Cole anyway.

And now Shawnee felt like a jerk for bringing it up.

She forced breezy humor into her voice. "Okay—that's numbers one through four on the list. What's five?"

"Wants babies. Except that should be number one. Cole is awesome with kids." Mariah linked her arm through his. "There are a whole lot of women in Texas who have no idea what they're missing. You just need a little coaching. Like charm school—"

Shawnee made a rude noise. "Don't go teaching him to smile and lie through his teeth. The best thing about Cole is never having to wonder if he means what he says."

Tyrell's eyebrows shot up. "Is that how you define charm?"

"In my experience? Yeah." And oh boy, did she have experience, and its name was Ace Pickett, otherwise known as Daddy Dearest. Self-centered bastard. Silver-tongued demon. She'd learned early and well that charm could turn on a dime and rip your face off if Ace didn't get what he considered his due.

They reached the park adjacent to the rodeo grounds and were swallowed by the crowd lining up to fill their plates with smoked chicken legs, pork chops, brisket, and heaping helpings of green beans, macaroni and cheese, and pinto beans. Hank popped up beside them, one pink bandana folded and tied on as a headband and another around his upper arm.

His gaze caught on Mariah and his mouth went slack, his eyes a little glassy—the standard male response, judging by the faces around them. "Oh. Hey. You're back."

"Hi, Hank." She flashed a carbon copy of her daddy's dimples at him, then waited to see if he had any remaining brain function. When he showed no signs, she asked, "Whatcha got there?"

"Here?" He looked stupidly down at the bag he was carrying, then jolted out of his Mariah-induced stupor and reached inside to pull out several more bandanas. "I'm supposed to make sure y'all get one of these for Tough Enough to Wear Pink night."

Analise tied one around her thigh, below the frayed hem of her plaid schoolgirl skirt. Mariah accepted hers with another smile that threatened to finish Hank, along with several bystanders who got caught in the overflow.

Hank blinked, then tore his eyes off her to hold a purple bandana out to Shawnee. "These are for survivors—"

She knocked his hand away as if he'd offered her a live scorpion. For an instant, they both stood in stunned surprise. Then she snatched one of the pink bandanas. "I'm gonna get something to eat before this mob licks the platters clean."

She felt all of their eyes boring into her as she walked away. Knew exactly what they'd be discussing when she was out of earshot. Cole and Hank were both aware that she'd gone a round with Hodgkin's lymphoma at fourteen. They might even know some of the rest. But they couldn't make her claim to be a survivor, any more than a soldier on leave between deployments.

That was just asking to get your ass blown up.

Chapter 9

SHAWNEE WOULDN'T MIND NEVER SEEING ANOTHER pink ribbon. And Tough Enough to Wear Pink days were bad enough without the dumb-ass T-shirts. *Save the Tatas. Free breast exams while you wait.* Whatever, asshole. Get your nuts smashed and irradiated every year and see if you still think it's cute. Damned ungrateful for the girl most likely to benefit from money raised for breast cancer research, but as the therapist at the children's hospital had told her, "Feelings are feelings—you don't have to justify them."

During cancer awareness events, what she felt was irritable. Tight. As if during one of the operations the doctors had implanted a steel band inside her rib cage that wouldn't allow her to take a full breath. On good days, she could ignore it, just the slightest constriction that she'd grown so used to, she barely noticed anymore.

On the very worst days, it sucked down tight around her lungs, her heart, until she had to resort to her happy pills to relieve the pressure.

Luckily, this week's rodeo committee had gone out of their way to provide her with a distraction. The Jacobs convoy had arrived to discover a stretch of fence along the front of the grandstand had been lowered to improve the view from shiny new VIP boxes. When Cole pointed out that it wasn't high enough to stop a bronc or bull determined to jump, the president had responded with a patronizing smile. "Isn't that why we have pickup men? To keep the stock under control?"

Shawnee and Hank had had to drag Cole away while Tyrell remained behind to be the voice of reason, for all the good *that* had done. Then the president had compounded the problem by giving them an extra helper—his round-assed moron of a son who was incredibly gifted at being in the wrong place at the wrong time.

Even Tyrell's powers of persuasion were no match for stupidity squared.

So for two performances Cole and Shawnee had been busting their butts, trying to take care of the cowboys while keeping one eye on the fence and trying *not* to mow down or strangle Idiot Jr. It was so exhausting they didn't even have time to snipe at each other.

And now they were fixin' to turn out a bull named for his inclination to make a break for freedom at the slightest opportunity.

"In chute number three," Tyrell boomed, "National Finals bucking bull and son of Jacobs Livestock's legendary Dirt Eater...meet Flight Risk!"

Cole shot Shawnee a warning look. She lifted her rope in response, to show him her loop was built and ready. Plan A was to get a rope on Flight Risk the instant the bull rider was clear. Plan B...

Things were gonna get western if they had to resort to Plan B.

The energy of the crowd built around her along with the beat of Foo Fighter's *Learn to Fly*. Salty pricked his ears in anticipation, as if he recognized the song. Like all of Cole's mounts, he was fast, strong, and knew where she wanted to go before she touched the

reins. Cole might suck at people, but the man had a way
with horses.

The cowboy nodded and Flight Risk fired out of the
chute, a fifteen-hundred-pound missile launching into
midair. His head whipped around to the left and his body
followed; the sheer power ripped the cowboy's hand out
of the rope. He shot backward, ending up astride the
bull's butt. On the next jump, Flight Risk slung him skyward, but instead of sailing free, the cowboy was jerked
down and slammed into the ground, one spur caught in
the flank strap.

Hung up in the worst possible way.

Cruz threw his body on top of the cowboy in hopes
that the extra weight would rip the spur free while Hank
grabbed for the tail of the flank strap to yank the slip
knot loose. As his hand closed around the rope, Flight
Risk kicked high, picking Hank up and tossing him a
dozen yards, right into Hammer's path, forcing Cole to
rein up hard. The flank strap and the cowboy came loose
and Flight Risk broke into a gallop, headed straight for
the luxury boxes.

Shawnee spurred after him. One, two, three swings
and—

A horse cut in front of her. *Son of a bitch*. Ignoring
Cole's strict instructions to stay the hell out of the way,
Idiot Jr. blundered straight into Shawnee's path, shouting and waving. The bull all but rolled his eyes as he
ducked around the moron. There was nothing Shawnee
could do but watch as Flight Risk reached the fence,
gathered himself, and leapt.

He landed in a narrow walkway between two of
the VIP boxes, greeted by screams and flailing bodies.

Flight Risk ignored them, focused on the tunnel that led under the grandstand and out to freedom—and the midway.

"Plan B!" Cole yelled.

He was already riding through a pass gate and into the stands. Shawnee was right on his tail. Hammer and Salty plowed through the chaos, impervious to dropped beers and flying nachos. When they clattered out the end of the tunnel, Flight Risk was twenty yards ahead, aimed straight for the line of shooting galleries and ring toss games. A mother grabbed her toddler and flung him over a low counter, face-first into the rubber duck pond, then dove in after him. A carny waved his oversized hammer in self-defense as the bull hooked a giant purple panda with one horn and flung it onto the lap of a bug-eyed girl on the Tilt-a-Whirl.

Flight Risk dodged left between a cotton candy booth and a trailer peddling funnel cakes and deep-fried pickles. Cole followed. Shawnee stayed right so the bull couldn't circle back. As they thundered past the mini donut truck, people scattered, shrieking and stumbling. Salty planted his fronts and swerved hard to dodge a stroller, knocking a candied apple out of a wide-eyed teenager's hand.

"'Scuse us!" Shawnee called over her shoulder.

As they came even with the next gap between vendors, Shawnee saw Cole's loop settle over the bull's horns, then heard Hammer's hooves scrabbling on the asphalt when Cole dallied up and attempted to bring the bull to a stop. As Flight Risk turned, Shawnee skidded around the shaved ice stand, took two swings, and laid her loop under his belly, snatching up both hind feet and whipping solid dallies around her saddle horn. Salty grunted but held as the bull stretched between the horses, teetered, then flopped onto his side a foot shy of a bouncy castle filled with squealing preschoolers.

Shawnee was blowing as hard as Salty. Ho-ly shit. That…was…so…*awesome*.

Cole didn't look nearly as thrilled, eyeing the pandemonium in their wake, and the flock of morons with cell phones already creeping closer. "We'll have to hold him until security clears these idiots out, then take him back to his pen and go ask that dickhead what he thinks of his fence now." Then, of all things, he grinned, and her heart gave an odd little *blippity-blip*. "Nice loop, by the way."

A warmth that had nothing to do with the heat rushed through her. It was just…okay, yeah, it meant more coming from Cole, *not* because she treasured his opinion, but because he was so stingy with his praise. That was all. Just a major ego stroke.

And maybe, just a little, that smile. Damn. She considered mentioning that if he broke it out a little more often, his wife hunt might go considerably better. But she'd had to earn it…and she didn't want to share.

Uh-oh.

She couldn't turn loose of Flight Risk and run, so she did the next best thing. She batted her eyes and leered at him. "See? I told you we'd be good together."

But this time, Cole didn't blush.

Cole wasn't allowed anywhere near the committee president. Instead, when he and Shawnee rode out of the arena gate after herding Flight Risk back to his pen and finishing the last three rides of the rodeo, lights flared in his face.

A woman with a microphone blocked their escape route. "Cole Jacobs? We're from Channel 5 News. We were out on the midway doing a feature on this year's fair food and were lucky enough to catch the dramatic capture of your bucking bull on film. Can we have a few words with you and Miz Pickett?"

Cole didn't drop many f-bombs, but…well, *fuck*. A news crew with footage of a Jacobs Livestock bull terrorizing women and children? And pointing their microphones at him? He could feel his brain grinding to a halt while he stared into the light like a paralyzed rabbit.

"Sure." Shawnee eased Salty near enough to lean over and hiss words directly into his ear. "You nod your face and say, 'We expressed our concern when we saw the fence had been lowered. You'll have to direct any other questions regarding the safety of the facilities to the committee.' I'll handle the rest. Got it?"

He nodded, downshifting from outright terror to mild panic. He had his lines. He just had to spit them out at semiappropriate moments. God save them from whatever Shawnee blurted, but she couldn't do worse than him.

The news lady positioned them side-by-side in front of their horses, then amped her smile up to a thousand watts as she turned to the camera. "Tonight's rodeo offered some unexpected thrills when a bull called Flight Risk lived up to his name, escaping from the arena and onto the midway. Our cameras were on hand for the dramatic capture of the bull by Jacobs Livestock pickup riders Cole Jacobs and Shawnee Pickett. Thanks to their immediate response and impressive skills, what could have been a disastrous incident resulted in only a few minor scrapes and bruises." She held the microphone up to Cole. "According to spectators, you didn't hesitate to ride your horses through the grandstand tunnel. That split-second decision may have saved lives."

Shawnee reached over and pulled the microphone down to her level. "Cole anticipated that if an animal jumped the fence it would go through the tunnel, so we practiced to be sure our horses could follow and asked the usher to be ready to open the gate for us."

"Really?" An avid gleam lit the woman's eyes. "You knew the arena might not be secure?"

Shawnee nudged Cole in the ribs. He started. That was his cue.

"We expressed our concern when we saw the fence had been lowered." His face was as stiff as frozen mud. "You'll have to direct any other questions regarding the safety of the facilities to the committee."

"But if you—"

"As Cole said," Shawnee cut in, "those are questions for the committee. If you don't have any more for us…"

The reporter hesitated, as if debating whether to push the point, then plastered on another smile. "It was an impressive display of horsemanship and roping skills. Especially for a woman."

Cole felt Shawnee stiffen, but her tone remained neutral. "Anyone willing to put in the time and effort could do the same."

"But you aren't just any woman. Your father, Ace Pickett, is a former world champion roper. He must have been a big help to you along the way. Not to mention having Cole's expert guidance."

Oh geezus. Shawnee went dead still, and Cole could feel her winding up. He had to say something before she blew.

"The most important thing is good horses," he blurted, to fill the awkward pause. He reached back to rub Hammer's ears. "These are the real heroes."

"You train your own horses?"

"Yes," he said.

"Cole is the best," Shawnee declared. "One of these days, he and his horses will be picking up broncs at the National Finals."

Cole shot her a surprised glance. She sounded so matter-of-fact, as if it was a given. Was she being sarcastic or trying to change the subject?

The news lady hit Cole and then Shawnee with a speculative look. "The two of you work extremely well together, almost like you read each other's minds. Have you been *partners* for long?"

Oh shit. Oh shit. Here it comes. Cole braced himself for the explosion. To his shock, Shawnee threw an arm around his waist, leaned her head on his shoulder, and poured syrup all over her voice. "We've only been together for three weeks, but like I said… Cole is *the* best."

Cole just stood there, stunned, his heart pounding so hard Shawnee must have been able to feel it. But somehow his arm found its way around Shawnee, and stayed there even after the news lady stepped away and turned to smile directly into the camera. "As we've said before, you can find almost anything at this year's fair—including drama and a little romance. For Channel 5 News…"

The instant the light on the camera went off, Shawnee pushed away and grabbed the news lady by the arm, yanking her around so they were nose to nose. "Listen, sweetheart, you may have fucked the boss to get your job, but I *earned* mine, and I didn't need my daddy's name to do it. Don't insult the entire female population by implying we can only get ahead if a man gives us a push."

She spun on her heel and strode away. Salty had to break into a trot to keep up. The newswoman stood, red-faced and stuttering, as the camera crew chewed their lips to stifle their laughter. Cole closed his eyes and let his chin drop to his chest. Honest to God. The woman was unbelievable.

But in this case, he wasn't sure he meant it in a bad way. The news lady had it coming. And the way Shawnee roped that bull…

An elbow nudged Cole's arm and he looked up to find Tyrell grinning beside him. "Just guessing, but that interview might put a serious crimp in your wife search. Unless you and Shawnee—"

"Don't even say it." But he still felt the shape of her pressed up against him. And a sneaky little part of his mind was already working out how he could go about getting her there again. Oh *hell*. He really was losing his mind. But on the other hand…

He gazed off in the direction of the midway and gave an appreciative sigh. "You should've seen the loop she threw out there."

Tyrell laughed and clapped him on the shoulder. "Eat your Wheaties, son. You're gonna need 'em if you go after that."

Chapter 10

THE PHONE DRAGGED SHAWNEE OUT OF THE DEPTHS of her afternoon siesta. She picked up and mumbled a profanity by way of greeting.

"Hello to you, too, sunshine," Tori chirped, intentionally, obnoxiously perky. "Look who's splashed all over the Internet now."

"What? Why?"

"That video of you and Cole riding to the rescue hit the national AP wire." Tori faked a Hollywood drawl. "You're famous, baby."

Shawnee groaned and flopped over onto her back. "Oh God."

"Yeah. Nice roping, by the way. Next thing I know, you'll decide you're too good for me."

"I always have been, princess. I just take pity on the poor little rich girl."

"Right. Violet talked to Cole and Tyrell first thing this morning to be sure they knew how to deal with any follow-up publicity or safety questions. Needless to say, she's thrilled with the exposure. But if I didn't know you and Cole better..."

"There is nothing going on there." But damn her and her big mouth. J.P. was roping at tonight's rodeo. Had he seen that bullshit, too? "It was just some dinky little local station. No one outside of Podunk County should've heard that interview."

"The Internet sees all. Especially if you don't want it to. You should know that by now, hanging around me."

"Your daddy was supposed to be president," Shawnee grumbled. "Mine is a bum. And it was just a joke."

One she'd been sure Cole wouldn't appreciate, but he hadn't said a word. Not last night during chores. Not this morning while they worked the stock. Not even the usual *what the hell is wrong with you?* glare. If anything, he seemed almost cheerful. Probably because Violet was happy with him for a change. And granted, Cole didn't always get the joke—another manifestation of his autism, Violet said. His brain took everything literally. But Shawnee hadn't exactly been subtle.

"I sure hope J.P.'s got a good sense of humor," Tori said.

Of course he did. Didn't he? With the language thing it wasn't like they sat around telling each other jokes. He laughed a lot, though. That must mean something.

Shawnee checked the clock. Only an hour and a half before she had to saddle up for the evening performance. "I've got to shower and primp. J.P.'s gonna be here by six."

He'd let her know via one of his infrequent texts, their primary means of communication because his roping partner could act as translator. Phone calls were a complete waste of air space. She knew how to say *Hello* and *How are you?* J.P. could manage about a dozen other common words and phrases, though he was getting better all the time. But between them, they could muddle through her explanation about the interview.

Shawnee crawled down out of the king-sized bed and

shuffled toward the bathroom. "It's not like J.P. and I are going steady."

But they weren't sleeping with other people, either. Despite what some of the pearl-clutchers might say, her standards were high. When she found a man who met them, she gave him her full attention for as long as they were both enjoying themselves, and asked that he do the same. She huffed out a breath. "J.P. is too laid-back to get upset about some stupid, smart-ass remark."

"Uh-huh. You may be underestimating the fragility of the male ego."

Shawnee rolled her eyes even though Tori wasn't there to appreciate the effect. "Whatever. I have to go. I have plans for the evening, and I will have to shave my legs for this."

There was nothing like her favorite Brazilian to distract her from Cole, his unexpected smiles, and the way he'd snuck that arm around her. A very strong, muscular arm, attached to a whole lot of hard male body.

But she wasn't thinking about Cole, dammit.

The shower only took ten minutes. Drying her hair was another matter. She stuffed it into a ponytail holder still damp, then dressed and took extra time with her makeup, even though she'd sweat most of it off before the end of the rodeo. She only had fifteen minutes to spare by the time she threaded her way through the maze of pickups and trailers in search of J.P. When she spotted his long, lanky frame, she broke into a grin. It really was good to see him. As she approached, he pulled a saddle out of the trailer and swung it onto his horse.

"*Olá*, handsome!"

He glanced at her over the horse's back, but instead

of the usual grin, his expression went stony. He ducked his head, tugging at the cinches.

"J.P.?" She stopped a few feet away, her heart sinking. "*Como ce ta?*" *How are you?*

His chin snapped up and he glowered at her, speaking so low and fast she couldn't catch a syllable let alone a word, but she could guess. She held her hands out, palms down, making an *easy, now* motion. "That interview wasn't what it looked like."

"You say...*ele é o melhor?*"

She had no clue what he'd said, but it must have something to do with Cole. "I was kidding. *Ha ha ha!*"

"Not funny to me. But others—" He flung an arm wide to indicate all of the cowboys milling around, many shooting curious glances their direction. "They laugh."

Oh *hell*. "I didn't mean—"

He cut her off with another stream of agitated Portuguese.

"J.P., if you'll just listen—"

When she took a step toward him, he spat a few emphatic words at her, then stomped off around the end of the trailer.

"I don't even know what that means," she called helplessly after him.

"He say there is nothing to talk about," a voice said behind her.

She swung around to face the cowboy who lounged against the fender of a nearby trailer, arms crossed, dimples winking even though he wasn't really smiling. "Marcus! Thank God. Can you please help me explain?"

"He won't listen. All day, people ask why his woman

says another man is the best." Marcus waggled his eyebrows. "They say Cole is very *big* man, you know?"

Shawnee gave a muffled shriek of frustration. "No! I do not. Because there is *nothing* going on between me and Cole."

"Doesn't matter. Once the talk goes out..." He made a gesture like trying to catch words and stuff them in his mouth.

"I was being a smart-ass!"

"When someone is an ass, they aren't always so smart."

"You're telling me."

He did one of those Brazilian shrugs that could have meant anything from *whatever* to *fuck off and die*.

Shawnee resisted the urge to shake him. "He's really not going to talk to me?"

"No."

"Not ever?"

Another inscrutable shrug, this time with a hint of a smile. "J.P. usually don't stay mad a long time."

Well, thank the Lord for small favors. She asked Marcus for a piece of paper and help translating a message. She left the paper tucked between the coils of the rope that J.P. had slung over his saddle horn. One single word.

Desculpe.

I'm sorry. Unless Marcus was screwing with her, in which case who knew what it said?

She stomped over to where the Jacobs Livestock rigs were parked. The pickup horses were already tied to Cole's trailer, so she grabbed a brush and attacked Salty's mane.

Cole stepped out of the living quarters, watched for a moment, then said, "You might want to go easy there. Salty's been known to bite if you irritate him."

"So have I," she muttered, but she took more care as she combed Salty's forelock. Cole tossed her a spray bottle of detangler and she worked it through Salty's long, flowing tail until every strand glistened. The repetitive movement took some of the edge off her jagged emotions, but with every stroke, her brain repeated—

Stupid. Stupid. Stupid.

So that reporter had jabbed the humongous red button labeled *Ace Pickett*. Right on cue, Shawnee had gone off and J.P., a genuinely nice guy, had been hurt and embarrassed.

And Cole…

Taking potshots at him around the crew was one thing. Trash talk was the rodeo way. But making a spectacle all over television and cyberspace? She gritted her teeth and turned to face him. "I guess I owe you an apology, too."

He gave her one of his patented blank looks as he untied his horse.

"For yesterday," she clarified. "The interview. I shouldn't have said…um, you know."

"That I'm the best?" He paused, frowning. "You didn't mean it?"

"Well, sure. The first part. You are the best with the horses, but the rest…" Dammit. He just kept staring at her like he couldn't fathom what she was talking about. "I practically announced that we're having sex!"

"Yeah."

She could actually feel her eyes bulging. "But we're not…we don't…it doesn't bother you?"

He tilted his head a fraction, looking thoughtful. Then he shrugged. "Guess not."

And for the second time in fifteen minutes, a man walked away and left Shawnee sputtering.

Chapter 11

JUST ONCE, COLE HAD WANTED TO RENDER SHAWNEE speechless—mostly to prove it was possible.

And he'd done it. He'd finally won one little skirmish, and all he'd had to do was keep quiet. She was bound to bring up the interview eventually. While he was waiting, he'd played every possible scenario through his head and practiced his lines. He was good at that—storing away bits and pieces of dialogue he thought he might need.

But the effect on Shawnee wasn't supposed to stick.

He scowled over the fence at her as she loped circles on the sorrel horse he'd taken to calling Sooner, because this one was far and away the most likely to amount to something in the foreseeable future, and not giving the two horses their own names made him a little crazy.

The gray remained Butthead, because that appeared to be where he stored his brain. By the time they left this rodeo, she'd have him behaving pretty well, but when he fell out of the trailer at the next rodeo he'd be a hot mess all over again. After two or three days he'd settle down and start paying attention, just in time to pack up and leave for the next show. Cole wasn't one to give up easily on a horse, but he was beginning to have serious doubts about this one.

Mariah gave him a mock queen wave and a smile as she jogged past on Shawnee's buckskin. She'd insisted on teaching him the barrel racing pattern, mostly because Mariah needed something to do. Shawnee just rolled her eyes and said Roy could exercise in little circles as easy as a straight line.

They'd crossed into northern New Mexico, climbing onto the lower flanks of the mountains where the air stayed cool well into the morning, eliminating the need for predawn training sessions. Analise had even started joining in. Over on the far side of the arena, she made a precise turn on Salty. She sat a horse pretty well after only a few lessons from Shawnee, her back ramrod straight, her black leggings and matching tank top making her look like one of those English riders—until she got close enough for him to see the tattoos.

The three of them congregated along the fence, pausing to chat. Cole folded his arms on the top of the gate and considered the odd trio. At first glance, a person might think they didn't have much to talk about. But underneath, they all had the same...well, grit, he supposed. Shawnee was a sandblaster, Analise slightly more subtle. Even Mariah, under that smooth, sweet surface, could be abrasive if you rubbed her wrong.

Cole scowled at Shawnee again. Had she actually been in love with J.P? He hadn't seen any sign of tears, but this funk of hers reminded Cole of how Violet had acted when Joe bailed out on her—temporarily. And dammit, Cole was just getting used to loud, proud, in-your-face Shawnee. What was he supposed to do with mopey?

Not that he had to do anything. Hell, he should be enjoying the silence.

But she was one of his crew. They were all his responsibility. He considered the piece of paper tucked in his shirt pocket. On one hand, he did owe her for covering his ass and making him look reasonably coherent in that interview. On the other, if he followed through, it would seriously mess up his schedule.

But as they said in the movies, "It's quiet. *Too* quiet."

Cole pushed back his sleeve to check his watch. He didn't want to be a jerk, but…

The PA system hummed to life, and Tyrell's deep voice boomed out. "Please clear the arena, ladies. The boss man is gettin' antsy."

Mariah rolled her eyes at Cole as she rode out the gate. Analise gave him a sarcastic salute.

Shawnee barely glanced at him as she said, "Give me a minute to change horses."

The perfect employee. Polite, obedient, and quiet. In other words, all wrong.

———

The stripping chute gate banged shut behind the first bunch of bulls and Katie flopped down in the dirt beside Hammer, tongue lolling, as Cole surveyed the action behind the scenes. The Leses herded the next group of four up the alley, but Mariah had paused to chat with Hank, who should've been pushing the bulls up into the chutes. He leaned on the pipe fence instead, grinning like a loon. Mariah smiled back. Something in the way they stood—together, but not quite—made Cole shift uncomfortably in his saddle.

Shawnee rode up beside him and stood tiptoe in her stirrups to see what had caught his attention. She glanced at his face and snorted. "Don't worry. She's too old for him."

Cole frowned. "She's sixteen."

"Going on forty. Did you know she designs most of her own clothes and already has a line of western shirts for sale on the Internet? Trademarked. Just something she does in her spare time between school and roping and plotting how she's gonna be the first black woman to compete at the National Finals. And then there's Hank."

As they watched, he tried to spin the sorting stick like a ninja staff and swatted himself in the side of the head.

Still…Cole started to make a mental note to have a word with Hank. But Mariah wasn't one of his crew. Plus, her father was fiddling with the sound system in the crow's nest directly above Cole's head, and Tyrell was more than capable of protecting his own. With a vengeance.

Maybe Cole should just remind Hank that it was hard to fight bulls with your kneecaps busted.

"Hey, Hank!" the nearest Les yelled. "Bulls comin' your way. Pull your head out of your ass, would ya?"

Hank flipped him the bird, then coaxed the bulls on up into the chutes and jogged up to slam the gates shut behind them. "Ready?" he asked Cole.

"Yep." Cole glanced over, but Shawnee had already moved into position. As always. "Turn 'em out."

Hank swung the gates open, one by one. Cole and Shawnee sat back and let the bulls find their own way around the arena, sniffing the dirt and spooking at a crumpled hamburger wrapper that tumbled in the breeze. At Cole's signal, both Shawnee and his dog closed in, gathering the stock into a small herd that the three of them pushed around the perimeter of the arena, then out the gate. Efficient. Organized.

And way too damn quiet.

When they were done, Cole hung back and let the others clear out. While Shawnee stepped off and loosened Roy's latigo, Cole loosened his own cinches, tied up his rope, and timed his exit so they met at the gate.

"Your sorrel horse is going good," Cole said.

Shawnee barely flicked him a glance. "He's coming along."

"I saw you roping the dummy on him yesterday morning." Cole reached down to scratch Katie's ears as she plopped beside his foot. "Looks like he has some potential."

Another slightly longer, more probing glance. "I think so."

"Helps that Mariah is here to pull the dummy steer around for you."

"Yeah. It's great." She stopped, fisting her hands and hooking her thumbs in the front pockets of her jeans, her eyes going squinty. "Is there a problem?"

"Huh?"

"With me roping the dummy. Am I disturbing the ground or something?"

He stared at her, perplexed. "With a roping dummy?"

"That's what I'm asking *you*."

He had the distinct impression that she was gritting her teeth. And she didn't seem sad at all. More like… stifled.

"Why are we talking about the dirt?" he asked.

"I have no idea. You started it."

"I did not! I said your horse looked good. And you—"
He threw up his hands in exasperation and hit Hammer in the nose. The horse fell back, burning the rein through

Cole's hand. He cursed when the snap at the end flipped around and smacked his knuckle. Rubbing an apologetic hand over the roan's forelock, he snapped, "I was just trying to make conversation."

"Why?"

"Beats the hell out of me." He yanked the folded flyer out of his pocket and shoved it at her. "Here. I saw this when I went to the feed store and I thought you might be interested."

She took it gingerly and shook it out with two fingers, as if it might be laced with anthrax. As she read the advertisement for a team roping jackpot that would be held in this very arena the day after the rodeo ended, the annoyance in her eyes turned to a gleam. Then her mouth tipped down at the corners. "This starts Sunday at noon. We're leaving that morning. Although—" The gleam returned. "I could stay and rope, and catch up with you later."

Cole stiffened. "It's a seven-hour drive. You're not doing it alone."

"I've driven from here to Oregon by myself."

"Not when you were working for us."

"Then why did you give this to me?" She waved the flyer at him. "Are you leaving the dog for protection?"

Katie's eyes popped open and she shot him a *you wouldn't dare* look. Cole could feel the muscles in his neck twitching with gathering tension. "We have a day to spare, and the committee doesn't mind if we stay until Monday."

"Seriously?" Shawnee's gaze jumped from the flyer to his face, shocked out of her politeness. "You'd re-arrange your precious schedule just so I can rope?"

He crouched to pet his dog, his voice gruff. "You gave up competing to help us out. We should return the favor."

"Oh. Well, if you put it that way."

Cole snuck a look at her face, but her expression was way too complicated for him. She squared up her shoulders and gave him a smile so polite it was almost creepy. "Thank you."

He should've left it at that, but instead he blurted, "What is wrong with you?"

"Nothing."

"Bullshit. You're being too nice. It's not normal."

She gave an aggravated huff. "Gee, thanks. Good to know I'm usually a jerk."

"Not…exactly."

"Then exactly what am I?"

Cole scowled. How had a simple conversation turned into what felt like hand-to-hand combat? "I don't know. Um, opinionated?"

"Well, there's a polite way of putting it." She angled her head away. "I thought I'd try something new and not say everything that pops into my head."

"You don't look very happy about it."

"It's a struggle," she said dryly.

He could imagine. Sort of. "I'll trade you."

"For what?"

He hitched a shoulder. "Most of the time, when I'm supposed to say something, nothing pops into my head."

She opened her mouth, closed it, and heaved a pained sigh. "You know you're killing me, right? One wide-open shot after another, and me with a shiny new vow not to take 'em."

"That's my evil plot."

She laughed, a single, surprised *Ha!* "Not bad. You've got more smart-ass potential than I figured."

He ducked his head, scratching Katie's chest to hide his ridiculously proud grin. "We're staying here until Monday morning. Rope if you want to."

He stood and started out the gate. She walked beside him, but let the conversation die into what felt like relieved silence on both of their parts. As they rounded the stock pens, a car whipped into the rodeo grounds, started for the contestant parking area, then swerved abruptly toward Cole and Shawnee. They scrambled back a few steps as the gold-trimmed Cadillac SUV skidded to a stop in front of them, sending dust and gravel flying.

The driver's door burst open and a woman jumped out. *Classy* was the first word that popped into Cole's head. Somewhere between her late fifties and a very well-preserved seventy. And furious.

As she stalked around to the back of the car, the passenger door opened and a cowboy climbed out. His right arm was in a sling and he moved with great care, as if not to jostle it. The woman dragged a beat-up suitcase out of the hatchback and tossed it on the road, followed by a rope bag and a pair of boots, which she sent sailing as far as she could in opposite directions. Then she slammed the door and stalked back to the front of the car.

"I'll see you—" the man began.

"Not if I see you first...and I've got my shotgun handy." She peeled out, the passenger door still swinging.

The cowboy raised his uninjured hand to wave. She stuck one arm out the window, diamond and gold bangles glinting in the sun as she extended an emphatic middle finger.

He watched until the car screeched onto the highway, then shrugged and turned to Shawnee, pasting a big smile onto his face. "Hey, darlin'. How've you been?"

Shawnee closed her eyes and swore—long, low, and filthy—while the infamous Ace Pickett beamed at her from the midst of his scattered baggage.

Chapter 12

ACE LOOKED ABOUT AS GOOD AS TROUBLE COULD, EVEN in day-old clothes and a dingy arm sling—broad-shouldered, narrow-hipped, with a lazy grin that had been fluttering female hearts since birth. Even Hollywood hadn't been able to resist him...until the third or fourth time he failed to show up on a set because he'd wandered off to rope and forgot to come back.

Shawnee folded her arms tight over the heart that was still stupid enough to skip a beat at the sight of Ace. "You can't borrow my horse and I'm not giving you money."

Beside her, Cole sucked in a breath, as if shocked at her rudeness. He didn't understand. With Ace you had to lay down the law before he had a chance to dazzle you with his bullshit.

He flashed her a sad, wounded smile. "Is that any way to talk to your daddy when I came all this way just to see you?"

Yes. "How did you know I was here?"

"Everybody's talkin' about you two." His eyes were measuring Cole even as he jabbed a thumb into his own chest. "That's my girl, I said. And it's been too long since I've seen her."

In other words, he was either flat broke or had some

scheme cooked up to cash in on her fifteen minutes of fame. Probably both.

"Well, here I am," she said. "And here I go. Glad you could see me."

And she walked away before she weakened and asked him if the sling was real or just a prop, or got sucked under by the wave of pity and disgust at seeing him that way—threadbare and abandoned by his latest sugar mama, all his worldly possessions tossed in the dirt.

"Shawnee, honey—"

In her peripheral vision she saw him move to follow her. Cole blocked Ace's path, Katie stepping up beside him with her ears pinned and lip curled. Shawnee could have told them not to bother. Ace would get to her eventually. He always did, on too many levels to contemplate. But she kept walking, knowing with absolute certainty that he wouldn't get past Cole right this minute. She was all for fighting her own battles, but she'd lost this one enough times to take advantage of every extra second to bolster her defenses. The silver-tongued devil was hard enough to resist when she saw him coming.

And they wondered why she didn't have much use for charm.

But what did you call a man who would sacrifice his precious schedule on her behalf? A smile tugged at her mouth and she realized she had the flyer Cole had given her clutched to her bosom like a damn bouquet. She scowled and jammed it into the back pocket of her jeans, but her heart did a fancy little swoop and spin of anticipation. Picking up broncs was way more of a rush than she'd anticipated, but God, she missed competing.

Sometimes she had to ride away from the arena during the team roping, out of sight and sound, because she couldn't stand being on the sidelines.

And Cole had not only noticed, but cared enough to do something about it.

She flattened another smile. Like he said, she was one of his crew. His responsibility. And they did owe her. There was no reason to take it personally. Or get all squishy in the head and start looking at Cole as anything but a giant favor she was doing for Violet.

Too late, a little voice whispered in her ear.

She shook it off and forced her attention back to the more immediate disaster. Getting rid of Ace was gonna cost her. It always did. She just had to decide how much she was willing to pay—and in what currency.

———

Ace didn't seem particularly alarmed when Cole stepped into his path. He just tipped his head back and flashed a friendly smile. "So you're Steve's nephew. Good man, your uncle."

"Yes." Cole folded his arms and took full advantage of his size to loom over the older man. "I don't think Shawnee wants to talk to you."

Another man might have been embarrassed, or shamed. Ace laughed. "Aw, that's just her way. She's gotta bust my balls for not keepin' in touch, but deep down she's happy to see me."

Very, very deep down, from what Cole could tell. "So that's all? Just a visit, then you're on your way?"

"Well, now, I suppose that depends."

"On?"

Ace flashed another good ol' boy smile. "How much catchin' up we have to do."

"Uh-huh." Cole surveyed the scatter of belongings on the ground. "You're travelin' pretty light."

"I like to keep things simple."

Somehow, Cole doubted that. He'd never had the dubious pleasure of meeting Ace personally, but from all accounts the man was a walking, talking complication. Before he could decide whether to tell him to gather his crap and keep on walking, Tyrell climbed down the stairs from the announcer's stand and strolled over, picking up a stray boot along the way and handing it to Ace.

"Did I miss all the excitement?"

"Nothing worth mentioning." Ace tucked the boot under his injured arm and extended his left hand in greeting. "I'm Shawnee's daddy. And you are…"

Cole made terse introductions. Tyrell and Ace both smiled their slickest smiles while sizing each other up. Then Tyrell turned to Cole. "I suppose it'll take, what, another hour or two for y'all to finish up with the stock?"

Cole frowned. What was Tyrell talking about? "We're just—"

"Getting started, right?" Tyrell cut in with a sharp elbow to the ribs. "Mariah and I are heading into town for lunch. Ace here might as well come along with us, if he doesn't mind a little shopping." He rolled his eyes skyward with a long-suffering sigh. "Daughters, right?"

"Uh, right." Ace glanced in the direction Shawnee had disappeared, his need to pursue her obviously warring with the offer of a free meal. "But I really should…"

"I'll talk to Shawnee," Cole said.

"I can wait—"

"*I'll* talk to Shawnee," Cole said again, with more emphasis and a hint of a threat.

Ace eyed him for a couple of beats, then relaxed into another of those devil-may-care smiles. "Sure. We'll have plenty of time to catch up later."

Unless Shawnee preferred not to be caught. As soon as Cole got his horse put away, he intended to make a beeline straight to her rig and find out what he was supposed to do with their uninvited guest.

———

Shawnee had barely set foot inside her trailer when her phone rang. A glance at the number confirmed what she'd already guessed. Her mother's Ace radar was still fully functional. And they'd have to slap a red-hot branding iron on Shawnee's bare ass before she'd confess that he was here.

She injected some sparkle into her voice when she answered. "Hey, Mama. How are you?"

"Fine." The word was a breath away from a sigh. "I saw you on television."

Shawnee toed off her boots, resisting the urge to kick them at the walls. "Yeah? Is it true what they say about chaps making your ass look big?"

"Shawnee!" Her mother sighed for real. "You looked good. And Cole Jacobs is such a nice-looking boy."

"He's thirty-five, Ma, and half the size of an elephant. I don't think *boy* is the word we're looking for."

"Hmm. And how is Joao Paolo?" Because of course her mother would pronounce his name in full, and properly, ever fearful of offending.

"That's over," Shawnee said breezily.

"Oh. Well. I suppose it had to be eventually. He is very young." She paused, then added hopefully, "Were you being sarcastic in that interview? About Cole, I mean."

"Of course."

"But you'll be working with him the rest of the summer, so there's always a chance…"

"Ma. Don't." Shawnee plopped down on the couch and scraped sweaty hair off her now-aching forehead. "They didn't save me a place in the happily ever after line."

"You don't know that! And Cole has always been so reliable…"

"He wants kids," Shawnee said flatly. "Of his own."

"Oh."

Yeah. That was always a conversation stopper. Shawnee put a deliberate leer in her voice. "But I suppose I could let him practice on me. He is very…large."

"Shawnee!"

"I'm kidding, Ma." But now she'd gone and planted the idea in her own head, where it immediately began to, um, grow. Ack. When was someone going to invent a safe and effective delete key for stupid thoughts? "I'm fine. And you'd be a whole lot better if you stopped worrying so much."

"You're all I have to worry about."

Shawnee swallowed a curse at the quaver in her mother's voice. Yet another sin for which Ace Pickett would burn, if there was any justice at all.

—◦◦◦—

Half an hour later, he still hadn't knocked on her door. She wasn't exactly hard to find with her name plastered on the side of the pickup. Should she worry what Cole had done with him? She dumped a blob of bread dough onto the scrubbed and floured counter top and began to take out her frustration on it. Of course, as soon as she was elbow deep, a knock came at the door.

Without even glancing over her shoulder, she knew it wasn't Ace. The knock was a familiar deep thud, and there was only one person big enough to make the whole trailer dip when he put his weight on the step after she yelled to come in.

And just how big *was* enough?

Shut up, shut UP, you stupid brain. "Did you knock him over the head and dump his body in a ditch?" she asked.

"Not yet."

Cole sounded so grim she turned to see if he was carrying a club. "What did you do with him?"

"Tyrell and Mariah took him into town. They'll keep him out of your hair until we can—" The words died as his gaze landed on the mound of dough. His voice dropped to a reverent whisper. "Are you baking *bread*?"

"Rolls, actually."

"I haven't had homemade rolls in almost two months." He swallowed audibly. "And *you* can make them? From scratch?"

Bristling, Shawnee folded her arms, then cursed when she smeared flour on her boobs. "They're edible. Better since Miz Iris taught me—"

He cut her off with a groan that sounded physically painful, and fumbled his wallet out of his back pocket. "I'll pay you for them. Name your price."

Shawnee gaped at him. "Are you insane?"

"Yes. It's the withdrawal." He gazed at her with more longing than she would've imagined him capable of. "Do you have any idea what it's like to get cut off after eating my aunt's cooking all these years?"

"That's…" She was going to say ridiculous, then she remembered the baked ham, biscuits, and mess of greens she'd inhaled the last time she was at the Jacobs ranch. And that apple pie…"I see your point."

"Then we have a deal?" He started to pull a bill from his wallet.

"No." At his stricken expression, she added, "I'm not taking your money. Just…" Geezus. She'd been braced to deal with Ace, and now this? She pointed at the table. "Stop looming while we figure something out."

He obeyed with an eagerness that would've made her laugh if this whole day hadn't been so damn bizarre. The dog followed on his heels, plunking her butt down and thumping her tail on the floor, suddenly friendly as hell. Cole plopped his forearms on the table and they both looked at her as if she was going to toss them a cookie.

"I'm not even done kneading the dough," she said. "Then it's gotta raise—twice—and I have to bake them."

"Okay." He didn't budge. Neither did the dog. Were they just gonna sit there and stare at her for two hours?

Shawnee stepped over to the sink, brushed the excess flour off her hands, then grabbed a full colander and an empty bowl. "Here. You can earn your first fix by snapping these beans. I assume you know how?"

"Of course." His big hands were surprisingly nimble as he plucked the first bean from the colander, snapped off the ends, then broke it into precise pieces. He cast her another hopeful look. "I don't suppose you got Aunt Iris's recipe for these, too?"

Shawnee huffed out a laugh. "My grandmother's. But I don't generally make enough to justify a ham hock, so I use bacon instead."

"I love bacon." Cole's eyes glazed over a little, then refocused with added determination. "Seriously. I will pay you to feed me. Even if it's only once a week."

"I can't…" Imagine sitting down to a meal with Cole, just the two—she glanced at the dog—okay, three of them.

"I'll buy the groceries," he added. "*And* I'll get rid of Ace."

Now she did laugh. "You can't just toss him off the rodeo grounds. It's public property."

"I can make it hard for him to stay."

Suddenly Shawnee was acutely aware of Cole's mass, and his strength. She had no doubt he could bundle Ace up, haul him out of town, and dump him on the side of the road. And she should let him. Dammit.

She heaved a deep sigh, ripe with contempt for her dear ol' daddy…and herself. "If he had anywhere else to go or a dime to get there, he wouldn't have come looking for me."

"How's that your problem?" Cole picked up another bean and snapped it into another series of uniformly sized pieces. "When did you see him last?"

"Three years ago." She went back to pummeling the dough. "When Tori and I won that big Turn 'Em and Burn 'Em roping in Abilene, he figured out who she was, realized I had connections, and showed up with all kinds of big ideas about how we could spend the

Patterson money—buying horses, training them, hauling them all over the country." She made a disdainful noise. "Ace's favorite kind of plan. Getting paid to rope."

"You said no?"

"Nah. I went ahead and let him try his sales pitch on Tori."

Cole winced. "Ouch."

"Yep. She sliced and diced him without even raising her voice." Shawnee smiled fiercely at the memory. "God, I love that woman."

"He hasn't been back since?"

Shawnee buried her fist in the dough. "No reason."

Another man might have pointed out that most fathers would just want to see their only child, but Cole wasn't one to waste words on the obvious. "Are you sure you won't let me run him off?"

"I know. I'm an idiot." Ace had abandoned her in an hour of desperate need. Why shouldn't she return the favor? She punched the dough again and blew out a sigh powerful enough to send flour poofing into the air. "It would make me no better than him."

For a few moments, there was no sound except the snap of beans and the thump of Shawnee's fists in the dough. Then Cole said, "He can sleep in one of the trucks. The Leses and Hank can take turns sharing the motel room."

"Way to cramp Hank's style," Shawnee said, falling back on sarcasm because she didn't know what else to say.

"Even better." Cole hesitated, as if he wanted to say more, then shrugged. "I can find some way for your daddy to earn his keep."

Shawnee fisted her hands, the dough squeezing out between her fingers. "Call him Ace."

Cole gave her a long look, then nodded. "Is he a drunk?"

"No. He's a gambling addict—but instead of cards or slots, team roping is his game. There's not much he won't do to feed his habit, but as far as I know, he doesn't steal outright. You may want to lock up any women of means over the age of fifty, though."

"Not the sweet young things?"

"Hah!" She rolled the mangled dough into a smooth ball and began to knead it properly. "Young women cost money. Ace *is* the trophy, custom-made for hanging on the arms of rich widows and divorcées. Unfortunately, he's also a lazy, self-centered bastard who is incapable of catering to anyone's whims but his own for very long. Hence—"

She gestured toward where Ace's latest had heaved him and his belongings out of her car.

Cole snapped the last of the beans and pushed the colander across the table toward her. The chunks looked as if he'd measured them with a ruler.

Shawnee gave the bread dough a final pat and covered it with a towel. "Come back in a couple of hours. I'll fix you a plate." At the almost inaudible whine, she added, "And a little extra for Katie."

Cole's smile was so bright it knocked Shawnee back on her heels. She grabbed the edge of the counter for balance. "Hey! Be careful where you point that thing."

"What?" The smile faded into puzzlement.

Right. Like she was gonna tell him. Shawnee flapped her hand. "Go. You and that dog take up too much air."

And way, *way* too much space, especially in her thoughts. And potentially, her dreams.

Which—given their completely opposite life goals—could turn into a total nightmare.

Chapter 13

COLE GLANCED AROUND TO BE SURE THE COAST WAS clear, then peeled up a corner of the foil on the square plastic storage tub Shawnee had shoved into his hands. His stomach gave a deep, happy rumble at the scent of warm bread. He had intended to grab his loot and hustle straight to his trailer, but the walk was too long, and the temptation too great. The three golden rolls she'd tucked in beside a grilled chicken breast and the pile of greens weren't quite as perfectly shaped as his aunt's, but they sure smelled right.

He extracted a roll from under the foil. The instant his teeth sank through the crisp, buttery crust, his taste buds began to sing the opening lines to "Hey, Good Lookin'." Not strictly appropriate, but it was the only song he knew about cooking. And Shawnee wasn't hard to look at. Especially in a wet T-shirt…

Okay, *that* was inappropriate. He took another bite of the roll, which obliterated everything except *Ahhh!*

"Hey, Cole, whatcha got there?"

Cole froze. He hadn't seen Hank lounging in the shade of the tarp they had stretched between Cole's trailer and the nearest truck. He stuffed the rest of the roll into his mouth, a lame attempt to hide the evidence. "Nuffin," he mumbled.

Hank sat forward in his chair, zeroing in on the

covered dish in Cole's hand. "Where'd you score a homemade roll? And what else have you got in there?"

Shit. Busted. He should've known better than to bring his booty here, where any of the crew might spot him. And, as usual, under pressure his brain gave him the equivalent of a pixelated computer screen.

He put a protective hand over the plate. "I, um, got it from a…friend."

Hank jumped up as if he intended to take a closer look. Katie bared her teeth and growled, bringing him to an abrupt halt. Hank glared at her, then turned accusing eyes on Cole. "Who do you know who can cook? Have you been holding out on us?"

"No. I just found…just ran into her, and she gave me dinner." Huh. Not too bad, by Cole's standards.

Hank drew a deep breath. "That smells awesome. I don't suppose there's enough—"

Katie growled again.

Hank heaved a dejected sigh, shoulders slumping like Cole's nephew Beni when Cole ate the last cookie. "Guess I'll have another rodeo burger."

"You're not guilting me into sharing." Cole wrapped his hands around the dish and tucked it close to his chest. "Lay off the buckle bunnies and you might meet a nice girl and score yourself a decent meal."

Hank's eyebrows shot up. "Is that what you did?"

No. Yes. Maybe? Not that he'd ever really done the buckle bunny thing. When he'd been young and dumb enough to be tempted, he'd demonstrated a real talent for scaring off even the most aggressive rodeo groupies. And if anyone called Shawnee a *nice girl* to her face, she'd bust out laughing. But she could cook. And he had scored. Big time.

He decided this was one of the rare times when a blank stare was the best answer.

"Fine. Keep it all for yourself." Hank jammed his hands in his pockets and hung his head, looking even more baby-faced than usual. "I sure do miss those big dinners Miz Iris made for the crew."

"I hear you." But he still wasn't sharing. Cole sidled toward the door to his living quarters with Katie stalking beside him like she was guarding an armored car full of cash. His hand was on the door latch when Hank brought him up short again.

"Have you talked to Shawnee?"

Cole's head jerked up, guilty. "About what?"

"Ace." Hank's lip curled. "He's got some nerve, showing up here and expecting her to take him in."

Hank wasn't just fishing for gossip this time, Cole realized. He was angry.

"Do you know him?" Cole asked.

"Not personally. But I've heard plenty from Melanie."

Hank's sister and truly Violet's best friend forever. She'd done her damnedest to look out for him when it became obvious their parents didn't have much interest in the surprise package that had shown up ten years after they'd decided Melanie should be an only child.

Shawnee had grown up south of Amarillo on her grandfather's ranch and had never left the Panhandle, but after college she'd drifted away in terms of contact. Shawnee stuck to team roping–only events. Violet threw herself into Jacobs Livestock and the rodeos they produced. Their orbits hadn't overlapped much until Shawnee had started roping with Tori, and Tori had married Delon and become Beni's stepmother.

Now they were all one big, happy…well, maybe not quite family, but crowd. Including Hank, who obviously knew things about Shawnee and Ace that Cole—big surprise—had missed.

"What did he do?" A greasy knot curled in Cole's stomach as he considered the worst of the possibilities.

"Nothin'. That's why Shawnee got so pissed off at that reporter. Ace never had time to waste coaching a kid. Her granddaddy taught her to rope, and how to handle a horse." Hank held up two entwined fingers. "Her and that old man were like this. Ace just showed her off and took credit whenever it suited him. Then she got cancer and he bailed."

Cole frowned, sure he must have misunderstood. "Like, didn't go with her to the hospital and stuff?"

"No. Like *left*." Hank made a *fly away* gesture. "Packed up his shit and cleared out. Said he couldn't handle being around sick people."

"She isn't *people*. She's his daughter."

How in the hell did a father abandon his child at a time like that? And why would Shawnee offer him anything more than a boot in the ass when *he* hit bottom?

It would make me no better than him.

"That ain't even the worst of it," Hank said. "After Shawnee was all done with treatment, Ace tried to come back, 'cuz he couldn't win shit without his father-in-law to keep a good horse under him. And her mama was gonna take him, but the old man said he'd shoot the bastard first. Ace convinced her Daddy would come around if they took off with his precious granddaughter, but Shawnee refused to go along, so her granddad just said good riddance to the two of them. A couple of months later her mom had a nervous breakdown and Ace dumped her at an emergency room in Waxahachie. Didn't even have the balls to call her parents. They brought her home, but after that she was always sort of, you know…delicate. At least for as long as they lived around Amarillo."

"Why did they leave?" Cole asked.

"Her granddaddy had to sell the ranch because of all the medical bills and shit. The Pattersons bought him out, then rented the place back to them until Shawnee was out of high school. Soon as she graduated the old folks and her ma moved up to Nebraska, by her grandmother's family. Wasn't a year later her granddad died of cancer. One of those deals where he was diagnosed and in a month he was dead. Shawnee was wrecked."

Cole knew that feeling. Dear God, did he ever. When he'd lost his parents and brother, he'd curled in upon himself until he'd barely found his way out again. Shawnee seemed like she'd done the opposite, turning her emotions loose on anything that got in her way.

"What about her mother and grandmother?" Cole asked, forcing words through what felt like a noose woven from pain…his and hers.

Hank shrugged. "Still in Nebraska, far as I know. Her mother never remarried. Lots of people think she never got over Ace."

Or at least what he'd done to her. And her daughter.

"Are you gonna let him hang around, using her?" Hank demanded, hands fisted in fury. Just when you were tempted to write him off, he'd remind you that, underneath, he had a decent heart.

Cole's fingers crumpled the foil at the edges of the plastic tub, his knuckles white with the urge to throttle

Ace Pickett. He'd be doing the world—and Shawnee—a favor. But…

"It's not my decision."

He had to respect Shawnee's decision—unless Ace became a detriment to Jacobs Livestock. As he sat down to eat, it occurred to him that he was constantly tripping over reasons to respect Shawnee.

—∕∕∕—

Cole had just polished off the last of his very excellent dinner when he heard voices outside his door—Tyrell's unmistakable baritone, Hank's chatter, and Ace Pickett's lazy drawl. Cole dumped his dishes in the sink and stepped outside. The three men were sprawled in lawn chairs, sipping sweet tea. He caught Tyrell's eye and gave a slight jerk of his head.

Tyrell pushed to his feet. "A couple of people complained that the sound was a little muddy up at the top of the big grandstand last night. Would you run on over there and listen for me, Hank, while I do a sound check?"

Ace didn't volunteer to help. Annoying, but convenient under the circumstances. Cole planted himself right in front of the older man's chair, forcing Ace to either stare at Cole's crotch or tilt his head back to see his face.

"I don't know what you've heard about me," Cole said. "But I'm not good with bullshit—dishing it out or taking it."

"Smart man," Ace said, with an easy smile that faltered when Cole only stared down at him, deliberately cold.

"We're not gonna pretend you're here to see a daughter you haven't bothered to visit in three years. But unfortunately I was raised right, and I wouldn't leave a stray cat to starve, so you get one chance to show me you're good for something."

Ace took his time, rubbing a hand over his chin as he thought it over. "Your boy there," he said, the inflection on the word *boy* making Cole's hackles rise when Ace nodded toward the chair Tyrell had vacated. "Got a great voice, but he's from up north. He could probably use someone in the crow's nest who knows the cowboys in this circuit."

It wasn't a terrible idea. Tyrell had been busting his butt to learn as much as possible about the contestants so he could add more color commentary, but with hundreds of entries in every rodeo it took time.

Cole inclined his head. "I'll ask. If he agrees, we can give it a try, and I'll pay you in room and board. In the meantime, Shawnee talks to you if and when she wants. You don't talk to her. You don't mooch off of her. If I catch you aggravating her in any way, I'll toss your ass in the pickup and dump you at the nearest bus station, with a ticket to anywhere we aren't going."

Ace gazed up at him with a wounded expression, testing to see if Cole would weaken, even a hair. Cole didn't.

Ace heaved a deep, put-upon sigh. "I'm sorry my daughter has given you such a low opinion of me. If it weren't for this—" He shifted the arm bound up in the sling. "But I guess talking is about all I'm good for right now."

Cole could've argued that, sling or no sling, being good for nothin' was a permanent state of affairs with Ace.

Chapter 14

"TOO BAD I'VE GOT THIS BUM SHOULDER," ACE SAID, as Shawnee saddled Roy for the roping on Sunday. "Looks like it's gonna be a nice little pot."

The sling was the reason they'd been saddled with Ace. His latest lady love was not the usual rich widow. She'd taken her MBA and her father's unambitious plumbing supply company and built a multimillion-dollar chain, tearing through a few husbands in the process. Bored with semiretirement, she'd invested her spoils in Quarter Horses—the best rodeo bloodlines her money could buy.

It was depressing to realize even a woman that smart could lose her head over a sweet-talkin', good-lookin' man.

She'd turned over one of her best prospects to Ace, who—with his complete lack of patience and inability to resist the quick score—had tried to make it rodeo-ready in six weeks so he could enter a big roping in Albuquerque. He'd pushed too hard, too fast. It had returned the favor by flipping over backward in the roping box, very nearly crushing him. He was damn lucky to escape with only a separated shoulder and a stiff back. Especially after the horse's owner got done with him.

Cole had kept his promise, though. He'd found a use for Ace. After the first performance, Tyrell had even given him a microphone and allowed him to chime in with color commentary—backstory about the cowboys, their careers, their parents' and grandparents' careers. Ace had bummed around Texas rodeos his entire life. He knew everybody and their daddy and had probably tried to sleep with their mothers.

He'd mostly steered clear of her, for which Shawnee was grateful. It wasn't out of respect for her feelings, she was sure. She hadn't asked Cole for details of their conversation. They all knew Ace was just biding his time, using them as his bolt-hole until his shoulder healed. Calculating all the angles until he figured out which one would get him what he needed to move on to better things.

"Been a long time since we roped together," he said.

And whose fault is that? Shawnee slipped Roy's bridle over his ears and bent to run the tie-down between his front legs and snap it to the cinch. "You don't have a horse."

"I can always find someone to mount me."

Sad truth. And he wasn't just talking about the ladies. Local cowboys would stand in line for bragging rights about how Ace Pickett had borrowed their horse that time. Even better if Ace happened to win something. Which was all they'd get, because Ace knew how to pick the ones who would happily decline the standard twenty-five percent mount money in exchange for a beer with the man of the hour.

And speaking of money…"I doubt you have enough cash to ante up for penny poker, let alone entry fees."

"I am a little short at the moment." He pitched her a sheepish smile with just the right amount of fatherly affection. "But I thought, for old times' sake…"

"That I'd pay to rope with you?"

She snorted her derision. It still pinched at her heart, though, that fleeting, ridiculous moment of imagining how it could have been. There had been a time when she'd been as starstruck as all the rest. She had insisted on learning to heel steers because Ace was a header, and that way they could be a team. Look out, here they come—Pickett and Pickett. She would be his pride and joy, and he'd take her to ropings and together they would—

Turning her back, she yanked a rope out of her bag. All of that was before. Now it was long, long *after*. Her cancer had struck the match, but Ace was the one who'd set fire to every bridge in sight. She refused to feel guilty or sorry or even bitterly triumphant as she slung her rope over her saddle horn and left him behind to go do the one thing he loved more than anything or anyone in the world.

Damn sure more than his daughter.

———

Plunging into the chatter and bustle of ropers and horses in and around the arena was like jumping into a lake after a long, parched day. Shawnee could feel her soul expanding as she soaked up the laid-back atmosphere, so different than the intensity of the rodeo performances. She owed Cole a hefty chunk of her sanity for this, but she could pay him back in fried chicken and dinner rolls.

As she started to join the parade of ropers circling the arena, a familiar white horse jogged up beside her. Mariah grinned from Salty's back. She was dressed almost exactly like Shawnee—jeans, T-shirt, curls corralled in the back loop of a baseball cap—but Mariah's jeans were the hundred-dollar super-bling variety, her cap was studded with rhinestones, and her turquoise T-shirt clung to her jaw-dropping curves. Beside her Shawnee felt like a dusty blob, even though she had made more than the usual effort with her makeup, and the peach-colored shirt was one of her favorites.

She focused on Mariah's horse instead. "You're roping on Salty?"

"Cole says he was a heading horse when they bought him and he probably hasn't forgotten how." Mariah lifted the nylon rope in her hand. "Wanna enter up with me?"

"Sure."

Barrel racing might be her ultimate end game, but Mariah had won high school championships as a roper, and it would give Shawnee one familiar partner. For the other four that she was allowed, she would be at the mercy of a random draw. Plus now she would have someone to talk to between runs. Short of having Tori appear, it was as good as the day could get.

Plus, Ace would be watching her rope for the first time since she was thirteen. She shoved that thought aside. She no longer gave a shit about impressing him. Right?

Right, goddammit.

Half an hour later, the draw lists were posted and the local announcer called for the ropers to clear the arena, then read off the names of the first twenty teams.

"Team number eighteen, Mariah Swift and Shawnee Pickett."

At the sound of their names, a cheer went up from the grandstand. Shawnee twisted around in her saddle to see the entire Jacobs crew parked in the shade high up under the roof. Yes, even Ace, who had joined the Leses in a card game, using the usual beer cooler as a table. She'd be worried that he might skin them, but Cole and Tyrell lounged against the upper railing, with their long legs stretched out across the benches below like two powerful lions keeping a lazy eye on their pride. Katie was planted between them, chin up, the coolest dog in five states.

The rest sprawled around a picnic lunch—buckets of chicken and what looked like the works, judging by the number of tubs. Analise toasted the ropers with one of her radioactive energy drinks. A person had to wonder if caffeine overload contributed to the girl's tendency to be verbally assaulted by prime digits. Or at least turned up the volume.

Hank did a *Huh! Huh! Huh! Huh!* football cheer, using a drumstick as a pom-pom. Mariah responded with one of her regal, mock rodeo queen waves. Half of the ropers in the arena turned to look. And Shawnee... *blushed?*

Swinging down off her horse, she did an unnecessary check of her cinches. She even had a lump in her throat. What the hell?

Maybe, she admitted grudgingly, she was a wee bit touched by the moral support. Granted, none of the crew had anything better to do, but a marathon team roping was most often likened to watching paint dry. Not exactly high drama if you weren't personally invested. In their place, she'd be shaded up cool, taking a nap. Instead, Analise and Hank were holding up a sign scrawled on the back of a rodeo poster that said *We Love S & M*.

Shawnee laughed, even as she blushed a little harder. It was bizarre, having a cheering squad. She'd had friends and college teammates who'd slap her on the back when she made a good run. And of course her mother and grandparents had always been there for her when she was younger, but they were more of the hold your breath and cross your fingers types. This—

She frowned. This felt like Cole's doing—the food, the whole happy family gathered together. If it had been her, it would have been part of a larger plot to irritate him, but the man was incapable of being truly devious. Which meant he was just being thoughtful. Or some other noble bullshit that made her squirm.

Nothing about Cole Jacobs should be making her *that* kind of squirmy.

The announcer called the first team to rope, and Shawnee gathered up her wayward thoughts and weird emotions and shoved them deep down into her pocket, where they wouldn't interfere with the moment. The sun was shining, she had a good horse underneath her and steers to rope. She intended to savor every minute of it.

When their turn came, Shawnee settled Roy into the box on the right hand side of the chute, and watched Mariah ride in on the left. Salty backed into the corner like an old pro, quiet but alert. Shawnee waited, focusing on the steer. Her job was to get out there and haze the animal so it ran as straight as possible, giving Mariah a better shot while putting Roy in position for Shawnee to have a quick throw.

The chute banged open and the steer lit out, straight and not too fast. Salty caught up easily and Mariah took a good, high percentage throw, her loop snapping around the horns. She wrapped the tail of her rope around the saddle horn and went left, towing the steer along. Shawnee swooped in, laid a wide open loop under its belly, and waited for him to hop into it. She held her slack high as the rope came snug around his back feet, then she dallied up as Mariah swung Salty around to face her.

As the judge's flag dropped to signal for time, a chorus of whoops and howls broke out from their cheering section. Shawnee pretended to ignore them, exchanging a thumbs-up with Mariah, instead. They weren't super fast, but they were solid, and if they could do it again in the second and third rounds, they'd get paid.

Hot *damn,* she loved this game.

Two hours later, two hundred and eighteen teams had been whittled down to twenty. Neither Mariah nor Shawnee had had any luck with their other partners, but together they were in third place, with a realistic shot at first if the teams ahead of them stubbed a toe. As their names were announced, they got more shouts of encouragement from their fan club. Though the others had wandered in and out during the interminable competition, the core group—Cole, Tyrell, Analise, and Hank—had hung tough through the whole thing.

Shawnee refused to glance their direction as she rode in the roping box. *Focus. Timing.* The familiar mantra beat in her head in time with the heavy thuds of her heart, the volume pumped up by adrenaline.

At the bang of the chute, Roy was off. Mariah's approach and throw were carbon copies of her first two loops. Shawnee rode Roy around the corner and into the sweet spot at the steer's hip, swinging in time with his strides so when she released her rope, his hind feet bounced right into the loop. She pulled her slack, dallied up, and felt the jolt as the steer hit the end.

Snap! The judge's flag dropped and he made a slicing motion through the air. Clean run. And the crowd went wild.

As she rode forward and released her dally, Shawnee looked up at the grandstand. The goofy bastards had arranged themselves in a single line, shortest to tallest, and when the announcer declared that Pickett and Swift had taken over the lead, they did a perfectly executed wave, with Cole at the peak.

Shawnee burst out laughing. Geezus. What a bunch of idiots. But the warm glow around her heart wasn't just about roping well. Then she looked again, and against all reason, her little happy bubble deflated with a pathetic hiss.

Ace was gone. And she shouldn't care, but damned if she could stop herself.

Besides, just because he'd left the grandstand didn't mean he'd walked away right before his daughter was due to rope in the short round. Maybe he'd headed down by the chutes to get a closer look. Shawnee rode out of the arena, exchanged a fist bump with Mariah, and forced herself not to scan the faces along the fences as she watched the last two teams go. One miss, then a good run that dropped her and Mariah to second place. They'd take it.

"Way to turn 'em, Hotshot," Shawnee said, punching Mariah lightly in the leg.

"Thank you! That was awesome." Mariah reached up to rub Salty's forelock. "This guy was a total stud."

"He always is."

Shawnee stepped off Roy, gave him some extra lovin', then loosened the cinches and started for her trailer. And that's when she saw Ace, holding court over a gaggle of old-timers under the awning of a nearby horse trailer.

He glanced up, saw her, and smiled. "Is it over? How did you do?"

Shawnee stared at him. How could he not...didn't he even...*fuck*.

"Not good, huh?" He grimaced sympathetically, then blessed her with a patronizing smile. "We can break it down later. Figure out what you're doing wrong."

As if he, oh wise and knowing Yoda, could fix anything that ailed her roping. She shook her head and kept walking before any of the raw, hateful words clawed out of her throat. Curses and accusations that would only embarrass her and anyone else caught in the crossfire, without leaving a mark on Ace. She ducked her head and blinked hard, fighting idiotic tears that should've dried up an eternity ago.

Geezus. She was no smarter than her mother.

"Hey!"

She came up short as she plowed into Cole, coming around from the grandstand side of the arena. He narrowed his eyes at her over the cooler he was carrying. "You're all red-faced. You didn't get overheated again, did you?"

"No, I just—" She glanced over her shoulder toward Ace, then up at Cole, all brawny and predictable and *there*—always there—and blurted, "Would you have dinner with me tonight?"

He blinked, then frowned, suspicious. "Why?"

Good question. With answers she'd rather not examine too closely, so she went with the easy one. "Ace won't dare come around if you're there."

Cole shot a dark look in Ace's direction. Obviously, he'd witnessed the utter lack of fatherly devotion, but he still hesitated.

"I won't even talk." Shawnee made a sign over her heart. "Scout's honor."

Cole's eyebrows shot up, and his mouth twitched. "That I've gotta see. What time?"

"Six." She jerked her chin at the cooler. "You bring the beer."

Chapter 15

COLE SHOWERED, SHAVED, AND CHANGED HIS SHIRT three times. Long sleeves, short sleeves, T-shirt? This wasn't exactly a date, but he was going to her place for dinner, so it seemed respectful to wear something decent. Katie rolled her eyes at his white button-down. She was right. Too formal. He stripped it off and hung it back in the closet.

All of his T-shirts were either dirty or faded, so he grabbed a royal blue polo with the Jacobs Livestock logo and yanked it over his head. There. He was practically in uniform.

And nervous as hell.

He ran a hand over his damp hair, trying to smooth down the cowlick that had tortured him since childhood. No sense putting on his hat when he'd just have to take it off again as soon as he got inside, but he felt naked without it. *Naked* and *Shawnee* was not a good combination.

Scratch that. Shawnee naked—the parts he'd seen, anyway—was just dandy. And him naked with Shawnee—

Nope. Not a chance. Shawnee didn't even like him with his clothes *on*. She was just using him as a shield in return for home cooking. But his brain just had to go there, and now he'd probably spend the whole evening thinking about nothing else, and sure as hell he'd blurt out something she did *not* want to hear. He might have to hold her to that vow of silence, for both of their sakes.

When he reached her trailer and raised his hand, the door opened before he could knock.

Shawnee smirked at him. "What did you do, pace off the distance after I invited you so you could show up exactly as the clock struck six?"

No need. Her trailer had become the last checkpoint on his nightly security rounds, so he already knew how many strides it was from her door to his. Give or take a half step. "Was I supposed to be fashionably late?"

"Not when you're the guy with the beer." She snagged the six-pack of Shiner out of his hand, pulling out two longnecks before stashing the rest in the fridge. She handed one bottle to him and twisted the top off the other. "Where's your best girl?"

Cole followed her gaze to the spot at his heels that Katie usually occupied. "I wasn't sure if she was invited."

"Oh, right. Like I want her hating on me."

She had a point. Katie could and usually did hold a grudge. Cole glanced back toward his rig. The team ropers were long gone and no other vehicles moved around the rodeo grounds, so he gave a shrill whistle. Katie popped out from under his pickup and trotted over. Instead of pausing at his side, she bounded up into the trailer and marched over to plunk down near the bathroom door, refusing to look at him, indignation radiating from every hair on her stocky body.

Shawnee laughed. "That's gonna be one cranky redheaded stepchild if you ever find a full-time night woman." Then she clapped a hand over her mouth, muffling her words. "Oops. Forgot. No running my mouth."

Cole cocked his head. "You've seen *Jeremiah Johnson*?"

"Seen?" She snorted. "It was Granddad's favorite movie. I swear, he must've watched it at least once a month."

"He had good taste."

Shawnee rolled her eyes, looking remarkably like Katie. "I should've known that'd be your favorite. There's only, like, fifty lines of dialogue in the whole movie."

She retreated to make room for Cole to step inside. Then they stood, neither of them sure what came next. She smoothed the fluttery hem of her blouse over her stomach. It was sleeveless, the peachy pink color of his aunt's favorite roses. Her skin looked as dewy fresh as one of those rose petals, and he had an insane urge to lean in and brush his lips over her cheek to see if it was also as soft. One more step forward...

She took a swig from her beer, then scowled up at him, her hair springing around her face like an independent life form, tiny, curling fingers that stroked her throat and bare shoulders. "You're looming again."

"I can't help it." But he usually didn't loom with intent. He angled past her, drawing a deep, appreciative breath as he slid onto one of the bench seats at the banquette table. "Do I smell meatloaf?"

"With new potatoes and corn on the cob. There's a great farmers market here."

Cole closed his eyes, his taste buds humming in anticipation as Shawnee pulled the meatloaf out of the oven and set it on a heat-proof pad on the table. For a woman he'd always thought of as a human bulldozer, she was light on her feet as she bustled around. Her bare feet. With red toenails. He opened his eyes and watched her fish ears of corn out of a pot of steaming water and set them on plates.

"I don't mind listening," he said.

Her tongs froze midair. "To what?"

"Talk." He ran his thumb back and forth along the edge of the table, the repetitive, tactile sensation grounding him. "People assume because I don't say much, I don't want anyone else to talk. But I like to listen."

"As long as you don't have to answer?"

"Depends. Ask me about feed supplements, I can go on all day."

She laughed in patent disbelief. "That I would have to hear."

"I used to talk a lot." He pressed the pad of his thumb harder into the edge of the table.

Shawnee turned, a plate in each hand. "And then?"

"I got old enough to figure out I was doing it wrong."

She paused for a beat, then set the plates on the table before fetching a third to set on the floor by Katie. The dog pretended she didn't notice until Shawnee turned her back, and even then she sniffed it suspiciously, just to be sure everyone knew she couldn't be bought off with a slice of meatloaf. "What flipped the switch?"

"Girls." He studied the way the pad of his thumb went white, then red, then white as he pressed and released. "Before that, I never noticed what other kids thought about me."

"That must've been awesome. Not caring, I mean."

He risked a quick glance at her. "You should know."

She made a noise of ripe self-disgust. "If that were true, you wouldn't be here."

Because if she truly didn't care, she wouldn't give a

damn whether Ace watched her rope. In a blink, Cole's perception of her shifted, revealing a nearly invisible web of cracks in her bulletproof armor. He could make an educated guess at what had put them there. And he had to wonder, what else was Shawnee only pretending not to care about?

"That man is a case study in narcissism," he said.

She plunked a bowl on the table, heaped with tiny new potatoes. "Listen to you with the fancy words."

"I read up on it."

"Because someone called *you* a narcissist?" Shawnee guessed, and hooted in derision. "Obviously, she's never experienced the real thing."

Cole didn't ask how she knew it was a woman. "I can be pretty self-centered."

"Single-minded and self-centered are not the same thing." Shawnee slathered her ear of corn with butter, then passed him the dish—the real stuff, no crappy margarine. "You obsess on particular details to the exclusion of all else, but every waking thought isn't for your sole benefit. Hell, I can't keep you out of my business. You even sat through an entire team roping today."

"My horse was there."

She blinked, then grabbed her beer and took a long gulp before thumping it down a little too hard. "Right. I forgot."

Was that hurt in her voice? More likely his imagination, because she was her usual, blunt self when she went on. "Anyway…when you get focused on something, it's like a boulder rolling downhill. If someone steps in front of you, their ass is probably getting run over, but if you looked up in time, you would try to avoid the collision."

"That's not much consolation to the people I mow down."

She shrugged, conceding the point. "Ace wouldn't even bother to put on the brakes unless they were holding out a stack of hundred dollar bills."

Cole scooped up a slab of meatloaf, laid it on his plate, then gestured toward the next piece. She nodded, and he dished it up for her. "Your mother and her family didn't have money."

Shawnee's lip curled. "He married her for the horses. Gramps had a pasture full of ropey sons a bitches. It's not a coincidence that Ace started kicking ass about the time he and my mother got engaged...and hasn't done shit since he left." She hesitated a beat, staring down at her plate. "You are not a narcissist. I'm not sure you even know how to be cruel. Ace, on the other hand...it's like in a horror movie, when there's this guy who's all handsome and smiling, and then bam! He morphs into a monster and hacks someone up with a meat cleaver." She huffed out a breath. "That's Ace when you call him too hard on his bullshit. Or say the wrong thing on the wrong day."

Spoken, Cole could tell, from painful experience. He shot her a puzzled glance as he doused his corn and potatoes with salt. "If you know all that, why do you still let him get to you?"

"Now there's the million-dollar question." She drove her fork through the heart of a potato. "It's genetic, I guess. Look at my mother. After all these years, she still believes they could've lived happily ever after if my grandparents hadn't been so hard on him, and if I would have forgiven him..." She spared Cole a glance, her eyes hard, but in a way that reminded him more of glass than steel. Brittle. Breakable. "I assume you know all the ugly details?"

He nodded. Then he frowned. "She blames you?"

"Not the way you mean." She used her knife to push the potato off her fork, then proceeded to mangle it with the tines. "She isn't angry at us. Well, not anymore. We're just a handy excuse not to blame Ace, so she can keep telling herself he really did love her. Maybe still does. And as long as she believes—"

"She doesn't," Cole said flatly. "I doubt she still did, even before you got sick."

Shawnee paused in the act of spearing another potato, cocking her head in question. "And you know this because…"

"There was a girl." He sighed, resigned. This was what happened when he started talking. Stuff spilled out, and then he had to keep talking, and the hole kept getting deeper and deeper. "Did you know my brother?"

"I saw him around. Y'all were hard to miss at the junior rodeos, running in a pack with the Sanchez brothers." She fluttered a hand over her heart in a fake swoon. "The girls *all* paid close attention to the Sanchez brothers. And Xander seemed nice. Fun."

Yep. That's what everybody said. Xander was the fun one. And Cole was…there.

Shawnee's brows crimped, puzzled. "I don't remember. Was he one grade or two ahead of you?"

"Neither. We were Irish twins. My mom got pregnant with him when I was only two months old. But Xander grew up a lot faster than I did—because of the autism, I guess—and everybody thought he was older. They didn't know what was wrong with me, but it was obvious school was gonna be a challenge. So we went together."

They'd gone everywhere together. It didn't matter if Cole was backward, because Xander was so funny and smart everyone just ignored his weird brother. And when Cole said something dumb, Xander always found a way to cover for him while Cole skulked back into the shadows.

"They were the cool crowd," he said. "Everybody wanted to hang out with Gil and Delon and Xander."

"Well, yeah. They were *hot*."

Emphasis on *they*, but Cole had been included by default, a big hulking fourth wheel, not that they'd ever treated him that way. Growing up, Gil and Delon had spent so much time at the Jacobs ranch that the four of them had melded into a seamless unit. Inseparable, everyone had said.

Until an out-of-control driver smashed their world into pieces.

But he wasn't going to let the memories tear open old wounds and ruin his appetite. Cole hacked off a chunk of meatloaf and popped it in his mouth. His taste buds had a minor orgasm. "Mmmm. That's good stuff."

"Thank you."

Shawnee picked up her corn and munched the full length of the cob before setting it down, licking the butter from each fingertip in turn, then her lips, her tongue sliding over them, slow and thorough. Heat bloomed in Cole's chest and trickled south as he stared, mesmerized.

"So there was this girl…" she prompted.

"Wha—oh, yeah." He gave his head a slight shake to jiggle some brain cells back into gear. "She was pretty and popular and she paid attention to me. But eventually I realized I was just her backstage pass." He cut a miniature potato into four precise quarters, then each quarter into half, then lined up the tiny wedges in a neat circle. "You can't *not* know, deep down, when you're being used. Not long term. Even *I* could tell."

"How?" Shawnee asked, almost gently.

"Mostly…" He hitched a shoulder. "They never look for excuses to be with you. Just the two of you, alone."

Shawnee was silent for a moment, waiting, but he didn't go on. "And then you dumped her?"

"No." He didn't explain why not. Shawnee could put it together. There was her mother, after all, hanging on way beyond reason.

They both stared at their food, the air humming with *Too Much Information,* every word of it a weapon she could sharpen to a sarcastic edge and use to slice him to ribbons. But somehow he trusted that she wouldn't.

"I would have watched you today anyway," he confessed, glancing up.

She blinked. "Why?"

"I like the way you rope. The way you ride your horse. I learn things from watching you."

"Oh."

Their gazes caught for a beat too long, and the tension shifted into an entirely different gear. Before Cole could open his mouth again and dig an even deeper grave, Shawnee grabbed her fork to scoop up mangled potatoes.

"So," she said. "What's new with feed supplements?"

Chapter 16

THAT WAS A MISTAKE.

But telling herself she never should've invited Cole to dinner didn't stop Shawnee from leaning against the door frame and enjoying the view as he strolled back to his own trailer, Katie toddling along at his heels. Lord, the man had a set of shoulders. And arms. And a whole lot more that wasn't nearly as apparent under his usual long-sleeved western shirts. That snug blue polo shirt wasn't keeping any secrets.

Huge mistake.

Sure, she'd noticed Cole before. But now she was *aware* of him. She knew herself, she knew her body, and this was a form of heatstroke that was not going to be cured by a few glasses of sweet tea. Not when she had to be in close proximity to the energy source every single day. She'd just get warmer and warmer, until—

"He's getting it from *you*!"

She jumped at the accusation, smacking her funny bone against the door frame as she whipped around to find Hank glaring at her from behind her trailer.

"What are you doing here?" she demanded, rubbing the sting from her elbow.

"Me and the Leses went out for dinner. I just brought them back, and I saw Cole sneaking out of your trailer, looking all smug and satisfied."

Oh hell. Just what they needed, Hank getting ideas. "He wasn't sneaking. And we weren't having sex."

"Duh." Hank rolled his eyes like an eighth grade girl. "He is *not* your type."

And even though she'd been telling herself the same thing, Shawnee bristled. "What's that supposed to mean?"

"You date guys like J.P., who just wanna have some fun. Cole doesn't do fun." Hank braced one hand on the side of the trailer, the other on his hip. "But you've been feeding him…and holding out on the rest of us. That is *cold*."

Shawnee felt her face go hot. Seriously? So what if she'd been caught trafficking in meatloaf? She worked up a powerful glare. "I did not hire on to be the camp cook."

"Then why does *he* get homemade rolls?"

Oh geezus. Now Hank was gonna pout. She folded her arms. "We have a deal. He's helping me out with, um, my horses."

"More like one particular jackass." Hank narrowed his eyes, his gaze uncharacteristically shrewd. "If you ever have a problem when Cole's not around, just let me know."

The offer, and the lump it raised in Shawnee's throat, caught her off guard. Hank was immature, sometimes a total dipshit, but once in a while he surprised you.

Then he waggled his eyebrows. "And *I'm* really good at casual, if you need someone to pick up where J.P. left off."

"Oh *gah*!" She actually gagged at the thought. "Stop before you make my brain puke. You're Melanie's little brother."

Hank laughed, unfazed. "Fine. I'll clean your

horse trailer, or wash your pickup. There must be something…"

She started to shake her head, but then she thought about how they'd all come to the team roping to cheer her and Mariah on. How every one of them had made a point of wandering by to say, "Good job" or "Nice roping" afterward, while she was putting up her horse. Would it kill her to show a little hospitality in return?

"Okay, fine. Tuesday's an off day. If everybody chips in a few bucks for groceries, I'll make a big ol' batch of Texas red." She could grab a bushel of that excellent corn at the farm stand on the way out of town in the morning, and whip up some corn bread to go with the chili. "Good enough?"

Hank wrapped both arms around his belly and squeezed, grinning. "You are my hero."

"Say that after you've chopped all the onions and peppers. Now go away."

Hank did, hustling to his car as if he was afraid she'd change her mind. Shawnee leaned against the doorframe again and sighed, her troubled gaze tracking over to Cole's trailer. Hank was a pain in the ass, but he was also right.

Cole wasn't a casual guy. And he sucked at letting go. He'd practically said so when he'd admitted how he'd let that girl keep using him. Who blurted that out over dinner? The way he kept people at arm's length wasn't disinterest, or coldness. It was pure self-preservation. He had no internal walls behind the stony facade. Everything he felt was right there, exposed and vulnerable.

Which meant Shawnee had to keep her hands off, despite knowing Cole was *aware* right back. If Cole did crawl into her bed—her breath hitched at the thought of getting her hands on everything under that snug blue polo shirt—he would very possibly want to stay. Maybe forever.

And forever was one of many things she didn't have to offer.

They started out early the next morning and drove until evening, into the heart of Texas's hill country. Half an hour short of their destination, the audiobook Mariah and Shawnee had been listening to ended. They rode in silence for a few morose moments.

"Do we feel more cultured now?" Shawnee asked.

"Not really," Mariah said. "Mostly we feel like people suck and civilization is doomed."

"Are we done with your summer reading list, or do I have to suffer through more of this depressing shit?"

"We're done." Mariah pumped a fist in celebration. "Next road trip is gonna be all sexy guys and smart-ass girls."

"Now *that's* my kind of book. I could use a good laugh."

Mariah contemplated the scenery for a couple of miles before asking, "Does it really suck, having your dad around?"

"Ace?" Shawnee corrected automatically. "Not so far, but he hasn't tried to con me into or out of anything yet."

"He's scared of Cole."

Or he realized Cole couldn't be charmed, and hadn't figured another way around him yet. Plus he was biding his time while his shoulder healed. Ace wouldn't make his move until he had one foot out the door. Usually, Shawnee would have been on pins and needles, waiting for the chips to fall, but her conversation with Cole had actually helped. Go figure.

Or maybe Cole was just turning into the bigger problem.

"Do you miss J.P.?" Mariah asked.

Shawnee thought about it, then sighed. "I wish it hadn't ended that way. I may have lost a friend, and that sucks."

"But you knew it was going to end?"

"Well, yeah." And all of the sudden, she found herself treading delicate moral ground. Her lifestyle was well and good given her situation, but Mariah was sixteen years old with the whole world waiting for her. Shawnee couldn't even remember what that felt like. She shook off the pang of self-pity and concentrated on choosing her words carefully. "J.P. is a great guy, and we had a lot in common, but neither of us was looking for a long-term relationship."

"Because of his age?"

"Not really. He's very mature."

"People say that about me," Mariah said. "They call me an old soul."

The edge of triumph in her voice triggered alarm bells. She had a stubborn set to her jaw, as if they were having an argument. One Shawnee had lost before knowing she was in it. "Don't be in such a rush to grow up," she said, grasping at a feeble straw. "I guarantee, it's not as much fun as you think it's gonna be."

Mariah's chin came up and her eyes flashed. "I can handle it."

Maybe, but like the inspirational poster in Shawnee's doctor's office said, *You don't know how strong you really are until strong is your only option.* She prayed Mariah never needed that kind of strength because, truthfully, it wasn't all that gratifying to prove how much you could bear.

It was just really fucking tiring.

Chapter 17

FOR THE FIRST TIME SINCE HE'D BEEN SENT OUT ON HIS own, Cole felt like it might actually be okay. Maybe even good. He didn't quite know what to do with the knowledge that Shawnee was a big part of his optimism, but he was working on it.

When they'd arrived at this week's rodeo, she'd parked just across the road from the rest of the Jacobs rigs instead of over in the contestant lot. It was like a piece of needle-grass plucked out of Cole's sock. He hadn't realized how much her separation had niggled at his sense of order until it was gone.

Now his whole crew was gathered up for dinner. Even Cruz had abandoned his latest rawhide project. They lounged in camp chairs scattered under the trailer awnings exchanging the usual gossip, tall tales, and friendly insults. Hank had hooked up a portable speaker to his smartphone and he and Analise and Mariah were arguing over the playlist. Katie sniffed around, searching for scraps on the empty plates that had been left on the ground.

Aunt Iris would be proud.

Cole soaked it all in as he strolled over to refill his sweet tea from a jug on the folding table beside Shawnee's door. He turned to tell her—again—how much he appreciated the effort, but hesitated when he saw her sitting with her chin in her hand, flip-flops kicked off, staring into the distance with a troubled crease between her brows. She had wadded her hair into a messy ball on top of her head, but long, curling strands had escaped, trailing across muscular shoulders and arms bared by her pale-green tank top.

His gaze gravitated down to equally powerful thighs and calves exposed by her khaki shorts. But her toes were…well, damn there wasn't really another word for it. Cute. She had cute toes. And if she could read his mind, she'd gut-punch him.

Cole dragged his attention off her body and followed her line of sight to the source of her frown—Butthead, pacing an agitated rut along the south side of his pen. The gray paused to sniff at the bucket hung on the fence, grab it with his teeth, and flip it upside down, dumping the water on the ground. Then he commenced pacing again.

"He's not getting any better," she said, as Cole settled into the chair beside her.

"Not so's you'd notice." He fought to keep his eyes pointed straight forward instead of straying toward all that firm flesh. And those cute, bronze-painted toes.

"I thought exposing him to all of these different places would desensitize him. If anything, he's getting more psychotic." Her mouth dragged down at the corners. "Got any bright ideas? One of your magic feed supplements that'll take the edge off?"

Cole had given it plenty of thought. He didn't have much to offer. "Magnesium, maybe. I've used it on horses that stress out in particular situations. Not something you can feed him every day for the rest of his life, though."

"By which you mean his condition is permanent?"

She made a sour face. "I suppose you have a name for this, too."

He dragged his attention off the satiny skin of her thighs and onto the conversation. Talking while ogling was just asking to blurt out something inappropriate. "Neophobia. The irrational fear of new places or situations. Documented in animals and humans."

She gave him a side-eye glance without turning her head. "Something else you had reason to look up?"

"Yeah."

He braced himself for a snide remark about how that explained so much about his anal tendencies, but she heaved a defeated sigh instead. "What am I gonna do with him? I can't sell a horse that loses his shit every time he leaves the round pen in my backyard."

"I suppose we could see if he'll buck," Cole said, without much enthusiasm. Rodeo broncs and bulls had to be road warriors, comfortable anywhere, or they burned out. The gray would never hold up.

Shawnee shook her head. "He doesn't have it in him."

They sat and watched him pace some more. The poor damn horse looked so miserable and anxious and there didn't seem to be anything they could do to make him feel better, short of a tranquilizer dart.

"I don't have room to keep him forever," Shawnee said. "I thought about sneaking down to the Patterson Ranch and kicking him loose in one of their back pastures, but he'd probably panic and run off a cliff. Plus if the stupid rubbed off on any of their colts, Tori would hang me with my own rope." She heaved another sigh. "I guess I'll just keep fighting the good fight and hope for a miracle."

She didn't sound optimistic.

"I'll pick up some magnesium paste when I go to the feed store tomorrow." Cole frowned, puzzled. Shawnee was too horse-savvy not to have seen what she was getting into. "How did you get stuck with him?

"Some friends bought him for their ten-year-old daughter because he was so pretty and sweet. He must've been doped to the eyeballs when they tried him out. *That* is not a kid horse. The little girl begged me to save him." She drove her fingers through the wayward curls at her temples with a groan. "She calls me at least every other week to see how he's doing."

"And you say…"

"I lie my ass off. Whatever I do with him has to be far, far away from Amarillo, or she'll want to visit."

Cole thought about that for a while. Then he said, "How about a distraction?"

"God, yes. How much tequila do you have?"

He laughed. "I meant for the kid. Have they found her another horse yet? Beni has decided Dozer is too slow, so he's laid claim to Cadillac."

"Violet's good horse?" Shawnee lifted her chin off her hand to stare at him in amazement. "How'd he swing that?"

"Oh, you know Beni. He's always got a plan. Since Violet hasn't been able to ride, he offered to keep Cadillac in shape for her."

"And she fell for it?"

Cole smiled. "Beni thinks so. Actually, her young horse is past ready to start earning his keep, and Cadillac is the perfect step up for Beni. He'll take good care of our little man."

Shawnee tossed a sullen glare at the gray. "That son of a bitch can't even take care of himself."

"Too bad we can't put him on anxiety meds, like a person."

"No kidding. They are a miracle." The words were barely out before she sucked in a breath, as if she could pull them back. Then she gave an overly casual shrug. "Imagine what a joy I'd be without them."

Before Cole could respond, she slapped her palms onto her thighs and pushed to her feet. "I'll give Violet a call about that horse. And if you don't mind, I'll ride along to the feed store tomorrow to see what they've got."

She grabbed the empty chili pot and disappeared into her trailer, the door slapping shut behind her. Conversation over. Topic closed for discussion.

Cole thought about that bottle of little blue pills in his own medicine cabinet, for the times when his body and mind turned on him and none of his usual tricks could pull him back from the edge. Something else he and Shawnee had in common. But mutual dependence on pharmaceuticals didn't seem like a great basis for a relationship.

A jolt ran through him like he'd been struck by lightning.

God help him. He'd just put *Shawnee* and *relationship* in the same sentence.

—∿∿—

Two days later, Shawnee reined Butthead to a stop and stepped off, rubbing a hand between his ears. He cocked his head, enjoying the scratch of her fingers. And it had only taken most of an hour to get to this point.

"Better," Cole called out from the fence. "It took four minutes less than average to get him to stop fighting and tuck his nose."

"You've been timing me?" Though on second thought, she shouldn't be surprised. It was classic Cole—his version of Butthead's precious round pen. Instead of fences, he coped by surrounding himself with walls of logic and routine.

She'd like to know how that brain of his made sense of the way she caught him looking at her when he thought she didn't notice.

Nothing was more illogical than her and Cole. Yeah, they worked well together in the arena, they were both horse trainers, and they came from similar backgrounds. But scratch a thumbnail across that very thin veneer and you'd uncover irreconcilable differences. Cole was a highway, cutting straight and true and solid, his destination mapped out to the nth degree. Shawnee was a cow path, meandering from one watering hole and patch of green grass to the next, letting the wind push her where it would.

He fell in beside her as she led Butthead out of the arena. "If we find a supplement or medication that reduces his anxiety in the short term, it may enable the desensitization process."

"Yes, Professor Jacobs," she drawled.

He hunched a shoulder, his jaw going tight. "Words and phrases stick in my head, so I use them. I know it makes me sound weird."

"Smart," she corrected.

He shot her a surprised look.

"Most people can't remember stuff like that," she

clarified, avoiding his gaze. Hearing Cole put himself down irritated her. "Maybe it was weird when you were a kid. Now you sound smart."

"Oh." His face relaxed into a slight smile. "Thanks."

"Don't let it go to your head. I said you *sounded* smart."

Instead of going all stiff and offended, he laughed. Shit. She couldn't even needle him anymore. When had she lost the edge?

She veered off toward her trailer. "Better go swap horses."

"See you in the arena in fifteen."

And weren't they ever so casual? Just good buddies, her and Cole. Until you scratched that paper-thin surface and saw what was threatening to come to a boil underneath.

But she was in a strangely Zen mood for the rest of the day. Even Ace couldn't get under her skin. For the most part he'd kept his distance, either afraid Cole would make good on the threat to ship him out or—more likely—just not all that interested in her as long as he had a place to sleep and three squares a day. And she didn't have to feel guilty about dragging along a freeloader. He'd turned out to be a pretty good rodeo announcer, with his bottomless well of insider information and the quick wit that had kept him from being murdered in his sleep for decades. Maybe Ace had finally stumbled into a legitimate career. Lord knew, it would suit his need to be the center of attention.

The sense of peace followed her to bed that night. She fell into a delicious, dreamless sleep so deep it took her a few moments to resurface when the pounding came at her door. Even then, she didn't panic, just yawned, stretched, and combed her fingers through her hair in a useless attempt to untangle the mess as she padded to the door to see what new excuse Cole had come up with to harass her in the wee hours.

She yanked the door open. "What do you—"

The words died abruptly as her heart lurched into her throat. It wasn't Cole. It was Hank. And he was covered in blood.

Chapter 18

THE CRASH HAD LAUNCHED COLE OUT OF BED A FEW minutes before his usual two-fifteen patrol. He'd scrambled into jeans and boots, shoving his phone into his pocket and grabbing a T-shirt as he burst out the door. A quick scan of the bucking stock showed a lot of wide eyes and flared nostrils, all pointed in one direction.

Toward the saddle horse pens.

Cole broke into a run as he rounded the front of his trailer, fear clawing at his chest. The scene was like something out of a horror movie. Shawnee's gray horse was groaning and thrashing in the dirt, blood streaming from a gash on top of his head where he must have slammed it into the fence.

Son of a bitch.

Cole didn't hesitate, his mind scrolling through the necessary steps even as he paused long enough to beat his fist on the door of the nearest truck before yanking it open. Hank's bleary face poked out from the sleeper. It was his weekend to stay on the grounds while both Leses took the motel room. Perfect.

"Whaa... ?" Hank mumbled, scrubbing a hand over his eyes.

"Shawnee's gray horse is down."

Hank was instantly awake and fumbling for his clothes. Cole didn't wait. He ran to his trailer to grab his vet kit.

"Stay, Katie," he ordered.

The dog whined, but dropped onto her belly beside the door.

Back at the pen, Butthead was wallowing on his side, kicking at his belly and banging his head against the ground. Blood streaked his face and jowls and spattered the ground around him, glistening black under the security lights. Cole dropped the vet kit and untied the halter that hung on the gate.

Hank trotted up, still pulling on a T-shirt. "Jesus Christ. Colic?"

"Looks like." Cole opened the gate and eased inside. "We've got to get him up before he hurts himself anymore."

Hank slid in behind Cole, giving the thrashing hooves a wide berth. "How do we do that without getting killed?"

Good question. The gray was unpredictable when he wasn't in blind agony. Cole took a precious moment to study the situation. The horse was lying perpendicular to the fence, so they had some room to operate, but there was only one option that he could see. "I'll pin him down. You put the halter on him."

"Be careful."

Cole wasn't sure it was possible. He handed Hank the halter, then moved around behind the gray. The horse didn't react to their presence, his eyes glazed, beyond seeing anything but the monster that tore at his guts. He flung his head back, nearly taking Cole out at the knees. Rather than jumping away, Cole dropped, splaying his legs and collapsing to pin the horse's neck down with his chest.

The horse squealed and thrashed, but didn't have the

strength or leverage to fight Cole off. Blood and sweat soaked through his T-shirt as Hank slid the halter on with swift, practiced motions. Thank God he was the one here tonight. The Leses didn't have a ranch kid's experience with doctoring large, uncooperative animals.

"Got it," Hank said, buckling the halter. He hopped over the horse's head and to the end of the lead rope, then braced himself.

Cole rolled off and well away before scrambling to his feet. Butthead gave a guttural groan and arched up, biting at his flank. Using the small amount of momentum, Hank hauled on the rope to rock the horse off his side. Cole bailed in, bracing his shoulder against the gray's and shoving him upright. They got him as far as his haunches, sitting like a dog on his butt, his front legs locked and trembling.

"Hold him there if you can." Cole hustled to the vet box, grabbed a syringe and a brown glass bottle, and drew a dose of Banamine. Hank had the lead rope hitched behind his hip and was leaning his full weight into it to keep the horse from flopping over. Cole eased up beside Butthead and latched an arm around his neck. The gray threw up his head and caught Cole on the chin with his rock-hard skull. Stars burst behind Cole's eyes and he felt blood spatter on his face. From the sharpness of the sting, he suspected some of it was his.

Hank moved hand over hand up the rope, shortening his grip so he could pull the horse's nose around and down, curving his neck around Cole's body and exposing the vein. Cole palpated quickly, found the vessel, and slid the needle into place, depressing the plunger. Then he jumped back while he still had all his teeth.

He took the halter rope from Hank with one hand as he retrieved his cell phone from the pocket of his jeans with the other. The first speed dial setting was always the official vet at the current rodeo, on twenty-four-hour call. "Go get Shawnee," he told Hank.

By the time they returned, Cole had managed to haul the gray up onto his feet where he stood, legs splayed, sides heaving.

Shawnee's first word was something not fit for polite company, but she didn't flinch. One look at Hank would've been enough to prepare her for the worst. She'd taken the time to get fully dressed in jeans, boots, and a long-sleeved T-shirt, and she'd wadded most of her hair into a rubber band. She was carrying her own vet kit in one hand and a flashlight in the other.

"Colic?" she asked.

"Looks like it. Hank, if you'll grab this—"

"My horse." Shawnee tossed the flashlight to Hank and strode through the gate to take the lead rope from Cole's hand. There was no sense arguing that she'd ruin her clothes. As if she would care, at this moment.

"Our on-call vet is clear down at the south end of the county doing a C-section on a cow, so it's going to take him at least an hour to get here. I'll get my stethoscope."

Shawnee nodded and murmured soft, encouraging words to the gray, stroking his bloody forehead. His head drooped, his eyelids sagging to half-mast—all those hours in the arena paying off. The horse trusted her, latching on to her touch and the sound of her voice like a lifeline. Plus the Banamine seemed to be knocking the razor edge off the pain.

A thought blinked into Cole's head—there and

gone—that if Shawnee whispered to him and touched him that way, he might not need pharmaceutical intervention for his anxiety attacks. Then he was back to business, pulling the stethoscope out of its leather pouch and clamping the rubber earpieces in his ears.

"Hank, go get two buckets out of my trailer, and fill one of them with warm water," he said as he settled a gentle hand on the horse's shoulder.

It didn't move, mesmerized by Shawnee's voice and rhythmic massage. She was oblivious to the blood that trickled down the bridge of its nose and dripped onto the front of her shirt. Cole pressed the disc of the stethoscope first to the horse's chest, timing the heart rate on his cell phone. Sixty-three beats per minute. High, but not in the danger zone. Yet. He worked his way back, pausing to listen at various points along the rib cage and belly.

When he straightened, Shawnee asked, "Well?"

"I don't hear any gut sounds."

She breathed another obscenity, well aware that it wasn't good news. No gurgles or grumbles meant food wasn't traveling through the intestines, and that most likely meant a blockage of some sort. With luck, it was an impaction—a lump of hay or bedding plugging up the works. But even that was an emergency. A horse was incapable of vomiting, and with the high volume of fluid secreted into their stomach to carry forage through their system, any blockage quickly became a critical condition that could result in a rupture.

Hank came back with the two buckets, moving as fast as possible without sloshing the water.

"Can you get him to move?" Cole asked Shawnee.

She pulled on the halter rope, a firm, steady pressure,

and Cole clapped a hand on the horse's butt. He took a couple of staggering steps. Then a couple more, becoming less unsteady as he went. Shawnee was solid as a rock. Like a good soldier, or a medical professional, her emotions locked behind a wall of calm, cool necessity.

"Good," Cole said. "Let's get him into the stripping chute."

With a combination of pulling and pushing, they were able to walk the gray to the narrow chute where riggings and saddles were pulled off the bucking horses after they exited the arena. With sliding gates front and back, it was a passable substitution for the stocks a veterinarian used to restrain a horse. Once Butthead was inside, Cole fetched his equipment.

Shawnee's eyes narrowed when she saw the nasogastric tube. "You know how to use that thing?"

"Yes." He handed her a roll of tape and one end of the flexible plastic tube, and set the empty bucket beside her. "I hang out with the vet in Dumas whenever I get the chance, and he's taught me the basics in case we have an emergency on the road."

As Cole climbed up onto the side of the chute, Hank wrapped the lead rope around one of the metal rails and snugged it up tight, anchoring the gray's head. He'd done this before, too. Shawnee angled the flashlight so it illuminated Cole's workspace without getting in his eyes. The horse strained against the rope, but couldn't budge as Cole eased the tube up one nostril.

"Be ready to catch anything that comes out," he told Shawnee. "The vet will want to see it."

Cole closed his eyes, his head filling with anatomical charts as he tried to feel each structure the tube encountered as he worked it in. That spongy resistance would be the esophagus. "Blow in the tube."

Shawnee blew, the force of the air opening the airway, and the tube moved past the obstruction. The horse swallowed, helping push the tube along its way.

"We should be almost"—a greenish brown slurry shot through the clear tube and out of the end Shawnee jammed into the bucket— there," Cole concluded.

As the rancid contents of its overfull stomach gushed out, the horse heaved what sounded like a sigh of relief. When the fluid stopped draining, Cole took the tape from Shawnee's hand, coiled the loose end of the tube and taped it up to the side of the halter, leaving the other end in place so it could be used again if necessary. "I'll go find some rags to clean that cut."

"Don't bother." Hank stripped off his T-shirt, balled it up, and dunked it in the bucket of warm water before handing it to Shawnee. "It was wrecked anyway."

As she pressed the makeshift bandage to the cut, Cole checked his watch. Only ten minutes had passed. Even if the on-call vet came immediately, there was nothing more he could do here at the rodeo grounds. "If we can get him into my trailer, it's about forty-five minutes from here to the equine hospital in Selma."

"We'll get him loaded," Shawnee said, grimly determined.

While Hank rousted Cruz to help, Cole called ahead to the hospital and gave them as much information as he could. Then he rigged a sling that passed under the horse's girth, and with Shawnee coaxing him forward and the three men putting every ounce of muscle into it, they hoisted him up, first front feet, then back. Unlike

Tori's trailer, Cole's was also used for hauling bucking stock. The rear compartment was one large open space with no stall dividers to get in their way.

The moment they slackened their hold, the gray's legs buckled. Hank and Cruz just managed to avoid being pinned against the trailer wall as Butthead collapsed onto his side. Shawnee held firm to the lead rope. "I'll ride back here with him."

The look on her face said there was no changing her mind—and no time to argue.

"Cruz, go get the seat cushions from the table in my living quarters." Cole strode around to grab a couple of saddle blankets from the tack room, tossing the pickup keys to Hank. "You drive."

When Cruz brought the cushions, Cole lifted the gray's head to put one underneath and tucked the other against the wall, the best he could do to stop the horse from inflicting any further damage on himself. For now, he was quiet except for the heaving of his flanks and an occasional groan.

"Stay here," he told Cruz. "Let the others know what happened. I'll give you a call when I have some idea what time we'll be back."

Shawnee took one of the blankets and dropped it on the floor before sitting down, close enough to reach out and stroke the horse's head but clear of the strike zone if he started to thrash. Cole took the second and settled in closer to the front of the trailer where he could lean back against the opposite wall and stretch out his legs. Katie jumped in and scampered up to hunker beside him as Hank shut and latched the door. Cole didn't try to talk over the rumble and clatter of the trailer and roar of the wind through the side slats. What was there to say? He had no meaningless assurances to offer. Shawnee knew better than to believe them if he did.

The drive blurred into a rush of sound and vibration increasingly punctuated by the bright slash of street-lights as they skirted the northern edge of San Antonio. Shawnee had brought the bucket of water along and gently dabbed blood from the horse's face and jowls, soothing him with words Cole couldn't make out. He could only see that it worked.

Then they slowed, turned onto a gravel surface, circled around, and stopped. The pickup engine cut off and the trailer door swung open and they were overrun by brisk, efficient hospital staff. The techs bustled around, positioning a stretcher, while the veterinarian checked Butthead's vital signs and peppered Cole and Shawnee with questions.

They'd made it this far and the horse was still alive. It remained to be seen whether they'd be able to keep him that way.

Chapter 19

BENEATH THE HARSH GLARE OF FLUORESCENT LIGHTS, Shawnee and Cole looked like escapees from a Texas Chainsaw Massacre movie. Hank looked slightly less gruesome in the clean T-shirt he'd grabbed to replace the one he'd given Shawnee to use as a bandage, but his hands, arms, and jeans were still streaked with blood.

Butthead was upright, supported by a web of harnessing and a hydraulic lift while the techs drained his stomach again. The vet was standing in front of Shawnee and saying words, but she was having trouble connecting them. *Impaction. Strangulation of the intestine. Not sure until we get inside…*

"How much is this going to cost?" she blurted, cutting him off midsentence.

"It depends on what we find. If it's a straightforward displacement with no complications during surgery, it could be as little as thirty-five hundred dollars. But if we find a segment with compromised circulation and we have to do a resection…"

As *little* as thirty-five hundred. Shawnee had spent the drive over praying that for once in his life Butthead would catch a break. Maybe he'd just have a blockage they could flush out. She'd heard enough colic stories to have a pretty good idea what surgery would cost, but hearing the vet confirm it…that fucking band tightened around her chest, making it nearly impossible to breathe.

If over three grand was chump change to this man, she shuddered to imagine what he considered expensive. He was droning on again about the risks, and chances of full recovery, and how the decision came down to the value of the horse, sentimental or otherwise.

Shawnee wanted to turn away, but she forced herself to look directly at Butthead as she delivered the verdict. "I can't afford it."

Not without taking a big bite out of the savings account that she considered untouchable. The sole safety net if the time came when it was her...when she couldn't...

Hands closed around her shoulders. Big, hard hands, warm in the air-conditioned chill of the clinic, that pulled her back from the edge. "Cost isn't an issue," Cole said. "The horse is included under the comprehensive policy that covers any stock that travels with Jacobs Rodeo."

Shawnee jerked her head around, tilting back to look up at him. There was a fresh scrape underneath his chin, no doubt inflicted by Butthead. "Are you serious?"

"Do I ever joke around? Especially at a time like this?" His face was a complete blank as he looked past her to the vet. "Shawnee has to decide whether it's worth the risk. But cost isn't an issue."

"He's a five-hundred-dollar horse with major psychological issues." She had to say the sensible thing, even if the implication made her stomach turn over. "You could spend thousands of dollars and he'll die anyway."

Cole just shrugged, so maddeningly noncommittal she wanted to stamp her foot. *Give me something, dammit.* An argument for or against. Where was all that fucking logic now, when her emotions were screaming at her to make the totally illogical choice?

Well, screw him, then. It was his dime. She turned back to the vet. "Do the surgery."

"We'll get him prepped right away. In the meantime, we have some paperwork to fill out." He made a sympathetic face. "You'll need to sign a release giving us permission to euthanize the animal if, in our opinion, there is no reasonable chance of recovery. But if it comes to that, I'll talk it over with you before proceeding. And you can be with him at the end if you wish."

She nodded mechanically. After all, there wasn't really a choice. If it reached that point, when the last sliver of hope had packed its bags and left town, there was no reason to prolong the suffering.

She knew better than anyone, and not just when it came to horses.

She'd talked it through for hours with her grandfather when she was fourteen and so sick she couldn't walk, or worse, ride. Rather than brushing her off with platitudes, he'd agreed. If this was all that was left of life, if there was nothing ahead but pain, the inability to do any of the things you loved, what was the point? Sitting side-by-side on her bed, they'd both put it in writing.

Five years later, she'd stood beside her grandmother and honored that agreement by not arguing when he'd declined treatment, even while her soul howled that there had to be a way.

There wasn't. There was only needless suffering, lingering beyond all pretense of dignity. If she wouldn't wish it on herself, or on her grandfather, she sure as hell didn't wish it on a horse.

She shook loose of Cole's grip and walked over to loop her arms around Butthead's neck to whisper in his ear. "Listen, moron. If you show half as much try as you do when you're fightin' me out in the arena, you'll come out of this just fine. But if you don't..."

She pressed her cheek to his and smoothed her hands down his neck, trying to project comfort and reassurance into him. *Be calm. Trust me. These people will take care of you.* The horse tipped his head to whuffle green slime into her shirt. She gave him one last pat, then stepped back, turned to the vet, and nodded.

God, she hated hospital waiting rooms. It was almost worse here, where the normal, healthy scent of animals was tainted by antiseptics and unhealthy sweat, combining into a deep wrongness. *Eau de fear and desperate prayers.*

And Lord knew, she'd smelled it often enough.

Cole had dragged her out to his trailer and tried to convince her to stretch out on the bed instead of perching on this stiff vinyl sofa, but that felt too much like abandoning Butthead. She had accepted his offer of a clean, incredibly soft T-shirt. She wanted to bunch it up and press it to her nose to block out the hospital smell, but that would look like she was trying to take a snort of Cole, and he and Hank were wedged on either side of her—silently, staunchly supportive. Even if Hank was dozing with his head on her shoulder. The contact felt good. Grounding.

She wondered if she could get away with pretending to do the same with Cole. Then he yawned, stretched, and extended his arm along the back of the sofa, behind her shoulders. Katie stirred, then resettled herself, wedged into the space between Cole's leg and Shawnee's, the hated leash clipped on her collar. Even the Queen of Jacobs Rodeo had to follow hospital rules.

Cole grimaced apologetically. "Sorry. I gotta get a little more comfortable."

"Damn. And here I thought you were makin' your slick first date move." Ah, shit. That almost sounded like flirting. Here. Of all places and times.

His mouth twitched. "I don't have any moves. Slick or otherwise."

He shouldn't be so sure. The back of the sofa was so narrow she had no choice but to lean against the hard warmth of his arm, bared by another of those clingy T-shirts. She closed her eyes, just for a minute. It would be so easy…

"Shawnee." The voice was deep and soft in her ear.

She opened her eyes. Then realized her face was buried in Cole's armpit and jolted upright, wincing at the painfully bright light. "Wha…I'm awake. What's wrong?"

"Nothing, for the time being." The vet smiled down at her, his eyes tired but his expression pleased. "Good news, actually. Your horse had an impaction in the long colon—it was a doozy, but about as uncomplicated as it gets in terms of colic surgery. We cleared the obstruction and flushed his system. He's being transferred to a recovery stall now. We'll keep him on IV fluids and monitor him closely as he comes out of the anesthesia, which will take an hour or so. And we'll need to hold him here for at least five days."

Five *days*? At least? By then they'd be five hundred miles down the road, in the far reaches of West Texas, gearing up for a four-day rodeo. And from there they were headed north into Utah. She racked her sludge-coated brain, trying to think of anyone she knew in this general area who might be willing to take care of Butthead until she could get back to pick him up. Then remembered that this *was* Butthead, who didn't tolerate new places or people.

"I can't leave him…" she began, shooting a helpless look at Cole. "You know how he is."

The vet cleared his throat. "I have a suggestion, if you're game. A friend of mine at Texas A&M is conducting a study aimed at developing a timed-release, antistress product for long-term use in performance horses. He's looking for test subjects. From what you've said about your horse's, um, disposition, I think he'd be a prime candidate. And if you agree, we'll waive our boarding fees until he's recovered sufficiently to travel."

Shawnee stared at him, trying to work out exactly what he was proposing. "So they're going to put him on…what? Horsey Prozac?"

"Not quite. It's actually a milk protein—maltose and casein—that's already on the market and proving both safe and effective. He's trying to tweak the formula to make it even better for horses with higher levels of stress or anxiety."

"And this is going to cost me how much?" Shawnee asked.

"Nothing. The university covers all costs including transportation to College Station, which they will arrange."

It sounded good. Too good. There had to be a catch. But she couldn't *think*…

Cole's arm slid down and tightened around her

shoulders, but his gaze was locked on the vet. "Get us the details. Shawnee can look it over and make a decision when she's had a few hours of sleep."

Hank strolled up, cradling three foam cups in his hands. Shawnee hadn't even realized he was gone. She scrubbed her hands over her face, then held one out. He put the blessed coffee cup in it and she took a careful sip. Ah. Now *that* hit the spot.

"Hot and sweet." Hank winked at her. "Just like you."

She curled her lip at him, then gave in and smiled as he handed Cole the second cup. "You know, sometimes I get to thinkin' you might actually be a decent guy."

"I can fake it now and then."

"You're not faking it, Hank." Impulsively, she reached out and grabbed his hand. "This is the real you, under all the cocky bullshit. You should let it show more often."

He hunched his shoulders, his cheeks going red as he looked away. "Whatever."

The moment got awkward in a hurry. Shawnee broke it short, turning her attention back to the vet. "Can I be with my horse when he comes out of the anesthesia? If he starts to freak out, it might help if I'm there."

"Sure. As long as you understand that we can't allow you to put yourself in danger."

She stayed until Butthead was safely, if unsteadily, on his feet in the padded recovery stall. And then she had to leave. *Had* to. It was already almost eight o'clock. Cole's schedule was shot to hell. But she remained rooted to the spot, one hand on Butthead's neck where she could feel his pulse tapping gently against her fingers.

Alive. Still alive.

"We'll give him a couple more hours, then move him to a regular stall," the infernally cheerful tech said. "We have visiting hours until six this evening if you want to come back later."

Shawnee shook her head. "We've got a rodeo performance tonight. I'll have to wait until morning."

"Oh." The tech frowned, then brightened immediately. "We've got your cell number. I can text you photos, so you can see how he's doing."

Shawnee gave her a grateful smile. "Thanks. That would be awesome."

But she still couldn't let go. Couldn't break that fragile connection that assured her his heart was still beating. Finally, the tech came over to stand in front of Butthead, gently placing a hand on his forehead.

"We'll be fine, won't we, handsome?" she cooed. "I'll be right here if you need any ol' thing."

His ears perked slightly at the tech's voice. She slid her hand down and let him sniff her fingers. He took his time debating whether he liked the smell of her, then sighed and lowered his nose into her palm as if he was too exhausted to hold his own head up.

"There, you see?" she said, stroking his muzzle with her thumb and reaching out with her other hand to squeeze Shawnee's arm. "You can trust us; we'll be right here when you get back."

Yeah. Where had she heard that before? She shook free of the memory that threatened to smother her like a black fog and checked the time on her phone. *Shit*. It was almost eight thirty. They should've been halfway done running stock and they still had a forty-five-minute drive to get back. Cole must be going insane.

She had to drag herself away, or force him to do it. She gave Butthead one last stroke. "You behave now, you hear?"

As she staggered outside, she gulped in fresh air, trying to scrub the hospital scent from her sinuses. Hank and Cole were leaning against the shady side of Cole's trailer, sipping coffee, paper plates and crumpled napkins stacked on the fender between them. Katie was licking pancake syrup from a plate of her own. They were both showered and shaved, Hank in borrowed surgical scrubs, Cole in his working uniform of long-sleeved shirt and cowboy hat. The benefit of hauling your house everywhere you went.

The only sign of impatience was the rapid *tap, tap, tap* of Cole's fingers on the fender. It stopped as soon as he caught sight of her. "Everything okay?"

"So far." She waved her phone. "They're going to keep me updated. We can go now."

Cole didn't bolt for the pickup, but it was obvious he wanted to. He did pause long enough to ask, "Do you want something to eat? We saved some scrambled eggs and sausage—I can heat it up."

Shawnee's stomach turned over at the thought of piling food on top of the stress of the night. "I'll grab a bite later."

She climbed into the passenger's seat, tipped the seat back, and closed her eyes, her hands clenching around her phone as they turned out onto the highway. *No complications. No signs of infection. Excellent prognosis for full recovery.* She repeated the vet's words like a mantra, but still the tension spiraled higher with every mile of separation, her mind conjuring images of returning to find an empty stall, nothing but sad, sympathetic faces.

Not the same. Not the same.

But last time they'd told her to go home, get some sleep, they'd been confident her grandfather would live through the night. He'd squeezed her hand, whispered that he'd see her in the morning. The only time she could recall that he'd failed to keep his word.

She shouldn't have left.

She checked her silent phone to be sure the battery hadn't gone dead. Too soon. The tech wouldn't text her for at least a few hours. Unless something went wrong…

No. She could not let herself imagine the worst. The minute they pulled into the rodeo grounds, they'd all have to hit the ground running. She would focus on that—every nitpicking step of Cole's routine—to carry her through this day.

But when they arrived, Tyrell and Mariah were just riding out of the arena aboard Hammer and Salty. Cruz and Analise strolled out behind them, closing the gate.

Cole stopped the pickup beside the stock pens and Shawnee rolled down her window. "What's up?"

"Just finished running the stock." The nearest Les flashed him a proud grin as the other latched a gate behind a pair of bulls. "You didn't think we'd been doing this long enough to manage without you?"

Analise marched over and did jazz hands with her leather gloves. "Cruz showed me how to run the gates. I want to do it again tomorrow. Except for the bulls. They reek."

"Weenie," Hank said.

Analise flipped him off. Cole actually laughed.

And inside Shawnee, the tiny thread she'd been cling-ing to snapped. Now what was she supposed to do? Just sit here and wait? Jump in her pickup and go straight back? And do what? Get in the way?

Distantly, she heard Cole saying something about slowing down. But that was stupid. She hadn't even moved. And then she realized…

Aw hell. She was hyperventilating.

Black spots pocked her vision, slowly expanding, eating the light and the air. Not good. It had been years since she'd had a full-on anxiety attack. These days she generally settled for an occasional crushing sense of dread—but the last few hours had punched every emotional button she owned. Her chest began to ache. She closed her eyes. Big mistake. The present faded out and she was sitting in an overheated, stuffy room, her grandfather's bony hand in hers. So frail. So wasted.

Such a fucking *waste*.

And then it was her hand being squeezed, and for a horrible instant it was her in the bed. Her, sliding down…down…

Cole squeezed harder, until her knuckles cracked and the pain yanked her back to the present. Not much of an improvement as far as she was concerned. Past, present, future…it all bore down on her as her mind and body turned traitor, her heart revving toward the red line—

"Sounds like it was a hell of night."

Her eyes popped open at the sound of Ace's voice. He'd climbed down out of the second truck, his jeans stuffed sloppily into the tops of his boots and his shirt unbuttoned, showing a thatch of graying chest hair. Just crawling out of bed, the only one of the crew who hadn't pitched in.

He ran a careless glance around the group. "Looks like I missed all the action."

Again.

The thought was a bucket of ice in Shawnee's face, jerking her upright. He couldn't see her fall apart. That bastard would not be able to sneer that she was just like her mother, and was it any wonder he'd bailed out on the whole batshit crazy of bunch of them? Ace would have to manufacture his own excuses for being a complete loss as a father. She wouldn't hand him anything.

"Don't worry," she said. "No one was expecting you to show up."

She kicked open the pickup door and slid out. Her knees buckled, and she had to grab the doorframe to stay upright. Hank was out of the backseat and behind her in a flash, his hands bracing her so she didn't fall backward. She gave herself a moment to get her legs under her.

And then—God knows how—she walked away. Her numb fingers fumbled with the door to her trailer. An arm reached around her, a hand flipping the latch and steadying her as it opened the door. She stumbled up the steps and bolted for the bathroom. The toilet lid magically popped opened and those same hands scraped her hair back and held it while she retched up everything she'd eaten in the last week, and then some.

When she couldn't dry heave anymore, Cole peeled her off the toilet and propped her up, sitting with her back against the shower door. "Are you done?"

"I dunno. There might be a chunk of my colon I haven't hacked up yet."

Her breathing was back to normal, at least. Hard to vomit and hyperventilate simultaneously. Her heart was still hammering, though, and the floor shimmied and whirled as if she was strapped into a fighter jet that had gone into a flat spin. Water splashed in the sink and something damp was pressed to her forehead.

"Do you have a thing about slapping girls in the face with wet washcloths?" she asked.

"Nope. You're a special case."

She snorted. "Ain't that the truth."

"Takes one to know one." He shoved a glass into her limp hand and closed her fingers around it. "Where are your meds?"

How did he...oh, right. Her big mouth, running off again. "Bottom shelf, cabinet above the sink."

Her hand trembled so violently, she had to wrap all ten fingers around the glass to guide it to her lips. She filled her mouth, sloshed it around, then leaned sideways to spit it into the toilet. Nice thing about trailer bathrooms, everything was close by. She rinsed and spit again, getting rid of the worst of the grossness, then slowly keeled over onto the floor, the rest of the water sloshing into a pool around her. She heard Cole's voice, a quiet rumble like he was talking on the phone. Then the bathroom door opened again.

"Geezus. I leave you alone for ten seconds..." Cole hitched his hands under her armpits again and hauled her into a seated position between his feet, his knees bracketing her shoulders. She squeezed her eyes tight, but it didn't help with the spinning. Pills rattled in a bottle, the faucet ran again, then the glass was back in her hand. "Open wide."

She did, intending to tell him to go screw himself, and he popped a tablet into her mouth. Even she wasn't hard-headed enough to spit it out. He helped guide the glass to her mouth so she could wash the tablet down, set it aside, then pulled off her boots.

"Okay. Up we go."

Once again he hoisted her up like an uncooperative toddler and half-dragged her out of the bathroom. Before she could lie and say she was perfectly capable of walking, he scooped her up, took three long strides, and dumped her on the couch.

She let her head flop back. "That would've been a lot more impressive if you hadn't grunted."

"Good thing you're not the kind of girl I have to impress."

That was probably an insult. She'd have to think about it later. For now, she just wanted everything to hold still, dammit, before it made her sick again. The trailer shook as Cole stomped around, sticking his big nose in the middle of her shit again. Half of her wanted to curl into a ball and scream at him to go away. The other wanted to whimper like a lost puppy and beg him not to leave her alone in the dark, even though brilliant sunlight streamed through the window and pressed against her eyelids.

"You're soaked." His hands grabbed the hem of her shirt and yanked it up to her neck.

"Whoa, now—"

"It's nothing I haven't already seen. Lift your arms."

She did. He yanked the shirt off, then immediately pulled an oversized football jersey over her head and guided her arms into the sleeves.

"You're pretty good at that," she mumbled.

"Practice. And you aren't half as squirmy as Beni." He hauled her up onto her feet and turned her around so her back was braced against his chest, his hands firm on her shoulders. "Kick off your jeans."

Again she considered protesting, but she reeked, and she was wet, so she stripped off the jeans. The jersey came to midthigh, so she didn't even have to wonder what underwear she'd put on that day. Cole stuck a pair of gym shorts in her hands. When she'd fumbled into them, he planted her back on the couch.

"I called the hospital. Butthead is doing great. Now try to get some rest. I need you out there in the arena tonight."

His arm scooped up her head and shoulders, then lowered her onto—whoa, not a pillow—a hard thigh. Then he was dabbing at her face, neck, and arms with that infernal washcloth. The man truly had an obsession. But it felt good, gentle and cool, and the slight rough-ness of the cloth gave her whirling brain an anchor. She focused all of her concentration on it as she felt the drugs kick in.

So tired. So, so tired…

Her heart slowed, and her mind drifted toward obliv-ion. She was aware of Cole moving, replacing his thigh with a pillow, but she couldn't pull herself back. Didn't want to. Cole rolled her onto her side, back against the couch cushions, then stretched out in the space he'd created, legs intertwined with hers, his big, warm body boxing her in. He cupped the back of her head, guiding her cheek to his shoulder. She was completely enclosed. Safe. Not even the whisper telling her this wasn't a good idea could penetrate her cocoon.

She could just let go, secure in the knowledge that there was no way she could fall.

Chapter 20

COLE OPENED HIS EYES AND LOOKED DIRECTLY IN Shawnee's, only inches away. Wide awake and sharply aware—of him. And of how very, *very* aware his body was of her. He half expected her to slam an elbow into his gut, but she was totally relaxed, contemplating his presence with no more concern than if Katie had snuck onto the couch while she was sleeping.

"Make yourself at home," she said.

He grimaced and turned his head away, catching a glimpse of the clock. Whoa. He'd slept for two hours? He dug in the pocket of his jeans for the plastic box of breath mints he always carried. Popping the top with his thumb, he offered it to her.

"Well, that's subtle," she said, but held out her palm.

He shook a couple of mints onto it, then two more into his own mouth before he snapped the top shut and stuffed it back in his pocket, using the delay to mentally rehearse his lines. Despite what Shawnee and certain of his body parts might think, his intentions had been honorable. He'd done for her what his uncle used to do for him in the early years after the accident...but he couldn't tell her that. He didn't trust anyone with the knowledge that gruff, burly Steve Jacobs had sometimes crawled into Cole's bed and wrapped his powerful arms around a devastated teenaged boy. God only knew what Cole might have done to escape the pain if Steve hadn't been there to stop him.

But there would always be some asshole who chose to interpret it otherwise, if they knew.

He said the first thing that popped into his head. "Sorry. These jeans aren't the cleanest."

Her gaze did a lazy stroll down to his chest, then back. "You didn't have to stay dressed on my account."

The low purr under her words brought his entire body to attention—waking up more than what was nudging her hip. She felt good against him, soft but substantial, like she would hold up even if someone as big as Cole had to lean on her. He liked how she filled all the space inside his arms. Liked it a lot, which was becoming more painfully obvious the longer he held her.

"Sounds like the patient has made a full recovery," he said, trying for casual and sounding like a bad soap opera actor.

"Courtesy of my magic potion." Her voice was flippant, but she shifted onto her back so she didn't have to look him in the eyes anymore, and he heard a breath mint crunch hard between her teeth. In profile, she wasn't near as intimidating. Her nose was too small and delicate, and tipped up at the end.

As cute as her toes.

"You take a sedative," he said, trying to ignore all that softness wiggling against him. "And it's been so long since you refilled the prescription it's almost outdated. You don't have chronic anxiety."

"No shit, Sherlock." When he just kept staring at her, waiting, she hunched her shoulders. "My anxiety is not random."

"The cancer?" he guessed, because it almost had to

be either that or Ace. "You've been in remission for what, fifteen years? Don't they consider that cured?"

"Yep. The chances of another bout of Hodgkin's are pretty slim."

"But?"

She drew a breath so deep he felt her rib cage expand. "My grandfather died of pancreatic cancer. My great-grandmother died of breast cancer, and my grandmother had a double mastectomy after finding a malignant lump when she was in her forties. And that's just my immediate family. One uncle is currently in treatment for prostate cancer, another has had polyps removed from his colon, and I won't even get started on my aunts and cousins. When you add in my personal history, the doctors give me a sixty to eighty percent chance of getting it again. Somewhere."

Her voice was matter-of-fact, but with their bodies all but plastered together, she couldn't hide the tension that rippled through her muscles. The light in the trailer seemed to dim, as if the damn disease had swooped in to hover over her. Suddenly, a lot of things about Shawnee made sense.

"I'm…" Sorry? Flabbergasted? Furious? All of those things, and more. "No wonder you hate Tough Enough to Wear Pink nights."

Her head jerked around in surprise. "Is it that obvious?"

"Because even I noticed?" He shook his head. "I just realized…it's gotta be hard enough not to obsess without having it shoved in your face."

"You would know about obsessing." She shifted toward him, her hand coming to rest on his shoulder as she studied his expression, looking for…what? "It's a piss-poor attitude on my part when these people are trying to save my life."

"Maybe." He pondered for a minute, trying to come up with a decent comparison. "It's like going to the dentist, I guess. You know it's for the best and you try not to be a whiner, but that doesn't mean you're gonna enjoy it."

Her mouth curled down at the corners. "Make that a mammogram and you nailed it."

Oh damn. Don't look at her boobs. Definitely not *a good time to look at her boobs.*

"You get, um, tested a lot?" he asked, his gaze glued to a spot in the middle of her forehead.

"Every reliable screening on the market." Her hand skimmed down his arm, where she paused and squeezed his biceps — a warning, not a caress. "I don't talk about this much."

As in never. He let his gaze drift down to meet hers. Huh. He'd always thought her eyes were brown, but close up they were lighter, almost gold, like that border collie he'd had before Katie. Probably not a good idea to make that comparison out loud.

"That's okay. I'm not much for talking." His body clenched, waiting for her to purr something about what he'd rather do instead. Geezus. All of the ways she'd ever tortured him were nothing compared to this. Especially when Shawnee kept wiggling, shifting, rubbing up against him in the close confines of the couch. Almost like she was doing it on purpose.

Then her eyes narrowed. "You *are* a much better liar than I thought."

"Me? When did I ever…" Oh yeah. That thing he'd told the vet…

"Your insurance wouldn't cover my horse unless he was injured in the line of duty." She shook her head in disgust. "I can't believe I fell for it."

"You were under a lot of stress." He could feel it building again now, muscle by muscle, as the memories of the previous night played in her mind. What were the chances that he could run his hand over her hair and smooth it out of her face without losing any blood? "Jacobs Livestock is responsible, either way. He was eating our hay, in a pen that I assigned to him."

"Oh, bullshit. The feed and the pen were fine. We both saw him tip his water bucket. He never drank as much as he should and you heard the vet—that kind of impaction can be caused by dehydration."

Cole felt his face settling into stubborn lines. "It doesn't matter. I lied. Therefore, Jacobs Livestock will take full responsibility for the bill."

"I'm sure they'll be thrilled to hear that y'all are now the proud owners of a thousand-pound neurotic lab rat." Shawnee curled her lip at him. "Have you called them yet? Because I would *love* to hear that explanation."

"They won't be surprised."

But it surprised Shawnee. "You've done this before?"

Close enough. On three different occasions, he and his uncle had faced a veterinarian who'd asked the same question—how much are you willing to spend to save this animal, with no guarantees that it would ever buck again? He couldn't deliver the death sentence then, so how could he stand back and force Shawnee to do it now?

Then he realized what she'd said. "What do you mean, we own him?"

She hitched a shoulder. "I can't afford to pay you back. So you get the horse."

"I don't *want* that horse."

"Too bad, so sad. Should've thought of that before you opened your trap." Her words were snarky, but they lacked the usual edge, and the way she was looking at him—he might not be very good at reading people, but he was pretty sure that wasn't anger. Did she realize that the thumb that had been clamped on his arm was now stroking his biceps, much like she'd stroked Butthead the night before? Except this small, delicious friction wasn't calming Cole down *at all*.

"We'll think of something else." When he could think at all.

And there it was, the sharp smile, that devilish gleam in her eyes. "Such as?"

He had no idea. His mind was too full of Shawnee. Her heat, the fullness of her body, her scent—okay, that still wasn't so great, with the smell of sick horse and veterinary antiseptic lingering in her hair. But her mouth. How could a woman so tough have such a soft, sexy mouth?

He didn't have words for any of those thoughts. So he kissed her instead.

She stiffened, sucked in a breath, but didn't pull away. Cole took that as a good sign and tilted his head, tracing the curve of her upper lip with his tongue, not brave enough to go any further. Her fingers dug into his arm, and for a second he thought she would pull him closer and take the kiss to another level.

She drew back, but he was gratified to hear that the breath she released wasn't quite steady. "Well, that was…interesting."

"I've been wanting to do it for a while." He slid his fingers into the tangle of curls at the nape of her neck, ready to repeat the kiss—or hold her back if she decided to head-butt him. "I was worried you might bite."

"I still could."

His stomach sank. "You didn't like it?"

"That's not the point."

That was the only point, as far as Cole was concerned, but Shawnee narrowed her eyes at him again. "We're not done chatting. You found my horse down and bleeding, and you woke Hank up before me."

Cole blinked, thrown by the change of subject. "He was closer."

"Twenty steps, at the most. And then—" She jabbed him hard with one fingertip. "You gave him an injection without asking me first."

Cole flattened his hand over his chest in self-defense. "Immediate administration of intravenous Banamine is the standard treatment protocol for suspected colic."

"Which is the only reason I didn't rip you a new one." She tapped the scrape on his chin hard enough to make him wince. "You might not have that if I'd been there to handle him."

Well, hell. She was right, on all counts. Cole tried to imagine what he would do if anyone touched one of his horses without his consent. Visions of the Incredible Hulk raging and roaring and busting out of his clothes came to mind.

"I didn't think...I mean, I have—"

"A list," she interrupted. "As always. You can't help yourself. Yet another reason your arms, legs, and family jewels are all still intact."

Cole tensed, aware that her knee was dangerously close to the jewels in question. "I'm sorry. We almost never travel with horses that don't belong to us, so I just followed the usual routine."

"I understand. But it better not happen again." She moved abruptly, untangling herself from him and swinging her legs around to sit on the edge of the couch, pushing at the thick, tangled mass of her hair. Cole had always thought it would be a lot more practical if she cut it shorter. Now he wondered if it was one more act of rebellion against the cancer that stalked her.

He reluctantly let his hand fall away from where it still rested on her hip. He should just shut up now, while he was still in one piece. "What about the kiss?"

"I'm gonna have to think on that." She scrubbed at her face. "Right now, I'm going to take a shower."

Shawnee stood, took a beat to get her balance, then grabbed her phone off the table. There would be messages waiting from the equine hospital. They'd promised to provide hourly updates after he'd guaranteed them it was either that or have Shawnee banging on their door the minute she could get there after tonight's rodeo, visiting hours be damned. A photo popped up on the phone and he saw her smile as she shuffled to the bathroom.

Cole pushed up onto one elbow. "What am I supposed to do while you're making up your mind about the kissing?"

"If you've got any sense at all?" She paused to cock an eyebrow at him. "Run like hell."

Chapter 21

BY THE END OF THE LAST PERFORMANCE ON SATURDAY night, Shawnee figured she deserved a whole pack of gold stars for good behavior. A bottle of Pendleton whiskey at the very least—so she could take a long swig, then use the thick-bottomed bottle to coldcock the next well-meaning soul who said, "Sure is lucky that wasn't your good horse."

Those were the boneheads who'd pat your shoulder at a funeral and whisper, "At least he wasn't your favorite uncle, bless his heart."

Of course she was glad she hadn't nearly lost Roy instead. She wasn't stupid. But she was getting tired of the smirks they thought she didn't see. *Can you believe she spent that much money on a head-fighting bastard that'll never amount to anything?*

But she'd managed to keep her lip zipped. And she'd also managed to keep her hands and, for the most part, her eyes off of Cole. Since resisting temptation wasn't a life skill she practiced much, she should definitely get extra credit.

She'd settled for extra calories instead. When she wasn't underfoot at the equine hospital—where Butthead was now settled in a regular stall and being eased back on to a regular diet—she'd resorted to stress baking in an attempt to bribe her body into shutting the hell up about how easy it would be to mosey over to

Cole's trailer for a little afternoon delight. If she kept it up, she was gonna have to spend her next paycheck on a new, larger-sized wardrobe, so she left bags of cookies on the table under her awning and told the crew to help themselves. The second day, Hank presented her with a book of crossword puzzles.

Shawnee scowled at it, flipping through the pages. "What's this for?"

"Chili, rolls, oatmeal cookies—it's starting to feel like the old days. But if you wanna be the next Miz Iris, you've gotta have all the props."

She nailed him between the shoulder blades with the book, but only because he paused to grab a cookie before he ran, and even then she had to put her whole arm into it. The little bastard was really fast.

Now she stepped into her trailer, hung her cowboy hat on the rack, kicked off her boots, and shucked her sweaty shirt and jeans on the way to the shower. One more rodeo in the books. Traveling town to town with their little crew was like her childhood dream of running away to be a carny, minus the greasy, leather-skinned dude who always operated the Tilt-a-Whirl.

She caught herself wishing the season wouldn't end—and that was not good.

This was supposed to be a lark. Another experience to add to the stockpile she held against her uncertain future. She wasn't supposed to love it. But who knew it would be such a rush, or that a big part of the thrill would be the moments when she and Cole operated not only on the same wavelength, but as if they were inside each other's heads? It was almost better than...

A great team roping run, maybe. Not sex. Please.

Nothing was better than sex, except more sex. As she stood under the lukewarm shower and soaped up, her body was more than happy to recall all that muscle wrapped around her. That excruciatingly sweet kiss, totally at odds with the erection he'd made no attempt to hide. How could he be so damn hard and so vulnerable at the same time?

But the hot tinglies weren't near as disturbing as how much she hadn't wanted him to let go. How his strength had drawn the anxiety out of her, like a human poultice. As long as he was holding her, she'd felt—

Horny. Anything more was out of bounds, so she shoved her head under the spray and forced her mind back to the good stuff.

Sex in the shower with Cole would be...well, impossible. First, the two of them would demolish the trailer shower if they started throwing their considerable weight around. Second, if he ever unwound enough to steam up a bathroom, he'd probably imprint on her like a baby duck. He'd already penciled her in on the *Stuff Cole Is Responsible For* list, and as far as she could tell, the man didn't own an eraser. And it wasn't even because she was so freaking irresistible.

Cole had decided he needed a wife, and once he set a goal, he became that boulder, rolling straight ahead until he reached his destination. Shawnee's life was all detours and winding back roads. But they would eventually collide. With five weeks of the rodeo season left, practically in each other's pockets all day, every day, and that kiss simmering between them? Yep, it was gonna happen. She'd just have to post all the hazards going in, like they did on arena gates. *Warning: the*

owner of this facility is not responsible for injuries.
Participate at your own risk.

She blew out an irritated sigh as she towel-dried her hair. Why couldn't he just be a regular guy? But no, he had to be…Cole, whatever *that* was.

She slipped into her most comfortable gym shorts and an extra baggy T-shirt and padded barefoot to the refrigerator. She'd picked up some excellent homemade hummus and pita chips at the farmer's market in New Mexico, and she intended to gorge while binge-watching *NCIS* reruns. And if she felt a little lonely, it was only because she'd let herself get used to hanging out at Tori's place when Delon was on the road. Roping, pigging out, and swilling beer—now that's what she called girl time.

She had just hunkered in when a tap at the door shot her heart straight into her esophagus. *Oh shit. Butthead.* Shoving her plate aside, she scrambled to answer.

Analise looked her up and back down again. "God. Mariah was right. You are in bad shape."

Only because Analise had damn near given her a heart attack, knocking at her door at this time of night.

"Says the girl with a…" Shawnee leaned closer, squinting at Analise's lip ring. "What the hell? Is that a real black widow spider?"

"No. But cool, right?"

Uh…that was one word for it. But she'd bet Analise didn't have men just up and kissing her without warning. Or permission. Or…or…

Oh hell, who was she kidding? She'd been pumping out *kiss me* vibes like a freaking lipstick commercial.

Analise gave her a shove. "Go on. Get dressed and

we'll go drink a toast to Butthead. May he find his bliss. Or least a really good buzz."

Shawnee folded her arms and didn't budge. "Who is this *we* you speak of?"

"Um…me and you, mostly, but Hank did promise to buy the first round. I tried to drag Cruz along, but he's got some horse thing he has to finish making. You know how he is."

Analise made a face that was at least partly admiration. Marcelino Miguel Ruiz de la Cruz had come straight out of the El Paso projects, one of Wyatt Darrington's first and most successful reclamation projects. He didn't waste time or money on dancing and beer. Inside the seventies vintage camper trailer he pulled behind a well-preserved El Camino from the same era, he created intricate rawhide masterpieces. Braided reins. Bridles. Halters. If you wanted it—and could afford the steep price tag—Cruz could build it. And every extra dollar went toward getting the rest of his family out of the ghetto.

"Tyrell and Mariah will be there for a while," Analise went on. "She found Cole a woman."

Shawnee's arms dropped, along with her jaw, too. Cole had a *date?* "What woman?"

Analise shrugged. "I guess we'll find out, won't we? If you get a move on."

Without thinking, Shawnee backed away to let Analise in the door. She was *not* jealous, dammit. Just…curious. And protective. As a friend. Violet would have to live with whatever woman Cole dragged home. It was Shawnee's duty to screen the prospects, that's all.

And she *had* told him to run. She just hadn't expected him to listen.

She eyed Analise, whose miniskirt was stretchy black lace to match her black lace gloves. Even her chunky high-heeled boots had lace insets on the sides and yes, more of those creepy black widows dangling from the laces.

"It'll be last call by the time I do something with this hair," Shawnee warned.

But she pulled out her best jeans—the ones that left no doubt how much junk she packed in her trunk—and a loose-fitting silky bronze tank top that slithered over her skin and showed enough cleavage to impair male judgment. "I'll just be a few—"

"Ooh, hummus!" Analise plopped her bony butt down on the couch and helped herself.

"I gotta quit answering the door," Shawnee said, and stomped into the bathroom.

She went heavier with the makeup than usual, especially on her eyes. A handful of magic goo worked through her damp hair tamed it from wild woman to a mussed-up *Yeah, I just got laid* look. She hardly ever wore it completely loose. The curls tickled her bare shoulders and smelled like an invitation to hot jungle sex. She added a necklace made of chunky amber glass beads with matching earrings, examined the result in the mirror, and smiled.

Yeah. That'd do.

When she stepped out of the bathroom, Analise's eyes popped wide, her gaze taking in the hair, the makeup, then zeroing in on Shawnee's chest. "Holy crap."

Shawnee propped a hand on her hip and struck a pose. "And honey, I know what to do with all of it."

"Do you give lessons?"

"Depends. Are we talking lecture or hands-on?"

Analise rolled her dark-rimmed eyes. "You're a little old for me, don't you think?"

"Gee, thanks." Shawnee grabbed her wallet, fished out cash and her ID—she wasn't too damn old to get carded—and shoved them in the back pocket of her jeans, then slid her feet into a pair of flip-flops blinged-up with rhinestones and turquoise. "If we're gonna do this, let's go."

Before this woman of Mariah's had too much time to get her hooks into Cole.

Chapter 22

COLE HAD TO ADMIT, THE WOMAN SEEMED NICE enough. Pretty, friendly, and very interested. Her face was vaguely familiar—one of the cluster of photographers who followed the rodeo circuit—and Cole had no doubt Mariah was telling the truth when she dragged the blonde over and said, "Of course, you two have met."

As if that meant he could pick her out of a lineup, let alone remember what she was called. Unlike so many other trivial bits of information, he was lousy with names and faces.

And the blonde had smiled and said, "Hi, Cole," as if they were old friends, so he couldn't very well say, "I'm sorry, what was your name?"

Worse, after Mariah shoved them onto the dance floor and disappeared, the blonde kept trying to strike up a conversation. She didn't seem satisfied with "Yep" and "Nope" answers, but he doubted she wanted a lecture on the role of selenium in horse nutrition, and that was all he had to offer at the moment. And every time she asked a question, he fumbled the steps.

"Oops," he muttered. "Can't talk and dance at the same time."

"Oh. Sorry."

For him, or for herself now that she was beginning to realize he had the personality of a brick wall? Cole only nodded and swung her around again, holding her close enough to avoid eye contact, but not so close as to give her ideas. The noise, the crowd, the constant movement bombarded his eyes and ears, and he could feel the anxiety coiling and hissing in his gut, like a snake preparing to strike.

He forced his mind to focus on one sound—the deep twang of the bass guitar—and let everything else fade to a blur. The blonde said something, but Cole was so zoned out he only caught one word. He blinked back to full reality. "Excuse me?"

"Shawnee," the blonde repeated, with a tilt of her head toward the fenced-off, adults-only section of the dance hall. "Who knew she could look like that?"

Cole whipped his head around, searching the mob. Then he saw her, and stumbled for real.

Whoa. Just…*whoa*.

She was bronzed, earthy, full-bodied, her hair an entity unto itself, like one of those ancient goddesses of fertility. Or lust. Was there a goddess of lust? If not, he had a nominee…

A hand tugged at his arm and he realized he'd come to a complete stop. Luckily, the song ended right then. Thank God. His focus was shot. Well, his focus on dancing, anyway. He zeroed right in on Shawnee, shouldering through the crowd until they were face-to-face.

"You do realize you just left your date standing alone in the middle of the dance floor," Analise pointed out.

"I…oh." Cole glanced back to see the blonde staring after him. Even he could decipher that expression. Lord knew he'd seen it often enough. "She's not my date."

"Well, that makes it okay, then," Analise said dryly.

Cole peeled his eyeballs off Shawnee to glance at her.
Was that an actual...no, never mind. He didn't want to
know. His gaze snapped back to Shawnee like a tractor
beam. "What are you doing?" he demanded.

"Having a beer." She held up her longneck.

"Why do you look like...that?"

She bristled so hard her hair practically crackled.
"What exactly is *that*?"

"All...girly."

Her mouth dropped open, but her eyes narrowed dangerously. "I *am* a girl. I sorta thought you noticed when
I showed you my tits."

Analise choked on her Coke. "You...showed him..."

"Not this kind of girl." Obviously, Cole knew she
was female, but like Violet. A cowboy who just happened to have a few extra curves. He could talk to a
cowboy. But this—

Shawnee very deliberately looked down, dragging
his gaze along to her cleavage, where it threatened to
burrow in and refuse to come out. "Are you implying
that I'm not properly dressed?"

"I..." He drew a blank, every single neuron too busy
shouting *WANT. NOW.*

Tyrell pushed through the crowd, dragging a sulky
Mariah with him. "Found her. And now we're turning in."

"It's not even midnight!" Mariah tugged at the hand
he had clamped around her wrist, scowling. "Why can't
I stay here with these guys?"

"You're sixteen, this is a bar that's getting drunker by
the minute, and these people aren't babysitters," Tyrell
said, reasonable enough to make any teenager scream.

Mariah muffled hers, but the sentiment came through

loud and clear. "I'm not a baby. I'm going to be a senior in high school. Nobody my age has a curfew."

"Or you can just skip going out altogether," Tyrell said.

Mariah clamped her mouth shut and seethed in silence for a few moments. Then she looked around. "Where's Tabitha?" she asked Cole.

"Who?"

"Tabitha!" Mariah threw up her free hand. "Blonde? Photographer? I left you dancing with her…"

"Oh. So that's her name."

Mariah gaped at him. "She said you've met at least half a dozen times."

Cole could only shrug. "Probably."

"And she is…" Mariah prompted.

"He forgot to bring her back from the dance floor," Analise said.

Shawnee smirked. "In case you were wondering why he's not already married…"

Mariah closed her eyes, shook her head, and heaved the eternal *Men!* sigh. "Fabulous. Come on, darling Daddy. If we have to go, let's make tracks before she hunts me down."

They squeezed out past a group of local college kids. A couple of them hooted and catcalled after Mariah, then clammed up under Tyrell's murderous glare. Back here in the bar everything was moving and shifting, closing in. The only constant Cole could find was Shawnee, but she wasn't right either. All the differences caught at his mind like tiny hooks.

Hank appeared in his peripheral vision, angling past a pair of drunk girls who were propping each other up while they howled an off-key version of "Hell on Heels." Cole hadn't seen him out on the dance floor earlier, or anywhere else for that matter, but this crowd could swallow up a full-grown bear.

Hank's face broke into a huge, leering grin when he saw Shawnee. He let his gaze zero in on her chest. "Well, *hello*, girls."

"They're out of your league, Junior," Shawnee said, cuffing him upside the head.

Hank grinned, rubbing his ear and straightening the cowboy hat she'd knocked sideways. "Can I at least take 'em out for a dance so I can enjoy the scenery?"

"No." Cole grabbed Shawnee's arm and pulled her toward the dance floor.

To his surprise, she followed, dropping her beer bottle into a trash can along the way. As he turned her into his arms, he looked back to see Hank scowling as he slapped what appeared to be a twenty-dollar bill into Analise's hand. She flashed him a superior smile and stuffed it down the front of her tank top.

The song was something Cole normally wouldn't choose, too fast for a decent two-step, with a lot of showy fiddle and steel guitar. Add the distraction of Shawnee not looking how she was supposed to, and he was too overwhelmed to find any kind of rhythm.

"If you don't approve of how I look, what are we doing out here?" she asked.

"Dancing." Cole tried staring off into the middle distance, but it was a whirl of faces and bodies. They did a half shuffle, half stumble around the corner of the floor, Cole's elbow missing an amplifier only because Shawnee steered him away. "I don't disapprove."

"That's sure as hell not your happy face."

"You changed." It came out as an accusation, as if she'd broken a sacred vow.

She glared up at him, her eyes all dark and smudgy like a makeup commercial. "This is how I dress when I go out."

His gaze strayed down the front of her shirt. From his height, he had an unobstructed view. He yanked his eyes back up again. "I got used to you the other way. Now you're different. It's…confusing."

"Seriously?" She huffed out a laugh. "It's just me. The one you don't have to impress, remember?"

He'd strayed off the dance floor, so when he swung her around she hip-checked a bowlegged buckaroo type. Beer shot out of his nose and soaked his fancy neckerchief. He whirled around to look up…and up…and up… and finally meet Cole's grim gaze.

"Sorry," Cole said.

After a brief moment's consideration, the buckaroo's handlebar mustache twitched into a grudging smile. "No problem."

When they were back on the dance floor, Shawnee stopped, forcing Cole to do the same. "I know you can dance. I've seen you. So why are we crashing around like somebody turned Flight Risk loose in here?"

"We're talking, and that"—he gestured toward her face—"is distracting, and I can't find the bass."

Her eyebrows crimped together. "Which base? First, second…home run? I didn't think you were that kind of a boy."

"The *bass*," he repeated, the static inside his head crackling louder, making his voice rise in pitch. "I need to follow it, but there's too much noise and…stuff."

This time, it was Cole left standing on the dance floor. He hooked his thumbs in his pockets and rocked back on his heels, watching as she marched straight over to Hank, snatched the beer out of his hand, and gulped down half of it.

Cole smiled. Yep. He was getting to her.

He considered going after her, but there was no rushing a woman that stubborn, and he could feel a migraine brewing, courtesy of the trailing ends of last night's disaster with Butthead and compounded by the racket in this damn bar. If he escaped and took his medication right away, maybe he could still dodge the worst of the headache.

He turned and walked out, into blissful solitude and darkness—and hummed that Aaron Watson song all the way to his trailer.

She stared up at him. "Okay, now I *have* to know what you're talking about."

"It's just something my mother taught me. To help shut out all the commotion. She told me to follow the bass guitar because it sets the rhythm."

He'd listened to hours of music, until he could pick that deep, resonant thread out of a song almost instantly. The bass was his optimal wavelength. He could feel it humming through his body, into his bones—and out through his feet. Like magic, he could dance…as long as nobody talked to him. As a bonus, he'd learned that finding a dark, quiet place, putting on his headphones and easing his mind along the pulsing path of the bass settled his anxiety.

Probably the only reason he'd been able to cope unmedicated for three decades.

He waited for another smart-ass remark. Instead, Shawnee cocked her head as she listened to the music, beginning to nod along with the beat.

"I get it. No talking." She tightened her grip on his hand and stepped in closer, her palm firm on his back. "Close your eyes so you can't see my fancy face, and I'll make sure we don't mow anybody down."

"You might shove me headfirst into a trash can."

"Tempting." She made a show of considering it, then shook her head. "Nah. I'm not feeling it tonight. You'll just have to trust me."

Trust Shawnee Pickett. A month ago, he would've laughed at the idea. But he'd been putting his faith in her every night in the arena, ride after ride, and she'd never let him down. Doing a job she'd only taken as a favor to Violet.

And Shawnee kept her word.

He drew in a deep breath of the dank beer- and body-scented air, and wished desperately for his stock pens and the good old smell of manure. At least the band had moved into his favorite Aaron Watson song. He closed his eyes and mentally caught the bass thread.

Shawnee gave him a moment, then a nudge. She didn't lead. Instead, she picked up his rhythm, using her hand on his back to direct him. He kept the steps small at first. The longer they moved without crashing, though, the more he loosened up. Breathed. Shawnee smelled different than the last time he'd held her. Better, obviously, minus the sweat and blood and horse puke. The noise and the crowd faded to the edge of his awareness, but unlike usual, Shawnee was inside the bubble with him, her feel and scent woven through the deep *bah-bah-bum* of the bass line, as if she'd dialed in to his frequency.

"What's it like?" she asked.

He opened his eyes and missed a beat.

"Don't stop." Her fingers dug into his back, urging him to keep moving. "Close your eyes and tell me what you see. How it feels."

"Why?"

Her gaze dropped to his chest. "Your whole body changed, like someone pulled a plug and drained out all the stress. I…" She flicked a quick glance up at him, then down again. "I was just curious."

He pictured her trying to fight off the anxiety attack and understood. One more possible weapon against the monster. "I can try."

He closed his eyes again and let himself sink into the music until he found the sweet spot. They danced for

a few minutes, while he tried to maintain enough consciousness to study the sensations without getting pulled out of the flow. Finally, he said, "Most autistic people are hypersensitive to things like noise, touch, light, color, movement. For me, this crowd is like drowning in a river of static, and the bass line is a rope. As long as I'm hanging on to it, the rest flows around me. But if I let go, I get washed away."

He opened his eyes and looked down to find her gaze fixed on his face, her eyes softer than he'd ever seen them. And somewhere during the time he'd been lost in the music, his mind had adjusted to this new version of Shawnee. She looked amazing. He'd just panicked when she turned herself into the kind of woman he'd never be able to talk to.

"I meant it as a compliment," he said.

She blinked, as if coming out of a haze. "What?"

"When I said I don't have to impress you. I don't have to fake normal. I can just…be. It's a relief. But I like this, too." He lifted a hand and skimmed it lightly down her hair, from the top of her head to her waist. The curls tickled his palm. Then he traced his fingertip along the inside of the chunky crystals of her necklace, from one bare collarbone to the other. "And this. I just had to get used to it."

She inhaled sharply when his finger made the return trip along the outside of her necklace, dipping dangerously low. Her lips parted and her eyes drifted almost shut as she exhaled, long and slow. God, he wanted to kiss her. He started to lean in, but she planted both hands on his chest and pushed out of his reach. "You should've stuck with the blonde."

Chapter 23

SHAWNEE SNATCHED HANK'S BEER OUT OF HIS HAND, took four big gulps, then let the air explode out of her lungs. Damn Cole! If she didn't know better, she'd think he did this crap on purpose. So vulnerable one minute, the next looking at her with such single-minded intent she could sympathize with every deer she'd ever caught in her headlights.

One touch and she'd damn near melted into a puddle of stupidity right there at his feet. But if he thought all he had to do was crook a finger, he'd better think again.

She spun around to say so, expecting to find him on her heels, but he was nowhere in sight. Where the—

"He's gone," Analise said.

Shawnee stared at the spot where she'd left him. "Just like that?"

"Well, you did practically shove him out the door."

No. She'd given him a little push. He'd chosen to leave. She'd told him he had the wrong woman and apparently he'd taken her at her word. Smart of him. Better for both of them. So why did she have this sick knot in her gut, as if she'd been ditched by her prom date?

"I can't believe Mariah dragged him here, as much as he hates crowds." Hank swiped the remainder of his beer out of Shawnee's hand and frowned at Analise. "Don't the lights and noise bother you?"

She shook her head. "My weirdness is all about

numbers. And not all of it is bad. Nines are the worst and fives can be real whiners, but sevens are wind chimes. Twos are my favorite—they gurgle like a rocky creek. And time has shapes." She smiled as she sketched them with her hands. "Tomorrows are bell curves, skinny at the beginning and end and fat in the middle. If you say July, I see a purple staircase with a step for each day. August is orange, and September is dark chocolate." Her expression went dreamy as she walked her fingers into the air. "The year just keeps climbing and climbing—a color-coded stairway to heaven."

Hank stared at her for a beat, then said, "They probably make a pill for that."

Analise screwed up her face, offended. "It's my superpower. Why would I want to make it go away? Speaking of which—" She made a shooing motion at him. "You promised us a round."

Shawnee took the opportunity to fight her way to the bathroom. When she got back, Hank was just returning with the drinks—another beer for her and a Coke for Analise, who, Shawnee realized with a start, was not legal drinking age. The bouncers had probably been so busy staring at the spider crawling around on her face they hadn't thought to check her ID. Pretty neat trick. Shawnee sort of wished she'd tried it back in college, except for the part about having needles shoved through her flesh.

Analise lifted her drink and waited for Shawnee and Hank to do the same. "To Butthead. May he finally be able to chill out and find some peace."

Shawnee tapped her bottle to the others and drank without comment. They stood for the requisite moment of respectful silence, then for a few more that grew increasingly uncomfortable as the three of them found nothing else to say. Damn Cole all over again for taking off. For once, he would've fit in. Awkward was right up his alley.

Analise set her cup on the nearest table and grabbed Hank's arm. "Come on. As long as you're just standing around, you can teach me how to two-step so I can blend."

"Blend. Hah!" But Hank set his beer aside and let himself be towed onto the dance floor. Also weird, now that Shawnee thought about it. Why wasn't Hank with his usual gang of baby-faced bull riders, on the prowl for groupies? Shawnee definitely wasn't the attraction here, despite his blatant appreciation of her assets. But Analise…

She watched as Hank guided Analise through the steps. He didn't treat her like the other girls. Because he saw her only as a co-worker? Or realized Analise would call his bullshit? They looked good together—both slender and graceful. Maybe this was the beginning of a positive thing. Even though Analise was two years younger, she could be a stabilizing influence on Hank.

Talk about old souls. She'd probably audited the hospital bill for her own birth.

But they had left Shawnee cooling her heels, the only bridesmaid at the dance who didn't bring a date. The contestants generally cleared out as soon as the performance ended, headed to the next competition. That left locals and tourists, none of whom Shawnee recognized. Time to make her own exit.

A hand tapped her shoulder. "Hey, gorgeous. I was hoping I'd find you here."

"Brady!" Her smile as she turned was brighter than it might have been if she hadn't been feeling so pathetic. "Excellent roping tonight."

Her former partner—roping and otherwise—grinned back. "Thanks. We got lucky, drew the best steer in the pen."

"And made it count. I thought you'd be halfway home to Bandera by now."

He shook his head—tanned and wiry, with a long, narrow face, unfortunate ears, and deadly aim with rope. "We're stopping in Victoria to deliver a horse tomorrow, so we stayed over. Plus, I wanted to see you."

Her scuffed ego lifted its chin. *Take that, Cole Jacobs*.

"Could we go outside where we can have a conversation without screaming?" Brady's smile was relaxed, not knitted together from the frayed ends of his nerves; his suggestion born from practicality, not a desperate need to escape. He was so totally…normal.

"Sure," she said.

He took her hand and broke a trail through the mob. Unlike someone else's she knew, his palm wasn't clammy, and his fingers didn't latch on to her wrist as if they were the sole humans in a crowd of newly turned vampires.

But those other fingers had also held her hair while she puked.

Not that Brady wouldn't have done the same— assuming he would have recognized the warning signs and followed her to the trailer—but she would rather have suffered alone than let him see her that way. Normal people didn't grasp how your brain could turn your body against you. Brady would have been kind, considerate—and totally freaked out.

They'd had a great thing for almost six months. Just over a year ago, he'd been offered a sweet job in upstate New York by an investment banker who had bailed out with his golden parachute right before the crash. With all that money to burn and time on his hands, he had decided to fulfill his fantasy of being a cowboy, and team roping was the most accessible of all the rodeo events. But a man like that didn't go to a clinic with the riffraff. He hired top-caliber ropers to be his coaches.

Brady had texted a few times to say it was working out better than he'd expected. As the filthy rich went, his boss was a reasonable man and had become a true roping addict. And since he'd started too late in life to be a world champion himself, he'd set his sights on the next best thing—he would own the horses that world champions rode.

With the price of elite horses climbing over the six figure mark, it was becoming more common for big name cowboys and rich breeders to partner up. The cowboy got to ride a horse he couldn't afford to buy. And when that cowboy won Houston or Fort Worth or hit it big at the National Finals, the owner got a cut of the money, invaluable exposure for his breeding program, and bragging rights. Gifted trainers like Brady got plum jobs, which included competing on the up-and-coming horses, preparing them for the big time.

In other words, he got paid to rope on the best prospects money could buy. Did it get any better?

As they passed the dance floor, Shawnee glanced over and caught Hank watching her over Analise's shoulder. His gaze dropped to her hand clasped in Brady's and his eyebrows shot up. Shawnee flipped him a middle finger,

irritated less at him than the sharp fingernail of guilt that
scratched at her conscience. No doubt Hank would run
tattling to Cole as fast as his scrawny little legs could
carry him.

Well, let him. Shawnee was a free agent. If she
wanted to drag Brady back to her trailer and have her
way with him, she damn well would. And if she didn't
want...well, that had nothing to do with Cole, either. So
Brady's touch didn't strike the old sparks. He'd caught
her by surprise, that's all. And besides, she didn't like
to repeat herself.

The moment they cleared the crowd, he dropped her
hand, but kept moving toward the picnic tables scattered
across the lawn for those who ordered up the barbecued
chicken with mac and cheese and potato salad also
served at the beer garden. The kitchen had closed for
the night, so only a few of the tables were occupied.
Brady chose one in the shadow of a massive pecan tree.
He made no move to touch her, circling around to sit
facing her instead.

"So you're the new Jacobs Livestock pickup girl." He
cocked his head, curious. "Do you like it?"

She gave a reluctant nod. "More than I expected."

"From what I hear, you're damned good. Is this a
permanent career move?"

"No!" The denial came out too sharp, and she tried to
soften it with a laugh. "I've made it to one roping in the
past month. I'd go stir-crazy at that rate."

"I was hoping you'd say that." He leaned forward,
bracing his forearms on the table. "How would you feel
about coming to New York?"

She gaped at him. Was he serious? Yeah, they'd had

fun. The sex was good and the roping was even better. But move halfway across the country to be with him? "And I would be your…"

"Assistant. Roping partner. Although other benefits are negotiable," he added with a grin.

She floundered, trying to get a grip on what he was offering. "Are we talking about a job?"

"Yes." Even in the dim light, she could see his eyes gleam. "The boss wants us to start giving private lessons. It's a good way to sell the lower-end horses. I need someone who is a good teacher and can really rope feet."

Shawnee made a skeptical noise. "This rich dude is gonna hire a girl?"

"Not just any girl. *You.* I showed him the TV footage of you and Cole roping that bull out on the midway and told him you're a genius with horses. He's sold. And that's not all." He bunched his fists and tapped them on the table, as if he could barely contain his excitement. "The First Frontier circuit has come a long way, but the northeast is not Texas. You and I are a good team, Shawnee. With the boss backing us, we could kick ass out there next year. Next stop—the National Circuit Finals."

Her adrenal glands revved up and set her blood pounding. Her and Brady. Taking a run at the Circuit Finals. It was…not impossible.

The circuit system was one of more confusing aspects of professional rodeo to an outsider. Basically, the governing body had recognized that a lot of great cowboys were either unable or unwilling to travel full time and compete for the world titles. But those same cowboys were the lifeblood of the mid- to small-sized rodeos, so the association had sketched out fifteen geographical regions—the circuits. The money won at those rodeos by the cowboys who called that region home was tallied toward the circuit championship.

Then they'd created the National Circuit Finals, where the champs from all over the country gathered to compete for a lot of cash and a national title.

For the majority of states, this meant competing primarily against people who had real jobs and rodeoed when they could. But Texas bred and attracted so many elite cowboys, winning the Lone Star circuit was as tough as making the cut for the National Finals Rodeo. Shawnee had given it a shot fresh out of college…and learned the hard way that she wasn't capable of competing head-to-head with the best men in the sport.

But the East Coast was a different matter. Pennsylvania, Connecticut, and New York combined didn't turn out as many arena sharks as Stephenville, Texas, alone.

Brady reached across the table and squeezed her hand as if he could inject his confidence into her. "Imagine the publicity we could generate if you were the first woman to ever rope steers at the National Circuit Finals. And if we won—"

Her heart leapt at the thought—then splatted back to earth. "I promised Violet I'd finish out the season with Jacobs Livestock."

"No problem." Brady made a broad gesture. "I'll be down here until after Labor Day, recruiting a few top ropers to haul our horses to the big shows next season. Then I'm going to spend some time with my family before I head back. We didn't schedule any clinics or lessons until the middle of October. That gives you plenty of time…" His gaze narrowed on her face. "Unless you're committed to more than just this job?"

It took her a beat to grasp what he meant. "Of course not! You know that isn't my style."

"Neither is Cole Jacobs."

"If you're talking about what I said in that interview—"

"More like what I just saw with my own eyes. He doesn't look at you like a guy who wants your contract to be up in a month." Brady flashed a quick grin. "That's part of the reason we're out here, where there are no witnesses. This might not be a real pretty face, but I'd prefer not to have it rearranged."

"Pfftt! Cole wouldn't punch anybody on my account."

But she couldn't help a glance over her shoulder, on the off chance that he was making his security rounds early. There was only a man and a woman strolling past, arms around each other's waists as he nuzzled her neck and murmured something that made her giggle. He lifted his head and the light caught his face.

Shawnee made a noise—close to gagging—and the man glanced her direction. Ace paused a beat, then tugged the woman along with him as he sauntered over to their table. Shawnee's dinner curdled in her stomach as he smiled, in full silver-tongued devil mode.

"Hey, sugar. Looks like you found a cure for the blues." He winked at Brady and Shawnee stifled another gag. Ace gave the woman a squeeze. "This is Cordelia. Her ranch is one of the major sponsors for the rodeo."

Naturally. And just as naturally, the donation had been made in honor of her dearly departed husband. The woman was the definition of Ace's target market.

Those boots would be hand-stitched, and all that chunky turquoise jewelry would be set in sterling silver. In this light, Cordelia could pass for fiftysomething, but Shawnee would bet she was closer to seventy—the age group ripest for the plucking.

"You know my daughter, right? The pickup woman?" Ace said, delivered with just the right touch of fatherly pride.

Cordelia's smile brightened. "Of course! We're all so impressed."

Shawnee inclined her head, afraid to open her mouth for fear of what might come spewing out, her dinner included. Sweet stinking hell, why couldn't these women see straight through him? Or were they so desperate for the attention they closed their eyes?

Then she realized Cordelia was snuggled up to Ace's right side. "You're not wearing the sling."

Cordelia's eyes widened. "Oh no! I forgot. Your poor shoulder, and you didn't say a word when I asked you to dance."

"Aw, it's fine." Ace made a show of lifting the arm, throwing in a slight grimace to be sure Cordelia knew he'd toughed it out for her. "There comes a point you've just gotta cowboy up."

This time Shawnee did gag, then covered it with a cough. Brady stood, grabbed her hand, and dragged her to her feet.

"Nice to meet you," he said, even though Shawnee hadn't bothered to introduce him. He knew Ace. *Everybody* knew Ace. And Brady knew enough to herd Shawnee away before she expressed any of her very pithy opinions.

"Have a lovely evening," Cordelia called to their retreating backs.

"You, too," Shawnee returned, saccharine sweet, then muttered, "Enjoy getting screwed five ways to Sunday before you even take your clothes off."

Brady choked on a laugh, but refrained from commenting until they were well beyond the beer garden, at the gate to the contestant parking area. "He is a piece of work."

Shawnee made a ripe, disgusted noise. They paused at the spot where she had to veer off toward the bucking chutes to reach her trailer. Brady was obviously reluctant to get any closer to the Jacobs Livestock camp. He tucked his hands in his pockets and stood a couple of steps back, making it clear to any observer—casual or otherwise—that his intentions were pure.

As they'd walked, she'd had time to consider the implications of his offer. "If I say yes, how long are we talking?"

"A year, minimum." At her silence, he nodded in understanding. "It's a big commitment. Upstate New York is beautiful, but it's a long way from home."

"I don't have any family in Texas," she said.

Brady opened his mouth, then snapped it shut again, reconsidering the wisdom of pointing out that they'd just had the pleasure of chatting with her father. Now *there* was a good reason to move halfway across the country. Ace would have to put some effort into tracking her down. But she'd also be abandoning Tori. And Violet. And Miz Iris and her orgasmic caramel rolls. And…a few other people.

"Take your time to think it over," Brady said. "I've

gotta be on the road by eight in the morning. Can we grab an early breakfast and go over the details? Say, six thirty?"

"Sure. And Brady…thanks for thinking of me."

His smile was warmed by memories of times when he wouldn't have left her to go inside alone. "I think of you a lot, Shawnee Pickett. And I also think a lot of you. I'm gonna make it real hard for you to say no."

"When has that ever been a challenge?"

He laughed. Then he glanced toward Cole's trailer and back at her. "I've got a feeling some things have changed."

He was wrong.

She wanted to yell it at him as he strolled away. At the alien crawling around in her chest, digging its claws into her guts when her gaze settled on the nearest truck, *Jacobs Livestock* in bold, blocky print running down the side of the trailer. Cole's rig was parked next door and hers across the road, the usual clutter of chairs under the awnings, waiting for a body to plop down and get comfortable.

This moving base camp had started to feel *way* too much like home.

In the past three years, since she had been engulfed by the sprawling mob that Iris Jacobs considered family, Shawnee had let herself get wrapped up, string by invisible string. That would not do. She had the potential to inflict too much damage. When her stint with Jacobs Livestock was done, she would have to cut herself loose. Create some distance.

She blew out a long, slow breath that felt as if it emptied a corner of her heart. New York should be just about far enough.

Chapter 24

TWO CUPS OF COFFEE WEREN'T ENOUGH TO LOOSEN the grip of the giant hand clenched around Cole's skull, digging bony fingers into his temples. The migraine meds he'd taken the night before had worn off before dawn, but he couldn't take any more on a driving day. This headache was a doozy, the kind that lingered for a day or two and made every noise and flicker of light an exercise in torture.

But his vision was plenty clear enough to see Brady's pickup stop beside Shawnee's trailer at seven forty-five in the morning.

"He showed up right after you left last night," Analise said behind him, causing him to jerk, which in turn shot silver needles of pain through his head.

Her arms were wrapped around a plastic storage bin that held the laptop and printer she used in the rodeo office. This morning, she was in goth light—black canvas high-top sneakers, tattered blue-jean shorts, and a delicate gold lip ring. Her hair was pulled up into two spiky ponytails on the sides of her head, making her look all of fourteen. She stepped up into Cole's living quarters to stow the bin under the banquette table, where it couldn't slide around when the rig was in motion.

She came back to stand in the doorway, openly observing Brady and Shawnee as they sat in the pickup, deep in conversation. "Hank says they were together for a few months, before Brady moved to New York."

Cole ground a curse word to dust between his teeth as Shawnee nodded, smiled, and climbed out of the pickup. Brady pulled away with a wave. Shawnee waved back, then flashed Cole a big, toothy smile before disappearing into her trailer. He stood rigid, the giant's right hand threatening to crush his skull, while the left squeezed the juice out of his guts. After their kiss, the dancing last night, how could she turn around and—

"She didn't sleep with him," Analise declared.

Cole frowned at her. "How do you know?"

"Different clothes. And most guys don't shake a woman's hand the morning after rocking her world."

She was right on both counts. Shawnee was fresh-scrubbed in jeans and a T-shirt, with her hair pulled back in a barrette. And instead of a good-bye kiss, they'd seemed more like two people sealing a business deal. The crushing grip on Cole's intestines relaxed slightly.

"Not that you would have had any right to complain." The ring glinted as Analise pushed out her bottom lip. "You didn't even stay to drink to Butthead's health."

The…oh shit. He'd assumed that was just an excuse Mariah had used to drag him to the beer garden. "Sorry," he muttered.

Analise made slitty eyes at him. "Don't apologize to me. It's not my horse. And I'm not the one you were cuddling up to before you disappeared without so much as a *screw off and die*. How exactly is a woman supposed to interpret that?"

As Cole being Cole. Shawnee knew that. She knew *him*. She understood why he had to get out of that zoo—but he'd totally blown the exit. Why hadn't it occurred to him to follow her off the dance floor and say good night like any functional human being?

Oh, right. Because he wasn't.

Cole squeezed his eyes shut and massaged his temples. He did not have time for this damn headache. There was equipment to pack, stock to sort, trucks to load, travel orders to be given. And instead of doing any of those things, he was rooted to the ground, staring at Shawnee's rig.

Her door opened. She stepped out and began to fold lawn chairs, stashing them in the bed of her pickup. Cole moved abruptly, covering the distance between them in a dozen long strides. He grabbed the chair out of her hands and tossed it in the pickup.

"What are you—"

"Apparently, I haven't made myself clear." He yanked the trailer door open, gesturing her inside. When she only folded her arms and glared at him, he huffed out a gust of air. "Please."

She hesitated, then scowled. "Fine, if it pries the burr out of your shorts."

He followed her in, banged the door shut—*ah, ouch, not smart*—and clamped his hands on her shoulders when she spun to face him. "You *are* the burr," he said, walking her back, step-by-step, until she came up against the closet door. "You go out of your way to be irritating and pushy and downright obnoxious, and unless you knee me in the nuts, I'm going to kiss you anyway."

Her eyes went wide. "I don't think—"

"Good. I'm probably safer that way."

He leaned in, giving her plenty of time to protest,

but she only stared at him, pupils flaring as he settled his mouth over hers, tasting one corner with the tip of his tongue. Blueberries. Waffles, he'd bet. The hint of whipped cream did crazy things to his ability to breathe.

He closed his eyes and risked another, deeper taste.

Her palms came up to his chest, but instead of another shove, she made a low, growling noise and dragged him closer. The kiss exploded like a firecracker in his hands, shooting streamers of flame through his body. Her hands slid up to latch behind his neck, her mouth taking him so high, so fast, he could've sworn he heard his ears pop. Or it might've been the closet door as he cupped her butt, lifted her almost off her feet, and pinned her there with his hips. She arched her back and did a little wriggle that was gasoline on an already roaring fire.

Cole fought to drag in enough oxygen to keep them both upright. It occurred to him that he had never been kissed. Not like this. No holds barred, *see if you can take it, cowboy*. Her fingers dug in, kneading his muscles in time with the hot, seeking plunge of her tongue. So much raw desire, all for him. His body picked up the rhythm, pulsing against her, his blood pounding in his groin, his chest, his head…

Oh geezus, his head. At that instant, something inside his skull cracked under the pressure.

He tore his mouth free with a tortured groan and pressed his forehead against the door, his breathing ragged. The need was so hard and desperate it could almost make him ignore the steel fangs sinking into the backs of his eyeballs. He heaved a shuddering breath, their bodies still pressed so tight together it felt as if their hearts were ping-ponging around inside the same chest. "I thought my head was gonna explode *before*."

"Which one?"

"Hah." He winced at a new stab of pain.

Shawnee rolled her head against the door, her breath hot against his cheek as she examined him from three inches away. She reached up to touch her fingertips to the tightly scrunched corner of his eye. "That doesn't look like the good kind of pain."

"There is such a thing?"

She flattened her palm and very gently patted his cheek. "So much to learn, grasshopper. But not today."

She wriggled again, this time with intent, and he loosened his grip. His vision went white from the exquisite friction as she slid down the length of him. Probably an aneurysm. That'd be his luck, just when he'd discovered the sexual equivalent of a new universe.

And all she'd done was kiss him.

Her fingers were on his neck again, gently massaging wire-tight muscles. "Migraine?"

"Yeah." He sighed the word as she found an especially tender spot.

Her voice was a soft murmur. "Did you take anything?"

"Last night."

His eyelids drooped as her fingertips worked small circles just behind his ears. "Nothing this morning?"

"Ibuprofen. I have to drive."

"Why?"

His eyes popped open. "We have four hundred miles to cover today."

"Last time I checked, there are at least three other people capable of piloting your rig."

"But—"

"You're the only one who can do it right, even when your eyes look like you've been mainlining heroin?" She slithered out of the space between him and the door so quick Cole had to throw up a hand to keep from face-planting into the wood. He was still trying to come to terms with the loss of her when she flung open the door and bounded down the steps. "I'm giving your keys to Tyrell. I'll take the brat pack so you can kick back and sleep while he drives. You go pop a pill and we'll get this circus on the road."

God, she was pushy. Bless her heart.

And in a minute, he would do as ordered. But first… he folded both forearms against the door and buried his face in them, concentrating on breathing. Slow. Steady. *Down, boy*. Katie hopped up into the trailer, cocking her head at him in question.

"Give me a minute," he muttered. "My, um, blood pressure's still a little high."

She plunked her butt down and gave him a look that would've done Miz Iris justice. In the distance, he could hear Shawnee barking orders. Cole relaxed enough to allow the pain to dial back a notch. After a few more settling breaths, he sighed, pushed himself upright, and went to take his drugs.

An hour later he was floating in a medicated haze, but the routine was so ingrained he could walk through it in his sleep. He finished the inventory, packing the last of the halters and flank straps into his trailer while Tyrell loaded Hammer, Salty, and the two backup horses in the rear stalls. Both trucks idled nearby, the horses and bulls already settled into their accustomed quarters on board.

Cole checked that all the doors were secure on his rig, then told Tyrell, "Pull around in front of the trucks. I'll go make sure Shawnee is set."

In the process, he took a head count. Cruz had pulled out the night before, headed home to El Paso until Wednesday, since their next rodeo was only an hour north. Analise was planted in the front seat of Shawnee's pickup. She got motion sickness if she rode anywhere else. That left Mariah to sulk in the back, her sunny disposition soured by a tiff with her father, who was more than happy to hand her over to Shawnee for the next few hours.

Ace rode shotgun in the first truck, having shown up just in time for all the work to be done, as usual. Hank climbed down from the second truck with a backpack in his hand. He wasn't allowed to ride in the trucks. The boy was allergic to silence and even the Leses couldn't tolerate his chatter. They'd be lucky if Shawnee didn't toss him out at a rest stop somewhere along the way. Cole went on around the rear of her rig. Sometimes she had trouble with the gray—

He stopped dead, reality and the sight of her smacking into him simultaneously. Her hand was clenched on the open back door of the trailer.

"I never thought I'd miss having to shove that neurotic bastard in here," she said.

"He'll be back to irritate you before you know it." But Cole folded her into his arms, back to chest, as they both gazed at the rear, now empty stall. Katie pressed into the side of his leg with a quiet sigh and Roy and Sooner craned their necks to look back, their eyes dark and questioning. *Aren't we missing someone?* For a moment, Shawnee leaned in and let him bear some of the weight. Then she shook him off to shut and latch the door with a brisk, no-nonsense clunk.

And in the time-honored tradition of the rodeo trail, they put one more show behind them and moved on.

Chapter 25

SHAWNEE HAD NEVER RESIDED ON THE CONTINENT OF discretion, let alone in the same neighborhood. There'd never been a need. She didn't do men who had reasons to sneak around, and by her reckoning, if she was embarrassed to be seen with a guy, why bother?

But that was before Cole.

All he had to do was give her one of those slow, deliberate looks and every cell in her body dissolved into slobbering lust. If he had actually touched her in the past three days, she probably would've torn his clothes off and taken him on the spot.

Except there'd always been at least one set of eyeballs observing every look and making note of every word that passed between them.

Honest to freaking hell, it was like trying to get laid at a church picnic, they had so many chaperones. On the travel days, when Mariah and Analise bunked with her and Tyrell and Hank shared Cole's quarters, privacy was getting to pee without anyone listening. And since they'd arrived and set up camp, *let's see what Cole and Shawnee do* had become the main form of entertainment. Hank had opted to stay in the truck again for fear he might miss something, even though it was his week to get the motel room. She'd even caught Cruz checking them out during what was threatening to become their weekly Tuesday night dinner. And Cruz never paid attention to anything but his rawhide projects until it was time to fight bulls.

Thank the Lord the rodeo had started tonight, and everyone finally had work to distract them.

The closest thing Cole and Shawnee had had to alone time was this very moment, sitting side-by-side in the arena, both staring at the bucking chutes and pretending they weren't intensely aware of each other. Or that might just be her. Cole's powers of concentration were legendary.

Then he turned his head, caught her gaze, and his eyes were hot blue smoke that went straight to her head when she sucked in a breath.

He smiled slightly and turned his attention back to the bucking chutes. Shawnee followed his example. She had to stay sharp. Tonight was a new experience for her. It was the first time she'd worked in an arena with a turn-back fence—a smaller U-shaped portable pen inside the larger arena, to keep the bull riding action close to the chute. It decreased the likelihood that a bull would decide to lope off into all that wide-open space instead of bucking. It was also better for the riders and the bullfighters, who didn't get caught fifty yards from the nearest safe haven if a bull turned on them.

Shawnee hated it. They had set up the fence when they worked the stock that morning so she and the bulls could get a feel for it, but she still felt like a fish in a barrel—and they were about to release a shark. This Brahma-cross wasn't named Master Assassin for nothing. But at least he didn't have horns. Talk about your small blessings.

Tyrell's voice poured out of the loudspeakers like

satin. "This next bull rider is a rookie out of Camp Woody, Texas, who drew his first professional paycheck at the Los Fresnos rodeo back in February."

"He may be young, but he's got a world of experience behind him," Ace chimed in, his easy tenor a nice counterpoint to Tyrell's bass. "A lot of our fans may remember his uncle, Sterling, who dominated this circuit back in the late eighties, and made two trips to the National Finals Rodeo."

In the nearby seats, Shawnee saw some of the older audience members nodding and sitting a little straighter, paying attention to a cowboy they might otherwise have overlooked. Deep in her chest, a tiny, warm bubble swelled. She wouldn't go so far as to call it pride. More like not-embarrassment. For once Ace was making a contribution to something other than her stress levels.

As the cowboy lowered himself into the chute, Hank gestured to Cruz to move farther left, where he would be in position to help if the rider got into trouble but wouldn't catch the bull's eye and distract him out of his standard right-handed spin. Amazing. When Hank stepped into the arena, he was a different person. The goofy knucklehead disappeared and he was all business. Last year he'd ditched the soccer shorts and gone retro—baggy Wrangler cutoffs and suspenders with yellow and red bandanas tied like flags to the belt loops—worn today over a flowered fuchsia pearl-snap shirt.

The bulls couldn't miss Hank, which was the point. His goal was to be a more attractive target than the cowboys. He stood now, hands on thighs, and shouted "Give 'im the gas!"

The rookie nodded his head. Master Assassin took

one jump, then cranked it back to the right only feet
from the chutes, just as advertised. The cowboy sat
square in the middle of a storm of spinning, head-
slinging beef, hips solid, chest out, feet hustling to
keep him there. Six seconds. Seven. With each lunge
the bull got him strung out a little farther, his chin
coming up and his free arm whipping back over his
head. Shawnee held her breath, willing the kid to hang
on just a little longer...

Right when the eight-second whistle blew, his hand
popped out of the rope. His feet flipped up and he flew
backward, heels over head, just as Assassin kicked high
and hard. His hips slammed into the kid's shoulders and
flung him into the front of a steel chute gate. He flopped
to the ground, limp.

When the bull swung around, Cruz was there, stepping between the cowboy and the irate animal. Assassin
caught him in the chest and tossed him against the
chutes, too. Cruz bounced off and sprawled, belly down,
shielding the cowboy with his body.

Shawnee spurred her horse into motion, a stride
behind Cole, as Hank jumped at the bull, yelling and
slapping its head. Assassin took the bait, charging after
him. Hank sprinted along the front of the chutes and
dove under the turn-back fence a whisker ahead of the
pounding hooves.

"Lead him off!" Cole yelled at Shawnee. "I'll get in
behind and rope him."

She and Salty sideswiped the enraged bull to get
his attention and make themselves his next target. He
wheeled around and charged after them. She hustled
Salty to stay ahead while Cole reined in behind, rope

swinging. Before he could release his loop, Assassin rammed his head into Salty's butt, blocking the shot.

"Look out!" Cole shouted.

Shawnee glanced ahead. *Fuck!* They were already at the fence. Salty skidded, then whirled, but the instant's hesitation was enough. The bull drove his head under the horse's flank, lifted him off his feet, and threw him onto his side, so fast Shawnee barely had time to think *oh shit* before she slammed into the dirt. She tried to kick free of the tangle of bull and horse, but her heavy chaps were pinned under the saddle. For an instant, she saw nothing but the bull's murderous eyes.

Then a flash of fuchsia cut through her field of vision. Hank leapt over Salty's thrashing legs and threw himself at the bull's face. Startled, Assassin jumped back and flung up his head, sending Hank hurtling through the air to crash into the turn-back fence. The distraction was just enough to allow Cole to whip a loop around the bull's neck. He dallied up and Hammer dug in. Master Assassin bellowed with rage as they dragged him away. Committeemen yanked down a section of the flimsy turn-back fence, allowing Cole and the bull out into the bigger arena, clear of the wreckage Assassin had left behind.

Salty scrambled to his feet and shook off the dirt. Since she couldn't feel any real damage, Shawnee did the same. Cowboys and committeemen came running from every direction, grabbing at her arms and trying to prop her up.

"I'm fine!" she snapped, swatting them off so she could get a look at her horse.

She grabbed the dangling bridle reins and led him

a few steps. He showed no sign of a limp. She ran a hand along his ribs and over his flank, probing with her fingers. He didn't flinch. There were no scrapes or signs of swelling. Shawnee dragged in a huge breath and let it out in a relieved gust.

Back at the chutes, the medical team was huddled around the cowboy. In response to their questions, he gestured with one dirt-streaked hand. At least conscious, then, and not seriously injured, judging by the body language of the medics. A few feet away, Hank paced circles, rubbing the back of his head and shaking out one leg.

"Anything broken?" she asked.

"The fence, maybe. It's no match for my head. You?"

"We're good."

She shooed away the horde of rescuers and climbed on Salty. The crowd roared when Hank gave them an *A-OK* wave. Salty showed no sign of ill effects as they trotted through the gap in the fence, over to the far corner of the big arena where Cole and Hammer held Master Assassin, thrashing around on the end of the rope. Cole lifted his chin in question. *Everybody all right?* She nodded and circled around to help herd the bull toward the exit.

She didn't start shaking until the gate swung shut behind him.

Cole's hand closed over hers on the reins before she could turn away. "Are you both okay to finish out these last three rides?"

"We're fine." She met his gaze and saw, behind the stoic mask, eyes dark with the dregs of fear. "Thanks to you and Hank."

And no thanks to Shawnee. Her mistake could've seriously injured or killed Salty.

"All in a day's work, right?" She forced her shoulders to square and her chin to come up, and pushed a mulish look onto her face. She could do it. She *had* to, for the sake of pride if nothing else.

Cole studied her, long and hard, before giving a clipped nod and letting her go.

By the time the final whistle blew, Shawnee had breathed through the worst of the aftershocks. Lord knew, it wasn't the first time she'd bit the dirt. It wouldn't be the last. She'd just never stared mutilation in the face while she was lying there, helpless. As Tyrell bid the crowd a good night and safe travels, she dismounted and followed Cole out of the arena, only to be mobbed by people. Cowboys, crew, committeemen, even a few spectators slapped her on the shoulder and patted Salty on the rump.

One drunk tried to do the opposite.

He was shoved aside, and Shawnee found herself face-to-face with her father. He stared at her for a beat, then pushed his hat to the back of his head to swipe at his damp forehead with his shirtsleeve. "I swear, girl, it took ten years off my life, seeing that bull standing over you."

Shawnee blinked. Had she ever seen Ace express an honest emotion? "Uh...well, it wasn't real pretty from my angle, either."

"I don't imagine." His arms came up, hesitated, and for a bizarre moment she thought he was going to hug her.

Then she was blindsided by a black-haired whirlwind.

"Oh…my…*GOD*!" Mariah squealed. "I thought you were dead. Or at least maimed."

"Not until now. If you'll just let me—"

She started to peel the girl off, but Mariah abruptly let go to fling herself at Hank. "Are you okay? When you hit that fence—"

Oh good Lord. Shawnee allowed herself a small eye roll as she turned back to Ace.

He had disappeared…along with the fleeting connection between them.

Chapter 26

COLE FORCED HIMSELF TO KEEP WALKING, HIS NEED TO get clear of the crowd warring with his instinct to scoop Shawnee up and haul her off to his trailer. He needed to *know* that she was all right. Run his hands over every inch of her. Every inch of Salty. Hands that wanted to shake as he pulled the bridle off of Hammer and replaced it with a halter. Cole loosened the cinches, tied them up, then pulled the saddle and blanket off and stowed them in the trailer, every movement tightly controlled.

Then he turned around, walked over to the nearest stock truck, and slammed his palm into the side of the aluminum trailer.

Stupid, stupid, *stupid!*

"I'm sorry," a voice said quietly behind him.

He whirled around to find Shawnee standing there, Salty at her side, watching him with her mouth pressed into a tight line. She stepped forward to tie Salty beside Hammer. The two horses touched noses, a silent *you okay?*

Shawnee stripped off her chaps and flung them over the tailgate of the pickup. "I screwed up. Lost my bearings. I'm just glad—" She braced both hands against the pickup and hissed a curse between gritted teeth. "Salty could've been seriously hurt because of my mistake."

"*Your* mistake? You followed orders." He was used to the tight quarters of the turn-back arena. And in his place, without a clear shot at the bull's head…"If I'd led him off and let you do the roping, you would've heeled him before he got to me."

She thought about it for a moment, then nodded. "Most likely. But that's not the way you're used to working with Violet."

"You're not Violet."

"Thank God for that. Leave me in charge of Beni for more than five minutes and your ranch would be a pile of smoking ruins." She drew in a long breath and let it hiss out, the tension easing from the line of her jaw. She angled him a look he couldn't quite read, but it made things go loop-de-loop in his stomach. "So I forgot where I was. You forgot *who* I was. But we all still lived happily ever after. How 'bout we don't do that again?"

Cole shocked them both by laughing, a single, choked *hah!* "Sounds like a plan."

"Excellent." She slapped the tailgate and turned back to her horse. "Let's get these guys put away. They earned their oats tonight, and I'm sure you want to inspect Salty from nose to tail."

Cole took a swift step forward to block her path. "What about you?"

"My nose and tail are fine, thanks."

"Are you sure? I'd be happy to look them over."

She made a shocked face. "Whoa! Are you actually flirting, Cole Jacobs?"

"I…might be." He had to stop and think about it. Yes. By God, he thought he was. He eased a little closer. "Is it working?"

His breath hitched as she pressed her palm to his

stomach, just above his belt buckle, and slid it slowly, *slowly* up until she reached the top button of his shirt. She dipped a finger inside and outlined the V of exposed skin at his throat. His heart jumped up to meet her touch.

"I dunno," she said, low and husky. "How's it working for you?"

He was paralyzed, a raccoon frozen in the spotlight by that brush of her fingertip. If he so much as breathed, she might stop.

Don't stop. Oh God, don't stop…

A throat cleared, loud and exaggerated, somewhere in the near vicinity. Cole paid no attention. Whoever it was could just go screw themselves. He almost whimpered when Shawnee's hand fell away.

"Don't mind me," Hank said. "Just grabbing some ice out of the cooler for my poor, aching knee."

Cole thought about offering to strangle the punk so he wouldn't have to suffer anymore, but Shawnee went to take a look.

"Ouch." She examined the rapidly purpling bruise under the floodlight on the side of Cole's trailer. "You're sure it's just a bruise? No ligament damage?"

"Nah." Hank scooped ice into a plastic bag, twisting and knotting the top with a swiftness born of long practice. "But you definitely owe me a beer."

Shawnee's expression went somber. "More than that."

"Yeah?" Hank shot Cole a sly glance, then grinned at her. "Sorry, but I don't think the boss man would be cool with me taking it out in trade."

The growl was out before Cole could stop it. Hank laughed gleefully and sauntered off, no doubt to spread the news far and wide that he'd seen Cole and Shawnee doing…something?

Shawnee stared after him, hands on hips. "How can he be so awesome one minute, and such a complete dipshit the next?"

Cole just shook his head.

Shawnee pulled a Gatorade out of the cooler, unscrewed the top, and took several long gulps. Then she strolled over and offered it to him, deliberately turning the bottle so his mouth would touch the same spot as hers. The tip of her tongue toyed with the corner of her top lip as she watched him drink. Heat shot through him, so white-hot he was surprised the Gatorade didn't turn to steam and shoot out his ears.

She smiled and reached up to flick a knuckle along his jaw. "Later for that, cowboy. We've got stock to feed."

And she sauntered off to unsaddle her horse.

If Cole had owned a bullwhip, he would've been cracking it that night, trying to hustle everyone through the chores. Geezus, could they move any slower? Then the president of the rodeo committee showed up because *of course* he'd told the local newspaper reporter that *of course* Salty would be examined by the official rodeo veterinarian. As if Cole couldn't be trusted to look after his own horse.

"I can't believe he went right back after that bull," the committee man said. "I thought he'd be traumatized for life."

Cole shook his head. "These are war horses. A bull hits one of 'em, it just pisses 'em off."

Once the vet was satisfied, they wanted to dissect the whole incident, quizzing Cole about how they could minimize the danger of a reoccurrence. When they finally cleared out, Cole practically ran for his trailer and dove into the shower. He took the time to shave and slap on something that smelled a whole lot better than horse sweat and manure. Then he considered his clothing options and was stymied all over again.

What exactly did you wear to a…whatever this was? Good underwear was a given. No saggy butts or fraying elastic. He hoped she liked boxer briefs because that's all he had. And jeans. Was clean good enough, or should he wear the new ones? And what kind of shirt? He didn't want to look like a slob, but it seemed silly to put on something he'd ironed when, with any luck, it'd get tossed on the floor two minutes after he stepped into Shawnee's trailer.

Katie rolled her eyes at him, heaved a massive, disgusted sigh, and flopped down on the rug by the table. Finally, Cole settled on a pair of almost new jeans and his Jacobs Livestock polo shirt. Not fancy, but respectable. He pulled on clean socks and boots and stood.

Katie stood, too, eyes bright and expectant.

"Not this time," he said. "You stay."

Her eyebrows lowered. She spun around and plunked down again, pointedly showing him her back.

He bailed out the door with only a twinge of guilt, then stopped dead in the middle of the road, stunned. He'd expected to see a light in Shawnee's window. Instead, her trailer was pitch dark and appeared to be buttoned down for the night. He eased closer, ears straining for the sound of the television or a radio. Nothing. Even when he stood outside her door, he couldn't detect any hint of movement.

If she was waiting for him, she'd see him standing there, right? Unless she'd given up and gone to bed because he'd dawdled too long. He waited. A minute. Then another. The trailer remained dark and silent. His heart sank, then crawled off into a corner to sulk. After another couple of minutes, Cole joined it, slinking back to his own trailer, flinging his clean clothes into a pile on the floor and crawling into bed to toss and turn and curse until, at two o'clock, he kicked off the single sheet.

Katie smirked at him while he yanked on his rattiest old T-shirt and jeans to make his nightly rounds. Being a Wednesday, the beer garden had closed at ten, so any partiers were long gone. The bulls and horses were all dozing contentedly—damn their smug hides—and he didn't hear a single voice as he made his tour of the arena and contestant parking areas.

He appeared to be the only living creature awake on the entire rodeo grounds, other than Katie. He stomped along, head down, kicking at pieces of gravel until he rounded the last corner of the grandstand. When he looked up, his pulse leapt into overdrive. It looked like he wasn't the only one awake after all.

The light in Shawnee's trailer was on.

Chapter 27

SHAWNEE'S HEART JOLTED WHEN SHE SAW THE BEAM of Cole's flashlight appear around the end of the grandstand. She flopped onto her back and pressed her palms into the mattress, barely able to hear his footsteps over the pounding in her ears. *Crunch, crunch, crunch…*closing in fast. Damn, the man could cover ground in a hurry when he put his mind to it. Every step was like the twist of a key, winding up a spring inside her.

Thud!

She shot off the bed at the single, deep knock. Her palms were damp as she smoothed one hand down her green nightshirt and the other over her hair. Geezus. You'd think she'd never done this before. She took a deep breath and forced herself to walk slowly to the door.

It was like kicking open the hatch of an airliner, midflight. The sight of him—a mountain of hard, rumpled male—sucked the air out of the trailer. Shawnee had to grab the door frame to keep from being dragged with it by his sheer gravity. A squiggle of unexpected apprehension tickled her chest.

Damn. That was a *lot* of man.

"Everything okay?" he asked.

She nodded, any cool, teasing words wiped from her mind as she stared at his chest. His T-shirt was ragged around the collar and worn so thin she could see the outline of his nipples. Suddenly, she absolutely got why men loved wet T-shirt contests. She dragged her gaze up to meet his and lost another chunk of her vocabulary. His eyes were doing that hot, smoking thing, and his hair looked like she'd already been running her fingers through it. Stiff, starched Cole was nowhere in sight, and she wasn't quite sure how to handle what had shown up in his place.

"I stopped by earlier."

"I know." There. She could speak. Sort of.

"Why didn't you answer?"

"You didn't knock." She knew, because she'd barely breathed the entire time he'd stood outside her window, hoping but not hoping he'd take the hint and go away.

"I thought you were sleeping."

Hah. Fat chance, when her body was revving like a dragster on the starting line. She could practically smell the burning hormones. If there'd been a snowball's chance in hell she wasn't going to jump Cole, it had melted the instant she realized he was furious—not at *her*—but at himself for not trusting in her ability. She'd always been attracted to men who respected her as a roper, but she'd never had one flat-out declare that she was, in this particular situation at least, the better hand for the job.

There was no bigger turn-on than a guy who thought you were a stud.

"I knew you'd be back," she said, in answer to his implied question, and angled her head toward the lighted digits on the microwave. "Right on schedule."

His eyes drifted down, over the shimmering silk nightshirt to her bare legs, and on to the toenails she'd painted a juicy purple. "Why not earlier?"

"I prefer not to have Hank outside doing play-by-play while we rock this trailer."

His head snapped up and his nostrils flared, like a stud horse scenting a willing mare. Shawnee's body responded with an equally primitive rush of heat. He started to step inside, then stopped. "I, uh, didn't bring…"

"Condoms?"

A hint of red stained his cheeks. "Yeah."

"Maybe you could get the dog to fetch them," she said, with a pointed look past his ankles.

"The…oh shit. I forgot." He jerked around. Katie's expression was somehow both mortally wounded and murderous. Cole gestured toward his trailer. "I'll just…"

"I'll be right here." Lord knew she wasn't setting a single bare toe outside, with Katie curling her lip and sending off death vibes.

He vaulted out of the trailer, not bothering to use the steps. The dog fired one last snarl over her shoulder as she stumped after him. Shawnee stood in the middle of the floor, left in awkward limbo. Did she just stand there, like he'd hit the pause button? Go sprawl on the bed and try to look seductive? Yeah, right. She folded her arms to contain the slow *ka-thud, ka-thud* of her heart and stared down at her feet, admiring the way the polish glittered when she wiggled her toes. Maybe she should—

She let out a squeak when Cole burst through the door and slammed it behind him as if the devil dog was on his heels. "What did you do, sprint?" she asked.

"I didn't want to give you time to reconsider." He was winded, and in one hand he clutched an entire box of condoms.

Shawnee raised her eyebrows. "I don't know whether to be flattered or intimidated."

"I wasn't planning on using them all tonight." He ducked his head and peeked through his eyelashes, which of course were long and dark, damn men and their genetics. "I thought I should leave them here, since my trailer is always parked right next to the trucks and all."

She probably should've been annoyed at his assumption that this was an open-ended invitation, but instead it was sort of, well, sweet. And that thought threw her totally off stride. She was prepared for hot and sweaty. Sweet, not so much. She glanced around, at a loss where to take this next. The couch? The bed?

She could just grab him and kiss him, and let it go from there.

He smiled, so pure and full of light it was as if a mist had lifted behind his eyes. Until this moment, when she saw him completely unguarded, she hadn't realized how many layers of protection Cole kept between himself and the world. And no wonder. Her heart twisted at the sight of the bashful boy who peered out from inside this massive man. Wary. Vulnerable. So very vulnerable.

Panic fluttered deep in her stomach. Oh God, what had she done?

The smile dropped away. "What's wrong?"

"I just…" She took a step back, found the edge of the counter, and braced her suddenly untrustworthy knees. It was too late to turn back. She'd already breached his defenses and been admitted into the secret garden. She hugged her arms tighter around herself and stuck out her chin. "You have to agree to the rules, first."

He swallowed visibly. His gaze swept around the

trailer, with special attention to the bed, then back to her. "Like establishing personal boundaries and safe words?"

"Safe...*what?*"

His cheeks colored again. "I read on the Internet if things are going to get a little, uh, rough, you should—"

She burst out laughing. "I'm not gonna chain you to the bed—unless you want me to. Otherwise...I meant that you need to understand my relationship ground rules. I don't do serious, and I don't do long-term. Ever." And because this was Cole, she had to be extra specific. "When my job with Jacobs Livestock is over, so are we. Agreed?"

"But—"

"No buts. No convincing yourself that I'll change my mind, or maybe you can drop by my place back home once in a while for old times' sake." She made her words deliberately hard and cold. "When September ends, I'm gone."

Cole frowned at her. "Why?"

"Because that's the way I roll." And explaining the reasons was a pit she had no desire to dive into. "Nothing personal. Same applies to everyone. Take it or leave it."

"Even if—"

Especially *if.* Her heart twinged, still beating its wings against the cage after all this time. "No exceptions."

Cole studied her intently, as if looking for a crack in her armor, or a loophole to wiggle through. After a long moment, he nodded. "Okay."

"Okay." There. She couldn't be any clearer. Cole was thirty-five years old and he might not date a lot, but this wasn't his first barbecue. If he chose to take his chances, any pain and suffering was on him. "So..."

"So."

When he didn't make a move, she shifted, one set of bare toes covering the other. "Well, this is awkward. Now that I've got you here, I can't decide what to do with you."

"No problem." He tossed the condom box up onto the bed, toed off his boots, and advanced on her, one deliberate stride and then another, until his scent drenched every molecule she breathed in—warm, spicy, and utterly male. He stopped a few excruciating inches short of touching her and his smile came again, this time slow and anything but pure. His voice rumbled so deep in his chest she could feel the vibration in her nipples. "I have a list."

Her laugh broke in the middle when he raised his hands, his fingers feathering over her cheeks, then threading into her hair. He turned his palms up and let the curls slide across them almost to the end, then trapped one with his thumb and brushed it over his upper lip, his eyelids drifting down as he inhaled. "Soft. Smells like cookies."

"Vanilla shampoo," she choked out. For some reason, she was having trouble breathing.

When he'd told her that autistic people tended to have heightened senses, she hadn't translated it into touch and scent. Or realized it could be contagious. Suddenly, every nerve ending was super-charged, the gentle tug of his fingers in her hair sending a rush of tingles across her scalp.

"Mmmm." He caught up a fistful and sniffed again. "Nice."

He draped the curtain of hair over her shoulders, then

cupped her elbows and all but lifted her off her feet. She
grabbed at his waist as he moved her over until her heels
bumped the steps to the bed, in the nose of the trailer.
"Step up."

She did. One step, then the next, too mesmerized to
argue. Strange, to be able to look Cole directly in the
eye. His were the color of misty summer mountains,
shot through with cobalt that brought to mind a secret
lake only a blessed few ever stumbled across. A place to
rest, and let your worries trickle away.

Or explore, the way Cole's fingers trailed sparks
down to her right wrist and closed over her hand. "Flex."

She blinked away the haze of lust and squinted at
him. "What?"

"Make a muscle."

She gave a baffled *huh*, but curled her fingers into his
belt loop and flexed her arm.

"That's where the magic lives," he said, cupping the
bulge of her biceps and squeezing gently.

"Not magic. Practice."

"Couldn't prove it by me." His thumb rubbed mind-
bending circles on the inside of her upper arm. "I tried
to learn to heel steers. As far as I'm concerned, any time
someone catches feet, it's magic."

"Maybe you need a better teacher."

He shook his head. "I'll stick with the horns and let
you clean up behind me."

"For now."

"For now." But something about his tone—agreeable
almost to the point of smugness—made Shawnee's
radar beep.

"Cole, I meant—" The warning was cut off by an

embarrassing squeal when he hitched his hands under her armpits and plunked her butt on the bed. She was not used to being tossed around like a lightweight. "Damn. You could warn a girl."

He flicked her a grin that was like striking a match to tinder. "Where's the fun in that?"

She started to scoot back and make room for him, but he caught her ankle, holding her in place. "What are you doing?" she asked.

"Moving on to the next item on the list." He lifted her foot to inspect her toes, then stroked each one between his fingers, massaging. "I had to pencil this one in, after I saw the purple toenails."

She groaned with pleasure. "Remind me to thank Mariah again for the polish."

"For both of us." He gave her a nudge, pushing her onto her back. "You have amazing legs."

She opened her mouth to argue. Her legs weren't long. They weren't skinny. In fact, they were...*oh God*.

He worked his way over her arch, her calf, and on to her thigh, his fingers kneading the muscles in a way that might have sent her into La-La Land if his thumb hadn't been trailing along, brushing the most sensitive spots— around her anklebone, behind her knee, along the tender inside of her thigh. The pressure inside her built with every touch, spiraling higher until she nearly whimpered from the intensity of the ache. He pushed the nightshirt up as he went, and gave a low, appreciative growl when he saw the matching underwear. For a long, breathless moment he just drank in the sight. Then he planted a hand on either side of her hips and lowered himself down to brush his lips over the barely there silk and lace.

Chapter 28

WHEN SHAWNEE'S ALARM WENT OFF AT SIX A.M., COLE balled up his fist to smash it, but destroying her phone didn't seem like the best start to their first morning after, even if the damn thing was blasting what sounded like a chipmunk wailing, "*Baby, oh baby*." Over and over and over. He pushed up onto one elbow.

Shawnee was facedown in her pillow, clear on the other side of the bed. When he'd attempted to snuggle, she'd wriggled away. "Either stay over there or go home. I don't do touching while I sleep."

Now she didn't even twitch. How could she sleep through that god-awful screeching? Cole blinked hard, shook his head, blinked again, and finally focused long enough to locate the phone on the shelf beside the television, at the foot of the bed.

He leaned down, killed the chipmunk, and flopped back with a groan.

"Bless you." One hand emerged from the sheets, wadded up her hair, and shoved it aside as she rolled over, eyes still shut. "God, I hate that song."

"Then…why?"

"Making it stop is the only thing that gets me out of bed."

She had a pillow crease down her cheek, her face was puffy from a scant three hours of sleep, and the minute he woke up enough to function, he was definitely moving

Fire shot through her, a scorching need that pooled beneath his lips. She shoved at his shoulders, pushing him upright as she jackknifed into a seated position. "Come here, dammit."

"But I'm not even halfway through—"

"You can finish later. Right now…" She grabbed the hem of his T-shirt.

He gave an exaggerated sigh, but lifted his arms obligingly so she could push the soft cotton up, pausing to admire the landscape. She leaned in and burrowed her nose into the wiry mat of dark hair, then flicked her tongue around one flat brown nipple. Cole sucked in a breath and yanked the shirt the rest of the way off. He flung it over his shoulder, then shucked his jeans and kicked them in the same general direction.

Oh *my*. If she'd still had ovaries, they would've starting spitting out eggs at the sight of him. Nearly naked, Cole seemed even larger, his body thick and muscular. And very well proportioned.

Shawnee gulped, sliding away from him. She'd never felt physically vulnerable with a man, and it wasn't that she didn't trust him, but with his size and strength, Cole could overpower her without breaking a sweat.

Either he read her body language or it was an effect he had on all women. He followed her onto the bed but touched only her chin, a featherlight brush of his fingertip, his expression grave. "If you need me to ease up—or even stop—just say the word."

"Same for you," she shot back.

He grinned, a brilliant flash that lit up his eyes and melted her brain—and several other vital parts of her anatomy. When he lowered his body over hers, he led with a kiss that picked up right where the last one had left off—on the edge of madness. Shawnee dug her fingers into his shoulders, then his back, dragging his weight down on her and reveling in the way he surrounded her, blocking out all other sensation except the crush of him against her. Hard where she was soft, and just as inflamed.

Suddenly, there was no more patience. No more teasing. They wriggled and shoved at underwear, hissed in approval when hands and fingers found hot, exposed flesh, muttered impatiently at the need to pause and deal with the condom. And then they were there, at the brink, gazes locked as he eased inside. Her breath hitched and her hips shifted, seeking to accommodate him, inch by inch. Sweat sheened his forehead and was salty on her tongue as she bit his shoulder, driven by an insane urge to leave a mark. Bury herself so deeply under his skin that this man, of all men, would never forget her.

And curse them both.

"Now," she breathed, digging her heels into the backs of his thighs, seeking oblivion in pure physical sensation.

He made a dark, triumphant noise and began to move—slow, strong, relentless. Shawnee grinned at the creak of metal and springs. Then she wrapped her hands around his butt and urged him deeper as they proceeded to rock that trailer *hard*. Not to mention her world.

Minutes or hours or half an eternity later, she floated lazily back to the surface, sprawled facedown across Cole's chest. He'd rolled over at some point, dragging her semiconscious body with him. Now she listened to the deep *thud-thud-thud* as his heart settled into a normal rhythm. His hand kept time, rubbing slow circles on her

back. She drifted along in the post-sex nirvana between sleep and awake, her entire system humming with pleasure. Who knew nitpicking attention to detail equaled cataclysmic orgasms?

"I'll do better next time," he murmured drowsily.

Geezus. Was that humanly possible? She slid her palm over his stomach and threaded her fingers through the springy curls of his chest hair. "I'd like to see you try."

"I'll bet you would." His laugh was a barely audible vibration against her ear—like so much about Cole, ninety percent below the surface. His hand migrated around to cup her breast, and she arched at the brush of his thumb over her silk-covered nipple. "We can pick up where I left off. Next on the list is getting your shirt off."

on to number six on his list, because there was way too much of that woman he hadn't got his hands on yet.

In one swift move, she threw aside the sheet and slid down to the end of the bed, out of reach. He got only a glimpse of her firm, round butt before the nightshirt dropped down to her thighs. The speed of her exit made him groan.

"Geezus. Slow down before you pull something."

"It's like jumping out of a plane. Can't do it one foot at a time."

He grunted in response as her footsteps padded off toward the bathroom. The shower came on. Imagining Shawnee wet and naked was almost enough to peel him off the mattress. He rolled onto his side, then paused to rest and dozed off.

His next conscious thought was *coffee*. He inhaled, willing the scent directly into his brain. It should work, dammit. Smells were just molecules of a substance floating around in the air. The bed dipped and something bumped his chin. He reeled up one eyelid to find a travel mug resting on the pillow in front of his face.

"Exactly two teaspoons of sugar, the way you always make it." Shawnee flicked the bendy straw she'd stuffed in the top. "And you won't even have to lift your head."

Cole wrapped his hand around the mug, inhaled again, then breathed out a sigh of pure bliss. "I don't even care if you're mocking me. You're still a goddess."

"As so few people recognize." She slithered away again, already dressed for her morning ride in a T-shirt and jeans. "I thought being a morning person came standard with the anal-retentive package."

He flipped her off. She laughed.

"I'll see you tonight, cowboy. Same time, same place, if I haven't ruined you already." She smirked, and then she was gone, the door slapping shut behind her.

Cole grabbed her pillow and used it to elevate his head enough to sip out of the straw. He closed his eyes, his body oozing contentment. Lord, this was one comfortable bed. Tori's stuff might not be fancy, but it was high quality. And now that he'd experienced the difference, he was gonna have to check the label on the pillowtop mattress and invest in one for his trailer.

Not that he intended to spend any more time there than necessary, unless Shawnee was with him. He took another sip of coffee and let the memory of her touch and taste wash through him along with the caffeine, slowly reviving his brain. And he smiled.

Goddess was right.

Shawnee was a long way from perfect, but she just might be perfect for him.

Half an hour later, Cole ambled—it was damn hard not to strut—over to his own trailer. The morning air was silky against his skin, ripe with the scent of horses, cattle, and dew-soaked dirt. Rodeo, distilled. He dragged in a huge breath of the elixir of his life and allowed himself what was undoubtedly a goofy grin.

His good mood deflated with a nearly audible *pop!* when he opened the door to his living quarters.

For an instant, Cole thought he'd been robbed and vandalized. Then he saw the culprit glaring at him from the nest she'd made in the laundry she'd dragged out of the upended hamper. Katie had shredded one pair of underwear, eaten the remains, and hurked them back up again, a pile of blue slime on one of his white shirts.

Cole sighed. "Point taken. *This* time."

She lifted her chin and glared harder.

"Get used to it," he advised, as he began picking through the wreckage. "This one's gonna be around a while."

He held his breath as he stuffed the ruined shirt and underwear in a trash bag. His gag reflex was a fickle bastard. Blood and pus and gaping wounds, no problem, but a pile of dog puke could drop him to his knees. And don't even come near him with a dirty diaper. He'd drawn that line in the good uncle sand before Beni was a week old.

If he had a kid of his own, though, he could learn…

He tried to shake off that thought. Getting *way* ahead of himself, and violating every one of Shawnee's ground rules. But the image of a little spitfire with a mop of her brown curls had taken up residence in his head, and just like Shawnee, refused to listen to reason.

By the time he cleaned up the mess, showered, dressed, and wolfed down half a box of Wheaties—because yes, he *was* gonna need them—he only had a few minutes to saddle his horse and get to the arena before Shawnee finished up for the morning. Sometime in the past month, watching her had snuck onto his daily schedule, one more item that had to be checked off or his whole day felt out of whack.

This morning, she'd brought out her roping dummy—a life-sized plastic steer mounted on a cart. Mariah was pulling the dummy with Roy while Shawnee trotted along behind on Sooner. Her wide open loop curled around the wooden legs and scooped them up, easy as netting goldfish out of a tank. She wrapped her rope around the saddle horn and stopped the sorrel. When the rope came tight, Mariah swung around to face her, as if they'd just completed a competition run.

"Perfect," Shawnee called out.

She released her dallies and walked Sooner forward. He dropped his head and stood, dead calm, as Shawnee flicked the loop free of the legs, coiled up her rope, and slung it over her saddle horn. He was clearly ready to rope some live steers, but she'd have to settle for the dummy until she got home at the end of the season and could hit the practice pen with Tori.

Cole frowned. The lack of opportunities to rope would be a problem if he decided to try to change her mind about taking a long-term chance on him.

Yeah, he'd heard her when she'd said they were finished as soon as her job here was done. But he also saw the way she lit up every night when Tyrell introduced the pickup men and they rode into the arena. Cole knew that look. That rush was *his* addiction, and she might not admit it under torture, but Shawnee was hooked, too.

She flipped the reins over Sooner's head and crouched to unbuckle the skid boot on his back leg. Her gaze met Cole's under the horse's belly and, without breaking eye contact, she yanked down the V-neck of her shirt and flashed him.

"What are you grinning about?" Mariah asked, glancing from Cole back to Shawnee, who might not even know he was there for all the attention she seemed to be paying as she unbuckled the second boot.

Cole shook his head. If he wasn't already a goner, he

would be before long. All the signs were there. Falling for her might not be smart, and it definitely wasn't going to be simple, but a happy ending wasn't impossible. He didn't even have to be an exception to her rule. If he wanted to keep Shawnee, he just had to hold her to her vow to be his for as long as she worked for Jacobs Livestock.

Then figure out how to persuade her to extend her contract…indefinitely.

As soon as they'd finished running the stock through and putting their horses up, Shawnee went straight to her trailer and pulled out first a jug of sweet tea, then her phone. Much as she'd like to put this conversation off, the friendship code dictated that it had to happen, the sooner the better.

Violet answered before the first ring ended. "Hot damn! I thought I'd have to call and pry the details out of you."

"What?" Shawnee fumbled the jug and sloshed sweet tea down the front of her shirt. *Ahhh!* Cold. "You already heard?"

"Heard, saw, read the comments. That was a mistake, by the way. Don't ever read the comments. Some people are complete dumb-asses."

Shawnee set the jug down with a thump and more tea shot out the spout and hit her square in the face. She cursed, sputtered, and wiped at it with her shirtsleeve. "It's on the *Internet?*"

How in the hell? Had Hank snuck a hidden camera into her trailer?

"Well, duh. A wreck that spectacular, you didn't expect every photographer and idiot with a cell phone to post it online ten seconds after you knocked the dirt off your ass?"

"Oh. That." The air huffed out of Shawnee's lungs. "There's not much to tell. It happened so fast, I didn't even have time to pee my pants. The worst part is having Hank lording it over me. I'm gonna have to figure out a way to save his life just to shut him up."

"That's what we pay him for." Violet took a breath, which was just long enough for the shoe to drop. "If that's not why you called…you're not quitting on me, are you?"

"Of course not! I said I'd stay until the end of September."

"Is something else wrong?"

Shawnee grabbed a towel and crouched to mop tea off the floor. "That depends."

"On?"

"How you feel about me sleeping with Cole."

Violet responded with one ripe syllable.

"Look, I didn't—"

"Hand me that sheet of paper," Violet commanded, her voice distant as if she'd set the phone down. "No, the other one. Who had yesterday?"

Shawnee held her own phone out, frowned at it, then put it back to her ear. "What are you—"

"Dammit!" Violet swore. "How does she *do* that?"

"How does who do what?" Shawnee yelled.

There was a rustle, then Violet came back on the phone. "My mother. She won again. And she's always so smug about it."

"Wait a minute." Shawnee gave her head a shake. "Your *mother* was betting on me getting laid?"

"Well, sure. Hank told Melanie that Cole had his eye on you, and I've gotta do something for entertainment. You should be proud of Tori. She gave you until after Labor Day. Said you'd have to inflict maximum discomfort before you gave in." Violet snorted a laugh. "Gil was the real loser, though. He bet Cole was too sensible to try you at all. Goes to prove, Gil never has been an expert on good sense."

Geezus. Even Tori's brother-in-law had been in on this thing? "What did you do, post it on the bulletin board at the Kwick Stop so the whole town could join in?"

"Of course not. We kept it in the family. Plus a couple of the mechanics at Sanchez Trucking. And Beth, at Tori's clinic. But not Tim—you know, Lily's husband? He didn't think it was seemly, gambling on extramarital sex, being a preacher and all." A voice spoke in the background. "Oh right. Tori's dad had you for this Sunday, because of the big Labor Day concert. And his executive assistant took Friday." Violet gave an annoyed huff. "You couldn't have jumped him last weekend? This thing is gonna pay pretty good."

Shawnee ground her teeth. Great. A former United States senator and a minister's wife were laying odds on her sex life. "So now I suppose you want a play-by-play?"

Violet made a gagging noise. "God, no! This is *Cole*."

"I do!" a voice called out.

"Oh gross, Lily," Violet said. "That's almost as bad as when Ma tries to tell me about her and Daddy. No, you can't have—"

There was the sound of scuffling, a few swear words, then a crow of triumph before Violet's sister came on the line, slightly winded. "Dang. She's a beast even when she's knocked up and flat on her back. Okay… tell. How'd he get to you?"

"I…" Shawnee gave up trying to pour herself some tea and plopped down on the couch. "How did you know he would?"

"Like Violet said…it's Cole. Once he sets his mind to something, he's like a slow motion landslide. He just keeps pushing and pushing, and next thing you know, he's managed to move you to right where you didn't intend to be."

Shawnee snorted in disbelief. "If that's the case, how come he doesn't have a wife and eight kids?"

"I assume he never really wanted them." In the pause, Shawnee could imagine Lily's soft brown eyes sharpening. "This is more serious than we thought, if the two of you have discussed kids."

Shawnee snapped upright. "No! We haven't…I mean, we have, but not like…shit. This is exactly why I should have steered clear. Y'all are gonna go making a big deal outta this."

"You're the one who brought up marriage," Lily pointed out.

"I didn't mean…oh, the hell with it." Shawnee jumped up and stomped to the refrigerator. "Think whatever you want. We'll be down here screwing each other's brains out until we get bored."

"Okay. I'll pass that along."

"Good."

No. Wait. Not good. She wasn't dealing with Violet

Chapter 29

"YOU SLY DOG."

Cole stiffened at the sound of Hank's voice, then slowly looked up from the flank strap buckle he was checking. He didn't have to ask what Hank was talking about. The grin said it all.

Cole took a breath, stared him straight in the eye, and asked, "Do you like fighting bulls?"

"Uh, yeah." The grin faltered. "Why?"

"You're not going to be very good at it if I have to bust more than your chops to get you to shut up."

Hank's eyes went wide. "Whoa. Dude. I was just kidding, but if you can't take a joke—"

"Do you see me laughing?" Cole made an effort to turn his face to pure, ice-coated granite.

Hank gave a slow shake of his head.

"Have I ever joked about a woman I was dating?"

"I don't know. I was only about ten years old the last time—" Hank broke off and threw up his hands when Cole took a step toward him. "Right. No jokes." He was quiet for all of five seconds. "Is it okay to talk about other people's girlfriends?"

"Is there some reason I would want to hear this?"

"Only if you'd like to know that Ace's woman is here. That Cordelia from last weekend."

Well, hell. While he contemplated how this could possibly become a problem for him, Cole hooked and here. Lily told her mother *everything*. Shawnee's face flamed as she imagined the next time she saw Miz Iris and had to look her in the eye knowing that she knew. And Violet's daddy knew. And Delon, and Joe, and hell, probably even Beni. The kid never missed anything.

Shawnee opened the refrigerator, remembered the sweet tea was still on the counter, and closed it again. "He caught me at a weak moment."

"Oh. Your horse." Lily's voice softened in sympathy. "How's he doing?"

"Good. They're moving him to College Station next week, for the research project. I need to talk to Violet about how I'm going to pay you back..."

Lily made a dismissive noise. "Consider it a bonus for saving our butts. Cole was really struggling before you showed up. Besides, as far as he's concerned, anything that happens on his watch is his responsibility. He's sure if he'd paid closer attention, he would've noticed sooner that the horse looked wrong or was acting funny or something. That's just Cole."

Yet another reason Shawnee was the last woman on earth he should get attached to. She was a wreck waiting to happen, and he would never believe he couldn't have stopped her from slamming into the wall.

"Did you want to talk to Violet again?" Lily asked.

Lord no. She'd said more than enough. Except...

"No." Shawnee's grin was pure evil. Because really, at this point she couldn't make it any worse. "But tell her for me that Cole is *amazing*. Especially that thing he does with his tongue—"

She hung up to the sound of Violet taking her name in vain, and Lily giggling like a loon.

tripped the quick-release on the flank strap a few times to be sure it worked properly. The woman was old enough to take care of herself. Maybe beyond? At what point did she fall into the vulnerable elderly woman category? And wasn't that her family's problem? Besides, if Ace's track record was anything to go by, he would shoot himself in the foot long before he got his hands on her kin's inheritance.

Still, Cole would have to keep an eye on them.

"Hey, Hank!" A trio of young bull riders paused, gear bags slung over their shoulders as they headed for the back of the chutes. "We're gonna tear it up later at the dance. See you there?"

"Uh…maybe. I'll see if I'm in the mood."

One of the guys hooted. "That'll be the day, when Hustlin' Hank isn't in the mood for hot girls and cold beer."

"Yeah, well…" Hank turned abruptly to climb up into the truck. "Guess I'm gettin' old. I gotta get my gear on."

The bull riders passed a glance among them, then shrugged and moved on. Cole stared at the truck door as it thumped shut. Hank bowing out of a party? Maybe he was actually growing up. Bigger miracles had happened, though Cole was hard put to think of one offhand.

Shawnee came strolling over from the stock pens, leading Salty. She flashed Cole a smile so bland he almost wondered if he'd imagined…but that wasn't possible. His imagination wasn't that good. The heat of the day was beginning to wane and all around them, the activity level was slowly ramping up. Contestants clomped past, leading or riding horses, chatting about tonight's draw or last night's runs. Cars rolled into spectator parking, spilling out families with toddlers, packs of cocky teenaged boys, and pairs of sleek, long-legged women, their clothes cut low on the top and high on the thigh with plenty of flash and fringe—what they considered cowgirl style.

Cole glanced over at Shawnee, in her royal blue Jacobs Livestock shirt and plain jeans, a rope slung over her arm and her hair corralled into a bushy ponytail— and imagined the shiny purple toenails inside those scuffed boots. Now *that* was his kind of cowgirl.

He waited until she stepped into the tack room of the trailer to get her saddle, then moved to block the door. "Hank already knows," he said quietly.

He braced himself for the explosion, but she only nodded. "I figured word would get back."

"Get *back*?"

"From home." She pulled Salty's bridle off a hook and hung it on the saddle horn. "As soon I hung up with Violet, I'm sure she called Melanie, and of course *she* called or texted Hank to see if he had any juicy details."

"You…Violet…what?"

Shawnee stacked blankets on top of the saddle. "I had to call her. It's the code. You don't sleep with a friend's brother—well, practically brother—and let her find out from someone else. Oh yeah, and Lily was there, too."

She hefted the saddle and turned, bumping him in the chest when he just stood there, gaping at her. She'd told Violet. And Lily. Which meant…

She bumped him again, harder. "This thing is kinda heavy, you know."

Cole grabbed the saddle out of her hands and

marched to where Salty was tied. Shawnee followed, propping one shoulder against the corner of the trailer while she watched him sling the blankets onto Salty's back. "I should have known you'd be the chivalrous type. Does this mean you're gonna saddle my horse for me every night now that you're gettin' to jump me? Because I'm all for emancipation but I'm also kinda lazy, so feel free."

"You are not lazy." Cole tossed the saddle on and straightened the cinches. "And I'm only doing this because I need to keep my hands busy so I don't throttle you."

"What? It's not like they weren't gonna find out. If I sneeze in my trailer, someone over here in the trucks yells 'Bless you!'"

Cole strode around Salty's butt and reached under his belly to grab the front cinch. "If that's the case, then why leave me hanging until two thirty in the damn morning, when we both could've got a decent night's sleep?"

"There's a difference between knowing and bearing witness." Her gaze went hot, sliding over him like melted caramel. "And if I'd let you in at eleven, we'd both be lucky to be standing upright right now."

Cole fumbled the latigo he was trying to thread through the cinch. He had to take a breath to clear the fog of lust from his head before he could speak. "What about tonight? You said same time, same place."

"I've reconsidered. You can show up after the rodeo, on one condition."

"Which is?" he asked warily, wondering what she'd dreamed up to torture him with now.

"I'm craving pizza. You show up at my door packin'

a large artichoke and sun-dried tomato with extra cheese and a six-pack of Shiner, I'll let you in no matter what time it is. I'll even throw in a movie. It can be like date night."

"A pizza." He took a deep breath, identifying the distinct aromas of hamburgers, barbecue, tacos, and popcorn, overlaid with the scent of hot grease. The concession stands were dishing up every other kind of fast food ever invented—and some that never should've been—but she wanted weird-ass pizza. And beer.

But she could've insisted on dragging him to the after-party instead, where one of the best indie bands in Texas was playing.

"I can do that," he said.

"Excellent." She ducked under Salty's neck and shouldered Cole out of the way, tugging the latigo from his hand. "And I can do this, unless it's an insult to your manly pride."

He braced one hand on the cantle of the saddle and the other on the side of the trailer, boxing her in against Salty, and leaned down so his breath ruffled the renegade curls escaping her barrette. "I think it's safe to say my *pride* is big enough to handle it."

Her breath hitched and he caught her slight quiver when he nipped the top of her ear.

As he sauntered back to get his own saddle, she called after him. "Hey, Cole? Exactly how long is that list of yours?"

At the rate he was finding new things to add? He smiled. "If I were you, I wouldn't make any other plans for the rest of the rodeo season."

—⁓—

After the rodeo that night, the crew set a land speed record for finishing up the chores, anxious to get to the concert. Or in Shawnee's case, to have time to dive through the shower before Cole showed up on her doorstep. The first crashing notes of the opening act rang out across the rodeo grounds as she chained the gate on Roy's pen and started for her trailer. She passed near the announcer's stand in time to see Mariah throw her arms around her father's neck.

"You are the best daddy in the whole world!"

Tyrell hugged her back, but his expression was pained. "Keep your cell phone turned on, don't take candy from strangers, and meet me at Cole's pickup no more than ten minutes after the last song ends."

"Ugh!" Mariah injected a gallon of exasperation into the sound, and topped it off with a spectacular eye roll. "I'm not a child. I've been to concerts before."

"Not with girls I don't know."

"You know their parents."

"I've seen them in the arena. That's not the same as actually *knowing* them."

"I'll be fine." She rose up on tiptoe to give him a smacking kiss on the cheek. "I'm spending time with kids my own age, just like you're always nagging me to do. Go have a nice, quiet dinner with your grown-up friends. I'll see you later."

And she was off, achingly fresh and beautiful as she all but skipped over to join the three girls who waited a safe distance away. Moments like this made Shawnee glad she'd never have to watch her own kids grow up.

She forced down the lump in her throat. Nostalgia, that's all. Remembering what it was like to be a teenager going unchaperoned to a concert. The definition of cool.

Tyrell sighed. "A year from now she'll be waltzing off to college. It scares the hell out of me."

"And rightly so."

He raised his eyebrows. "Everyone else tells me how mature and driven she is, and I shouldn't worry so much."

"They have apparently forgotten their first year of college," Shawnee said dryly. "And I didn't look like *that*."

Tyrell grunted a laugh. "Wow. You really know how to make a guy feel better."

"Just keepin' it real." She cocked her head toward the noise and lights. "You could spy on her."

"Right. A tall black man wouldn't stand out in that crowd at all. Besides…" He smiled, his dimples winking sheepishly. "I don't like going out without my wife. It's hard enough, being apart this long. She doesn't need to hear I've been drinking or dancing or whatever the gossips will manufacture if I give them a chance."

Shawnee slugged him in the arm. "You are a good man, Tyrell Swift. And you've raised a good kid. She'll be okay."

"That makes one of us." He rubbed a hand over his heart, then shot her a hopeful look. "I don't suppose, if you're going, you'd keep an eye—"

"Sorry. I have other plans."

Big ones. About six and half feet worth, in fact. She grinned at her own wit as she waved good night and made a dash for her trailer before anyone else could sidetrack her.

She was just stepping out of the shower when the knock came at her door. After a two-second debate, she wrapped a bath sheet around her and went to let Cole in.

He didn't even blink. Just stared intently at where the towel was tucked between her breasts, then said, "Let me find a place to set this stuff down."

"You can do that while I put some clothes on."

His gaze finally made it up to her face. "Don't bother on my account."

"I'm not. Unlike the pizza, the sex will get hotter if we set it aside for a bit."

Cole grinned, and her heart did a crazy *boom-chicka-boom*. His hair was damp and he'd opted for another of those soft, clingy T-shirts that made her want to rub her face against him like a cat. Heavenly aromas of garlic, tomato, and yeasty crust wafted from the two boxes he balanced on one hand. A six-pack of Shiner longnecks dangled from two fingers of the other.

A great big hunk of man on her doorstep, bearing pizza and beer. Welcome to her wildest dreams. Shawnee inhaled so deeply she had to clutch at the towel to keep it from falling. "Give me two minutes."

She locked herself in the bathroom before she could change her mind about the order of events. Still, there was no sense putting on a whole lot of clothes, so she pulled on a black racer-back tank with a built-in bra, bikini underwear to match, and a pair of cuffed denim shorts. She took the time to smooth lotion on every inch of exposed skin, run a wide-toothed comb through her hair, and curse the fact that men looked sexier straight out of the shower, while she just looked pasty. Oh well. He wasn't here to admire her eyeliner.

Cole was kicked back on the couch with a beer in his hand. She snagged a Shiner from the fridge, twisted off the top, and made herself comfortable. Cole retrieved a stack of napkins and the pizzas from the table and sat down right beside her, hip to hip.

"If I can't have you in a towel, I'll settle for this." Balancing the pizzas on his lap, he reached up to trace the curving edge of the tank top across her upper back, trailing sparks. Then he pushed aside her hair to press a warm, lingering kiss at the base of her neck, putting a little tongue into it. "You have really great shoulders," he breathed against her skin.

She gasped out a laugh. "That's supposed to be my line."

He drew back, some of the heat leaching out of his eyes as a crease formed between his brows. "I'm sorry. I guess that's one of those things women don't like to hear."

"No! I mean…maybe some women would take it wrong, but I…" *Cannot speak in full sentences because I'm on the verge of spontaneous combustion.* But her lust was muted by how, in a blink, his pleasure had dissolved into uncertainty. What idiotic bitch—or series of them— had done this to a man who could convince a woman that she had the world's sexiest kneecaps? She let loose an aggravated breath. "Do you hear me complaining?"

"You're just being polite."

"Hah!" She practically spit beer. "I realize the sex was mind-blowing last night, but have you forgotten who you're talking to?"

He blinked, stared at her for a beat, and then gave his head a shake. "Yeah. I guess I did." Then his grin crept back. "Mind-blowing, huh?"

"Begging for compliments?" She poked him in the arm. "*That* is lame. Now tell me why we have two pizzas."

"You didn't expect me to eat pickled vegetables and shriveled up red leather?"

"Have you ever even tasted them?"

"Why would I do that, when there's so much perfectly good pepperoni in the world?" He passed her the top box, then flipped his open and pulled out the first slice.

Shawnee did the same, and waved hers under his nose. "Are you sure you don't want to try a bite?"

He squashed back into the couch and screwed up his face like a first grader threatened with a brussels sprout. "Yuck. I don't know if I can even kiss you after seeing that stuff."

She stuck out her tongue, then took a huge bite.

Cole gave her a sidelong look that strolled from her bare toes to the top of her head. Then he flicked her a smug grin. "Still leaves me plenty of room to work."

All the available territory was hit by an instant heat wave at the thought of being invaded by Cole's hands, and Cole's mouth, and…

She took another swig of her beer, but it didn't do a thing to bring her internal temperature down, especially when he slung his arm around her and started sketching circles on her upper arm. He had her tucked up against him, knee to hip to shoulder, as close as they could get without sharing molecules.

She frowned. "I thought autistic people didn't like to be touched."

He shrugged, unoffended. "We're all different. And it seems to matter where you are on the spectrum. I was a real cuddler when I was kid. I wanted someone to hold my hand everywhere we walked and I used to beg my mom or dad to come and lay with me at night, when I went to bed, just for five minutes so we could whisper secrets about any silly thing. Which Ninja Turtle I wanted to be, or whether there was a Disneyland in heaven." His hand went still, as if he'd been struck by the thought that they might be able to answer now. Then he shook his head. "And touching a girl you're dating is different. Like, I can't handle it with Violet or Lily. I never know where to put my hands so I don't grab the wrong thing. But I figure you and I are to the point where you might not knee me in the nuts for an accidental butt squeeze."

Shawnee had to swallow hard, tangled up in visions of Cole as a…well, smaller boy. She couldn't imagine him ever being little. "So that's why that miserable mutt is so spoiled. Nothing like a dog when you need a cuddle."

"Or a baby." His expression went soft. "There's nothing like cuddling a baby."

Shawnee dropped her pizza slice, then tried to pretend she'd tossed it down on purpose by grabbing for a napkin.

"The way they curl up on your shoulder…" He sighed wistfully. "I used to offer to watch Beni just so I could hold him, but he outgrew that a long time ago. It's too bad Lily and her husband haven't been able to have kids. But pretty soon we'll have the new baby."

Geezus. He really did need to find a wife who wanted to pop out half a dozen rug rats. Shawnee closed the lid on her pizza, her appetite destroyed. She should tell him. Right now. Just spit it out.

Sorry, darlin', but this ol' mare's been spayed.

And ruin not only this night, but all of the others they might have. He'd start looking at her *that way*. The way people always looked at her when they found out. *Oh, you poor thing. Bless your heart.*

Worse, if they realized she'd had a choice.

Cole's hand tightened on her shoulder as she moved to rise. "That's all you're eating?"

"I'll save it to gross you out later." She pushed to her feet and made a show of batting her eyes at him. "I just *love* pizza in bed after a good workout."

He made another brussels sprout face. "Food in bed is just *wrong*."

"Well, damn. Guess I bought that whipped cream for nothing."

His eyes lit up. "Could we make strawberry waffles instead?"

Shawnee burst out laughing. Honest to Pete, he was such a goofball. She could see why Violet didn't like turning him loose. She tossed the box on the counter, then went looking for the television remote.

"We have five movie channels, or…" She angled him a hopeful look. "*NCIS* marathon?"

"*NCIS*. Gibbs is my hero."

"Somehow not surprising." She flicked to the right channel and fetched another beer for each of them. The first scene that came on was in the lab, with the goth forensics chick, which reminded Shawnee. "I asked Analise if she was going to the concert tonight, but she made a face like you did at my pizza and said she had plans that didn't include country music."

Cole polished off his fourth slice and washed it down

with the last of his beer. "Hank said he wasn't going, either."

"Really?" Shawnee drew out the word as her mind put two and two together...or should that be one and one? "They were dancing when I left the beer garden last weekend. I wonder..."

Cole's eyebrows rose. "Might explain why Hank's friends are bitching that he's been making himself scarce. She wouldn't be impressed by that bunch of yahoos."

"And wouldn't be afraid to tell them so." It was one of the things Shawnee loved about the girl.

She settled in beside Cole again. He immediately wrapped his arm around her. She made a token effort to concentrate on the television while Cole plowed through the rest of his pizza, then tossed the empty box on the table without getting up. Her blood hummed, but for now it was only pleasant background noise, like the music echoing across the rodeo grounds from the concert. It must be like this for Violet and Joe or Tori and Delon at the end of a long rodeo day. Relaxed, comfortable, but with the ever-present potential for fireworks if either of them decided to strike a match. The reason people got married, she supposed.

And had babies.

"What?" Cole asked, when she stiffened.

"Nothing. I just...I had an itch."

"Where?" He gave her a leering grin. "I'd be glad to scratch *all* of your itches."

She forced an answering, suggestive smile. "How 'bout you try to guess, and I'll let you know if you're getting warmer or colder?"

"It may take me a while," he warned, plucking the

bottle out of her hand and then pressing her back on the couch. "I've always been a little slow when it comes to games."

His mouth found the most tender spot on the underside of her jaw, and her blood went from humming to singing through her veins. She let her hands rove over his broad back, his arms, his shoulders, learning the contours she'd missed in their previous explosive encounter. Meanwhile, he continued his search, his mouth and fingers making her breath come in hitches and gasps as he worked his way south, and she kept mumbling, "Warmer. Warmer. Oh *yeah*, definitely warmer..."

He had just crossed the equator when they heard the first scream.

Chapter 30

Shawnee sat up and jerked her top down so fast she nearly brained Cole with her elbow. He rolled off her and landed with a thud on the floor. She scrambled over him, buttoning her shorts and shoving her feet into flip-flops while Cole gathered himself up and staggered after her. His head spun as another scream rang out and he tried to shift gears from mindless desire to possible danger. Shawnee grabbed a frying pan off the stove as she passed and was out the door.

Damn crazy woman. She didn't have any idea what she was jumping into.

He bailed out into the darkness and slammed into her where she'd paused near the front of her pickup, frying pan cocked as she peered into the shadows, toward the sound of raised voices. Cole recognized one of them immediately. He stepped in front of Shawnee and held out an arm to hold her back while he tried to make sense of what he saw and heard.

"Tyrell?" he called.

The man ignored him, bellowing in rage as Mariah clung to one arm, shrieking at him in what seemed to be a combination of fear and fury. Cruz had both hands planted on Tyrell's chest, trying to hold him back. Above them, the door to the truck cab hung open, the dome light dimly illuminating the chaos. Three steps closer and Cole could see someone splayed out on the ground, with Analise crouched over him. Two more strides and Cole saw it was Hank.

In the second it took for the pieces to click into place, a pair of uniformed county deputies came jogging down the road. "What's going on here?" one of them barked.

For an instant, they all froze, and the only sound was Katie yipping and scratching frantically at the door of Cole's trailer. Then Mariah flung herself away from her father. "*He* is out of control."

When they saw Tyrell, both cops shifted into high alert. Both dropped their hands to their weapons. The taller one drew his revolver. Oh shit. Cole leapt forward, raising both hands as he put his body in front of Tyrell's. "Let's not get excited—"

"I can date whoever I want!" Mariah raged. "I'm—"

Shawnee threw an arm around the girl and clamped a hand over her mouth. "Now, sugar, these fine officers don't wanna listen your caterwaulin'," she said, laying on the backwoods southern accent.

Mariah squealed in protest as Shawnee put her in a headlock, speaking low and fast into her ear as she dragged her away from her father. And away from the gun, its black, deadly eye focused on Cole's chest. Fear congealed the air in his lungs. One twitch of a finger…

"But I'm not from—" Mariah began.

"We'll talk about it later," Shawnee cut in. "You just hush up now. You're makin' the officers nervous."

And God knew, they did not want to alarm the man with the gun. Cole was acutely aware of Tyrell standing behind him, silent and motionless. Of Cruz moving to add his body to Cole's human barricade as off in the periphery, Hank struggled to sit up.

"Step aside," the taller cop ordered.

They stood their ground. Words. He needed words, and they had to be the right ones. "I'm Cole Jacobs. All of these people work for me. This is just a little family squabble. I've got it under control."

"That's for us to decide." The shorter cop took a step closer, angling for a better look at Hank. "Is he seriously injured?"

Analise waved off the question with a sneer. "Nah. He's a bullfighter. He gets smacked harder than that every day."

The cop transferred his gaze to Mariah, obviously summing up the situation just as Cole had, and getting the same answer. "What about you, ma'am?"

"I...I'm fine," she stuttered. "We were...I mean, I was..."

"She was sneakin' around with that blockhead." Shawnee jabbed a finger at Hank. "Even though she knew full well her daddy would not approve...and with good reason. Can't blame a father for lookin' out for his own."

The cops relaxed slightly, and the pent-up air whooshed out of Cole's chest when the tall one put his gun away, pulling a face that suggested he knew all about trying to keep a daughter in line.

The short cop fished out a small notebook. "We're gonna have to write this up. I need names."

Tyrell swore softly. Shawnee shot Cole a look even he could decipher. *Fix this!*

"No problem." Cole edged closer to the cop and tried a reassuring smile that felt stiff and cracked as an old tire. "Like I said, I'm Cole Jacobs, the stock contractor for the rodeo. This is Shawnee Pickett…"

Cole went on around the circle. Hank was sitting up now, head hanging, but he lifted a hand when he heard his name. Cole deliberately left Tyrell for last. When he finally turned aside and gestured toward the other man, Tyrell had regained his dignity. He managed a shadow of his usual smile. The cops relaxed another few degrees, but their eyes were still suspicious.

Come on, come on. If Cole didn't talk them out of an official report, this was going to turn into a nightmare in about three seconds flat.

"Look, we've been on the road all summer," he said. "People rub each other wrong, things get tense, and sometimes we have a squabble. But if this shows up in the police report, it's gonna give us a real black eye with the committee."

The cops exchanged a dubious look. "We have to at least see some ID. We can't just take your word…"

"Here." Cole yanked out his wallet, fumbled for his driver's license, and shoved it at them. If they would just be satisfied with his—

"I'll need the others," the tall cop insisted.

Cole made an exaggerated, pained face. "Like I said, we'd really like to keep this out of the sheriff's report. Especially names—"

"What if we gave you a reference, instead?" Shawnee cut in. "Someone who will vouch for Cole?"

The cop shined his flashlight on Cole's license and shook his head. "We can't rely on the word of anyone clear up in the Panhandle. We wouldn't know them from Adam."

"Give me two minutes." Shawnee released Mariah to jog to her trailer.

The shorter cop maneuvered around Cole and crouched beside Hank. "Do you need medical attention?"

"No." The reply was grunted between clenched teeth. "Jus' a bruise."

"Can you stand up?"

Hank nodded, but before the cop could attempt to assist him, Cruz materialized beside them in that uncanny way of his. He grabbed one side and Analise the other and they hoisted Hank to his feet, subtly bracing him so he couldn't sway.

"Let me see your eyes," the cop said.

Hank lifted his chin and stared straight ahead, wincing when the cop flashed a light in his eyes. "Don't need no doc," he muttered.

"Macho idiot," Analise said, with just the right amount of disgust. "You wouldn't get him to admit he's hurt if he was missing an arm."

The cop shook his head and smiled slightly—*those crazy cowboys*—as Shawnee hustled back and shoved her phone into the shorter cop's hand. "Senator Patterson would like to speak to you."

Every head jerked around as the goggle-eyed cop held up the phone to stare at the face on the screen, immediately recognizable to anyone who'd lived in Texas in the last thirty years. "Uh…yes sir. Deputy Herndon here, sir."

"Good evening." Even over the phone's tinny speaker, Richard Patterson's voice resonated with power. "I understand we've had a little scuffle down there. Cole Jacobs is a close friend of mine. You can trust him to be sure the matter is handled properly, but I'm happy to assist in any way, including speaking to your superiors…if necessary."

There was the slightest emphasis on the *necessary* that made it sound less helpful than cautionary. *You really don't want that, do you?*

"Um…yes, sir. Thank you, sir."

"I will personally review this matter with Cole, and if I feel it is appropriate for charges of any kind to be filed, we will do so immediately. But we don't want to waste your time or the court's. Is that acceptable?"

The short cop looked to the other. He shrugged, loath to disagree with one of the most respected men in the state. "Of course. Thank you, sir."

"No, thank *you*." The retired senator flashed a broad smile. "I appreciate your service, deputies. Men like you are the backbone of our state. Best of luck."

The screen went blank and Shawnee tugged the phone out of the flummoxed cop's hand. "Satisfied?"

"Um…yeah." He shook off the cloud of awe and snapped to attention, sending a warning glare around the group. "But if we have to come back here…"

Cole's whole body went rubbery with relief, but he put iron in his voice. "You won't."

The cops looked him up and down, then nodded. Everyone stood silent while the deputies walked away. Mariah was the first to move, whirling to face Shawnee. "I didn't know. I swear to God—"

"Obviously." Shawnee gave Hank a deadly glare. "But he did."

Tyrell looked from one to the other, confused. "I don't understand."

"The age of consent in Texas is seventeen," Analise said. "Mariah is still jailbait here."

"That is so stupid!" Mariah exploded. "He didn't force me to do anything. And we didn't even…"

Cole glared at Hank, who hung his head and refused to make eye contact. "Doesn't matter. If he's more than three years older and touched you in a sexual way, even over your clothes, it's considered indecency with a child. Mandatory minimum two-year sentence. No exceptions."

And Hank should know, dammit. Just last winter a star basketball player from Amarillo had lost everything in a similar case—including a scholarship to A&M and a shot at the pros.

"Are you talking about statutory rape?" Tyrell asked, stunned.

"Basically, yeah." Cole transferred his gaze to the other man. "You have the right to press charges, if you choose."

"You wouldn't!" Mariah grabbed his arm, pleading. "Daddy, you can't."

Tyrell shook his head again, flexing his hand, which was swelling as fast as Hank's jaw. "This is too…I need to think."

"We all do," Shawnee said.

And they had to get Hank checked out. He had a concussion, minimum, and the way his jaw was swelling, that was more than a bruise. Tyrell's hand might be broken, too, but that would keep until morning. Hank, though…if they took him to the local ER the cops might find out, and they'd be screwed. Or at least Hank would be. Cole turned to Cruz. "It's an hour into El Paso and you know the city. Can you take him there for x-rays?"

Cruz nodded. "We can take my car."

"I'll go with them," Analise said.

Everyone burst into motion. The instant Cole opened his trailer door, Katie bailed out, running frantic circles, yipping and whining and generally adding to the chaos. Analise and Cruz started to drag Hank toward the car but he jerked free, staggering toward Mariah.

"Don' go," he slurred, reaching for her. "I didn't mean for this—"

"Oh, Hank." Mariah took a step toward him. Shawnee jerked her back as Cole grabbed Tyrell's arm.

Shawnee pushed Mariah behind her and slapped a palm on Hank's chest. "I realize your brain is more scrambled than usual, but we're not screwing around here, Hank. You can't touch her—unless you want to be labeled a child molester for the rest of your life?"

He shook his head, swaying. "It's not like that. I wouldn't hurt her!"

"Then leave her be."

"But we need to—"

"You *need* to back off, Hank, before this turns into something that wrecks your entire life. And hers."

Shawnee gave him another shove, then dragged Mariah off toward her trailer.

"Mariah!" he begged. "Please…"

The girl paused, glanced over her shoulder, then gave a helpless shrug and let herself be pulled away.

Hank stared after her for a long moment, then his chin dropped and his whole body sagged. "I would never hurt her," he insisted, his voice cracking.

"Not on purpose. But Hank…you just can't. No matter how you feel about her." Analise wrapped an arm around him and squeezed as they steered him toward Cruz's car. "We have to take care of you right now."

Shawnee slammed her trailer door behind Mariah and slumped back against it.

"Okay." She drew in a huge breath, then huffed it out. "I've got this one for the night. Tyrell, take my pickup to the motel and get some ice on that hand. Give everybody 'til morning to simmer down."

"If Hank comes back…"

"He'll have to get through me," Shawnee promised.

Tyrell held for a beat, then nodded. "Yeah. That's probably best. Anything I say tonight…" He shook his head. "I'd better call her mother first."

Cole didn't envy him that conversation. Tyrell's footsteps dragged, his shoulders slumped as he crossed the road, accepted Shawnee's keys, and drove away. Suddenly, fatherhood wasn't looking quite as appealing as it had half an hour earlier. Cole closed his eyes. Jesus Christ. What a mess. Katie pressed against his leg and whined, as if in agreement.

"You okay?" Shawnee asked.

His eyes popped open. She was still leaning on her door, watching him. Was he okay? Other than the tremors every time he pictured that gun aimed at him, and the knowledge that he, who had never so much as swiped a candy bar, had just covered up a felony?

"I will be. Eventually." Although he was no doubt gonna have some dandy dreams for who knew how long. "Thank you for calling the senator. I don't know why he would put his reputation on the line for Hank—"

"He did it for *you*. For Jacobs Livestock." She pushed

away from the trailer and strode up to him, hands balled into fists. "You dumb-ass."

"I know. I should have kept a better eye on Hank—"

She lunged, and for an instant he thought she was going for his throat. Instead, her hand latched onto either side of his neck, fingers digging in like claws, and tried to shake him. "You could have been shot! What the hell were you thinking?"

He tried to shrug, but her grip had him paralyzed. "I wasn't. I just…well, I'm white. And Tyrell's black. My odds were better."

"Your odds." She stared up at him in disbelief. "Like that was gonna stop a bullet."

Truthfully, he hadn't had time to think about it. But he was now. Another tremor ran through his blessedly intact innards. "I had to do something."

"God! You are so—"

She yanked his head down and kissed him, her mouth taking his as if she was trying to dive straight to the center of him. There was nothing sexual about this kiss. It was a punishment. And somehow, a prayer of thanksgiving.

She broke it off and hugged his neck so hard his vertebrae creaked. Her words were low, unsteady. "For the record, they shoot white men too. Especially large, potentially threatening white men." She loosened her death grip, leaned back to gaze up at him, and huffed out a sigh. "We might as well give you a cape, you're so damn determined to be a hero."

Cole couldn't find a trace of sarcasm in her voice. Or the soft press of her lips on his cheek.

Then she turned him loose, scowling. "But I get to

spend the night with Miss Washington instead. See you tomorrow, Captain America."

Cole was tempted to point out that Captain America had a shield, not a cape, but this probably wasn't the time to nitpick. He watched her disappear into her trailer, then looked down to find Katie staring up at him, head cocked.

What now, Einstein?

Damned if he knew. He had a disaster of potentially epic proportions on his hands, and all he could do was stand there and stare at the light in Shawnee's window and curse the fact that he was on the wrong side of the door.

Chapter 31

When Shawnee stepped into the trailer, she found Mariah slumped on the couch, staring at her knees. From the dazed look on her face, the full implications of what could have happened had finally smacked her upside the head.

"Is my dad okay?" she asked in a small voice, sounding younger than her years for the first time.

"His hand is probably broken," Shawnee said bluntly. "Along with Hank's jaw. Was it worth it?"

"I didn't know!" Mariah burst out.

"That your dad would go ballistic? Bullshit."

The momentary flash of fire died and Mariah ducked her head. "He's so overprotective," she muttered.

"For good reason, obviously." Shawnee plopped down on one of the banquette seats, her legs folding up camp for the night. "Seriously, Mariah? Hank?"

"He's sweet," she said defensively. "Sort of goofy, but…he listened to me and my crazy dreams. And he's been places—really big rodeos, and hanging out with Joe at the National Finals. He made me feel like I could be there, too. At first, we just hung out. Friends, you know? I don't really know anyone else down here except you and Analise, and you're both—"

Boring? Weird? Grown-ups?

"He never told me…" The beginnings of anger were

sketched in the pleat between Mariah's eyebrows. "Why didn't he tell me it was illegal?"

"Because he's Hank, and using his brain has never been one of his talents."

"But he could have gone to jail!"

Shawnee didn't bother to point out that it wasn't necessarily past tense. If the cops decided to take a closer look, or if Tyrell or his wife insisted on pressing charges…

But the odds were low, in Shawnee's estimation. The sad fact was, the Swifts couldn't afford to raise a fuss. In a situation like this, the victim stood to suffer as much or more as the accused. Especially a girl who looked like Mariah. The world would be quick to blame her—attack her—regardless of the circumstances.

Hank had a lot of friends who were as bone-headed as he was, and enough of a name in rodeo for his arrest to reverberate across the country, laying waste to the career Mariah hadn't even started. Not to mention Tyrell. Breaking into the upper ranks as a rodeo announcer was a bitch for anyone. There wasn't much room at the top—and all of those golden microphones were held by white men. Tyrell had the voice, the talent, the brains, but he had no room for error. Something like this could bury him.

It wasn't just unfair—it sucked balls. Goddamn Hank. That bastard had a *lot* to answer for.

Mariah took a deep, shuddering breath. "I can't believe they would send him to prison. If I told them—"

"It wouldn't matter. Until you turn seventeen, your opinion is irrelevant."

Mariah's face twisted with disgust. "Like I'm going to be so much smarter in six weeks."

"Oh, I don't know. Look how much you've learned in just one night."

Mariah dropped her face into her hands. "If he gets in trouble, everyone will hate me."

Yep. And Hank's life as he knew it would be finished. He was immature, thoughtless, and occasionally downright obnoxious, but the thought of him in prison for two years, branded as a pervert for life, made Shawnee ill. The mandatory sentence made no distinction between him and creepy uncles who liked to slip their hands up little girls' dresses.

But if he'd truly taken advantage of Mariah…

"Have you been drinking?" Shawnee asked abruptly.

Mariah's head snapped up. "What?"

"Did Hank give you a beer, a shot, anything?"

"No! He didn't even come to the concert. I met him outside and we snuck back here. We didn't even grab a Coke."

Shawnee breathed a sigh of relief. She didn't really think Hank would slip anything into a girl's drink and Mariah didn't smell like alcohol or act drugged, but it was good to have the possibility off the table. "Whose bright idea was the truck?"

"Mine." Mariah made a face. "Cole was over here with you, and everybody else was gone. We planned to slip out before Daddy came back from dinner, but he was early."

"How did he catch you?"

Mariah's pout deepened. "The window was open a crack. On the side toward Cole's rig, where everybody hangs out under the awning."

Oh dear Lord. Shawnee cringed, imagining what Tyrell might have overheard.

Mariah rolled her eyes and huffed. "It wasn't like that. Hank said we couldn't have sex because I'm too young. I told him I'm not a virgin. I had a boyfriend for, like, three years. But he still said no. We were just fooling around."

Shawnee heaved a sigh that drained the last of her energy. "Look, you want to show everyone how grown up you are? Tell your dad what you just told me—maybe minus the part about not being a virgin—and beg his forgiveness. Then buck up and take whatever punishment he dishes out."

Mariah's face went mulish. She pushed out her bottom lip—then sucked it back in and squared her shoulders. "Okay."

"Awesome." Shawnee massaged the ache in her forehead. "Let's get some sleep."

"What about Hank?"

Shawnee paused in the act of prying her heavier than usual ass off the seat. "You can't go near him."

Mariah grimaced, but nodded. "Will you at least tell me what the doctor says?"

"I can do that." Shawnee checked her phone, but there were no texts or missed calls. "They've barely had time to get to a hospital, and God knows how long the lines are at an ER in El Paso on a Saturday night. We won't know anything until morning."

And it wouldn't hurt Mariah to stew for a while. She damn sure wouldn't be the only one. Shawnee hauled herself up and toward her bed. "You can have the couch. And if you decide to get all weepy, put a pillow over your head. I don't want to hear it."

When Shawnee crawled out of her trailer the next morning, the clean-up crew was just beginning to work their way around the grounds, picking up cracked plastic beer cups and crumpled rodeo programs. Shawnee fed her horses, then kicked aside a broken string of red Mardi Gras beads as she shuffled to the office. She stopped in the open doorway, staring dumbly at a stranger in plain boy-cut jeans, a white sleeveless blouse, and red canvas Keds. Her face was scrubbed clean and a pair of delicate silver crosses swung from her ears, her hair pulled into a neat ponytail at the nape of her neck.

But she spoke in Analise's voice. "Concussion. Three loose teeth. Minor fracture of his jaw. He's probably having it wired up right about now."

Shawnee frowned. "You left him there alone?"

"No. His sister showed up at five o'clock this morning. Apparently Hank's brain came unscrambled enough to figure out he might be in deep shit, and he called her for help. When she showed up, we cut and ran." Analise made wide, scared eyes. "Cruz said he's happy to step in front of Master Assassin, but no way he was gettin' between that woman and Hank."

"Wise choice," Shawnee said. Her friend and former roommate was no one you wanted to mess with when she was on a tear. "So…you and Cruz?"

"He's a very centered person. I like his company."

The answer was delivered with such a dignified air, Shawnee couldn't even work up a smart-ass remark. Analise went back to coiling and stowing computer and printer cords.

Shawnee squeezed her eyes shut for a count of five, then opened them again, but the view didn't change. "Who are you supposed to be?"

Analise straightened and looked down at herself. "These are my emergency normal clothes. In case I have to, you know, talk to cops or something. I can fake it for a while."

Shawnee shook her head. "Well, knock it off. You're freakin' me out."

Analise smiled angelically and continued on about her work. "Cole said if he didn't see you first, text him when you're up."

Shawnee did and was instructed to come to the announcer's stand. Cole was waiting for her at the bottom of the steps. He looked like the Cole she'd thought she knew, what seemed like years ago, stiff through the shoulders and tight around the mouth. But he softened when he saw her.

"I need backup," he said, apologetic.

She pinched his butt. "I'll watch your backside any day, cowboy."

He smiled, ever so slightly, and dropped a quick kiss on her forehead. Then he turned to trudge up the stairs. As they stepped through the door, Tyrell latched a hard-sided equipment case, then looked up, haggard and hollow-eyed.

"How's Mariah?" he asked, a complicated mixture of concern and anger playing across his handsome face.

"Embarrassed," Shawnee said. "Mad. Sorry, even if she doesn't sound like she means it. Might help if you didn't look like you could chew glass."

"How am I supposed to look? She lied to me!" Tyrell

slammed bunched fists against his thighs, then winced and shook his swollen hand as he gazed out the open front of the crow's nest. "I have to take her home."

"Okay," Cole said.

"We can fly out today, then I'll drive down to meet you at the next rodeo." Tyrell flicked him a glance. "I need a day or two at home, but then I'll miss the timed event slack on Wednesday."

"We'll manage," Cole said.

"Ace can handle it easy enough." Tyrell stared back across the arena, where the flags above the grandstand hung limp in the breathless morning air. "I understand if you want to replace me at the rest of the rodeos."

"No," Cole said.

Tyrell's head jerked around, his dark eyes wary. "We could have caused serious trouble. If rumor gets around to the committee that the cops were here—"

"You're not the first. Won't be the last."

Tyrell flexed his bruised knuckles. "When will Hank be able to work?"

"Don't know yet. At the very least he'll have to pass the concussion protocol before we'll let him in the arena."

Tyrell nodded slowly. Then he blew out a long, thin stream of air. "And then I guess we'll see."

"You're not pressing charges?" Shawnee asked.

Tyrell's mouth tightened. "We all know how ugly it would get. Especially for Mariah."

Just like they all knew Hank didn't deserve to walk away, free and clear. Shawnee glanced at Cole. His eyes were bleak, his jaw clenched, as if he was in physical pain. She had a pretty good idea why, and wished there was some way she could make it hurt a little less.

But when had she ever been the kind to kiss anything better?

Tyrell looked at Shawnee and forced a sliver of a smile. "Thank you for last night. You were right…we needed a time-out. But I still have no idea what to say."

"Try 'I love you no matter what, but I swear to God, girl, if you don't start applyin' some common sense I might have to wring your neck.'" Shawnee hitched a shoulder at Tyrell's expression. "Worked for my granddaddy."

This time Tyrell's smile was a shade closer to normal. "I'll give it a try. She's still in your trailer?"

"I told her she was under house arrest until you came to get her."

Tyrell heaved a sigh so deep it sounded like it might turn him inside out, then shuffled out the door. Cole slumped onto one of the wooden stools, making it creak dangerously.

"So Hank just keeps on skatin' by?" Shawnee asked.

Cole lifted his gaze to hers. She studied his face for a long moment—the grooves around his mouth that hadn't been there a day earlier, the emptiness in his eyes.

"That's what I thought," she said softly.

She ran a hand down his arm and squeezed his fingers. Then she left him to come to grips with the only decision he could possibly make. At the bottom of the announcer's stand steps, she cut around the front of the truck backed up to the loading chute and collided with Ace as he jumped down from the cab. He had his battered duffel slung over one shoulder. A silver Lincoln pickup idled in the road, Cordelia at the wheel.

"Where are you off to?" Shawnee asked, more out of habit than any particular interest.

"Back to Texas," Ace declared. "My shoulder's almost good as new and Cordelia…well, she's quite a woman."

Shawnee gaped at him. "Didn't you hear what happened last night?"

"Yeah." He shook his head with a rueful grin. "Boys and girls. Always gonna be trouble."

"Tyrell is taking his daughter home. He won't be back in time to announce the slack. Cole is counting on you to cover for him."

Ace shrugged. "He'll work it out."

Don't do it. Don't even go there. You know how he gets…

But today she didn't have it in her to turn the other cheek.

"That's it? You mooch off of us for three weeks, then walk away when we need you?" Her voice had climbed to an embarrassing octave. She clenched her teeth and dragged it back down again. "Why am I even surprised? Like you've ever cared what anyone else needed."

His silver eyes glinted. *Danger! Danger!* "And you've got so much room to talk."

"Me? What have I ever—"

"You came out of that cancer thing just fine." He thumped a fist to his chest. "*I* lost everything."

"You threw it away!"

"I wouldn't have had to if you hadn't been such a baby." His lip curled in disgust. "Why should I sit around the hospital? Wasn't a damn thing I could do. But if I had the nerve to go to a roping, your mama pitched a fit."

"You didn't just go to a roping," Shawnee shot back. "You took off to California for over a month and left her to deal with everything."

"She had her parents. And you always liked your granddaddy better anyway. I couldn't take all the wailin' and moanin' anymore. So, yeah. I left. And when I tried to come back, you forced your mama to choose." He took a step toward her, his voice low and vicious. "*You* drove her over the edge. Now she's a basket case and the rest is all gone, thanks to *you*."

Shawnee staggered back a step, his hatred a visceral blow. She should have just kept her mouth shut. She knew better. But she was his *daughter*. How could he—

"Get out." Cole's voice sounded behind her, his words dense with threat. "Don't you ever come near her again."

"You can't tell me what—"

Cole took one heavy step down the stairs, fists like sledgehammers at his sides.

Ace hitched his duffel higher on his shoulder and backed away with one last venomous sneer. "You can have the fat bitch. I'll be happy to say I told you so when she wrecks your life too."

He swung around and strode to Cordelia's pickup. As they drove away, he slung an arm along the back of the seat and smiled at the woman as if his conversation with Shawnee was already forgotten. Cole's hands closed on her shoulders and turned her, gathering her tight against him.

Ace actually hated her. And she couldn't stop shaking.

"Do you need your meds?" Cole murmured, one palm stroking her back while the other hand cradled her head, pressing it into his shoulder.

She gathered her shattered thoughts and pieced together enough to take stock. Her heart was thudding, but her chest didn't feel like an alien creature was tearing her rib cage open from the inside. And her breath was choppy, broken by something perilously close to sobs, but she wasn't hyperventilating. She just needed a minute to regroup. To let Cole's warm bulk absorb the blood from the wounds inflicted by Ace's words.

All the more lethal because they were true.

Chapter 32

COLE HAD NEVER DREAMED HE WAS CAPABLE OF beating a man to death, but if he'd been close enough to reach Ace Pickett...

Instead, he nearly crushed Shawnee in a belated attempt to protect her from that...that...Christ, there wasn't even a word for him. She allowed it longer than he expected, but was already pushing away when a car rumbled to a stop in the space Ace's woman had vacated. Cole didn't recognize the silver Dodge Charger. The man who swung out of the passenger's side was another matter.

Cole blinked. "Joe?"

Shawnee spun away from him as the driver and backseat passenger also emerged, both tall, slender, and unmistakably Patterson bred.

"Mornin'," Joe Cassidy said.

"What—" Cole began, then didn't bother. He knew why they were here. He could even guess how, given Richard Patterson's fleet of three private aircraft.

Tori braced one arm on the driver's door and the other on the roof of the car as her gaze narrowed on Shawnee. "Was that Ace we met on the way in?"

"Yes." The word sizzled as Shawnee spit it out.

Cole breathed a sigh of relief. Mad was good. Infinitely better than what he'd seen on her face in that awful moment..."He was just leaving," Cole said. "For good."

Tori studied Shawnee for another long moment, then nodded. "About time."

"So what are you, the damage control team?" Shawnee asked.

"Something like that." Joe opened the back door on his side of the car, dragged out a gear bag, and held it up. "Rumor is you could use a bullfighter."

"But Violet—" Cole began.

Joe made a rueful face. "Booted me out the door. She says I'm driving her nuts with the hovering."

Maybe so. Or it might be the story they'd concocted so Cole didn't feel guilty for dragging Joe away. Or— more accurately—they'd sent him to clean up Cole's mess. Joe had celebrated his first wedding anniversary by presenting Jacobs Livestock with a check big enough to make him an equal partner. He had as much say in what happened here as Cole did.

But this was Cole's crew, dammit.

Slumped on his couch through what had remained of the night, Cole had considered every possible angle, every course of action, while desperately wishing it was Shawnee snuggled up against him instead of his dog. Katie was an excellent listener, but she wasn't much for feedback. Despite all of the excuses and justifications, he kept circling around to the same place. He couldn't even call it a decision. The proper word would be *consequences*.

The early morning call to his aunt and uncle was the hardest he'd ever made. The story sounded even uglier in the clear, clean light of day. Steve had been outraged, but he'd brushed off Cole's apologies—as if he hadn't completely failed to justify the trust they'd put in him. Still, Cole knew what his uncle had to be thinking.

If only Violet had been there.

They had been in complete agreement on what had to be done. Steve had offered to make the call to Violet, but Cole had declined. His crew. His responsibility. Of course, she'd already known. Word had passed along the chain from Richard Patterson to Tori to Violet. She'd said she was already working on recruiting a bullfighter to fill in for Hank.

She hadn't mentioned that she didn't intend to look further than the other side of her bed.

"I came along in case you needed any assistance on the legal front," Richard Patterson said, failing to look like an average guy despite jeans, boots, and a polo shirt. There was something about his posture. The haircut. The camera-ready smiles. A man couldn't scrape off a lifetime of polish in a couple of years.

"And I'm just nosy." Tori's blatantly curious stare slid from Shawnee to Cole. "All kinds of interesting things going on down here."

"Make yourself comfortable." Shawnee waved at the chairs clustered under Cole's awning. "I'll grab the sweet tea and cookies."

As they settled in, Cole gave the senator an apologetic look. "I'm sorry for dragging you down here."

Richard gave him one of those patented smiles. "I am more than happy to lend a hand after the hospitality your family has extended to me."

As if Easter dinner at the Jacobs ranch was a huge honor. The man must have piles of invitations—but possibly a shortage of true friends. Money and power had a way of isolating a person. Look at Tori—

Except Cole couldn't, because he was suddenly,

intensely aware that she knew what he and Shawnee had done in her trailer. On her couch. In her bed. He risked a quick glance. She smirked at him. His face flamed, and he dropped his gaze to his boots.

"Well, we sure do appreciate your help," he told her father.

Shawnee rescued him, returning from her rig with a jug of sweet tea and a Dr. Pepper for Tori. She passed around glasses, poured one for herself, then took a seat off to the side, as if she wasn't a part of the discussion. And Cole couldn't very well drag her over next to him where she belonged.

"I should have stopped this," he said. "I saw the two of them...I should have said something then."

"I told you not to worry about it," Shawnee reminded him. "I honestly thought even Hank was smarter than this."

Joe's face went hard with contempt. "And we thought he'd learned his lesson at Fort Worth. Those stitches and the two black eyes didn't come from a bull. He got the shit kicked out of him by a big-ass steer wrestler who didn't appreciated Hank foolin' around with his girlfriend. He was damn lucky he wasn't too beat up to finish the rodeo."

Tori came to attention. "That's why Wyatt refused to work with Hank the rest of this year?"

"It wasn't Wyatt," Joe said. "I wanted to can him right then and there. There are too many guys like Cruz who appreciate every opportunity...but Wyatt talked me into giving Hank another chance. And he insisted on playing the hard-ass so it didn't stir up trouble between Violet and Melanie. You know how she is about her brother."

Oh yeah. Everyone knew Melanie wasn't entirely rational when it came to Hank. As if it was her fault, and her responsibility to make up for all the fucks their parents hadn't given about her much younger brother. If Joe *had* fired Hank, and Melanie had been forced to choose sides...

Joe shook his head. "The only thing Hank is serious about is fighting bulls. And he's got what it takes to be one of the best—if he'd stop shooting himself in the foot outside the arena. Wyatt thought he could scare him straight. Kick his ass down a few notches and threaten to make sure he never worked another major rodeo if he didn't smarten up."

"Could Wyatt do that?" Shawnee asked.

"Without breaking a sweat," Tori said. "Not everybody likes Wyatt, but they respect him. He always brings his A game and puts it all out there every time. Throw in that pretty face and the way he can work a room? Sponsors and committees love him. A few whispers in the right ears about Hank being unreliable..."

"*Would* he do that?" Cole asked.

"No." Joe's answer was immediate and certain. "Wyatt is into lifting people up, not knocking them down. And why bother? Hank's doing a damn good job all on his own. But Wyatt's still gonna be pissed at himself. He's not used to being wrong."

The way they'd all been wrong. Too tolerant. Too forgiving. Too...hell. Cole didn't even know anymore. He could barely remember a time when Hank hadn't been underfoot. No, his parents hadn't been the greatest, but he'd had plenty of other perfectly good role models. Dozens of people who'd given him a hand along the way. A sister who'd slay dragons for him. Truth be told, Hank had run out of excuses a long time ago.

But how did you just turn your back on a human being?

Richard Patterson heaved a resigned sigh. "You have to let him go."

Cole saw agreement in the tight set of Joe's mouth. Heard it in the grim silence that fell over the group. The dog let out a dejected groan and plopped her chin glumly on her paws.

My thoughts exactly.

"I'll talk to him," Joe said.

"No." Cole said. "My crew. My job."

Surprised glances ricocheted around the circle. *Cole wants to do the talking?* His irritation swelled—with them, and with himself. Hank wasn't the only one who'd been dodging responsibility. It was time for both of them to grow up.

"Are you sure?" Joe said. "He's practically one of your family."

"It's your family, too. This isn't going to make things easy between Violet and Melanie." Cole brought the discussion to an end by looking at Tori. "Would you give Tyrell and Mariah a ride to the airport?"

"Sure."

He met Shawnee's gaze, not sure what to make of her expression. Was that concern? Or pride? "Can you gather up the crew for a meeting?" he asked her. "I have to talk to Joe."

"I'm on it."

Shawnee drained her glass and stood as Tyrell and Mariah came out of her trailer. Tori and Richard also rose. Introductions were made, then the four of them went off to gather luggage and load it in the Charger.

Shawnee poked at her phone. "I'm texting the Leses and Analise, and I'll go knock on Cruz's door. I'll tell them all to come to the office, where we won't be overheard."

"Thanks." Cole wanted to reach for her as she passed. Drag her into his trailer and bury himself in her until everything else went away. Unfortunately, his days of hiding when the going got tough were over. These were his people and, God help them, he was their leader.

But at least Shawnee would be watching his backside.

Tori caught Shawnee inside her trailer, rinsing sweet tea glasses. She shut the door, then folded her arms and leaned back against it. "You suck."

Shawnee raised her eyebrows. "Did you fly down here special to let me know?"

"Yes." Tori tipped the last few drops out of her Dr. Pepper can and tossed it into the trash. "Your dad has been mooching around here for three weeks, you've been jumping Cole, your gray horse damn near died, and I have to hear it all from Violet? What kind of friend are you?"

"Lousy. I told you from the start—I don't do the BFF thing. And my sex life is none of your business."

"Since when?" Tori's eyebrows arched, incredulous. "You're the damn poster child for too much information. And you had your nose stuck in the middle of everything when Delon and I were dating."

"Somebody had to. The two of you were manufacturing ways to screw it up."

"And now you owe me. What's going on between you and Cole?"

Shawnee forced her mouth into the smirk Tori would expect. "I sort of figured after being married twice you'd know about this stuff, but...boys have boy parts, and girls have girl parts, and when you rub them together—" She made an exploding motion with her fingers and a *kapow!* noise. "Magic!"

Tori gave her a dead-eyed stare. "What I saw when we drove up had nothing to do with sex."

Right. Tori would have to see that touching little moment. Shawnee yanked open a cupboard door to hide her face and took great care in stowing the glasses so they wouldn't rattle around on the road. "That was just Cole thinking he needs to play lord and protector."

Tori straightened, her gaze sharpening. "Did Ace say something to you?"

Only that I'm a walking wrecking ball. Which we all knew. Shawnee wrung the dishcloth tight between her hands. "He was his usual asshole self. I was an asshole back. Turns out he's better at it than I am. Cole thought"—and rightly so—"that I was upset, so he gave me a hug."

"Cole...gave you...a hug." Tori spoke in segments, like she had to process it bit by bit.

Shawnee hitched a shoulder. "He's the affectionate type."

"Cole," Tori repeated. "The guy didn't speak directly to me until three months after we met."

"Must not've had anything to say."

Tori angled around to look into Shawnee's face. "You're messing with me, right?"

"What do you think?" Shawnee asked, batting her eyes.

Tori growled, spun away, and flung herself on the couch. "You are such a pain in the ass."

"And this is why we don't have sleepovers and play Magic 8 Ball. How's your daddy getting along with his new horse?"

Tori glared at her for a beat, then gave up with an irritated huff. "Great. We went to the club roping in Canyon last week and he caught five out of six steers."

"Awesome. He must've been pumped."

Tori smiled. "Yeah. It was pretty cool."

Upon exiting the U.S. Senate, Tori's father had made learning to rope his first objective. After two years, his appearance at ropings in the Panhandle hardly caused a stir anymore, except among single women of a certain age, and most of them were too scared of Tori to do anything about it.

"Lord, I'm tired. Daddy called me right after he got off the phone with you." Tori let her head fall back against the couch cushions. "Was last night as scary as I'm imagining?"

"You have no idea." Shawnee still felt a little sick, remembering the screaming. The gun. Cole and Cruz putting themselves in the line of fire. "When your daddy gave me his cell phone number, I figured I'd only need it if I got drunk and disorderly on the wrong side of the border. I couldn't believe he jumped right in."

Tori studied her for a moment that stretched long enough to get uncomfortable. "That's what real friends are, you know. People who want to be there for you in the hard times. And tend to get irritated when you don't let them."

Yep, Tori was pissed. And it was only gonna get worse when she found out about New York. Shawnee opened her mouth, but before she could spill the beans, there was a familiar deep thud on the door.

Cole stuck his head in. "Everybody's over at the office. You ready?"

"Yeah." She wiped her hands on a dishtowel and glanced at Tori. "Wanna have lunch after we're done?"

Tori shook her head. "As long as we dragged the jet out of the hangar, Daddy figured we might as well fly on up to Ellensburg and watch Delon ride in the finals."

"Why ever wouldn't you?" Shawnee drawled. "It's only a couple thousand miles out of the way."

Tori stood and sauntered to the door, making deliberate eye contact with Shawnee as she passed. "We can finish this conversation when you bring me back my trailer."

"Yes, princess." Shawnee sketched a mocking curtsy.

Tori flipped her off. Now that was the kind of girl chat Shawnee appreciated.

Unlike the one they'd be having when she got home.

Chapter 33

TICK, TICK, TICK, TICK...

Even now, his palms damp and his heart pounding as he looked at the expectant faces looking back at him, Cole was intensely aware of every second that they weren't on the road, putting miles behind them. It was ten hours to the next rodeo in southern Utah. Every minute they delayed was a minute of rest lost for the stock.

But this was more important than his schedule, dammit.

What remained of Cole's crew were waiting in the confines of the rodeo offices—the Leses, Analise, and Cruz. Shawnee grabbed the chair closest to the door. Joe took a seat in the corner, leaving Cole alone at the front of the room, the focus of all those eyes. Waiting for him to say something. The sweat beaded along his hairline and in his armpits. He could feel his face stiffening to the point of cracking, like Play-Doh left out in the hot sun.

He met Shawnee's gaze. She lifted her pointy eyebrows as if to say, *Well?* But then she smiled, just a little, and nodded. *You can do this.*

He drew in a huge breath. The first words gushed out with it. "Mariah and her father have decided not to press charges. However..." Cole had to stop and take another breath. "A law was broken. Analise, Cruz, Shawnee... you were all witnesses. I won't ask any of you to commit a crime of omission by keeping quiet if your conscience tells you otherwise."

Chairs squeaked and feet shuffled as glances were exchanged.

"What does the senator say?" one of the Leses asked.

Cole searched through the phrases he'd memorized, trying to anticipate every question or concern. "He is comfortable with their choice."

Another lengthy silence. Then Analise. "Is Tyrell gone for good?"

"No. He'll meet us in Utah."

More silence. More shuffling. Then Cruz piped up. "What happens when Hank's ready to come back?"

Cole drew another deep breath, forcing himself to look from face to face, meeting every eye in the room. "Hank won't be coming back to work for Jacobs Livestock."

What air was left in the room disappeared in one giant inhalation. Cole braced himself for the outrage. Instead, there were only quiet sighs, slow nods, resigned shakes of the head. And, if he wasn't completely off base, a whisper of relief. Cole had offered up a punishment severe enough to soothe a guilty conscience, without ruining Hank's life.

Something like grief tore through Cole's chest. These people had considered Hank one of their own, jumped to his rescue despite his flaws. And now...even if they forgave him, none of them would ever quite feel the same about him.

And Hank would never understand how much he'd lost.

"So that's it?" Cruz asked, his near-black eyes impenetrable. "Tyrell stays. Hank goes."

"Yeah."

Cruz considered for a beat. "Okay," he said.

No one said another word, but the pact they had made might as well have been carved in stone. *We don't speak of this again*.

As they rose and scuffed out the door, Cole propped his elbows on the table, laced his fingers tight together, and stared at the creases in his knuckles. He heard Joe get up and leave and thought he was alone. Then a chair scraped on the dusty wood floor. Shawnee walked over, pulled another chair close to his, and wrapped her arms around him, ignoring Katie's low growl. They sat that way for a long time, the woman pressed against his shoulder, the dog against his leg. Again something tore inside Cole's chest, but this time it felt like a good kind of pain. Scar tissue ripping away, giving the soft, tender parts of his heart room to expand.

Shawnee kissed his temple, then stood. "I owed you one."

Three hours later, Melanie Brookman's white SUV whipped into the rodeo grounds and parked behind Cole's trailer. There was no mistaking the family resemblance. She had the same brown hair, worn long and straight, and the same lean, athletic body, which had made her the defensive player of the year in their high school basketball conference.

But unlike Hank, her brown eyes were sharp, her posture radiating *don't even try to mess with me*. A dozen years in the business world had carved away any softness from back when she and Violet had raised their fair share of hell. She didn't waste a meaningless smile on Cole or Joe when she climbed out of the car.

"I'm taking him home until he's fit to work again," she said abruptly.

Hank slouched out of the car, jerked a nod of greeting toward Joe, and mumbled something to his sister. Melanie shot him a quelling glare.

"Come on inside," Cole said, and led the way to the office.

He dragged over chairs for Melanie and Hank, then took a seat with Joe on the opposite side of the single long table. Melanie eyed them, head up, nostrils flared, like a horse that scented a threat. Hank slumped in his chair and stared at his knees.

There was no sense beating around the bush. "Hank won't be coming back."

"You're *firing* him?" Melanie came almost out of her chair. "He has a contract!"

"Which has a moral turpitude clause," Cole said. "You should know. You helped Violet write it."

"He hasn't been convicted of a crime," Melanie shot back. "You have no legal grounds for his dismissal."

Cole steeled himself against her fury. And worse, the bewildered hurt in Hank's eyes. "So sue us for breach of contract."

Melanie opened her mouth. Then she clamped it shut with an audible click of her teeth. Any such suit would require describing the circumstances under which Hank was let go.

"Tha's bullshit," Hank slurred, his confusion morphing into anger, with an edge of panic. "I been with you since I was a kid…"

And you still act like one. Cole shook his head, chest aching. "I don't want to do this, Hank, but you didn't leave me any choice."

"I'll call Steve—"

"We all agree," Joe broke in. "We warned you at Fort Worth. No more second chances."

Hank stared at him for a long moment. Then he stood and very deliberately kicked his chair over with a resounding crash. "Go to hell. I don' need any of you. I can make it jus' fine on my own."

Katie bolted to her feet and growled, low and menacing, as he stalked out the door. Cole put a hand on her head and pushed an envelope across the table. "Mariah left this for Hank. That's the last he'll hear from her. If he tries to contact her in any way, or so much as mentions her name online or to his friends, Tyrell will reconsider pressing charges."

Melanie snatched up the letter and stared down at it, her fingers flexing as if she wanted to rip it to shreds. When she spoke, her voice was low, her temper tightly reined. "You've made your point. He gets it now. Give him a few weeks to stew, then talk to him about next season. I promise…"

"We can't, Mel. Not after this. I'm sorry."

She sat, head bowed, for a long moment. Then she pushed out of the chair and turned to leave without a word.

"I hope he's right," Cole blurted.

She paused to glance at him, questioning.

"I hope he goes out and proves to everyone just how good he can be," Cole said.

Her lips pressed together and her eyes shimmered.

She jerked a quick nod, then turned and strode out the door.

Cole dropped his face into his hands, feeling as if he was going to be sick.

"That was impressive," Joe said.

Cole made a rude noise. "Me and my great people skills."

"Three years ago you would've hightailed it for the border if anyone suggested you should get up in front of the crew and talk."

"I sounded like an asshole."

Joe gave an impatient huff. "You left out all the bullshit. That's what they expect from you. It's what they needed. And they were ready to follow wherever you led. Like I said, impressive."

Cole leaned back in his chair and considered Joe. He'd changed too. He was…not softer, but less edgy. Less cocky, more confident. Year by year, more of Steve Jacobs's dignity seemed to rub off on him.

With any luck, Cole had absorbed a little too. He could always hope.

Joe blew out a gusty breath. "Holy hell, I need a beer."

"Follow me."

~~~

Shawnee was dozing on the couch when Melanie slammed into the trailer, scaring the bejeezus out of her.

Melanie punched the closet hard enough that Shawnee feared for her hand. "They fired him!"

"Yep."

Melanie turned on her, snarling. "You *knew*?"

"Yep. And for the record, I agree completely."

"Three days ago he saved your ass!"

Shawnee pushed up on her elbows, still groggy. "And last night I kept him from being hauled away in handcuffs. I'd say we're even."

"He did not assault that girl."

Shawnee swung her feet to the floor and scrubbed both hands through her hair. "She's sixteen, Melanie."

"Almost seventeen." Melanie folded her arms, hip and chin jutting. "And she was all for it. What was he supposed to do?"

"Say no."

"Oh, right." Melanie snorted in derision. "How many guys are gonna turn down a girl who looks like that?"

"The ones with a brain?" Shawnee stood up, planted both hands on Melanie's shoulders, and gave her a shake. "He was one wrong word away from prison, Mel. *One word.*"

The anger leached out of Melanie's face, along with some of the color. She knocked away Shawnee's hands. "I can't even think about it."

"Well, Hank had better, or eventually he's going to screw something up beyond repair."

Temper sparked in Melanie's eyes again. "You mean like Wyatt blackballing him?"

"He won't—"

"Bullshit. Hank told me about Fort Worth. *One more screw-up,* Wyatt said. We both know he'll do it if he decides it's for the *greater good*, the self-righteous bastard." Melanie's lip curled, her eyes going dark with loathing. "You watch. Even if Hank doesn't set so much as a toe out of line from here on out, every time he tries to take a step up, he'll get kicked back down again. Wyatt will make sure of it."

Shawnee wanted to argue. Tell Melanie the truth about what Joe had confessed. But it wasn't her place to shift the blame to Joe, and she sure as hell didn't want to be the one who blew up a friendship between Violet and Melanie that had lasted over three decades.

"Did Hank tell you everything that happened last night?" she demanded instead. A shiver of leftover fear raced across her skin. "I watched Cole step in front of a loaded gun to protect Tyrell. I'm gonna keep seeing that in my dreams for a long, *long* time."

They stared at each other for several breaths. Then Melanie let out a sour *hah*. "I'll be damned. You're actually sweet on him."

"I am not!" Shawnee recoiled as if Melanie had taken a swing at her. She regrouped and squared her shoulders. "I respect him. And I hate seeing him beat himself up for something he couldn't have stopped, short of firing Hank two weeks ago."

Melanie had the nerve to laugh outright. "Oh my *God*! You are! You're in love."

"Don't be stupid!"

"Hah! I think that's my line, sugar pie." Melanie did a little shimmy and sang, "Shawnee's in lo-ove, Shawnee's in lo-ove…"

Panic scorched Shawnee's veins, leaving behind a scent like burned rubber. She whirled and stomped over to grab a cookie from the bag she'd left out to send with Cole and Joe. "Don't you have a brother to babysit?"

Melanie went quiet. Then she heaved a huge, tired sigh. "What am I going to do with him?"

"Haul him to the ranch and dump him off?"

"I can't. Daddy threw him out."

Shawnee almost dropped her cookie. "When?"

"At the beginning of the summer." Melanie wandered over to the couch, plunked down, and dropped her face into her hands. "You know Daddy. The ranch is everything, and it's his way or the highway. They fought every time Hank went on the road instead of staying home to do *real* work."

"What about your mom?"

"Same old song, one-millionth verse. All about how she never intended to get stuck being a ranch wife, so she can understand why Hank doesn't want to spend his whole life staring at the ass end of a bunch of cows. You'd think a woman who was so dead set on being a nurse would've had a better grasp of birth control. Not that I'm complaining, obviously." Melanie twisted the turquoise ring on her right hand. "The three of them had a huge blowout back in May, when Hank showed them his schedule for the summer. Daddy told him if he left, don't bother to come back. So Hank said fine and walked out. Ma left right behind him. And this time, it's for good."

Oh hell. Shawnee grabbed another cookie and walked over to sit beside her. "So you're stuck with him."

"Yep."

"Geezus." She held out the cookie. "You want a shot of whiskey instead?"

Melanie laughed, a harsh, broken sound. "You don't know the half of it. On the drive up here from El Paso, I was yelling at him and…" Her face twisted up at the memory. "He cried, Shawnee. *Cried*. It was all Mariah this, Mariah that…I swear, he really thinks he's in love with her."

Son of a bitch. How was Shawnee supposed to stay pissed at him? Stupid Hank was one thing. But heartbroken, homeless, and unemployed Hank…

"I am the goddess of marketing. I can write copy that will make gnarly old ranchers line up to buy tons of calf pellets from an upstart company like Westwind Feeds, but I can't persuade my own brother that he's so much better than this." Melanie blew out a shaky breath and for a horrible moment Shawnee thought she might cry, too. "I didn't raise him to be this way."

Shawnee scowled. "*You* shouldn't have had to raise him. He had two parents."

"So did you, and where would you have been without your grandparents? At least Ace had the decency to leave, instead of hanging around making everyone miserable."

Now, there was what Tori would call some positive spin. "You think Hank would've learned some sense if your parents had split?"

"Lord help him." Melanie scrunched her eyes shut against the thought. "How awful is it that I can't imagine the poor kid surviving alone with either of them? Daddy would've ignored him except when he needed help with the cows, then spent the whole time hollering at Hank for doing it wrong. And Ma would've sulked nonstop about how she's never had a chance to have a life of her own, let Hank run wild, then made excuses for him when he got in trouble." She heaved a disgusted sigh. "Which is pretty much how it worked when they were together, except with a shitload of snide remarks and cheap shots thrown in. And I just ran off and left him there."

"You went to college, not the Foreign Legion."

"And it was *wonderful*. But I should have…"

"What? Taken him with you?" Shawnee had to resist the urge to grab Melanie and shake her again, but sarcasm was less likely to get her punched in the chops. "You think he's screwed up now, imagine an eight-year-old living in that crappy apartment with the two of us. Talk about seeing some things that would scar him for life. Just that one night, with the llamas and the rented hot tub…"

For an instant, humor sparked in Melanie's eyes at the memory. Then she sighed. "I could have gone home more."

"You *deserved* your own life, Mel." If she'd been a different person, Shawnee would've patted Melanie's knee or even put an arm around her. Lord knew she looked like she could use it, and Shawnee had recently gained an appreciation for the restorative powers of a good hug. "Besides, he spent as much time with Violet's parents as he did with yours. That should've done something to set him right."

Melanie broke her cookie in half. "So I told myself. And kept on telling myself after I graduated and got a town job and steered clear of the ranch as much as I could."

"Nobody could blame you."

"*I* do." Melanie's head jerked up, her expression fierce. "I blame me for not staying as close to my brother as possible."

"Well, look on the bright side. You're gonna get to see plenty of him now."

Melanie huffed a laugh, scattering cookie crumbs along with her frustration. "Are you sure you couldn't talk Cole into taking him back?"

"You know he can't. And I won't try, even for you."
Even as repayment for the way Melanie and Violet had
stood by her, held her together after Gramps died. "It's
gonna take Cole months to get over this—if he ever does."

Melanie stopped nibbling her cookie to eye Shawnee.
"Can you even hear yourself when you talk about him?
You are in it so deep. With *Cole*."

Shawnee wanted to shout, sneer, anything to convince them both that Melanie was wrong. But she just
stuffed a cookie in her mouth. There was no sense trying
to argue with the woman once she got something in that
thick skull of hers.

Not to mention, the last thing Shawnee wanted was to
look any closer at her feelings for Cole.

Chapter 34

FOR THE SECOND WEEK IN A ROW, JACOBS LIVESTOCK left pieces of itself behind as the rigs rolled out onto the highway. Even with Joe to ride shotgun in Tyrell's place, Cole felt the empty spaces. They gnawed inside him, nibbling down his nerves like mice chewing on electrical wires, threatening to short circuit his system.

So he talked.

About the stock. Violet. What a great season Delon was having and what were his chances of repeating as the world champ? Any and every subject he and Joe had in common. At first, Joe was startled. Then wary. Then he seemed to recognize why Cole was suddenly as chatty as a sugared-up third grader and played along, asking questions, nudging out stories from when they were all kids.

Violet was going to wring his neck for some of those.

So why hadn't Cole told them before? Even with Joe, with his family and closest friends, all the people he would trust with his life let alone his pride, he'd fallen into the habit of keeping one finger on the mute button. Letting go felt like relaxing a muscle that had been clenched for years.

Four hours down the road, the exhaustion slammed into Cole. He turned the wheel over to Joe, tilted back the passenger seat, and fell into a fitful half sleep, peppered with dreams and memories that twisted together and apart and together again, exposing more internal wiring, overcharged and throwing sparks.

He woke with a lurch to the flash and boom of lightning.

"Just a thunderstorm." Joe slowed the rig as the first fat drops smacked the windshield, building to a deluge. "No severe weather warnings."

But it had caught Cole completely off guard. In the turmoil of the morning, he had forgotten to check the weather along their route. Somehow, that was the last straw. The final failure that threatened to tip him over the edge. He dug his fingers into the armrest, struggling to swallow the ball of emotion that choked off his airway. It hurt enough to make his eyes water.

"It'll be okay," Joe said, his gaze fixed on the rain-slick road. "The worst is over."

He could've been talking about the storm, which was already slackening off to a steady drizzle, but Cole thought there was more to the assurance. He only nodded as he checked the weather app on his phone. A slow-moving green blotch stretched over the Texas border and into Utah, covering the town where they planned to stop for the night.

As predicted, there was still a steady patter at one a.m. when they pulled into the rodeo grounds where Violet had arranged for them to unload and bed down. Normally, the sweet, clean smell of it would've lifted Cole's spirits. Tonight every drop was a tiny dart against his skin. One more complication he'd failed to anticipate.

But the horses threw up their heads and snorted, frolicking like kids in a sprinkler. The bulls lumbered out of the trucks and drew in deep breaths, grunting their appreciation.

"They won't melt," Shawnee said, noticing Cole's expression as she passed by leading Roy and Sooner to their pens.

But they wouldn't rest. Not like usual.

Raindrops continued to slant across the headlights of the trucks and glisten on bright-yellow slickers as bodies strode in and out of darkness, hauling hay bales and checking water tanks. It was close to two a.m. before everything was fed and settled and the humans began straggling toward their various bunks. Cole watched Shawnee dump grain into buckets for her horses, give them a final pat, and start for her trailer, where Analise was already sleeping. And Cole had Joe rooming with him. But he wanted Shawnee, warm and soft and solid.

A hand clapped on his shoulder. "I'm out," Joe said. "See you in the morning."

Cole jerked his gaze away from Shawnee. "What?"

"I'm bunking with Cruz." Joe grinned at Cole's confusion. "Give me some credit, buddy."

Cole didn't know what to say, so he just nodded. Then he all but sprinted to catch Shawnee. He grabbed her arm to swing her around to face him. "Stay with me," he blurted.

She hesitated. For the first time he could recall, Shawnee looked indecisive. As if she truly wasn't sure if it was a good idea. Or she was trying to figure out how to tell him to get lost. Apprehension coiled through his chest. Somehow, he'd done it again. Said or done something wrong without even knowing.

Then her jaw set and her eyes narrowed. "It's just sex," she said, so forcefully he blinked.

"Okay." He would've said anything right then if it got Shawnee into his bed.

"Okay." She reached for the door handle. "I'll grab my toothbrush and be right over."

The knot inside him let go in a hot rush of relief. "I'll wait here."

When she came out of the trailer carrying nothing but her toothbrush, his thoughts disintegrated. They walked the ten yards to his trailer in silence. He opened the door and held it for her, then moved the dog bed to the tack room and ordered a disgruntled Katie inside. Her malevolent glare promised he'd pay. He made a mental note to keep his clothes picked up and his closets locked for the next year, minimum.

Back inside the living quarters, Shawnee was in the bathroom, brushing her teeth. With his toothpaste. He shivered a little at that small intimacy. First his bed. Then his toothpaste. Then…

She came out of the bathroom, walked straight up to him, and pulled him down into a kiss that was cool and minty and hot enough to sear his synapses. "Don't take your time," she said, and peeled her shirt off as she walked toward his bed, her bra following close behind.

He practically ripped his clothes off in the rush to wash up and get to her.

But when he stepped out of the bathroom, he stopped dead. So did his heart, for a full beat. She was on her belly, on his bed, naked. Her hair cascaded over her shoulders, a few long curls trailing down to nestle in the curve of her lower back, fingering the dimples above her butt. In the soft yellow glow from the light above the sink, the parts of her skin that hadn't been touched by the sun glowed like a pearl in contrast to her golden-brown arms and legs.

Lord, he was a sucker for a woman with a farmer's tan.

Music began to play, low and mellow. Shawnee set her phone aside, then propped her head on one hand to tilt an eyebrow at him. "So are you just gonna stand there and stare?"

"Yes." No. He had to touch her.

She smiled. It broadened into a grin as he stumbled toward her, trying to kick off his underwear without stopping. Even the insistent tap of raindrops on the metal roof of the trailer receded into the distance as she rolled onto her back and exposed every inch of gorgeous nakedness to his greedy eyes.

He forced himself to slow down and slide onto the bed with a little finesse, instead of falling on her like a starving coyote. Then he couldn't decide where to put his hands first. Breasts were the obvious choice, but it seemed like he should work his way up to that, so he started with her shoulders, shaping the muscles with his palms as he traced her tan line with his thumbs. He bent his head to bury his face in all that fabulous hair. It was damp, smelling of rain and shampoo and wet horses.

"So soft," he whispered, burrowing in deeper so the curls tickled his face and throat. "I like when you don't put stuff in it."

She snorted. "My dragged-through-the-bushes-backward look?"

"You look fine. Besides, I didn't fall for you 'cuz you're pretty."

She jerked away from him, her jaw dropping. "Excuse me?"

"I didn't mean…it isn't that you're not…" He screwed up his face, cursing silently as he scrambled for the right words. "I like you better without all that stuff."

She stared at him for several excruciating seconds. Then she huffed out a laugh, shaking her head. "It's a miracle you've survived this long."

"I know." And he kissed her, because it was a whole lot safer than talking.

And much, *much* more fun.

He turned his hands loose, letting them roam where they wanted, exploring all those lush curves and valleys while she did the same, until they were both gasping and groaning. She plucked the condom from his fumbling fingers and took her time doing the honors—payback for the "not 'cuz you're pretty" crack, she said—then shoved him onto his back, straddled his hips, and took him in one smooth, heart-stopping move. But instead of riding him, she lowered herself so she was stretched out full length, her weight pressing him down into the mattress so they were connected, chest to chest, thigh to thigh.

Closer than he'd ever been to another human being.

When she began to move, it was an intensely intimate slide of body against body, breath tangled with breath, his hands stroking her back and butt in time with the small, exquisitely slow movements that generated enough friction to heat his blood to boiling and blow his mind into the stratosphere, taking Shawnee along with him.

On the way to the bathroom to dispose of the condom,

he tossed her one of his T-shirts and grabbed his underwear. When he crawled into bed beside her, she pressed a lazy kiss to his shoulder before rolling away and pulling up the sheet. "If you're done poking me, Gus, I'm gonna sleep now."

He laughed at the *Lonesome Dove* reference, then settled back and listened, cataloging her going to sleep noises—soft rustles and breaths and the quiet creak of the mattress as she got comfortable. Up here in the nose of the trailer, with the ceiling only three feet above his head, the steady *tap tap tap* of raindrops became more and more of an irritant, as if each struck his own skin. He imagined the horses and bulls hunched against the rain. More hours of rest lost...

Nothing you can do about it. He tried to concentrate on the sound of Shawnee's breathing instead, waiting...waiting...

When she hadn't stirred for a full two minutes, he eased his hand over until his pinky finger found skin. A tiny point of contact, like a ground wire. More minutes passed as he focused his entire being on that one warm spot. It was almost enough.

"Oh, for God's sake!" He jerked as Shawnee flung onto her back. "Roll over."

Cole tugged his arm from underneath her. "Why?"

"Let it be known that I only cuddle in emergencies. And being the inside spoon makes me claustrophobic, so roll over."

He did. She wrapped one arm around him, spread her palm over his heart, and burrowed in close, a miracle of warm, silky flesh curled around him. Once again, she literally had his back.

"Listen to the bass," she ordered.

He focused on the music still spilling from her phone, picking out the bass line and following it like a winding trail into a shady summer forest. Cole smiled as her breath tickled the nape of his neck. He was nearly asleep when he realized he'd told Shawnee that he had fallen for her.

Oh shit.

Then another, deeper warmth blossomed in his chest. He'd told her…and she was still here.

Chapter 35

TEN DAYS LATER, SHAWNEE LOUNGED IN A CHAIR under her awning and watched Cole's dog belly-crawl from underneath the trailer toward one of her flip-flops, intentions obvious. Despite his best efforts to keep everything locked up and out of reach, Cole had lost two more pairs of underwear and a pillow to the green-eyed monster. He was still picking feathers out of stray corners of his living quarters. Shawnee sort of admired the mutt. You had to give it to a woman who took her revenge seriously.

But there were limits. "Touch that shoe, dog, and you've have your last taste of meatloaf until you get home."

Katie froze, her snout a bare inch from the toe of the nearest flip-flop. Her eyes swiveled toward Shawnee, narrowing as she debated whether the threat was serious and worth the trade-off. Then she heaved an infuriated sigh and crept backward, out of sight.

"Hard to figure why you don't date more," Joe told Cole, who reclined in a lounger in one of those soft, clingy T-shirts, eyes half-closed, as relaxed as Shawnee had ever seen him with his clothes on.

She'd been seeing a lot of Cole looking very relaxed lately.

I didn't fall for you…

Shawnee fought off a skitter of panic, mixed with

something she wasn't *even* going to put a name to. In any other situation, Cole's words would have sent her running far and fast. But he hadn't repeated them and besides, even if she assumed *fall for you* wasn't just a figure of speech, where was she gonna go? She didn't welch on a promise, so she was stuck with Jacobs Livestock for the duration. Breaking it off with Cole before the end of the season would only make life miserable for everyone.

And if he had meant it the way it sounded—well, it was already too late, wasn't it? Indulging herself for two short weeks wouldn't do any more damage. Especially when the indulgence was so, so delicious.

A low growl sounded from under the trailer, as if Katie could smell the pheromones. Shawnee grinned and lolled her head to the side.

Joe was sprawled on the chunk of outdoor carpet, loafing through a series of stretches, his skin glistening with sweat from his morning run. As usual, he'd tied a bandana around his head to contain his shaggy hair. This one was acid green, paired with a purple T-shirt and faded red shorts. Color coordination didn't rank high on Joe's priority list. As he spread his legs wide and reached for his toes, pulling miles of long, sleek muscles taut, Shawnee decided it was good that drooling over a friend's husband was some kind of mortal sin. Otherwise, she might need a bib.

His presence had more than filled whatever awkward gap Hank might've left. Joe had been trapped at home for most of the summer. His slightly guilt-ridden delight at his sudden freedom and the unapologetic joy he took in every aspect of every rodeo performance was contagious. Watching him from inside the arena was a rare treat. Damn, that man could *move*. Cruz was in heaven, working side-by-side with one of his idols—and more than holding his own.

Of course, he'd been trained by the best. Cruz was the product of one of the bullfighting clinics that occupied Wyatt Darrington's free time these days. Like the youth horse camps at the Patterson ranch, there was no fee to attend Wyatt's clinics. Unlike the ranch, though, Wyatt didn't offer a week of hugs and feel-goods. He recruited his students from the El Paso projects, the poverty-stricken Navajo Nation, the poorest pockets of Appalachia, even the urban ghettos of LA and Chicago. They were wary-eyed predators who had existed on little more than guts for most of their lives. Wyatt tore them down, and if their toughness went deeper than bravado, rebuilt them into budding rodeo superheroes.

Cruz had been a star pupil.

Despite Cole's anxiety, the rodeo in Utah had been a resounding success. The stock had been energized by the rain and the cool desert evenings, and the committee was elated when they realized they were getting Joe Cassidy, future Pro Rodeo Hall of Fame inductee, for the price of Hank.

They'd rolled out of town with a contract for next year practically in hand. This week found them in the southern Colorado foothills, another respite from the Texas heat and humidity. Cole had grilled steaks for the Tuesday crew dinner while Joe and Tyrell took to the outdoor basketball court at the adjacent park to play a full combat one-on-one, Joe making up for Tyrell's superior talent with shameless cheap shots. They'd invited

Cruz and Cole to join them, but both had declined on the grounds of having an allergy to asphalt burns.

Currently, Cruz was holed up in his camper working. Analise was in the office, preparing tonight's stock draw sheets and uploading last night's scores to the Pro Rodeo website. The Leses and Tyrell wouldn't wander in from the motel for a while yet. Shawnee, Cole, and Joe were recharging after two hours of signing autographs at the local western store. Yes, even Shawnee—and wasn't that a kick in the ass. There'd been a whole line of women from eight to eighty who thought her scribble was worth waiting for since all that viral online video crap.

She used to wonder how Violet could choose to produce rodeos over the adrenaline blast of competition. Now she understood a little too well. Each hour flowed into the next, slowly gathering momentum from the laid-back routine of the mornings to the hectic, hoof- and heart-pounding unpredictability of the performances—all spiced with anticipation of the nights with Cole.

Yeah, she could live like this.

Shawnee tensed again, then forced herself to relax before Cole noticed. For a guy who could be so oblivious, he was incredibly tuned in to every nuance of her body language. Like she was a bucking horse or bull. *His*.

No. She couldn't be. Not long-term. But the last rodeo of the season was rushing toward them. How could it already be the third week of September? She wasn't ready for it to end. For Cole to end. But she had to cut him loose, as planned. And thank the Lord for New York, forcing her to make a clean break. With their proximity—only an hour from her place outside

Amarillo to his near Earnest—it would be far too easy to open the door when he inevitably came knocking.

Besides, there wasn't nearly enough roping in her life these days. Her gaze focused on Roy, dozing in his pen with his bottom lip hanging slack. The craving curled like a fist and punched her in the gut. Since Mariah's departure, Cole had been coming out in the mornings to tow the dummy steer around for her on either Salty or Hammer, but it wasn't the same as roping live steers.

As competing.

Her heart thumped hard against her sternum, a prisoner banging on the bars of the cell. Ace Pickett wasn't the only addict in the family, and Shawnee was in dire need of a fix. She scowled at Cole, suddenly annoyed at how much he reminded her of one of his precious bulls, a massive pile of man-flesh all smug and content. All he needed was a tail to switch at the flies.

"Do you ever do anything just for fun?" she demanded.

His sleepy gaze traveled down the length of her and back up again, and he raised his eyebrows.

"Besides me," she snapped.

Joe choked, coughed, and sat up, holding his back. "Shit. I think I just pulled something." If so, it didn't seem to bother him as he sprang to his feet. "It's bad enough, being cut off for months because of the baby. I don't need to breathe your lust fumes."

Cole, now fully awake and wary, eyed Shawnee as Joe ambled away. "Did I do something wrong?"

Dammit! She hated how he was so quick to assume that if there was a problem, he must be lacking in some way. She upped the heat in her scowl. "I don't like to brag, but I have been called the Queen of both Obnoxious and Impossible. Her Highness does not appreciate you implying that I require a man to bring out the worst in me."

He grinned, just as she'd intended. She hadn't meant to feel this good about it, though.

"So…fun?" she repeated. "Got any hobbies? Guilty pleasures? Interesting vices?"

He gave her another long, slow appraisal that raised her body temperature several degrees. "All of the above."

Oh, the hell with it. If he was going to be that way… She jumped out of her chair, grabbed his wrist, and hauled him into her trailer.

Saturday morning, Cole showed up as usual to help Shawnee work her horses. He found Joe sitting in one of the rodeo committee's snazzy four-seater ATVs, the dummy steer hooked to its hitch. Why…

"Don't blame me, I'm just following orders," Joe said.

Shawnee looked up from tightening Roy's cinch and flashed Cole one of those toothy smiles that made his warning antennae quiver. "Oh good. You brought Salty."

"What's up?"

"There's a team roping tomorrow morning over at the saddle club arena. I need a partner. You need a bad habit. Time to create the monster."

She handed Cole a brand-new rope. "Here. You can figure out what weight and stiffness suits you later, but this'll work for starters."

"But I don't…" Compete. Not since his brother—his built-in partner and moral support—had died. When

Shawnee pressed the rope into his hands, the memories slammed into him like an avalanche. Xander, grinning, joking, flipping him a pile of shit even as his eyes said, *Hey, you got this, bro.*

For a moment, it was all Cole could do to breathe as he clawed his way to the surface. Xander had understood his debilitating nerves. His abject fear of failing his partner. In public. A simple miss that anyone else shrugged off was, for Cole, one more reason for folks to shake their heads in something posing as sympathy. *Ah, well, at least he's trying. And his brother is so patient, bless his heart.*

Xander never got upset, even though Cole's miscues as a header meant his brother, as the heeler, didn't get a chance to throw his rope. Team roping was a lark to Xander. Just a throwaway event to kill time until the bull riding.

To ultracompetitive Shawnee, it was life.

"I've never roped steers with anyone but my brother," he said, the words choppy and uneven. "I haven't…not in years…"

"Then it's time you got started again." Shawnee braced her hands on her hips, impatient. "Just pretend you're chasing this thing down the midway."

But…

But. Shawnee was and would always be a roper first and everything else second. Forced to pick one or the other, she would not choose Jacobs Livestock. So she was right. He had to suck it up, if he wanted any chance at persuading her to stick around.

He dragged air into reluctant lungs, his hands clumsy as he built a loop and took a few tentative swings. The new rope was stiff and waxy, with the peculiar aroma of all tack stores—a potent mix of leather, rosin, and dreams.

He coiled the rope and hooked it over his elbow as he tightened Salty's cinches. Then he swung aboard and faced Shawnee. "Tell me what to do, Coach."

Chapter 36

As Shawnee piloted her rig across town the next morning, it occurred to her that she'd never been alone in a vehicle with Cole. Despite everything they'd done to and with each other—and she did mean *everything*—she felt weirdly awkward, like they were headed to a drive-in for their first date. Possibly because Cole was so tense she could feel it rolling off him in ultrasonic waves.

And if you wanted to distract Cole, you asked about his stock. "Joe said they rode one of your bulls to win first at the Extreme Bulls event in Albuquerque."

"Yep."

Okay. This was gonna take a little more prodding. "One of Dirt Eater's sons?"

"Nope." But despite his nerves, he couldn't leave it at that. "It was Texas Smackdown. He's out of a daughter of Carrot Top, crossed with one of Chad Berger's best sires. They don't make the whistle on him very often."

"It must be amazing, seeing your stock compete at that level." Especially after decades of clinging to the very bottom rung of professional rodeo, producing the smallest, least profitable shows. In the past three years, with some savvy financial scheming on Violet's part and the connections and influence Joe had brought to the table, they were moving up fast. "I bet you wish you could be there to see it."

Cole shook his head. "I get my fill at the National Finals and a few of the early winter rodeos. Besides, my aunt and uncle have earned it. They almost lost it all after my parents died. It took years just to get back to even."

Shawnee had never thought of the Jacobs family tragedy in financial terms, but of course it would have had an impact. One thing they hadn't had to worry about when her grandfather died. Between her illness and his, there was nothing left to lose.

She couldn't even afford to fall in love.

The ache was sharper than usual, when she was sitting this close to what might have been—in another, better life. But she could live with the pain of letting him go. She refused to die knowing she'd tarnished the bright, shiny future he and his family had fought so hard to rebuild.

And on that cheery note…

"I'd rather be the pickup man," he blurted. When she stared at him, uncomprehending, he added, "At one of those big rodeos. Or the National Finals."

Okay. Wow. That was news. As far as Shawnee knew, Cole had never mentioned the possibility to anyone in his family.

"Have you…applied or whatever?" She didn't even know how you got those jobs.

"No."

"Why not? You're good enough."

"Maybe." He spread his hands on his thighs and studied them. "I, um, don't always work well with others."

She couldn't argue. On the other hand…

"You've managed to work with me. That must be

worth something. And we've being doing our damnedest to put together an Internet highlight reel this summer.
I think you should go for it."

He hunched his shoulders, Cole-speak for *ain't gonna
happen*. Dumb-ass. Shawnee made a mental note to talk
to Joe. He'd know what it took to get on the short list
for those jobs.

And if she had a hand in making this dream come true
for Cole, it might help soothe her conscience for what
she was going to do to him when she left.

She slowed and turned into the driveway of the
saddle club. The parking lot was already crowded and
a good number of riders circled the arena, warming up.
Her pulse did an eager shimmy of anticipation.

Cole gulped audibly. "I thought this was just some
little local deal."

"It is." Shawnee wheeled into an empty slot and shut
off the engine. "Looks like there are a lot of locals."

Cole trailed behind her like a bewildered child as she
strolled over to the entry office/concession stand. He
got a Coke while she gave the secretary their names.
They both paid their entry fees. As they stepped aside
to make way for the next in line, Cole froze, staring at
the poster that described the roping, taped to the table
for quick reference.

"It's progressive?" The horror in his voice suggested
she'd invited him to a ritual sacrifice.

"Almost all of the ropings are nowadays," she said,
ignoring the curious glances from the others in the line
to enter.

"If I miss the first steer, we're done. You won't even
get to rope."

He sounded so desperate, on the verge of panic. "Well, then, don't miss," she said, and walked away.

If only it were that simple. When the position draw was posted, she and Cole were the fifty-seventh team out of ninety-eight, and with each successive bang of the chute gate, he got a little paler, sat a little more rigid in his saddle, until Shawnee was afraid if she tapped his arm he'd keel over.

As team number fifty-one rode into the roping boxes, she nudged Roy closer until her knee bumped Cole's. His eyes were glazed and he was barely breathing. She crooked a finger. When he leaned down within reach, she clenched her fist in the front of his shirt and slapped a long, hot kiss on him. By the time she let go, he had regained some of his color.

"Just a reminder," she said. "What you get later for being a sport."

"Even if I miss?"

"Especially if you miss. Then you'll owe me. Big. And I already know how I plan to collect."

His smile was a pitiful thing, but at least he seemed to be taking in air again.

And he didn't miss. The loop wasn't a thing of beauty, but it fit. Cole dallied up and went left, and Shawnee was able to snag both hind feet. Roy buried his rear end and the big steer hit the end hard enough to jerk two feet of rope through her gloved hand. Like a junkie snorting a line, her blood sang at the hot slide of nylon against her palm and the smell of burning rubber from her saddle horn.

God, she loved this game.

Her grin was made of pure joy. Cole's held the

petrified relief of a man who'd taken a single step into a minefield and hadn't blown up...yet.

While they waited for their next run, Shawnee wallowed in the singular aroma of horses and ropes and dirt, Roy's quiet strength beneath her, the laughter and banter of the other ropers filling the air. Not a particularly friendly bunch. Or Cole was scaring them away with his Grim Reaper face. Shawnee stuck by him, rather than wandering around to chat up strangers. Funny, how much easier it was to make friends after they saw her double-hock a steer or two.

Yeah, kiss this, boys.

Almost half of the teams dropped out in the first round, so their turn came up quicker the second time. As the team ahead of them tracked their steer to the catch pen, Shawnee stuck out her chest and flipped back one side of her button-down shirt to flash Cole some cleavage. "Don't forget. Catch now, or pay later."

He caught. Farther down the arena than Shawnee would have preferred, but her own loop was quick and deadly, so their time was still respectable. The two runs combined put them eleventh out of the top twenty that got to rope a third and final steer. Not bad. And as the saying went, a bad day roping was better than the best day doing anything else. Shawnee was buzzing with adrenaline. Cole looked like he was going to puke.

Shawnee put her hand on his thigh and squeezed. "Dude. It's a fifty-dollar jackpot. We're not roping to win the world."

He just shook his head and rode over to the corner where he sat alone, muttering to himself.

By the time they backed into the roping boxes for

their final steer, he'd gone from pale to green. He nodded his head, took three swings, and threw a balled-up mess of a loop that swatted the steer on the side of the head and fell on the ground. Cole dropped his head, reined Salty up, and turned to ride straight out the gate, his rope trailing behind, without even glancing at Shawnee. He was already off his horse and jerking at the cinches when she caught up with him at the trailer.

"Cole—"

"Don't try to tell me it doesn't matter." He wadded up the rope and slung it in the general direction of the tack room. "I've heard Tori talk. You rope to win, not just show up."

Shawnee paused, knowing she needed to tread carefully. Not exactly at the top of her skill set. She listened instead—to the times being announced while Cole yanked his saddle off and slammed it onto the rack so hard it almost went through the wall. Finally, she said, "You did rope to win."

Cole made a noise packed so full of disgust it practically turned the air purple.

"Quit your tantruming and pay attention."

"I am not—"

"Oh please. You're two seconds away from throwing yourself on the ground and holding your breath until you turn blue." Shawnee pointed at the nearest loudspeaker, now droning out the final results of the roping. "Listen to the placings."

Cole scowled, but listened, then punched a frustrated fist into the other palm. "If I'd caught, we would've won third or fourth."

"Assuming I caught two feet."

He glared at her. "You never miss."

She laughed outright. "If only. Then I'd be a legend in something other than my own mind." She hitched her thumbs in his belt loops and dragged him close, wishing she had a bucket to stand on so she could glare straight into those stony blue eyes. She gave him a shake instead. "You threw to win. Gave it your best shot. *That's* what matters. I know how hard this was for you, and I really appreciate it. If you hadn't gutted it out, I wouldn't have been able to rope at all."

He shook his head, jaw set, rejecting every word.

Shawnee sighed. "How long do you intend to mope about this?"

"Forever."

She laughed again, then realized he wasn't joking.

"I can list every steer I ever missed for Xander at a rodeo," he said, his voice flat. "And every free throw in basketball in high school. This is why I don't play team games. I don't forget anything."

She had to blink a few times to take it in. "What about the good runs? The shots you made? Do you remember those?"

"Well…yeah."

"But you focus on the mistakes."

"I can't help—"

She wanted to call bullshit—would've if it had been anyone else—but Cole's brain didn't work like other brains, so maybe he couldn't stop himself from obsessing. Either way, he'd known this day would be torture and he'd come with her anyway. Her heart did a complicated, slightly terrifying whirl and swoop. This man. This strange, wonderful, maddening man.

What the hell was she going to do with him?

She shied away from the question and kissed his chin instead. "You realize this leaves me no choice."

"Except?" he asked, worry puckering his brows.

"I'll just have to blow your mind so hard tonight you can't even remember your name, let alone some stupid team roping."

He had to grin at that.

And the next morning, when she strolled into the rodeo arena, she found Joe once again behind the wheel of the ATV and Cole on Salty, looking grim but determined.

"Your sentence as my partner has been served," she said.

Cole got busy building the perfect loop. "There could be another roping next week. Or…after."

Her heart felt as if it stopped—one second, two, three—while she stared at him stupidly. Was he insane? He'd suffered through every minute of the roping, and had admitted he would continue to suffer indefinitely from the aftereffects. No reasonable human being would put himself through that again. And again. And again. As many times as she asked.

But this wasn't a reasonable man. This was Cole. And he was talking about *after*.

I didn't fall for you because you're pretty.

It was possibly the most romantic thing a man had ever said—at least as far as she was concerned. Cole didn't care about the surface. He had seen her sweaty, dusty, covered in horse puke, blood, and manure, an emotional disaster. He'd even had to deal with *Ace*. And he kept coming after her anyway.

What woman didn't dream of a man who loved her from the inside out?

Love. Shawnee clamped down on her quivering heart. She had to be the strong one here. Realistic. Nothing had changed. She would have to walk away, the way she always had before. Because—dammit—she probably did love the big galoot, and he deserved so much more.

"You don't want to do this," she said, jerking her head toward the roping dummy, but thinking of that *after*.

His face went stony, but his eyes...God, the sheer determination in his eyes was going to kill her. "Yes, I do."

One more week. Seven days. Then she would have to tell him why he was wrong. Why *she* was wrong. She could make a list. He liked lists.

He wouldn't like hers.

But she deserved something, too. Even if it was only a lousy week of pretending she could be the woman that a man—*this* man—could want for all of his afters.

"Okay. Let's rope." She turned to flip the reins over Roy's head, pausing to blink away the prickling heat in her eyes. "Just remember, I warned you."

As if that was going to do either of them any good.

Chapter 37

COLE LEANED AGAINST THE HOOD OF HIS PICKUP AT A desolate municipal airport and watched a sleek twin engine Cessna execute a butter-smooth landing and taxi toward him. Joe had flown home as soon as the previous rodeo ended. Now Wyatt was flying him back for the Thursday performance of their last summer rodeo.

Unlike the old days, the end of the regular season didn't mean they would be parked at the ranch until after the first of the year. Jacobs horses and bulls had been selected for no less than four big invitational rodeos in the next two months and at least a dozen head were a shoe-in for the National Finals in December. They'd come a very long way, and Violet and Joe weren't close to satisfied.

But standing here, nearly at the end of his sentence as sole custodian of this branch of Jacobs Livestock, Cole realized he no longer dreaded the idea of constant change. He'd shown everyone he could handle it. Himself most of all.

Before the plane came to a full stop, Cole saw a flurry of activity in the cabin. The instant the props went still, the door flew open and a small body leapt out and hit the pavement running.

"Beni!" Cole crouched and opened his arms.

Violet's son barreled into him with enough force to almost bowl him over. He got a nanosecond of full body contact and a whiff of boy scent before Beni remembered he was ten now, and too cool for hugs.

He wriggled loose and punched Cole in the arm, instead. "Hey, dude."

"Dude?" Cole's eyebrows shot up at the skater drawl.

"He has discovered the *Teenage Mutant Ninja Turtles*," Joe said, with a mix of amusement and exasperation.

Beni scowled. "Mama banned them for a whole month after I told Mrs. Domingo to *chillax* when she yelled at me for running in the hall."

Cole stood, smothering a grin as he imagined the cheery little principal trying to scold Beni while keeping a straight face. The kid had been a constant challenge and source of entertainment at Earnest Elementary since the first day he was dragged through the front door. "Why aren't you in school?"

"They said I could afford to take a couple of days off."

Translation: Beni was so far ahead of his class the teachers struggled to keep him occupied. And the whole staff could probably use a break.

Cole mussed his inky black hair. "How come we get stuck with you?"

Joe tossed their bags into the back of the pickup. His duffel had a *Justin Boots* logo. Joe never bought anything that he might get free from a sponsor. Beni's hard-sided carry-on was covered in cartoon stickers in various stages of disintegration, charting his course from the *PAW Patrol* through *Phineas and Ferb* to his current *Turtle* obsession.

"Delon's riding in Omaha this weekend," Joe said, in answer to Cole's question. "Tori has a continuing education seminar in Seattle, and Lily says she has her hands full just trying to keep Violet in line."

"And I haven't seen you for, like, months! Or Katie."
Beni dropped to his knees to fling his arms around
the dog. She gritted her teeth and tolerated the attack.
Beni was on his feet again in an instant, dancing circles
around Cole and tugging at his sleeve. "I brought my
Jacobs Livestock shirt. Can I help the rodeo queens
chase steers and stuff out of the arena?"

"We'll have to check with the committee." But Cole
already knew the answer. Beni had inherited his father's
striking Navajo good looks and his irresistible smile.
Like Delon, he knew how to use them.

Wyatt had made his usual circle around the plane,
doing a quick visual inspection. Now he strolled over to
join them, walking without any sign of a limp, a major
accomplishment this late in the season. This summer's
limited schedule appeared to agree with him as much as
it did Joe. Today he looked like an endorsement for silver
spoons, wearing pale-green shorts, a matching plaid sport
shirt, and canvas sneakers with no socks and a price tag
that would no doubt send Cole into cardiac arrest.

He and Cole exchanged a quick, hard handshake and
shoulder slaps. "You're looking pretty pleased with life,
considering. I figured you'd have a few bald spots, or
gray hair at least."

Cole ran a hand over his head. "Not for lack of trying."

But the past two weeks had been as good as any he'd
spent on the rodeo circuit. Better. He roped every morning with Shawnee, relaxing enough to enjoy himself
when there was no competition looming over his head.
He loved watching the way she worked with her horses.
How Sooner improved day by day.

Every evening they were in the arena, galloping

through the barely controlled chaos. And every night...
he stuffed his hands in his pockets and fought off a grin.
Yep. It had been a really good two weeks.

He dragged his mind back to the present and found
Wyatt watching him in that intense, off-putting way, as
if his laser-blue gaze could carve a hole in Cole's skull
and see his thoughts. If so, Wyatt was getting an eyeful.
Heat rose under Cole's skin at the idea of anyone view-
ing that particular slide show.

"So...who are my bullfighters going to be next year?"
he asked.

Wyatt cocked his head, eyebrows climbing. "I
expected more resistance."

"Doesn't do me any good," Cole said. "I'm surprised
you let Joe have these rodeos instead of dumping another
one of your teacher's pets on us."

"He was gonna," Beni piped up. "But Mommy said
Joe better get out of the house because if he didn't quit
makin' a fuss every time she got up to pee, he was gonna
be the one who needed bed rest."

Joe scowled. "I caught her cleaning the toilet. And
folding towels."

"Shame on her," Cole said dryly.

"You've changed over the summer," Wyatt said, still
eyeing Cole closely.

"I've been practicing my coping skills." Whether he
wanted to or not. "Besides, the only bullfighter *you've*
ever sent that caused any trouble was Joe, and we got
him lined out pretty quick."

Wyatt laughed, but under the surface the wheels were
spinning. He seemed to approve of whatever he saw,
though Cole got the distinct impression he was also

amused. Or just happy he had guaranteed jobs for at least two of his prize pupils. You could never tell with Wyatt. Tori claimed he always operated on at least three levels of intention. Cole wasn't even sure what that meant.

"Got any prospects for your next pickup man?" Wyatt asked.

Joe shot him a look even Cole could interpret. *Shut. Up.* "We're waiting until we all get home to discuss next year."

"Violet will be back by March, at the latest," Cole said, letting his inflection turn it into a question.

"The doctor said even if she has to have a C-section, she'll be able to ride by February," Joe agreed. But there was something in his voice…and for once it wasn't Cole dodging eye contact.

Then it hit him.

Violet wasn't coming back. Not as a pickup man. He should have seen it coming—the business end of things had been running her ragged before she tossed a new baby into the mix. But the promise that he only had to survive this one season alone had been his lifeline, and he'd clung to it like a barnacle. Until recently.

He tamped down another grin, keeping his face blank. "If she's got too much on her plate, Shawnee might be willing to stay on."

Something flashed between Joe and Wyatt, too quick and subtle for Cole to catch. "Maybe," Joe agreed, a few beats too late.

They all shuffled around, trying to kick dust over the awkward moment, but as they waved Wyatt off on his way to Omaha and climbed into the pickup, Cole couldn't help fretting at Joe's lack of enthusiasm.

Because they didn't want to keep Shawnee—and why the hell not?—or didn't think they could?

Didn't think *Cole* could.

Back at the rodeo grounds, she was lounging in the shade of her awning, looking round and lush in a tank top and shorts as she waited for Cole to come back so they could run downtown and buy groceries for the last crew dinner of the season.

When Beni ejected from the backseat, she tipped her sunglasses down to scowl at him. "Oh geezus. What did we do to deserve this?"

Beni stuck his tongue out. Shawnee returned the gesture, once again making that little brown-haired girl dance through Cole's head, bursting with mischief. He let out a breath and smiled at Shawnee. She smiled back, making his blood go hot. See? He wasn't crazy. She loved being a pickup man. And there was a possibility, judging by the way he caught her watching him sometimes, that she might love Cole, too.

Stranger things had happened, right?

"I'm here to work," Beni declared. "I'm gonna help clear the arena during the timed events."

Shawnee's brows peaked. "Are you, now? I suppose you could use a good cow horse, then. And Roy *is* just standing around bored."

"Your buckskin?" Beni's eyes went round, his voice reverent. He'd been begging Violet for a horse like Roy since the first time he'd laid eyes on the line-back dun, with his golden coat and jet-black mane.

"If you promise not to teach him any bad habits."

"No, ma'am!" Beni jittered in place, then shot off toward the horse pens. "I gotta go tell him!"

"I'm sure he'll be thrilled," Shawnee drawled. But she couldn't completely squelch her smile.

"Thanks," Joe said.

She shrugged. "Like I said, Roy's bored."

And Shawnee was a lot more generous than she liked to let on. Cole sauntered over and kissed her on the top of the head. She swatted him. He grinned.

Tomorrow night, after the last performance of this last rodeo on her contract, he'd pop the question. *Will you stay? Be my partner indefinitely?* He had his speech memorized, and now he could argue that they needed her to replace Violet long-term. She had to say yes, he'd tell her. Who else could put up with him?

That would make her laugh. He knew better than to get mushy, or even hint at love or marriage or kids this early in the game. But they were good together in the arena. Why break up a great team?

Logic was his secret weapon. And her hidden weakness.

For all that she mocked his schedule, Shawnee liked routines, and she had a strict personal code of conduct, even if it didn't always line up with what polite society dictated. Yes, she was explosive and confrontational and occasionally obscene, but never random. After all these weeks, Cole could anticipate almost without fail what would set her off. Like him, she had zero tolerance for fools and incompetence. While he retreated behind his shell, Shawnee blew up, a volcano of blistering sarcasm.

But pity the fools who stood in either of their paths.

So he'd keep his fantasies to himself and appeal to her practical side. If he could buy enough time, he

could keep just being there until she couldn't imagine
life without him. He'd sketched it out, how they could
arrange the schedule so she had plenty of chances to
go roping between and during rodeos, and he would
find a way to conquer his nerves and be the partner she
deserved whenever she needed him.

His gut clenched in anticipation. Tomorrow night. He
had it all planned. As soon as the rodeo was over, he'd
go knock on her door with her favorite pizza and her
favorite beer and show her all the reasons staying with
Jacobs Livestock made perfect sense.

Chapter 38

COLE DROPPED A BUNCH OF KALE INTO THE SHOPPING cart, wrinkling his nose. "No wonder those things you drink look so disgusting."

"But that's where I get my superhuman sex drive." She cocked an eyebrow at him. "You should try it."

He snorted like one of his stud horses. "I'm keepin' up just fine, thanks."

Yes. Yes, he was. The memory of just how well gave her a hot flash, even standing in the chilly produce aisle. She'd been playing a dangerous game of house with him—sleeping, shopping, eating dinner together every evening like a real couple. Inviting Joe—and now Beni—to share their meals should have made it less intimate. Instead, she had drawn Cole's family circle more tightly around her.

And it was a frighteningly comfortable fit.

Talk was easy—of horses and bulls, the best and worst rides of the night before, how the coming night's cowboys would match up with the stock they'd drawn. There were friendly bets on which bareback rider would have the high score, how many jumps past the end of the gate before Master Assassin drilled the poor fool who'd drawn him.

They argued about scores, and whether a former world champion had been gifted a few points because the shine off that gold buckle got in the judges' eyes. Lately, Cole had started paying attention to the team roping, asking Shawnee's opinion of the contestants, their horses, how the headers handled the steers to give their heeler the best shot. His obvious effort to learn her event was touching…and scary.

She tried to tell herself this was just his compulsive side rearing its head. She'd thrown out a challenge and he was incapable of letting it go until he had mastered it to his satisfaction. Hell, maybe she *had* created a monster. He might be hooked on team roping for life.

Or he might be hooked on her.

Her heart gave a sharp little blip, an annoying habit it had developed lately. Probably lack of sleep and some kind of hormonal imbalance from excess sexual stimulation.

Cole paused in the midst of contemplating watermelons to glance over at her, a thoughtful pleat between his brows. "Is that why you cook your own meals? Because it's healthier?"

"We're having fried chicken," she pointed out.

"In olive oil. With greens. You eat a lot of vegetables and drink those smoothie things. Is it because of the cancer?"

Leave it to Cole to stomp right to the point, no dancing around. She picked through the cartons of strawberries. "If I make it myself, I know what's in my food."

And she did try to keep the processed crap to a minimum—as if she could reconstruct her DNA by avoiding Twinkies. But she liked to cook, and who knew? Maybe she could stall the inevitable with a few extra antioxidants.

"That's what Aunt Iris says, too." Cole thumped a melon with his knuckle, weighed it in his hands, then hefted it into the cart. "At least you're not on some crazy diet."

"For my health…or my weight?" she asked dangerously.

Cole went still, holding four ears of corn in each big hand. After a long, pregnant pause, he sighed. "Nothing I say right now is going to save me, is it?"

"Depends. What are you thinking?"

He clasped the corn to his chest like a shield. "That starving yourself would be dumb. Skinny wouldn't suit you. Or me."

The practiced, scathing retort congealed into a lump in her throat. "It wasn't my best look," she quipped, without thinking.

"You used to be…" Then comprehension dawned. "When you were sick?"

She forced a mocking smile. "I was practically a supermodel. Not an ounce of fat on me."

The chubby thighs and round face she'd cursed since she'd been old enough to be teased had melted away, leaving nothing but bone and pasty skin. And now, for her, thin would never be beautiful or sexy. In her mind, knobby wrists and razor-sharp hip bones would always equal sickness. Other people might look at her now and see a fat girl. *She* saw every meal that hadn't tasted like copper going down, then turned around and come right back up. Healthy flesh that covered the grotesque skeleton she had become as a result—and probably would be again.

Until then, she was damn well gonna eat.

She thought she'd kept the morbid thoughts off her face, but Cole stepped over and wrapped his arms around her, still holding the stupid corn. She considered resisting on principle, but he felt too damn good. He made *her* feel good. Quiet. Not weaker, or pitiful, just less…raw. She couldn't help rubbing her cheek against his chest, that killer combination of baby-soft cotton and hard muscle. "You may be the only cowboy in Texas who isn't a starch addict."

His voice rumbled under her ear. "It chafes. Anything that rubs or scratches drives me nuts. When I buy new clothes, the first thing I do is cut off all the tags and run them through the washing machine a dozen times to soften them up."

That explained why the Jacobs Livestock shirts were silky, instead of the usual stiffly pressed cotton. She mustered her willpower and pushed him away. "Unless you're planning to do me right here on the apple cart, we should keep moving."

He grinned as he handed her the corn, and she lost her breath for a moment while her heart did that blipping thing again. Definitely dangerous, playing house with this man. It made her mind wander down garden paths and past picket fences. Made her wish…

Her phone rang. Her mother. Again. When they'd just talked a couple of days ago. And that had been a weird conversation, peppered with more than the usual uncomfortable pauses. Alarms jangled in Shawnee's head. She shoved the grocery list at Cole and gestured for him to go on without her.

When he had rounded the end of the aisle, she answered, bracing herself for the latest family disaster. "Hey, Ma. Is something wrong?"

"No! I just…I hope I'm not bothering you. Is this a bad time?"

Shawnee glanced over at an old lady who was poking through the bananas. "No. This is fine. What's up?"

"I was just wondering...well, hoping...I mean, you're done with the rodeos this weekend, and I know your schedule is pretty tight, but..."

Spit it out, Ma. "I have a little extra time." She glanced around to be sure Cole hadn't wandered back into earshot, but lowered her voice anyway. "I plan to swing by for a visit on my way to New York."

"Oh! That's great."

"And..."

"Nothing. I've missed you, and you're going so far away."

Shawnee fingered the silky tassel of one of the ears of corn, not reassured by her mother's bright voice. "I couldn't leave without seeing you and Gran."

"Well, good. We'll have dinner, and you can...um, see all the cousins. And stuff."

"Sure. That'll be great."

But Shawnee's stomach jittered uneasily as they said goodbye. Her mother was wound up. And that rarely meant good news.

As soon as the groceries were stowed in her trailer and Cole had gone off to find Joe and do boss man stuff, Shawnee snatched up her phone and dialed her grandmother's number.

"What's going on with Ma?" she demanded, skipping straight past the *how are you*s? "She keeps calling me and saying nothing, but I can tell there's something."

Gran laughed. "She's trying to work up the nerve to tell you that she's seeing someone."

"Seeing...a...*man*?" Shawnee collapsed onto the couch, taken out at the knees. Her mother. *Dating*.

"She wants you to meet him."

"Wait. This is *serious*? Like, bring home to meet the daughter serious?"

Her grandmother laughed again, the low, musical sound that had carried them all through the worst of everything. She had always found the humor or flat-out ridiculousness in any situation. One of the best lessons she'd ever taught Shawnee. "First she had to bring him home to meet her mother. And I approve. He's a good person, and he makes her…steadier. You know?"

Shawnee closed her eyes and thought of that moment in the grocery store, Cole's arms strong around her. Yes. She knew.

"That's…wow. I don't know what to say."

"Congratulations will suffice." It was more of an order than a suggestion. "It's way past time she started living instead of just biding her time, waiting to die. She deserves to have a man who loves her right." There was a weighty pause. "So do you."

"Gran—"

"I know." Her tone was the verbal equivalent of throwing up her hands. "I'm not meddling. Just saying."

Every one of the uncountable times before, the conversation had ended there. But today the ever-present question would not be muted, even if what came out wasn't exactly what she wanted to ask. "Are you…happy?"

"More often than I'm not," Gran said. "And I figure that's better than a lot of people. I'm not saying I don't have sad times. You don't love a man for forty-seven years without feeling like you've lost a part of yourself when he's gone, but I've got family and friends all around me. I have a daughter who is one of the sweetest souls I've ever known, and a granddaughter who kicks ass."

Shawnee choked on a laugh. "I get it from you."

"We're a tough bunch, Shawnee girl. If you find a man who's your match, grab him. They're thin on the ground."

"It's a big risk, taking me on."

"Have you checked the divorce rate lately?" her grandmother asked dryly. "Fifty-fifty, at best."

"I'm more like drawing to an inside straight."

Gran laughed softly. "Maybe. But you never let anyone stick around long enough to ante up. A man should get to decide for himself if he's up for it. And the thing about long odds…when you do win, the payoff is huge."

After she hung up, Shawnee just sat and stared blankly at the clock on the opposite wall. She'd have to start dinner soon. Fried chicken and all the fixin's. Cole would wander back this way to shuck corn and slice strawberries for the shortcake. She could count on him. He was the kind of man a woman could always count on. But how could he say the same for her? Next week, next year—the boom could come down at any time. And her precarious health probably wasn't even the deal breaker.

Cole could be a father, or he could be with her. He couldn't have both.

But what if he chose her? Fear and elation and a whole raft of emotions she could barely identify raged in her chest at the prospect. Cole was already close enough to decide whether she was worth what he'd have to give up. Who was she to make that choice for him? And really, how much worse could it be if he walked away, compared to never knowing what he might have done if she'd given him a chance?

Tonight. After the rodeo. She would tell him everything.

And then...she'd have to find a way to deal with the consequences, one way or the other.

Chapter 39

THAT NIGHT, COLE GOT CHOKED UP DURING THE national anthem.

He sat in the middle of the arena at the end of a row of horses—dignitaries and personnel introduced during the grand entry—his cowboy hat pressed to his heart, with Shawnee on one side of him and Beni on the other. The soaring notes of the anthem floated up and away, into the azure sky, and as the rodeo queen loped around the end of the arena, the setting sun caught the rippling American flag and set it aglow.

Cole's throat knotted so tight it nearly brought tears to his eyes. *This*. Exactly this. The whole day, beginning to end, had been perfect. An amazing woman, good food, a great kid, and a grandstand full of people here to watch a rodeo produced by *his* crew.

And this was the end. Last night. Last rodeo. The season would make its official exit with the last bull that left the arena.

He glanced over at Shawnee. Instead of the usual smirk, she flashed a quick, tilted smile, then her gaze immediately dropped to her hand on Salty's reins. Yeah, she felt it, too. The bittersweet tangle of endings and beginnings. This season might be over, but for the two of them there could be another. And another. And another. Anyone who'd grown up with Ace Pickett was bound to be head-shy, but eventually she would realize how much sense they made together.

He let his gaze slide over to Beni, straight and proud in the saddle, dressed in the Jacobs Livestock uniform right down to miniature blue and white chaps. Cole's throat tightened another notch. Give it ten years and that could be his little brown-haired girl, her chin in the air as she mouthed the words to "The Star-Spangled Banner." Lord knows, any child of Shawnee's would insist on being in the middle of everything.

Cole grinned at the image, then bowed his head as Tyrell recited the Cowboy's Prayer in a voice that sounded as if God himself were speaking.

"…help us to live our lives in such a manner that when we make that last inevitable ride to the country up there, where the grass grows lush, green, and stirrup high and the water runs cool and clear, You will take us by the hand and tell us our entry fees are paid."

There was a moment of silence as the final words echoed in the still evening air. Then, with a whoop and a holler, the flag bearers spurred their horses into a gallop and led the riders from the arena. Only Cole and Shawnee stayed put. He no longer had to check that she was in the right position for each horse. She knew them all as well as he did.

Now he looked over because he liked seeing her there.

They hadn't even bucked the first horse and her hair was already a mess, springing free of the barrette to coil in little hooks around her face, and she was jawing with the cowboys on the back of the chutes as they waited for the first bareback rider to wedge his gloved hand into the rigging.

"Hey, Cody, you gonna spur one to the whistle so I can actually pick you up for a change?"

The cowboy in question rolled his eyes. "I get bucked off one time…and you'll probably drop me on my head, anyway."

"Just aimin' for the one body part I know you can't break," Shawnee shot back.

Cole chuckled, then did a double take. Six weeks ago, he would've been irritated half to death. Now he just sat back and smiled at how none of them could get the best of her. Damn. There might be hope for his sense of humor yet.

"You gonna tell *her* how her butt looks in those chaps, Joe?" one of the cowboys yelled.

Joe paused in the midst of adjusting a flank strap to grin and shake his head. He'd learned that lesson the hard way with Violet.

"How 'bout you meet me out back and you can kiss it?" Shawnee yelled in return.

All of the cowboys and a sizable portion of the crowd busted up laughing. The moment fixed in Cole's brain, like an image in one of those old Polaroid cameras. Shawnee—defined. Bold, brash, and bigger than life. Around them, the air hummed with potential. Significance. This was one of those nights. A time you'd remember, crystal clear, twenty years from now, when you were tipping back a cold one with a few good friends. Or one special woman.

Remember? That was the night…

Then the bareback rider scooted up on his rigging, cocked his free arm and nodded, and there was no more time to think. Thunder Bay took two long, lunging jumps, then swooped left so hard his hooves skidded in the dirt. Cole sucked in a breath as the horse dropped onto his left shoulder, jacking the cowboy up and over the rigging. The horse slid, flailed, then regained his balance. The cowboy wasn't so lucky. The stumble had thrown him off the left side of the horse, his weight clamping his hand around the rigging. He fought to keep his feet under him while the bronc lunged and kicked.

"Go!" Cole shouted.

Shawnee was already two strides ahead of him, her loop sailing through the air to settle neatly around Thunder Bay's neck. She dallied up short, leaving only a few feet of rope between Salty and the bronc, and reined in hard. The bronc grunted and threw its head, but Shawnee turned in a tight circle to stay out of range of his lashing front hooves as Cole tripped the flank strap. Then he leaned across and grabbed the cowboy by the back of his protective vest, hauling him up high enough to release the bind on his glove. His hand came free and he dropped to his knees in the dirt.

Shawnee kicked up and herded the bronc safely away, toward the catch pen. Cole followed. Behind them, Cruz and Joe had sprinted out to help the cowboy. They hoisted him up with a hand under each elbow, then he waved them off and stumbled to the chutes under his own steam.

The crowd roared. Drama over. No casualties.

As Thunder Bay ducked into the exit gate, Shawnee tossed the tail of her rope in the air and let the bronc take it with him to the stripping chute. She swung close to the chutes to grab a replacement from one of the Leses, then took up her position for the next ride. No big deal. Just a day in the life. Cruz slapped her thigh as he passed. Joe offered a fist bump.

Cole gave her a brisk, approving nod.

But as they rode side-by-side out of the arena and around the back of the chutes to Cole's trailer, he leaned over, snagged an arm around her shoulders, and planted a big, smacking kiss on her cheek. "You are amazing."

"Ew," Beni said, as he passed going the other direction, to chase team roping and steer wrestling stock out of the arena.

Shawnee...blushed? "Stop sexually harassing the help. People are gonna talk."

"Let 'em," Cole said, and kissed her again.

The rest of the performance was a highlight reel filmed in high definition—image after image etched into Cole's brain—until that final, inevitable eight-second whistle blew. Cole wasn't ready for it to be over. Not quite yet. Instead of making a beeline for his trailer, he crossed his arms over the saddle horn and took it all in.

Fans jostled toward the exits, clutching the hands of sticky, tired children. The bright-yellow running lights of the pickups and horse trailers shone as they rolled out of the parking lot and away, one more year of hopes and dreams either achieved or dashed on the cold, hard rocks of the rodeo trail. Behind the chutes, cowboys hitched bronc saddles or gear bags over shoulders thrown back in triumph or slumped in defeat.

Shawnee reined her horse up next to his and mimicked his posture. "Well. I guess that's that. But don't expect me to sing about it."

Cole gave her a blank look, his brain too busy

screaming, *Now! Ask her now, when she gave you the perfect opening*.

"It isn't over 'til..." She made a gesture toward herself.

"I don't..."

She rolled her eyes. "Forget it. You already killed the punch line."

Oh. Now he got it. He frowned. "You're not fat."

"Bless your heart." She patted his arm. "At least you didn't say, 'You're no lady.'"

"I would never—oh, you're joking again." Geezus. This was bad. Even for him. It was the nerves, tying him into knots. And now he'd started doubting himself. Wondering why a funny, sarcastic woman like Shawnee would ever choose a man who literally couldn't take a joke.

Before he could fight off the attack of insecurity, Beni trotted over to join them. "Thank you for letting me ride your horse. He's awesome."

Shawnee smiled. "You're welcome. I think so, too."

"You're almost as cool as my mommy. Or Tori, if you had your own jet. And Uncle Cole likes kissing you." He heaved a disappointed sigh. "I wish you could have babies, so you could get married and I could ride Roy all the time."

Shawnee sucked in a breath that was like a spear through Cole's gut.

"What are you talking about?" he demanded. "Of course she can have babies."

Beni shrunk from Cole's sharp words. "But Mommy said she had an operation—"

Cole turned on Shawnee, icy shock radiating from the

point of impact and frosting his words. "What does he mean? What kind of operation?"

"A hysterectomy," she said flatly. "My second year of college, when Violet and I were roommates."

"A hyst—" He couldn't even force out the rest of the word, as the icy burn crawled up into his chest, sending needle-sharp spikes into his heart.

Her gaze remained level, her voice stony. "I had a cyst that destroyed my right ovary, so I told them to go ahead and take the left one while they were at it."

Just. . . *take* it. Like it was a hangnail. A minor inconvenience. Even as a part of his mind warned that he was being irrational, that he had no right, that she'd tried to tell him and he'd chosen not to listen, he heard himself saying, "You just decided, *That's it. I'm never having kids*? You didn't stop to consider that someday you might meet someone who wanted a family?"

"I considered a lot of things." She bared her teeth, snarling back at him. "Like how after all the chemo and crap, my baby-making odds were in the crapper with two ovaries. And how I should probably *consider* minimizing the number of body parts that might try to kill me someday. And that I shouldn't pass these lousy genes down to some poor kid, anyway. And if you're wondering about these..." She hefted one boob in her palm. "Yes, I've *considered* getting rid of them, too, given the chances it's gonna happen anyway. But I'm afraid the scar tissue would screw up my roping. Because yeah, I'm that obsessed. Just like my old man. So *consider* yourself lucky that you dodged this bullet."

Cole and Beni sat in stunned silence as she kicked Salty up and trotted out the gate and into the shadows beyond the arena lights. Cole was vaguely aware that he should follow and say…or do…or…something. But he was shaking. Tremors that started deep, deep in his core, the fissures radiating through his soul. That picture he'd been carrying around in his head—the little girl with Shawnee's grin and her wild hair—curled up like an old, fragile newspaper clipping and crumbled into dust. The shock was so intense it was as if a real person had died.

"I didn't mean to make her mad. I heard Mama and Aunt Lily talking…" Beni sniffed, tears welling in his eyes. "Mama keeps telling me I shouldn't repeat everything the grown-ups say. I have to tell Shawnee I'm sorry."

Beni clucked at Roy and went after her. Cole couldn't move. Couldn't *think*. Five minutes ago his world had been a shiny, happy place, full of hopes and plans and dreams, and now…

Now it had gone dark and empty, as suddenly as if someone had killed the arena lights. He could still hear the voices of the cowboys, feel Hammer shifting impatiently beneath him and tugging at the reins, but it was all drowned out by memories. Distant, muffled screams inside his head.

No! No! No! You're lying. They can't be gone.

But his family had been taken from him then. And the one he'd manufactured in his head had been ripped away now. He had to go after her. Didn't he? But then…what? He had no list. No rehearsed dialogue for this scene. If he went to her now, he would only make it worse.

If worse was even possible.

Chapter 40

SHAWNEE TROTTED ALL THE WAY TO COLE'S TRAILER, ignoring everyone who spoke to or looked at her. *Go. Go now. Go fast.* As long as she kept moving, she could outrun the roaring, swirling tornado of emotions bearing down on her. Once it swallowed her up...

She bailed off Salty, yanked blindly at the cinches, and threw the saddle in the tack room, then tossed her chaps in on top. Let Cole put them where he wanted, the son of a bitch. He had no right to tell her...

She flung Salty's bridle in after the saddle, replaying what he'd said, using each and every word to fan the flames. Anger would keep her moving. Get her gone enough to be out of sight before she ran out of fuel for the fire.

"I'm sorry," a small voice said behind her.

She whirled around to find Beni, his eyes wide and dark, tears dribbling down his cheeks. Oh, dammit.

"I didn't mean to make you sad," he said, choking on a sob.

"I'm fine." She had to soften her voice, wipe the rage from her face, and the flames flickered. Threatened to die. "What you said was true, and I was planning to tell Cole tonight anyway. You just saved me the trouble."

Beni gave a huge sniff. "Are you sure?"

"Yep. Now you'd better go find Joe while I get that saddle off of Roy. He's ready for some grain."

Beni was more than happy to make himself scarce, thank God. She heaved his saddle onto the pile and all but ran for her trailer, Roy trotting along behind. She tied him up, then scrambled around, rolling and securing the awning, tossing the lawn chairs aside for Cole to gather in the morning.

Inside, she heaped the coffeepot and spare dishes in the sink and flipped the switch for the slide-out. As it slowly retracted, she all but tore off her blue shirt and yanked on the first thing that came to hand, a grubby, wrinkled tank top from that morning's horse training session. Sooner was really coming along, and it was amazing how well Cole—

She slammed the closet door on that thought, wadded her hair up in a ball at the back of her head and strangled it with a ponytail holder. That oughta hold it for about five minutes.

Five more minutes was all she needed.

Outside, she dropped the blue shirt on top of a lawn chair, grabbed Sooner's halter from the tack room, and strode to his stall, trying to look purposeful instead of panicked. The saddle horses were in a barn separate from where the bucking stock was penned, so she was able to retrieve the sorrel and hustle back to the trailer without tripping over any of the crew. She didn't see Cole's massive shape jostling through the post-rodeo commotion, searching for her. He'd obviously learned everything he needed to know out in the arena. The bastard.

She jumped Roy into the trailer, latched the divider, and sent Sooner in behind him. Almost there. Just double-check the safety latches on the back door, grab that one bucket she'd left tied on the side of the trailer…

"What are you doing?"

Her heart crashed into her ribs. She spun around to find Cole standing beside the driver's door of her pickup. No getting around him. No way to read his expression in the flickering shadows as the headlights of departing rigs swung over them.

"Rodeo's over." She tossed the bucket in the bed of the truck. "Time to move on."

"You're going *now*?"

She put everything she had into a don't-give-a-shit shrug. "No reason to hang around."

"It's late. You'll be alone. And I…we…" He made a helpless gesture. "You can't just go."

"Actually, I can. As of about half an hour ago, I no longer work for you. I'm a free woman."

"Shawnee." He reached out a hand, then let it fall. Another pair of headlights swung over them, throwing his face into stark relief, pain and desperation etched into every line. "I didn't mean to…I don't know what to say."

Well, there's a shock. But the snide comment stuck in her throat. The fury she'd worked up died in a giant *whoosh*. All she had left was the pain. The guilt. She'd done this to both of them. Plowed ahead, knowing he wasn't like the others. Cole and his damn list. *What I want in a wife.* And on the surface, she could check all the boxes. *Loves bucking stock. Good cook. Doesn't care about football. Tolerates the damn dog.*

But number five was the kicker.

She'd told him flat-out that she was never getting married. Wasn't even sticking around after the end of the season. But she'd known, deep down, that he wasn't listening. Cole had reckoned it all out in that rock-hard skull of his and concluded that it made sense. *They* made sense. She'd known he would. She *knew* him. The way he'd only thought he knew her.

She wanted to press her hand over his heart to stop the bleeding, but she was the knife shoved between his ribs. "There's nothing to say. This is always how it was going to end."

Tears welled in his eyes. "But I love you. And I know you—"

"Can't be the one you need," she cut in, before he completely destroyed her. "The one you deserve. Along with that family. That's *your* future, Cole. But it's not mine."

She stepped closer and gently shoved him back a step—*don't breathe him in, don't notice how he feels*—so she could open the pickup door. It was better this way. Fast, like an amputation. With a dull ax.

"How can I just stand here and watch you leave?" The raw anguish in his voice tore at her guts. And God, the way he looked. She'd done that to him. Stupid, selfish bitch.

She took his wrists and raised those big, beautiful hands to his face. "Cover your eyes," she whispered.

Then she got in the pickup and drove away.

Cole did watch her leave. Stood right there and stared until her rig disappeared behind the grandstand, headed for the highway. Kept standing as people and cars veered around him. He was oblivious to the stares. The whispers. He had no idea what to do next, so he did nothing.

"Um, excuse me?" A nervous clearing of a throat, young and feminine. "They said you're Cole?"

He swiveled his head, one slow degree at a time, to find a teenager in a pizza delivery uniform eyeing him uncertainly.

She held up an insulated bag. "You ordered a couple of pizzas?"

He had. Called it in right before the bull riding. An hour…or a lifetime ago. He stared at the girl, unable to react.

She retreated a step toward her car, the sign on top glowing obscenely bright. "If I got the wrong guy…"

"No." Cole fumbled for his wallet, his fingers thick and numb as he dragged out two twenties and thrust them at her.

She took them and passed him the pizza in return. There was something he should say now, but he couldn't think what it was so he walked past the girl toward his trailer.

"Hey! You got, like, fourteen dollars change coming."

He ignored her. *Pepperoni* was scrawled across the top box in black letters. He tossed the bottom box— Shawnee's veggie pizza—in a trash can as he passed. Katie popped out from under the trailer, took a good look at him, and dropped to her belly, whining as if she'd been kicked. He let them both into his living quarters without turning on the lights, opened the pizza box and dropped it on one end of the couch. The dog looked from him to the pizza and back again, as if she suspected this was some kind of trick.

"It's all yours," he said.

She sniffed at it, then turned away to watch him

instead. Cole grabbed the six-pack of Shiner from the
fridge and twisted the top off the first beer. When he
dropped onto the couch, Katie jumped up beside him.
He sat, one hand on his dog, the other wrapped around a
bottle, and stared into the darkness.

Shawnee was out there somewhere. Alone. Hurting.
He grabbed his phone, started to dial, then stopped. He
still had nothing to say. But he had to know...

Please be careful, he typed.

The reply took so long he didn't think she was going
to answer. Finally, the phone vibrated in his hand. Don't
worry. I've got Roy and Sooner with me.

And no matter how upset she was, Shawnee would
never put her horses at risk. Wherever she'd gone, it
would be someplace safe for all of them. Small comfort,
but as much as he could expect. Cole drained the last of
the first beer, tossed the bottle in the general direction of
the trash can, and reached for another.

Shawnee had driven east, to the next ink spot of a town,
where there was a saddle club arena often used by cowboys as a stopping off point between far-flung Texas
rodeos. It was off the main highway, where she could
hunker down without the Jacobs convoy rolling past in
the morning and seeing her.

She could not handle seeing Cole again.

When the horses were penned, fed, and watered, she
climbed into the trailer, stripped down, and pulled on
shorts and a T-shirt. Then she fished out a prescription
bottle. She dropped the first pill she shook onto her
palm. Leaving it to roll into some corner, she shook out

a second, popped it in her mouth, and washed it down with lukewarm water from the tap.

God, what she'd give for a sleeping potion she could shoot straight into her vein, like anesthesia. *One, two, three...lights out*. Instead, she crawled onto the middle of the huge, empty bed to wait for blessed oblivion. The sheets and pillows still smelled like Cole. Squeezing her eyes shut, she wrapped her arms around her knees and curled into a ball.

Once again, it was up to her to hold herself together. No more stupid hugs. No big strong arms to wrap up in. At least Cole would have his damn dog to cuddle with.

Her chin began to shake. And then her shoulders. And then her entire body. She gave in to the misery and sobbed until the pill finally worked its magic and took her under.

Chapter 41

THE BUZZ OF SHAWNEE'S PHONE WOKE HER EARLY THE next morning. A text from Violet.

Where are you?

She stared blearily at the screen, trying to decide how to play this out. The old Shawnee would've had some smart-ass remark. Blown it off as just another fling. But she wasn't going to fool anyone, least of all herself. Or Violet, who knew better than to even ask if she was okay. So she dodged the question.

I'm going to see Butthead. Be home in a few days.

There. That would give her some breathing room. They didn't have to know that she'd be *seeing* Butthead via a live video feed, not in person. The horse was in hog heaven at A&M, with vet students standing in line to cater to his every need.

Be careful, Violet wrote back. Let me know as soon as you're back in town.

Not likely. She couldn't have any of them knocking on her door while she was clearing out her place, a care-taker's apartment above a barn where she'd lived longer than any place other than her grandparent's ranch.

The next text was from Tori. Shawnee fed her the

same information, guaranteeing no one would show up on her doorstep for at least a few days. Then she got dressed and loaded her horses. By her reckoning, she was no more than three hours behind the Jacobs trucks when she rolled into Amarillo.

Violet checked in a couple more times. So did Tori, and even Melanie. But not Cole. Thank God. It was hard enough, knowing he was only an hour away. If he'd actually tried to reach her...

She gave notice to her landlords, who were only slightly mollified by the short list of names she gave them, acquaintances who would jump at the chance to take her place.

"I can't imagine finding anyone as reliable as you," the old lady said, sounding a little choked up. "It's been so wonderful, to be able to leave and never once worry that everything here would be taken care of better than we could do it ourselves. And we'll miss you."

Shawnee swallowed hard and gave a *yeah, me too* nod. Yet another sign that she'd stayed in one place too long. Another string to be cut. How had she let herself get tangled in so many?

And how had she, who prided herself on traveling light, accumulated so much stuff? The apartment was no big deal. She pared her clothes down to what would fit in the closet in her trailer—her wardrobe was due for an update anyway—then the rest along with boxes of bits and pieces of household crap to the homeless shelter. Everything they couldn't use went to the dump.

But the tack room—she stared in helpless despair at the rows of bridles and rope bags, saddles and blankets, the majority trophies from ropings. She started to sort through it all, but every piece she picked up had a memory stuck on it like a sand burr. There were the halters she and Granddad had won when she was fifteen, her official comeback after treatment. Gran had a picture of the award presentation that Shawnee hated. Granddad looked great—strong and proud—but her hair had barely started to come back in and she was still gaunt. Hollow-cheeked. A refugee from a war with her own body.

One whole corner was crammed full of stuff she'd won in the past three years with Tori. Back in college, she never would've imagined that the girl she'd mockingly called Cowgirl Barbie would end up being the best partner she'd ever had. The strongest, truest of all the ties that bound her to the Panhandle.

Not counting Cole. Which she didn't, because those strings had been woven from delusions that had evaporated in the harsh light of reality.

She'd meant to sort through, pick out the must-keeps, then haul the rest to a used tack shop. Apparently, though, her fucked-up emotions had failed to get the memo. She threw in the towel when she teared up at the sight of a cheap, ugly breast collar from a roping in Hereford of all the damn places. But it was the first trophy of any kind she'd won on Roy...

A dozen bridles with various bits—snaffles, D-rings, different sizes and styles of ports and shanks to suit individual horses—went into her trailer, along with five kinds of saddle pads, a couple of insulated horse blankets for the cold New York winter, splint boots, skid boots, plus buckets and hay bags for the trip. And her ropes, of course. Brady had promised to provide anything else she might need.

She got a flash of Cole's hands sliding over her skin, his glorious weight settling over her, and gave a short, harsh laugh. That was one need she wasn't gonna be able to fill at the tack store.

Tuesday she scrubbed Tori's trailer, top to bottom, front to back, until there wasn't a trace that Shawnee had ever used it. Then she texted to say she'd be dropping it off that evening.

I'll be there, Tori replied.

That afternoon Shawnee backed up her pickup to the tack room door, loaded everything that wasn't going to New York, and hauled it all to a storage unit. She started to pay a year's rent, then reconsidered and made it two. She had no idea when she would be back. Or if. Maybe, with time and distance, she'd get over herself, call the owners, and tell them to auction off the works.

It was just after five o'clock when she rolled down the garage-style door and snapped the padlock shut on what was left of a lifetime in the Panhandle. Almost done. But this last part was going to be a bitch.

When Shawnee pulled into Tori's yard, Delon's red Charger was gone. Tori's generic *I'm-not-anybody-important* four-door was parked in the driveway, under a thriving young pecan tree. New siding gleamed on what had been an ugly concrete box, surrounded by a patch of lush green lawn and a blaze of flowers, planted and maintained under Miz Iris's strict supervision. She was worse than Cole, taking charge of everyone who wandered into her orbit. Shawnee fought off a pang of regret that there would be no more cooking lessons.

But she would always have Miz Iris's rolls.

She drove on past the house and backed the trailer into

its usual spot, alongside the indoor arena. The heaviness
in her chest condensed into a lead weight. How many
thousands of practice runs had she and Tori made in that
building? All the hours, curses, bickering. The laughter
and moments of triumph when they pulled off a flawless
run. Tori was no piece of fluff these days. The moment
she had decided to own her legacy as Panhandle royalty,
she had become a force to be reckoned with.

Tonight, Shawnee would've rather faced Cowgirl
Barbie.

Tori strolled out of the house, dressed for the barn in
a *Rope Like a Girl* T-shirt and grubby jeans. She walked
directly to the front of Shawnee's pickup, crossed her
arms, and waited.

Shawnee got out and slammed the door. "Yes.
I screwed up. I should have told Cole about the
hysterectomy."

"Is that normally how it works?" Tori mimed a
handshake. "Hi. I'm Shawnee, and I can't have your
children."

"Cole isn't a normal kind of guy."

"Now *that* I can't argue with."

Shawnee waited for the *what the hell were you thinking?,* but it didn't come. Tori was supposed to be mad,
dammit. Cole was family now, by way of Tori being
Beni's stepmother. But she just stood there, doing a
perfect impression of her father's bland politician face.
What did she expect Shawnee to do with…nothing?

Open her trap and dig herself a deeper hole, most
likely.

She clambered into the bed of the pickup to release
the gooseneck hitch from the steel ball. "Home alone?"

"Delon's at the ranch. The annual end of season barbecue."

Ah, yes. Shawnee's invitation had been in the pile of mail her landlady had collected while she was gone. A letter bomb hidden amongst the bank statements and grocery store flyers. She jumped down from the pickup and set a wooden block under the trailer jack. "Shouldn't you be there?"

"In the interests of family peace, we decided it was best if I sent my regards."

Shawnee started cranking down the jack. "Can you repeat that in regular people words?"

"I'm steering clear because Violet and I got into it yesterday when I dropped Beni off."

Shawnee paused midcrank. "About what?"

"You. And Cole." When Shawnee stared at her, open-mouthed, Tori shrugged. "You told him you didn't want a husband or kids. There are witnesses. If he chose to build some fantasy world, that's his problem."

"And you said so."

"Naturally."

Shawnee's initial reaction was gratitude. At least one person was on her side. Then the guilt sucker-punched her. Just what she needed. One more burning ember to dump on her personal hellfire. Tori and Violet got along pretty well, but that hadn't always been the case, and no truce involving stepparents was unbreakable. The damage Shawnee had done to Cole was bad enough. She shouldn't have to live with being a wrench in the works between Violet, Tori, Joe, and Delon.

She cranked the jack with a vengeance. "I can take

care of myself, princess. Go party with your people. And try to play nice."

"Excuse the hell out of me," Tori drawled, sounding more amused than pissed off. "My daddy raised me to have my partner's back."

"Yeah, well, we both know how my daddy raised me." Or, more precisely, didn't. Shawnee gave the jack one last turn to be sure the hitch was clear of the ball, took a deep breath, and faced Tori. "You're gonna need to find a new heeler. It's been great and all, but I'm ready for a change."

Tori's arms dropped to her sides. "A *change*?"

"We're getting kinda stale, ya know?" She made a show of brushing the dust off her hands. "Don't take it personally. It's not you, it's me…blah, blah."

Tori stared, incredulous. "You're breaking up with me?"

The underlying hurt made Shawnee want to take it back, but she only gave an elaborate shrug. "It had to happen sooner or later."

Tori just kept staring at her, for so long Shawnee was holding onto her cool by the tattered edges when she finally asked, "Why?"

"Huh?"

"Why did it have to happen?" Tori's eyes narrowed, her gaze sharpening to a steely razor that could dissect flesh and bone. "Why does everything have to end with you? Is this some kind of trust issue courtesy of Ace?"

"No!" She would not give the bastard even that much credit. Or blame.

"Then why? What are you scared of?"

"Scared?" Shawnee scoffed, despite the twist in her gut. Tori folded her arms again and gave a slow, disbelieving shake of her head. "Wow, I am slow. You're a textbook case. Parent abandons child at a critical time in her life. Child vows never to allow anyone to wield that kind of emotional power over her again. Thus follows a string of meaningless relationships—"

"*It has nothing to do with Ace!*" Shawnee yelled, so loud Tori took a step back. "My life is exactly what I want it to be."

"Yeah. I can see how happy it's making you. Did I mention you look like shit? Almost as bad as Cole."

Shawnee stopped dead. She had to know…"He'll get over it, right? Eventually."

"What do you care?" Tori curled her lip, mocking. "You're moving on. Big, tough Shawnee Pickett doesn't need anybody but herself."

"No one can afford to need *me*!" Shawnee clamped her mouth shut, but it was too late. She couldn't leave the words just hanging there, shrill and pathetic, so she went with a carefully blended mix of sarcasm and self-contempt. "If I was a car, there would be a mandatory recall due to a fatal design flaw. I've already been wrecked, I'm missing a few parts, and it's only a matter of time before something else goes to shit. Who wants that in their life?"

"People who love you?"

Shawnee scoffed again, harsher. "And in return, they get what? A stack of medical bills. The pleasure of watching me—"

She cut off sharply and bent to unplug the trailer light cord from the socket in the pickup bumper. Crap. Sweat had broken out along her hairline, and her stomach was already a wreck from three days of inhaling the junk food she normally avoided except in small, celebratory doses. Much more of this and she'd be heaving banana Moon Pies in the grass.

Tori was quiet for too long. Thinking. Shit.

"I see," she said, in her snotty rich bitch drawl. "You're just watching out for everyone else. How selfless of you."

Shawnee jerked upright too fast and whacked her head on the underside of the gooseneck. She cursed the insult to her already aching head. "Medical expenses are the leading cause of bankruptcy in this country. How do you figure Violet and the rest of the family would feel about Cole tying himself to a woman who's already brought down one ranch?"

"Been there, almost done that when Cole's parents died," Tori said. "As a result, Jacobs Livestock is now financially structured in a way that protects the corporation from the debt—or death—of any of the individual partners."

Oh. Shawnee rubbed the knot on her head, feeling as if the rug had been jerked out from under one of her feet. So she couldn't ruin the company. She could still ruin Cole.

Tori cocked her head. "So…you've at least considered the long-term with Cole."

"I've considered that it's impossible." And that she wouldn't have this nest of rattlesnakes in her gut if she hadn't allowed herself to wander into that particular dreamland. "Even if I could give him kids, I can't promise anything beyond my next six-month checkup."

"So you don't even try." Tori's words dripped with disgust. "All those times you rode my ass about pushing myself, never settling—it was just a massive pile of bullshit."

Shawnee yanked the latch on the tailgate and let it fall open with a bang. "No, it was *not*. I always rope for first place."

"But when it comes to real life, you won't even enter up."

"Don't tell me about real." Shawnee stomped up to Tori and jabbed a finger at her, stopping just short of making contact. "I've got so much fucking reality, I oughta be a television star by now. Do you have any idea what it's like, never knowing which day will be the one when you're taking a shower and find a lump? Which time the doctor is going to walk in with your lab results and that *look* on his face? Well, in case you can't guess, it sucks. I wouldn't inflict this on Ace, let alone Cole."

"You're scared. I get it." Tori leveled that cold blue gaze on her. "Again—been there, done that after I lost Willy. And you're right, it's a piss-poor way to live, waiting for the next disaster. But do you really think not letting yourself have anything that matters is going to make it easier to die?"

The blunt words hit Shawnee like a fist, driving her back a step and flattening her lungs as she pictured her grandfather—his withered body and the bottomless grief in his eyes as he whispered, "I'm going to miss seeing all the things you turn out to be."

And Gran, trying to be strong and cheerful while the other half of her wasted away until there was just…nothing. How could she stand to see Cole that way, feel him squeezing her hand, desperate to hold on as long as possible and losing. Again. And she'd know she'd done this to him because she was Ace's selfish bitch of a daughter who took what she wanted, no matter the cost.

Shawnee shook her head violently, scrambling the images.

"Just tell me one thing." Tori's voice was quiet, but penetrating. "What if you don't get sick again? You just wake up twenty or thirty years from now and realize you spent your whole life bracing yourself for a wreck that never happened?"

Shawnee made a harsh, bitter sound. "There's not a bookie in Vegas who'd take those odds."

Tori set a hand on the *Turn 'Em and Burn 'Em* logo scrawled across the hood of Shawnee's pickup. "When you made me enter this roping, I looked at the number of entries, how many really good ropers would be competing, and told you our chances of winning were about five hundred to one. And you told me I'd never be a winner if I kept planning to lose." She gave another disgusted shake of her head. "How did you, of all people, let hope become the enemy?"

Another sucker punch, this time right to the heart. Shawnee spun around and grappled blindly for the door handle. "Fuck. You."

Tori didn't even pause. "I've never been dumped before. How does this work? Do I pretend I don't know you next time we both show up at the same roping?"

Shawnee finally got the damn door open. "We won't. Brady offered me a job in New York and I accepted. Tomorrow morning, I'm gone."

She slammed into her pickup and revved the engine. Tori stood square in her path for a long moment, staring her down through the windshield, before taking a few leisurely steps to the side. She tucked her hands in the back pockets of her jeans and continued to stare as Shawnee drove away.

Neither of them lifted a hand to wave goodbye.

Chapter 42

COLE WAS AVERAGING SIX PACKS OF GUM A DAY. THE rhythmic chewing drowned out his thoughts and soothed his anxiety, and the wrappers…

He stroked the one on his thigh until the foil was nearly mirror smooth. Then he folded it precisely in half, matching the serrations along the edges, and stroked that smaller square until it was also smooth, the fold as sharp as a blade.

Around him, at a safe distance, people chatted and laughed, ate and drank at the year-end barbecue. Even Katie had abandoned him to trail Beni and his herd of friends, who had a habit of leaving plates unguarded. Cole folded the gum wrapper again, and then again, the same way he had folded his emotions in and in and in, where he could keep them contained.

He frowned as he reached the last possible fold in the current wrapper. The one that was never quite right. No matter how hard he squeezed, he could never make the edges match on that last fold. He'd even tried using the vise in the shop. He could mash it as hard as he wanted, but parts of the white underside of the wrapper would still be exposed.

He squeezed until the nugget of foil dug into his fingertips, then examined the result. No good. He began to reverse the process. When it was flat again, he plucked the gum out of his mouth, set it in the middle of the wrapper, and carefully folded up the sides to cover the gum. Then he dropped it into his shirt pocket with three others, pulled out a fresh stick, and started over.

No one had to tell him this was not a thing rational people did. And lucky for him, no one would. They'd made their support known, each in their own way, since he'd been home. A single hard squeeze on the shoulder from his uncle. A plate of his favorite oatmeal cookies left in his cabin by his aunt when he didn't stop by for his usual afternoon coffee. From Violet, regular assurances that yes, she'd been in touch with Shawnee and she seemed to be okay. Plus a spreadsheet with the season's buck-off percentages and average scores for every horse and bull in the herd. He could analyze and rearrange the numbers for hours on end. And from Joe... blessed silence as they'd worked side-by-side checking and repairing fences.

If he wanted to talk, they were ready to listen. But he still had no words.

If he had, he would have given them to Shawnee. Made her understand that he knew he was the one with a piece missing. He was the one in mourning for a child—an entire life—that had never existed. Cole was profoundly aware that this was also not rational. Knowing didn't make it easier to stop.

Any easier than it was to stop craving the smell and the taste and the feel of Shawnee. The way he reached out at night expecting to find her. The sickening jolt when there was nothing but empty, cold space.

Once again, he reached that final, critical fold in the gum wrapper. He tried smashing it between the flats of his thumbnails this time. Closer, but not perfect.

He unfolded the wrapper, spit out the gum, and started again. Family and crew flowed around him as if he was a boulder planted under the huge oak in the corner of the backyard. When he crawled back out of that deep, dark center of himself, they would treat him as if he'd never been gone. Until then, they knew enough to steer clear.

All except Analise.

She marched toward him, intent in every stomp of her black boots. He scrunched down in his chair, but he hadn't mastered the art of becoming one with nature, so she planted herself in front of him and braced her hands on her narrow hips.

"Why is Hank in Florida?" she demanded, her glare making it an accusation.

"To fight bulls."

Cole knew because the contractor had called Violet for a reference. Which she had given, no mention made of circumstances under which Hank had left Jacobs Livestock. To their surprise—and Cole's immense relief—Melanie had reported that Hank seemed determined to do exactly as he'd said...prove that he could do just fine without them.

Analise wrinkled her nose, doubtful. "There are rodeos in Florida?"

"And ranches. It's a good place for Hank."

He could work all winter down there, and Florida was as far as he could get from Idaho and Mariah without falling off of the continent, which should keep him out of trouble. At least, that particular trouble.

Analise's brows puckered. "But he's alone. And hurting. I don't think he's ever been in love before."

"In *what*?"

"It was *so* obvious." Analise did one of her finer eye rolls. "He was a totally different person with her— polite and funny and sweet. When she was around, *I* almost wanted to date him." Analise gave a melancholy sigh and braced her back against the oak. "I've always thought that was the ultimate goal, you know? To find someone who makes you the best version of yourself. And then to not be able to be with them…it seems like such a waste."

"Not if it wasn't mutual." When Analise scowled at him, he hunched a shoulder. "It has to be two people who make each other better."

"Like you and Shawnee," she said, so quick he suspected this was where she'd been leading the whole time.

Cole looked away, his fingers smoothing and smoothing the latest gum wrapper on his thigh. Over by the beer cooler, his uncle Steve was in deep conversation with Joe and Delon, his hand palm down with four fingers extended, bucking like a horse through the air as he described some ride or other. Violet was planted on a lounger, with her mother and her sister taking turns keeping an eagle eye on her.

Music rippled through the air—Delon's brother, Gil, and a couple of friends picking guitars and singing on the rear deck of the big white farmhouse, doing everything from Lynyrd Skynyrd to Ernest Tubb to a few songs Cole didn't recognize. Gil's own, probably. In the past couple of years he'd started performing occasionally—informal, unpaid, but damn good. If he weren't so dead set on turning Sanchez Trucking into a world power, he could—

"Ignore me as long as you want," Analise said. "I won't go away."

"What about you and Cruz?" he asked, trying to throw her off the trail.

"We're going to keep in touch…until one or both of us stops feeling like making the effort." She shrugged one shoulder, bare beneath the skinny strap of what looked to Cole like a black feed sack. "If it was meant to be more, it wouldn't have been so easy to leave it at that. Unlike you and Shawnee."

Another shard of pain sliced through him. Shawnee had never pretended there could be a happily ever after for them. That was all Cole. His screwed-up head and his idiot heart, latching on and refusing to listen to reason. Because he was good with his hands. Hadn't she told him so? He'd been convinced he could put all of her pieces back together, one by one. Fix the damage Ace and that damn disease had done.

But he couldn't give her back what was gone forever.

He made that last, impossible fold in the gum wrapper and ground it onto the arm of his chair. Instead of better, he made it worse, peeling away the thin foil, baring a ragged patch of white. He swore silently.

"It's not that simple," he told Analise.

She gave him a long, implacable look. "It can be. You just have to decide what matters most."

A car came zooming down the highway, whipped around the corner and into their driveway, its abrupt halt sending puffs of dust into the air. Alarm rippled through the crowd as Tori kicked the door open, vaulted out, and slammed it behind her. Delon and Joe hustled over as she bore down on Cole.

Her normally cool eyes were spitting sparks. "She *dumped* me!"

Cole stared up at her, confounded. *Who? What?*

"Shawnee?" Delon asked.

"Of course, Shawnee. You think there's some other woman I sneak around with behind your back?"

"No, I just don't understand…" Delon frowned, baffled. "She doesn't want to rope with you anymore? Or be friends at all?"

"Both. She says it's for our own good," Tori snarled. "So we don't have to worry our little heads if—oh, excuse me, *when* she gets cancer again. Like we're all too feeble to cope, while she goes around pretending she's so tough—"

"She's not pretending," Cole said.

A dozen sets of eyes locked on him. The guests had gone quiet, and the family had gathered around to see what the kerfuffle was about. Even the music had stopped, the better for all of them to eavesdrop. Cole sank deeper in his chair, as if he could squeeze between the slats and crawl off through the grass.

"No?" Tori challenged. "Then why is she running scared?"

"Of what?" Cole asked.

"You. Me." She made a wide, sweeping gesture to include the entire crowd. "Anyone she might slip up and actually start to care about."

Delon laid a careful hand on her shoulder, as if he was afraid she might bite. "Give her a few days—"

"Not an option. She's leaving tomorrow for upstate New York and some job Brady offered her. I came to tell *him*." Tori jabbed a finger at Cole. "If you were planning to stop moping around at some point, you're gonna have to do it before morning."

New York? Brady? The words bounced around inside Cole's head, refusing to sink in.

Tori turned on her heel and strode back toward her car.

Delon scrambled after her. "Where are you going?"

"Home. To call my sister. Elizabeth is one of the top cancer researchers in the world. What she doesn't know, her friends do." She paused, turned, and flashed a smile so filled with icy determination Cole felt his testicles retract in reflex. "I don't care if I have to drag Shawnee into clinical trials by that damn hair of hers, I'm gonna make sure the bitch lives to be ninety."

They all watched her slam back into her car, wheel around, and gun the engine, spattering the driveway with gravel. No one spoke until she had disappeared over the rise.

"If Elizabeth is anything like Tori…" Miz Iris glanced at Delon. "What do you think?"

He rubbed a hand across the back of his neck. "If I was Shawnee, I'd start saving up for a real long retirement."

Chuckles and murmurs rippled through the crowd and they began to disperse, wandering back to the food table for another slice of pie, or the cooler for another beer. Only Joe and Analise lingered. Joe gave her a pointed look. She scowled, but stomped off while Joe pulled up a lawn chair and settled in beside Cole. No comment. No questions. Just there, in case.

Leaving. New York.

Tori was right. Cole had been indulging himself, taking the time to sort his feelings into safe little boxes. Grief here. Lust there. Affection over in this corner. And in that one…he took a quick peek, then slammed the lid, but the emotion inside kept swelling, refusing to be locked away. Everything he wanted to feel some day. Fatherly pride. The soul-altering love for a child. *His* child.

But never, ever Shawnee's child. He didn't know if he could let go of that dream to reach for another. And he had to *know*. He couldn't give her anything less than complete acceptance. If she would take it.

"Does it still hurt?" he asked.

Joe started. "What?"

"Dick Browning had his stroke less than a year after you left Oregon." Cole pulled out another piece of gum, turned it between his fingers, then slid it back into the pack. "If you'd stayed, he would've made you a partner in Browning Rodeo instead of turning it over to his kid. Do you ever regret coming to Texas instead?"

"Those are two different questions." Joe gazed out over the dusty plains beyond the oasis that was Miz Iris's yard. "I will never stop missing Oregon, the same way you would never stop missing this place, no matter where you went or for how long. It's in here." Joe pressed his palm flat over his heart. Then he searched out Violet, who was watching them intently from across the lawn, and what Cole saw in his eyes was so deep, so true, it was almost painful to witness. "But regrets? None."

And in that single look, Cole found his answer. There was no decision to be made because there wouldn't be another woman. No children. Shawnee was his one and only shot at getting this right. If he lost her, he would just keep folding in and in, until no one could reach him ever again.

He couldn't lose her. But how could he make her stay? "If Violet hadn't come after you, would you have come back?"

"I don't know." Joe dipped his chin and worried a barbed wire scratch on his wrist. "I'd like to say yes—I imagine Wyatt would've found some way to make me—but on my own? I'm not sure I could have convinced myself that I deserved this."

Cole nodded slowly, thought for a while longer, then stood up and started for his pickup.

"Cole?"

He paused, half-turning to look at Joe.

"You probably can't stop her from leaving, but it's not because she doesn't love you and want to be with you. Make sure she knows she can always come back."

"Okay," Cole said.

As if it was as easy as that.

Chapter 43

SHAWNEE COULD NOT MAKE ONE MORE DECISION.

She stared at the heap of stuff piled on the kitchen table, and her brain refused to compute what to do with it. For two days, every move she'd made had required a choice. Did she pack this, or that? Close the checking account she'd had since high school to open a new one in New York? Get her oil changed now, or at her uncle's shop during her stopover in Kansas, even though the pickup would be five hundred miles past due when she got there?

And now, *this*.

She plopped down in a chair, too tired to even scowl at the mess on the table. Half-eaten boxes of cereal, open bags of pasta, plastic tubs of flour and sugar, a jar with two lonely dill pickles floating in the brine, a barely used squirt bottle of ketchup—all the odds and ends from her cupboards and refrigerator that she hadn't been able to donate anywhere. It seemed wrong to throw it all away, but she had no one to give it to. If she'd been thinking, she would've unloaded the leftovers on Tori before…

She squeezed her eyes shut tight, as if she could wring that whole conversation out of her brain.

As if she'd needed to be told. Yes, Shawnee was scared. Every minute of every waking hour, at some level. On the good days, when she was busy with her horse or roping, that level was eight floors below the basement of her subconscious. The fear was always there, though, with one finger poised over the *up* button for the express elevator to the surface.

But that *hope is the enemy* line was pure bullshit.

Shawnee had plenty of hope. Every time she rode into the arena, she hoped her partner would turn the steer in the money, and she'd do her part by roping both feet. She hoped Sooner would keep improving, so he'd be good enough to sell by the end of the year. She hoped she could live up to Brady's expectations.

She hoped she hadn't cursed herself by making promises that could extend clear into next fall.

She hoped—Lord, how she hoped—that she hadn't done any permanent damage to Cole. Her goal had always been to leave any man at least as good, if not better, than when she'd found him. *Please, God, don't let Cole be the exception.* She didn't want to be the reason that when the right woman did come along—her breath hitched at the stab of pain—he refused to take another chance. She should have told him...what?

I love you, you big idiot. Now go find someone who can give you what you need.

Yep. She'd fallen in love with Cole Jacobs, of all the damn people. It was so ridiculous, she laughed out loud. An ugly, rasping sound, echoing around the barren apartment. If the two of them hadn't been so impossible, he couldn't have snuck up on her. It was *Cole,* for crying out loud. What danger could there possibly be? And then there he was, taking up all the space inside her head, in her chest, so there didn't seem to be enough room to breathe anymore and her heart felt squashed.

And now all she had was leftovers. Literally.

She kicked the table leg and clamped her mouth tight against another of those gross, sobby laughs. If it weren't for this table full of crap, she could load up the horses and leave right now. She'd have to camp in the trailer tonight anyway, since all of her bedding was packed. She wouldn't sleep tonight unless she tranqued herself into oblivion. Why waste a perfectly good pill when she could just climb behind the wheel and drive until she was too tired to keep going? Out of here. Out of Texas.

Away from Cole, so she didn't show up some horrible night, begging on his doorstep.

With a sudden burst of anger, she heaved out of the chair, grabbed the last empty box, and shoveled everything from the table into it. She'd just…just…cram it in the trailer somewhere. Gran could always use extra groceries. If any of the cold stuff went bad, she'd toss it out along the way. Lighten her load as she went.

Who knew—by the time she left Kansas, she might not feel like her bones were made of lead.

She jumped at the heavy thud on her front door. Her heart felt as if the fist had made direct contact. She knew that knock. For an insane moment, she couldn't decide whether to fling herself toward the door or out her bedroom window. Luckily—for her bones, at least, since her apartment *was* above the barn—common sense elbowed aside the panic. Every light was on and her rig was parked out front. Kinda tough to pretend she wasn't home.

Thud! "Shawnee?"

She drew a breath, braced herself as best she could, and opened the door. And was still staggered by the sight of him. The sheer *size* of him, blocking the sun and the sky and every single brain wave. At the rodeos everything was bigger than life. The stock. The arenas. The grandstands. Cole hadn't seemed quite so massive by comparison. But here…she just stared at him, too overwhelmed to make words.

He braced a hand on each side of the doorframe as if to block her exit. "You're going to New York."

His voice gave no clue as to how he felt about the news.

"And…what?" she asked, dredging up some sass. "You wanted to be sure I was actually leaving the state?"

His expression didn't shift one iota. "I'll be here."

"No shit." She squinted at him, trying to extrapolate some kind of meaning from his statement. "And you needed to tell me this because…"

"For you," he said. "I'll be here for you."

Her laugh was sharp with disbelief. "Keepin' the porch light on?"

"Yes."

Was he drunk? She leaned closer to sniff, but only caught a hint of mint gum. "I'm not even gonna ask if you're insane, because we both know that's a slippery slope." Then a thought struck her—the same one that had been sneaking around, whispering impossibilities into her ear. "Oh hell. I suppose you've decided that if I can't pop out a few kids, we could adopt instead. Well, forget it. I can't make that kind of commitment, and even if I could, who would want me raising their kids?"

"Me." He didn't even hesitate. "They'd be tough, and ballsy, and know how to handle a horse."

She snorted to cover the spurt of warmth. "Well, that'll get 'em into Harvard for sure. Sorry, but I'm not mama material."

"Okay."

What? He was giving up, just like that? Not likely. He probably figured he could wear her down. "You're not gonna change my mind."

"That's okay. If I can't have both, I choose you."

She blinked, stunned, then glared at him. "I'm leaving, remember? And you're staying."

He nodded gravely. "Right here. Anytime you need me. Any reason. Flat tire. Sick horse. Friend. Lover. Fix your toilet. Whatever."

She laughed. How could she not? Only Cole would put love somewhere on a list between colic and plumbing.

Only Cole.

"I told you, marriage and family isn't in my cards." She made her voice cold, so it couldn't be mistaken for a whine. "And before you go spouting off about how it can all end at any minute for any one of us and nobody knows better than you…well, I'm sorry for your loss and all, but it's not the same."

"I know. I want you anyway." He had that look. The one that said he was ready to bust through fences and tear down walls to get his way.

She stepped back, shaking her head. "No. You want me *now*. But eventually you'll realize it wasn't worth everything you gave up and you'll hate me for it."

"I'm not Ace." He gave her a long, steady stare that she couldn't refuse to meet, if only for an instant. "I make my own choices and I stand by them. And I want you."

Damn him. He had to quit saying that. Suddenly furious, she cupped a hand under each boob and shoved them up for inspection. "And what about when these are gone? What's left then?"

"All the important stuff," he said, so certain she wanted to punch him. "I'm gonna fall apart too, you know. My belly will get bigger and my ass will shrink up to nothing. Happens to all the Jacobs men. Are you gonna quit me then?"

"Of course not." Then she slapped herself upside the head, realizing the trap he'd laid for her. "I mean, I wouldn't. *If* we were gonna stick together."

"I am sticking."

Agh! It was like talking to a rock. "What if I never come back from New York?"

"That'd be a damn shame. We'll probably never find anything this good again."

"Because I'm *not looking*." But she'd stumbled over him anyway. Just one more way life had decided to torture her. And now he stood there making the two of them sound like a perfectly rational choice. Holding a match to a candle she'd snuffed out years ago.

The one called hope, Tori's voice mocked.

Shawnee cursed, words she normally reserved for Ace and idiot drivers. "How can you be so calm about this?"

"Do you want me to come unglued? Because I can." And buried in the deep rumble of his voice, she heard a note of desperation.

Finally, *finally,* she let herself really look at him. His eyes were dilated and the knuckles of the hand clenched on the doorframe were bone white. His chest rose and fell with deep, deliberate breaths. The kind she took when she was fighting off the anxiety demons. They were both holding on by a thread, and it was a dead heat whose was gonna snap first. And then…well, God help them.

She closed her eyes. Shook her head. "Don't do this to us, Cole. You're only making it harder."

"I love you," he said. "It can't get much worse than that."

She choked out a laugh. "That's the first thing you've said that made any sense." She could feel the tears coming. Damned if she'd make them both suffer through that, too. She blew out a shaky sigh. "Do you really want to know what I want?"

"Yes."

"Fine. I want to know that you're going to move on."

He started to open his mouth. She gave her head a quick shake and stepped up to put her hands on his shoulders. Those broad shoulders that would be so easy to lean on. She slid her hands down, her breath catching at the piercing pleasure of touching him one last time. Then she slid her arms around him and hugged him so hard that if it had been anyone else, she might have cracked a rib. In the process of letting go, she ducked under his arm and out the door. "And I really, *really* need you to go."

"Shawnee—"

Halfway down the exterior staircase, she stopped to glance past him into the apartment. "While you're at it, take that box of crap on the kitchen table with you."

—⁓—

Cole left. It was what she wanted, and there was nothing more to say. He loved her. He was ninety percent sure she loved him. And she was leaving.

He took the box. It weighed a ton. After checking out the contents, he hauled it into his aunt's kitchen, where she and Lily were scrubbing pots and pans while his uncle, Delon, and Joe cleaned up the backyard with Beni's assistance—which consisted mostly of balling up stray napkins and tossing them basketball-style at the trash can. When Cole plunked the box on the table, Iris turned to give him a searching look. He shook his head. She sighed and went back to scraping leftover chili from a slow-cooker into a plastic tub.

"What are you going to do?" Lily asked.

Cole thought about it for a moment. "Chores," he said, then carefully folded his emotions up, stuffed them back into their boxes, and walked down to the barn.

That was the best thing about lists and routines. You always knew what to do next. One step after another. Didn't matter if your mind and heart shut down, your body would just keep on moving out of habit. By the time he tossed hay to the saddle horses, he had retreated so far into himself he barely noticed the odd, buzzing sensation in his chest.

He pulled the phone out of his shirt pocket. His pulse jumped, hard and fast, as he answered. "What's wrong?" he demanded.

Shawnee made a choked sound. "Well. That's just perfect. You see my number and immediately think *disaster*."

"Habit," he said. "Where are you?"

"Texhoma. I can't…" She took an audible gulp of air. "I had to pull over. My pickup won't go."

"It just quit?"

"Yeah. Sort of."

He was already headed for his own pickup. "I'm on my way. Forty-five minutes, max."

As he passed the shop, he grabbed a toolbox. He was almost to Earnest before his phone rang and he realized he hadn't told anyone where he was going or why. He let it go to voice mail. He didn't talk or text while he was driving and he refused to stop, even for a minute.

Shawnee wasn't hurt. Wasn't sick. But there'd been something in her voice that made his muscles jump and his hands clench around the steering wheel. He wasn't operating on autopilot anymore. Every one of his senses was wide open and so hyperalert he could swear he heard the *whoompf-whoompf-whoompf* of the giant blades as he roared past a row of windmills. Felt it in his chest.

He spotted her rig before he even reached the city limits of what little there was of Texhoma. She'd limped to a stop alongside the only patch of grass in a mostly empty lot directly across from a row of huge grain silos, fifty yards short of the Oklahoma border. Both horses were contentedly munching hay inside the portable pen that attached to the side of her trailer. She'd also unloaded her roping dummy. As Cole pulled up, she took two swings, laid her loop under its belly, and scooped up the hind feet. Then she stepped forward, pulled the rope off, rebuilt the loop, and did it again. And again.

Without even glancing his direction.

Cole had watched her rope that dummy almost every day they'd been on the road. Usually, every throw was different. Five swings. Then one. Then three. Throw from a couple of steps farther back. Off to the right. Or the left. She changed it up every time, practicing for every possible situation.

This was not that kind of practice. This was rhythmic,

almost robotic, the same exact steps, swings, and throws, one after another after another.

It made him think of folding gum wrappers.

She didn't pause as he parked and stepped out into the soft evening air. Her hair was loose, a wild cloud of curls she'd made no attempt to tame with goop or a barrette, and she'd traded jeans and a dusty T-shirt for shorts, rhinestone-studded flip-flops, and a sleeveless black polo shirt.

He ached to touch her. Bury his hands in all that baby-soft hair, slide them down her bare arms…

And if he tried, he'd get whacked by the rope she was still swinging. *Whish, whish, crack!* The loop sucked tight around the wooden legs. She still hadn't acknowledged his presence.

"Are the keys in the pickup?" he asked.

"Yep." *Whish, whish, crack!* Retrieve her rope. Build a new loop.

"I'll just…" He gestured toward the pickup.

She nodded without missing a beat. *Whish, whish, crack!*

The tailgate was down. As he walked to the driver's door, he glanced into the bed and saw that she'd unhitched the trailer. Before climbing behind the wheel, he slid the seat all the way back to accommodate his height. When he pushed in the clutch and turned the key, the engine fired right up and ran smooth as butter. He revved it a couple of times. Not a tick or a rattle.

He put it in first gear and eased out the clutch. The transmission engaged and the pickup rolled forward. When he was clear of the trailer, he sped up a little. Still nothing out of the ordinary. He shifted into second, checked for traffic, and pulled out onto the street. The pickup accelerated easily. Third gear, on through the tiny town, then fourth as he cleared the other side and hit open highway. Fifth gear, sixth, steadily gaining speed until he hit sixty.

Two miles out of town he turned around and went back. Shawnee was still roping the dummy. He parked the pickup beside his own, turned it off, and got out. "It seems to be fine."

"Yep." *Whish, whish, crack!*

"You said it quit."

"Nope." She built another loop with those precise, mechanical movements. "I said it wouldn't go."

"It ran just fine for me."

Whish, whish, crack! "Probably 'cuz you were pushing on the gas pedal."

Cole gawked at her. "And you weren't?"

"Nope." She paused in the act of retrieving her loop to point at a sign that said *Welcome to Oklahoma.* "I saw that and I just sort of…vapor-locked. I couldn't make myself cross that line." She braced her fists on her hips, loop clenched in one hand and the coils of her rope in the other, gaze fixed on the sign. "I've never left Texas. Not indefinitely. I just…couldn't."

She seemed confused, and more than a little angry. As if someone had thrown up a roadblock at the Texas border and refused to let her pass.

"I don't know what to say," he said.

"There's a shock." She rolled her eyes and huffed out a breath. "I have to go to New York. I promised. And you're gonna have to figure out how to get me there, since this is your fault."

"*Mine?*"

"You and Tori." She kept staring at the sign, her scowl deepening. "You win, okay? I'm tired of letting this cancer bullshit push me around. And I'm really tired of going it alone. So if you're crazy enough to want to take this on…" She spread her arms wide in a *check it out* gesture. "It's all yours. Just don't come whinin' to me when you realize you got a sucker deal."

His? Cole felt as if the earth had bucked beneath him, taking out his knees and slamming him into the dirt. He actually saw stars. Moons. A whole damn galaxy whirling through his head. It was a surprise to realize he was still standing.

His.

"So, uh, yeah," she said, eyes still fixed and slightly glazed. "In case you hadn't noticed, I'm sort of freaking out here. It would help if you would—I don't know—speak? Shoot me with a tranquilizer dart? Knock me in the head and put me out of my misery?"

He closed his hands over hers instead, prying the rope out of her fingers and hanging it on the roping dummy. Her eyes were wide, the pupils dilated, as he threaded his fingers into her hair. He lowered his cheek to the top of her head, bracing against the storm of emotions that raged through him.

After a few moments, Shawnee sighed and wrapped her arms around his waist. "I suppose it was too much to expect that you'd actually *say* something."

He nodded, savoring the rub of his cheek against her hair. When he did eventually speak, it was to ask, "Do you have to leave right now?"

"Tomorrow."

"Good." He slid his hands down to her hips and began

backing toward the door to the trailer's living quarters, tugging her along.

She dragged her feet, but it was a token resistance. "What are you doing?"

"We're in shock. We need to lie down."

Her eyebrows quirked, the sass already making a comeback. "Oh, really?" she drawled. "For how long?"

"At least eight hours. Maybe twelve. Depends on whether you have any food in there."

He opened the door, pulled her inside, and closed it behind them before planting his mouth on hers. A long, deep kiss that was the equivalent of that first drink of water at the end of a dry, dusty trail. His entire being gave a huge *ahhhh*. Her hair tickled across the backs of his hands as he molded her close against him. He could spend at least two hours just running his fingers through that hair. Another three or four kissing her.

She drew back, her mouth soft and slick from his kisses, her expression still not entirely certain. "What happens when you've recovered from this terrible shock?"

"I doubt I ever will."

"Even while I'm halfway across the country for the next year or so?"

"Even if you were halfway around the world."

But tomorrow would come, regardless. He thought about the next day's schedule. Young bulls to gather. Salt and mineral supplements to haul out to the pastures. Fences to check. The first fall practice session late in the afternoon. Then he looked at Shawnee.

No contest.

He pulled his phone out of his pocket and dialed. "Hey, Violet."

He kicked off his boots while she ranted about his disappearance, finishing with, "You even drove off and left Katie sitting in the middle of the driveway!"

Oh. Shit. That was gonna cost him. "Tell her I'm sorry. Give her a steak. And whatever you do, don't let her in my cabin. Or the tack room. Oh, and let everyone know I won't be home for a few days."

"You *what*?"

"Could be longer. I have to drive to New York," he said, grinning as he heard Shawnee gasp. "I don't know how long it will take. We'll just have to wing it."

"*Wing* it?" Violet practically screeched. "Since when do you—"

"Gotta go," he said, and hung up.

He turned off the ringer before tossing the phone on the table. Shawnee looped her arms around his neck, and as he gazed down into her whiskey-brown eyes, his heart nearly exploded from what he saw there. "I love you," he said. "And I'm sticking. No matter what."

"Same here." She shook her head in disbelief. "And ain't that just a kick in the ass."

He laughed. And then he kissed her until neither of them could talk.

Just how he liked it.

Chapter 44

Fifteen months later—National Circuit Finals Rodeo

AS THE LIGHTS DIMMED, LASERS DANCED AROUND THE coliseum to a pounding rock beat. Shawnee sat in the wide alley leading up to the arena gate with the three most important men in her life. Brady, her team roping partner, on one side. Roy standing patient and calm beneath her. And Cole on the other side, aboard Hammer, all duded up in a white shirt, red silk bandana, and red and white chaps with the National Circuit Finals logo.

It was so damn perfect it made her shiver.

"Nervous?" Brady asked.

"Pumped." The shiver boogied up and down her spine. "I've never roped on television before."

He angled her a sly grin. "Well, you'll definitely be the star of the show tonight...especially after you make your grand entrance."

She kicked him in the shin. He snickered. Not that it mattered. Cole wasn't paying attention, too busy watching his uncle and Violet on the back of the chutes. They set the flank strap and hovered protectively while a bareback rider prepared to climb down on one of the nine Jacobs horses that had been selected to buck at the second-most prestigious event in professional rodeo.

And Cole had been chosen to be one of the pickup men.

Shawnee had put the bug in Joe's ear and he'd taken it from there. He knew everyone who mattered, and no one could argue that Cole didn't deserve to be here. All the publicity he and Shawnee had generated last year hadn't hurt. Plus, Jacobs Livestock as a whole kept grabbing more and more of the spotlight—most recently with Riata Rose being named Bareback Horse of the Year in all of pro rodeo.

As far as Shawnee was concerned, Violet should be working in the arena, too, but that might be more than the old boys' club could handle all at once. A black man announcing the National Circuit Finals *and* a woman competing in the team roping? Their heads were probably already on the verge of exploding.

Well, they'd better brace themselves. When this rodeo was over, Shawnee's obligation to Brady and New York was done. As of Monday she was officially back on the Jacobs Livestock payroll. Violet was so caught up in wheeling and dealing—not to mention diapers—she was more than happy to hand over her chaps. Since the moment she'd learned to crawl, Rosie Cassidy had kept them all on the run. Even her big brother, who got regular baby-chasing duty.

"She never *stops*," Beni complained.

He didn't find this nearly as amusing as all the adults in his life did. Then Cole would scoop her up with one big hand and she'd cuddle against his chest and bat her eyes at him, sweet as honey. Just like that little girl with Down syndrome at today's Exceptional Kids Rodeo. She'd been terrified by the commotion, the other rug rats, the horses, and the cowboys with their big hats. Cole took his off, squatted down, spoke to her softly, and offered her his hand. After a few moments, she took it. By the end of the event, he'd had her up on Roy, squealing with delight as he held her in the saddle while Shawnee walked them slowly around a miniature barrel racing pattern.

It seemed damn selfish to rob some kid of a father like that, even if it meant having Shawnee for a mother. So, yeah, she might be reconsidering her stand on adoption.

Someday.

The fear still flared up. She had *so much* to lose now. But overall, she was feeling a lot more optimistic about her somedays. It was hard not to, since Tori's sister Elizabeth and Elizabeth's wife, Pratimi, had taken charge of Shawnee and everyone they could hunt down who shared her DNA. They were absolutely giddy, finding a large family with a pronounced history of malignancies to include in their study on the genetic roots of cancer. Elizabeth extracted tissue samples and unraveled the DNA while Pratimi drilled them with health history questions, then cross-matched the results in some superpowered computer program that would, they hoped, eventually be able to diagnose cancer before it happened, just from a drop of blood.

They'd already caught an early-stage case of lung cancer in one of her cousins, undoubtedly saving his life.

Shawnee might have to battle the beast again, but she was poked, prodded, and scanned so often it was nearly impossible for it to sneak up on her. And *if* the time came—she was working hard on *if* instead of *when*—she'd have the medical equivalent of the Avengers on her side.

The music reached a crescendo as the alley gate swung open and a pair of flag bearers burst into the arena, galloped a full lap, and skidded to a stop on either side of the far end.

Tyrell's golden voice boomed from the rafters. "Ladies and gentlemen, welcome to the first performance of the National Circuit Finals Rodeo! We begin tonight by introducing you to the men and women from across the nation who've qualified to compete, beginning in the Northwest with the Columbia Circuit!"

One by one, the twelve circuits were introduced. The Badlands Circuit of North and South Dakota, the Turquoise Circuit of Arizona and New Mexico, followed by California, Texas, and Montana. Each delegation galloped in and took their places in the two lines that stretched the length of the arena. And finally, "Last but certainly not least, our cowboys and cowgirls from the Northeast, the First Frontier Circuit!"

Shawnee and Brady thundered in behind the rest of the contestants and stopped at the very end of one of the lines.

"Our bullfighters—" Tyrell continued. "Joe Cassidy, Wyatt Darrington, and Shorty Edwards!" The three stepped out and saluted the crowd. "And our pickup men, Brent Sutton and Cole Jacobs."

Cole and Brent trotted out and took their places, one at the end of each line, which put Cole conveniently— and purposely—right next to Shawnee.

"And now, friends, we're going to pause for a moment to recognize history in the making. Tonight, Shawnee Pickett will be the first woman to ever compete in the team roping at the National Circuit Finals." Tyrell paused until the round of applause died down. "I am proud to call this woman a friend, and honored to turn the spotlight over to her for a special presentation."

Shawnee froze when an actual spotlight trained on her. Oh God. So many people. And cameras. Her heart started scrabbling around in her chest like a frantic rat. What had possessed her...

Brady reached over and tugged the reins away out of her fist. Everyone was staring. Waiting. She had no choice. She got off her horse. Then she turned to Cole and said, "Come down here."

He frowned at her, suspicious. "Why?"

"Get off your damn horse, Cole."

He stared at her as if she'd lost her mind—which was a fairly accurate assessment—huffed out an exasperated breath, and stepped off his horse. Shawnee grabbed the hand that wasn't holding Hammer's reins, sank down on one knee, and tilted her head back to look way, way up at him as a murmur rippled through the crowd, slowly swelling to a roar. Above the bucking chutes, the massive video screen flashed: *Marry me, Cole*.

Cole looked as if he'd swallowed a thistle. "Did you *have* to?"

"Hey, if I wait around for you to calculate the exact right time and place, we'll be honeymooning in a nursing home." She pushed her mouth into a smile that felt like it might crack down the middle. "So? What's it gonna be? Do I get to spend the rest of my life being your *for worse*?"

Cole swore. Then he latched both hands under her arms and dragged her up and into a hug that lifted her clean off the ground, and capped it with a quick, hard kiss.

"Does that mean yes?" she gasped, crushed against him.

"*Hell* yes." Then he plunked her back down on her feet. "Now, quit screwing around and go kick ass."

She grinned. "Yes, dear."

And for once, Shawnee did exactly as she was told.

Keep reading for a sneak peek of the next book in the Texas Rodeo series

FEARLESS *in* TEXAS

Chapter 1

THE INSTANT HIS FINGERS CAME TO REST ON HER BARE skin, they both cursed. A mutual, almost silent hiss, too quiet for any of the crowd encircling the nearly empty dance floor to hear. Their steps didn't falter. They didn't blink. But Wyatt also didn't pretend he couldn't feel the jolt at the inevitable, unavoidable contact…and neither did Melanie.

He smiled—a generic, just making conversation smile that would fool anyone not looking directly into the hot blue of his eyes. "Well. This is inconvenient."

"Extremely," Melanie agreed with a matching bland smile.

He didn't bother to move his hand. The cut of her emerald-green halter-top bridesmaid dress left him with no alternatives but her exposed back or her satin-covered butt. Her long, straight chestnut hair had been pinned into a tousled updo with tendrils that trailed down her neck, begging a man to twirl them around his finger.

Damn Violet for being the one woman on earth who was determined to make her maid of honor look hot as sin.

As they circled the floor, eyebrows were raised and glances exchanged. He was aware of the picture they made—him blond and elegant, at ease in the tuxedo that made the other cowboys tug at neckties and fidget with cummerbunds; her following his lead as effortlessly if they'd been dancing together for years. They were sleek and athletic, glowing with the pheromones that had been accumulating, molecule by molecule, over the enforced proximity of two days of the standard pre-wedding hullabaloo.

He flicked a glance toward the bride and groom, so wrapped up in each other they wouldn't have noticed if their attendants had broken into a tango. "Joe is the closest thing I have to a brother."

Despite the fact that he did have a male sibling.

"Violet is my sister," she countered. "Her family is my family."

Despite the fact that her own parents were sitting at a table only a few feet away, pointedly ignoring each other.

He studied the circle of faces that surrounded them, let his gaze settle for a beat on Joe and Violet, then focused on Melanie again, his voice hardening. "I'm not giving them up."

"Neither am I."

"So this…" His fingers flexed, a slight, dangerous increase in pressure. "Would be incredibly stupid. Especially for us."

She tilted her head in question.

"You don't trust me," he said.

"Depending on the circumstances. You are a good friend. If you hadn't forced Joe to come to Texas in the first place, he wouldn't be over there trying not to fall face-first into Violet's cleavage—which is pretty damn impressive in that dress." She smiled fondly at the two of them, then slid her gaze back to meet Wyatt's. "I've seen you risk life and limb for him in the arena."

He shrugged. "I'm a bullfighter. You do what it takes to make sure the cowboy and your partner walk away."

He didn't have to explain. She'd been on the rodeo trail long before she took her first steps, and her brother was also a bullfighter. But she shook her head. "You'd do the same for a complete stranger in a back alley. If I ever got caught in the middle of a convenience store robbery, you'd be the person I wanted standing at the Slurpee machine."

"But not sitting across the breakfast table."

She pursed glossy red lips as she considered the question. "It could be crowded—you, me, and whatever agendas you're working. I'd have a hard time deciding where I fit into the scheme of the day."

"Says the woman who makes a living parting the unsuspecting public from their hard-earned dollars."

"Ouch." But the edge in her voice was more amusement than offense. "I'll have to tell Human Resources to add that to the marketing director's job description."

"And this conversation is a perfect example of why we would be a disaster. Despite this." He traced a featherlight arc across her skin with his thumb, just to feel her shiver.

She let her lashes flutter lower, to match her voice. "We could sneak off for one night of depraved wedding sex. Get it out of our systems."

For a moment the possibility hovered between them like a heat mirage. They both inhaled sharply, then exhaled slowly.

"Been there, done that, have the divorce papers to prove it." He flashed a smile, bright and lethal. "And I have it on good authority that you can—and will—hold a grudge."

"Every girl needs a superpower," she said, with an equally toothy smile.

"Yours could make future Thanksgiving dinners a little awkward, don't you think?"

Her eyes narrowed. "I *think* I am both reasonable and mature enough to handle myself."

"History begs to differ."

Color flared in her cheeks, a visible gauge of her rising temper. "Are you trying to irritate me?"

"Yes."

She blinked. Then laughed in disbelief. "You really think that's going to help?"

"Can't hurt. And it comes so naturally. Just like your reaction." He twirled her, then pulled her close again, nearly eye to eye with her in heels. "We can't be friends."

The song was winding down. One more chorus and he would have to step away to dutifully tap the groom on the shoulder and cut in for the best man's traditional dance with the bride.

Her gaze drifted to her hand as it rested on his arm, nails bloodred against his black jacket. "We also can't avoid each other completely."

"Close enough. Between your job and mine, we've barely crossed paths since Joe and Violet got together.

If we work at it, we shouldn't have to see each other except at the holidays."

"Not a problem for me. I've had years of practice behaving myself at Miz Iris's house."

He raised his eyebrows. "Also not what I've heard."

"Hey, it was all at least half Violet's fault." Her soft laugh was laced with affection. Then her eyes narrowed again as she scraped a fingernail lightly down his neck on the pretense of flicking off a speck of the infernal glitter Violet's son had blasted them with upon arrival at the reception hall. "So we agree on one thing. This—"

"—is not worth the risk." Wyatt kept his voice cool, despite the sizzle in his blood.

"And we swear never to speak of it to any of them." Her gaze sharpened on his face, suspicious. "Ever."

He curled his lip. "Would you like to spit on our hands and shake to seal the deal?"

"Sunshine," she drawled, "if I decide to swap spit with you, I guarantee it'll get a lot messier than that."

He gave a strangled laugh, dropped his hands, and took a step back as a passing waiter shoved plastic champagne flutes at them for the latest in an endless series of toasts.

Ignoring the drunken ramblings of some distant cousin, Melanie lifted her glass. "Here's to no lovin' between *this* man and *this* woman."

"For as long as we both shall live," he agreed mockingly.

They tapped their glasses together and both tossed back the champagne in a single long swig.

She handed him her empty glass before sauntering over to join Joe and Violet. Wyatt rocked back on his heels, appreciating the view...as he was sure she had intended. Then he turned and walked in the opposite direction—straight to the bar.

Rodeo 101

Professional Rodeo: Also known as pro rodeo, refers to rodeos that have been approved by the Professional Rodeo Cowboys Association. The PRCA sanctions around 600 rodeos each year across the U.S. and Canada, establishing the rules for competition, requirements for membership, and standards of care for livestock. Money won at rodeos throughout the season is tracked via the World Standings, and at the end of the season the top fifteen money winners in each event qualify to compete at the National Finals Rodeo.

National Finals Rodeo: Also referred to as the NFR or just the Finals. It is the culmination of the rodeo season, and qualifying is the goal of every full-time cowboy. The nationally televised NFR stretches over ten days in early December, with the money won during the ten rounds of competition added to a contestant's season earnings to determine the World Champion in each event. Since 1985, the NFR has been held in Las Vegas, and is contracted to remain there through 2024.

Circuit: A large percentage of cowboys and cowgirls who compete at pro rodeos are not able to travel extensively due to work or family commitments. For their benefit, the 600+ rodeos of the PRCA are divided into twelve regional circuits (e.g., the

Texas Circuit, the Montana Circuit, the Great Lakes Circuit). Money won by members within each circuit is tallied in a separate set of standings, and at the end of the season the top contestants qualify for their regional circuit finals. Champions of the twelve circuits then qualify to compete in the **National Circuit Finals Rodeo**. Usually held in April, the National Circuit Finals Rodeo provides an opportunity for these skilled part-time cowboys to win a national championship.

Would You Like to Know More?

For more information on the sport of professional rodeo, the events, athletes, stock contractors, and the rodeo nearest you, visit **prorodeo.com**.

And for live streaming action online from some of the biggest events of the rodeo season, visit **wrangler network.com**.

Acknowledgments

To my publisher, Sourcebooks, for their incredible support and their amazing art department. Thank you, Dawn and company, along with photographer David Wagner, for allowing my covers to showcase authentic rodeo gear used by myself, my family, and friends. It makes this whole crazy ride even more special.

To Rhonda, Vincent, and Beau Michael and Black Eagle Rodeo for providing the gear for this specific cover and letting us feature their logo. The trophy saddle I won at the first Tal Michael Memorial Rodeo remains one of my most treasured possessions.

To all of the people who make it possible for me to continue to tell my stories, and the readers who make it worth all the times I've wondered why I didn't just keep selling insurance.

To my son, Logan, who has shown us that autism can be simply a unique set of abilities, and the world is a pretty cool place when you quit worrying about "normal."

And finally, for all of those who have gone a round with cancer and know that, deep inside, the battle never ends. Here's to hope, and to everyone who makes a contribution that helps researchers around the world in their race to win the war. Yes, even on Tough Enough to Wear Pink nights.